SIGHT UNSEEN

DAN GILROY

Carroll & Graf Publishers, Inc.
New York

First Carroll & Graf edition 1989

Carroll & Graf Publishers, Inc
260 Fifth Avenue
New York, NY 10001

Library of Congress Cataloging-in-Publication Data
Gilroy, Dan.
  Sight unseen : a novel / Dan Gilroy.—1st Carroll & Graf ed.
    p. cm.
  ISBN: 0-88184-469-1 : $18.95
  I. Title.
PS3557.I467S5 1989
813'54—dc19   89-30221
                                                       CIP

Manufactured in the United States of America

With special thanks to Tony Gilroy, who cowrote a significant portion of this book.

Prologue

May 1954

Pressure forced cold seawater through chinks in the aging hull, condensed it into beads on the bulkheads making the dark steel seem sweaty, and sent it finally, glistening, along the submarine's brittle electrical cables and down into the control room, where every *drip . . . drip . . . drip . . .* seemed to mock Captain Carl Avery's command.

The tarnished brass dials and gauges packed into the cramped space had proven unreliable from the moment Avery and his skeleton crew had slipped beneath the waves six days earlier. The equipment couldn't be trusted. The situation was worsening, reaching a crisis point. Avery was doing all he could to keep his growing apprehension to himself, but the sub was staggering through every maneuver, and the crew, far too small and already stale from lack of sleep in unfamiliar quarters, was growing dangerously shaky.

And now, at this most critical juncture, they were terribly lost.

Avery glanced down at his watch, a present from his wife, and performed a quick calculation in his head.

7

"So what is it?" the captain anxiously asked his navigator.

Ensign Walter Lamm had been staring nearly eighteen hours straight at a half-inch-thick circle of scratched ground glass. Beneath this pie-size cataract, the sonar's green finger swept out its turn. A crippled *ping* issued forth every few seconds. For the past fifteen minutes, with each groggy revolution, the source unnervingly seemed to change.

Ensign Lamm was past being tired. He had taken a methedrine with Atkins and Sussman hours before. For a while the drug had kept him awake and sharp, but now it had settled into his neck. His head ached. His jaw was tight. And for the first time in some eight years—the first time since his maiden cruise—Walter Lamm was losing his grip to the panicky clutch of doubt, fatigue, and lurking terror.

"I don't know. . . ." He nervously toyed with the dog tags around his neck. "It's all over the place. Without tools—"

Avery cut in: "Put it up. Full extension."

First Mate Lyle Atkins had been nervously awaiting the command. He quickly raised the periscope into place and almost tripped over himself backing out of the way.

Avery again checked his watch and then climbed the two-step scaling. He spun the beak of his cap 180 degrees, rested his forearms on the scope's handles, and peered uneasily into the outside world.

It was night. To the west, open seas; to the east—

"Jesus! Ninety degrees starboard! Now!"

The full moon silhouetting a jagged, wooded coastline a mere half mile away made Avery's voice razor-sharp. The suddenness of the command sent a keen chill through the steel room. Avery angrily pulled away from the scope. "Christ, Walter, we're right up on the goddamned shore!"

Chief Engineer William Furrows already had his large hands on the throttle levers and was leaning them out with powerful and steady force. His disgust with the sub's inferior equipment had been well voiced over the last few days. The right turbine lever jammed and Furrows impatiently slammed it forward with enough force to shake the entire housing. *"I've run tractors better built than this."*

His comment went unheard as the loud rumbling of twin diesels sent a heavy drone through the control room. The sub pitched forward, banking steeply to one side, and the crew instinctively grabbed at pens and coffee cups, holding them for a few moments until the vibration and angle had settled.

Second Mate James Dilling, bare-chested and soaked with sweat, ducked through the bulkhead door.

"This isn't a pie cruise, Dilling," Avery snapped. "Put the damn shirt on!"

Dilling's greasy hands loosened the oil-stained T-shirt tucked around his waist and pulled it over his head.

"Captain, there's some kind of compression problem with the starboard eng—"

Avery stiffened, senses suddenly yanked elsewhere. One hand on the scope, he turned apprehensively back toward the navigation bank.

"What's that smell?"

The entire control room froze. It was the one question nobody wanted to hear. Five men shifted instantly, subtly, all of them drawing at the stale air, each one hoping to God there'd be no confirmation of that worst of fears.

Brows furrowed over a confused grimace, Ensign Lamm sniffed at the air above the sonar and slowly, incredulously, touched the radar's green glass. As his fingers recoiled from the extreme heat—a cry still forming on his lips—smoke began to wisp up through the seams. In the moment it took for the word to stick in his throat, the entire instrument panel before him ignited.

"Fire on the bridge!" Avery thundered.

Lamm, struck dumb, stared blankly as the sheet-metal casing before him came alive, blistering almost instantly.

"All hands forward!" Dilling screamed back toward the engine room. "Fire on the bridge!"

Already—just these few seconds later—the entire control room was soured with the harsh, bitter haze of electrical fire. Glass gauge lenses began shattering. Angry short circuits, like roman candles, shot streams of sparks across the grated floor. Acrid smoke thickened under the red lights and the control room took on the hellish cast of each man's worst nightmare.

The crew charged into a rush of frantic activity.

"Furrows, Sussman, shut down that panel! Shut down the whole damn side!" Avery wheeled backward. "Dilling, give me full bridge ventilation!"

Furrows and Ensign Sussman waded stoically into the roiling black smoke and vanished into the instrumentation closet.

Seaman Durso, sprinting forward from the engine room, smelled steam, paused briefly, heard a *bang*, and looked up just in time to be hit by an explosion of seawater as a seam gave way in the overcharged starboard ballast trimming tank.

The sub pitched suddenly starboard, writhing in the night sea like a whale taking a harpoon.

Avery just managed to catch himself as he fell. Dilling, off balance in the bulkhead doorway, struck his head hard falling back into the gangway. Sparks and flaming bits of burning wire shook free from the panel and rained down over Ensign Lamm. A fire extinguisher in Atkins's hand jerked free and crashed against the wall, spilling its wasted contents in wild release as it snaked around the room. Black, velvety smoke poured from the bonfire that had been the main control panel. The heat on the bridge was rising by the second, its insistent caress searing lungs and burning eyes.

"Permission to radio position, sir!" Atkins cried, unable to wait any longer for the captain's order.

"Permission denied!—Report, Furrows!"

The chief engineer called out from somewhere in the darkness, bravely enduring a deep, hacking cough, "It looks . . . like it's running through . . . everything . . ."

Lamm, wide-eyed, beat frantically with a seat cushion at the little fires that were sweeping across his uniform.

"Prepare to surface, sir?" Atkins called out, nearly pleading. Avery did not respond, trying to focus astern through badly tearing eyes.

"Dilling!"

"Request permission to radio position, sir!" Atkins's fear

was no longer disguised. They were close enough to the surface! His trembling hand was poised over the transmit switch.

"Denied!" Avery yelled. "Dilling! . . . *Dilling!*"

A small explosion suddenly ignited the far wall and sent a hissing stream of burning black fluid across the control-room floor. Atkins watched in horror and fascination as his captain tried dancing around the branching streams of liquid flame. Avery presented a hellishly comical figure as he barked orders while flailing at the fire running up the legs of his pants.

". . . Bring it up!" Avery's voice struggled to be heard above the confusion. "*Surface!*" He screamed.

"Prepare to surface," Atkins recited, clinging to regulations in his unbridled terror, and he pulled frantically at the main wheel.

Lamm screamed as a bright shower of sparks erupted from the auxiliary panel behind him.

"Sir!" Atkins shrieked through the smoke. "We've got to radio our position!"

And from the blackness, stripped of all authority, left naked with only his anger and fear, Captain Carl Owen Avery bellowed out his final reply:

"They didn't give us a fucking transmitter!"

Silver moonlight played over the dark rolling waves as they drove east toward the densely wooded coastline. A lone gull skimming the night swells cawed at the unsteady rumbling rising from the sea and gracefully lifted as the submarine's conning tower crashed into the air like a diver gasping for breath.

Then it stopped.

Barely moving in the moon's blue-white glow, the soaking steel mass hung there precariously—hesitant, trembling, rising no farther—as the engines below struggled desperately to surface.

The sudden muffled thud and flash of an underwater explosion shook the dripping black tower so harshly it nearly broke from the pressure hull. The tremor faded, and the submarine slowly, forlornly, began dropping back into the shimmering waves.

And if someone had been on that near but deserted coast and had glanced out at this closing struggle, he would have briefly seen the bright red star of the Soviet Navy as the conning tower disappeared into the dancing ocean shadows.

Chapter One

The Present

The earth seems a magically beautiful place from one hundred and fifty miles up: the glowing mystery of a bright blue ball floating against a scrim of black, its jagged polar ice caps clinging like remnants of some newly broken shell, the continents visible under an eddied veil of clouds, vast and fragile, inexorably turning—the curved stage of countless conflict and endeavor.

From just such a height, a fifty-two-foot-long, ten-foot-wide black cylinder was hurtling over central Russia. Sky-high over smoky tearooms and factories changing shift; gliding silently above wet forests and sunny cobblestone squares, the invisible presence soared on.

The two men controlling the satellite were arguing in a small windowless room outside Washington, D.C.

"Matt, it's Ginnie's sister, for chrissake. She's here for two days. All I'm asking, it's not much, you take her to a movie or something—"

"I don't do blind dates, Harry."

"I'm saying a movie. I'm not asking you to take a blood test."

13

"Blind dates are for losers."

Harry swiveled to a control panel just over his shoulder and punctuated his annoyance by sharply clicking a series of twelve switches. He spun back to the console and typed out a rapid statement on the keyboard before him, logging it onto the system. This task complete, he turned back to Matt. "I think you're getting the wrong idea, that I'm pushing this girl because she can't get a date on her—"

"Can we concentrate here?" Matt cut in. "I've got T-minus eighty on the shoot."

Eight months earlier, Matthew Clarke had specifically asked to see the KH-12 Ikon satellite before it was launched. And now he was remembering the large black cylinder, lovingly balanced on white work scaffolding in the center of an all-white room in TRW's Redondo Beach plant. With a white cotton cap over his straight sandy hair and a surgical mask covering his face, Matt stood for hours watching identically clad men and women fuss over their exotic creation. The black alloy shell had been removed, exposing thousands of multicolored sinews, each one of them an artery, linked and layered over a series of gold foil-wrapped organs; to Matt, the perfect example of progressive engineering repeating—being forced to repeat—organic design: computers with circuitry so advanced they demanded a frame that resembled the cerebral cortex, this satellite with its spine and brain and central nervous system of gallium arsenide circuitry.

Matt had edged steadily closer, finally unable to stop himself from reaching out, instinctively, to touch the steel skin that housed this fragile intelligence.

Matt pictured that satellite now, dutifully circling the earth like an electron around a nucleus.

But Harry Ingram was insistent. "I all but promised her, Matty—"

Matt chose not to answer, focusing instead on the three computer screens before him, scanning for hints of anomalies among the constantly changing coordinates.

This looked like a smooth run. It had taken dozens of precisely timed firings of the satellite's hydrazine thrusters over the last eighteen hours, but Matt and Harry and the three other station-keeping teams that constantly monitored and controlled

KH-12 Ikon 5603 had finessed its ground track to accommodate this particular shoot. The boxcar-size satellite read stable on all three axes, was generating 93 percent power from its large rectangular, rotorlike solar paddles, and was rapidly approaching its 141-mile perigee.

On the wall above them, small numbered lights passed with varying speed and arc across a highlighted Mercator projection of the globe. Matt was silently concentrating on the work, and Harry Ingram's impatient stare finally fell away. He was older, nearly forty, with dark weepy eyes and a fallen chin that gave him a constantly idle look.

"You think I'd risk having to pull the whole fall tour with you if Ginnie's sister was some kind of gargoyle?" asked Harry, rolling himself up closer to the console.

Matt took his eyes from the screens, as a driver briefly turns his attention from the road to a passenger, and regarded Harry. The idea of him having promised fresh meat to his sister-in-law was amusing. Matt almost smiled.

"T minus forty-seven four," Matt said. "Cover Open Sequence."

"Cover Open Sequence loaded," Harry intoned with an irritating edge to his voice.

"Check Cover Open Sequence."

"Check."

The electronic waltz began. A digital request, deftly sent from the keyboard at Matt's fingertips, leaped at the speed of light across thousands of miles of vacuum. The spacecraft spoke the precise language of numbers, responding to encoded, multidigit sequences that were transmitted to execute specific commands. It was a task of exacting delicacy, as the beams of data were then perfectly targeted, processed, and relayed from one TDRSS satellite to the next. As the Rolls-Royce of U.S. imaging reconnaissance satellites, the KH-12's sophisticated on-board VHIC microprocessors almost instantly deciphered the command. On the far side of the world, a circular alloy shield on the spacecraft's undercarriage silently slid from view, revealing a large, perfectly sparkling, unblinking eye.

Until recently, the United States' fleet of some fifty-plus spy satellites had been exclusively controlled from seven widely separated ground stations around the world. Then, sending instructions to a satellite was like standing on a roadside and yelling commands to someone in a passing car, there was only a brief period, when the satellite was right overhead—a window of approximately ten minutes for the low-altitude reconnaissance platforms—that it could hear you. You had to quickly and specifically tell it what to do, and from there it was operating on its own until it passed over the next ground station.

With recent technological advances, however, such was no longer the case.

Matt and Harry were housekeepers, or satellite controllers. At present they were part of an eighteen-month trial run involving the newly launched Tracking Data and Relay Satellite System, which allowed continuous transmission and reception from hardened control facilities safely ensconced in the U.S.

The control facility where Matt and Harry sat had taken years of interagency wrangling to establish and was buried deep within the NSA's Headquarters-Operations Building at Fort Meade, outside Washington, D.C. It had been placed there in a wildly bold effort to capitalize on the well-known bureaucratic improbability of finding such a facility within the NSA—in effect the last place someone would look, and was designed to supplement the Satellite Control Facility in Sunnyvale, California, and the Consolidated Space Operations Center (CSOC), being constructed outside Colorado Springs. Only a relative handful knew of the NSA satellite control facility's existence, and, barring another Christopher Boyce, or Ronald Pelton, or William Kampiles, it would hopefully stay that way for a long, long time. Simply titled the Auxiliary Space Operations Center (ASOC), its astronomical budget had been hidden by a complex accounting sleight-of-hand, and was actually split by the NSA and the National Reconnaissance Organization, which, despite officially not existing, oversees most of the actual operation of America's eyes and ears in the sky.

"T minus thirty-two seconds and . . . clear for Shutter Sequence . . ."

Matt waited, his eyes reflecting the green glow of the screen, as the whirring, unseen emissary sailed over Russia.

Harry coughed.

Matt shifted in his seat, was about to say something, when Harry fell in line.

"Sorry . . . Shutter Sequence loaded."

"Check Shutter Sequence."

"Ah . . . check."

An East German defector had been debriefed ten days earlier in Stockholm. In the course of questioning he mentioned rumors of an airfield being extended to handle heavy bombers near the Yakutskayan city of Verhoyansk. An analyst from the CIA's Intelligence Directorate passed the information to his section intelligence officer, who dutifully sent the report to the Committee on Imagery Requirements and Exploitation. COMIREX passed its operational request to the NRO with a high-grade priority rating. The NRO quickly included it in the Joint Reconnaissance Schedule and time was budgeted and scheduled on the next available KH-12 fly-by. ASOC was given control of the shoot.

Matt focused on the digital clock running in the corner of the center computer screen before him. "T minus seven, six, five, four, three, two . . . say cheese—"

Some nine thousand miles away, several dozen sharp clicks were swallowed by the silence of space, as the KH-12's hyper-sensitive charge-coupled devices were focused on the radiated energy emitted by the landscape below.

"I've gotta ask you," Harry said a half world away. "I'm interested now, from a personal point of view. I mean, what the hell is one night?"

"Close Cover Sequence."

"Out of all the nights in your life . . ."

Matt was losing concentration. He squinted at the screen, nervously pushed his glasses back toward his forehead, and very quietly, very sternly, repeated his prior request: "Close Cover Sequence. *Finish the shot, Harry.*"

"Close Cover Sequence is loaded."

"Check Close Cover Sequence."

". . . Check," Harry said after a deep, grudging yawn.

Matt transmitted the sequence. Seconds after he sent the order, the satellite's cover slid into the closed position.

The satellite had been maneuvered down to 141 miles to get maximum photographic detail. The price for going low was atmospheric friction—heat—which, if sustained, would drag the satellite into a still lower orbit, generating more heat and ultimately, if not corrected, burning up an extremely expensive spacecraft.

"Computer mark for seven-point-six-two-second full-altitude boost," said Matt, eyes darting over the constantly updated screens before him.

"I'm not blind, Matt. Boost burn time's loaded."

"Coming up on mark—"

"Mark—"

"I read positive on full boost."

"Check on full boost," Harry said.

A 7.62-second burn from the KH-12's primary altitude thrusters would lift the satellite into a higher, less rigorous orbit until it was needed again, which, since the lingering shortage of launch platforms created by the *Challenger* explosion, was immediately.

The digital clock was running. Matt blinked when the thrusters didn't stop firing at 7.62 seconds. At 8.94 seconds his mouth dropped open. At 9.46 seconds he quickly leaned forward, scanning all three screens, searching for a verification stop code that should have been there by now.

"It's still firing, Harry!"

"Oh shit—"

"Wha—"

"Cancel it, Matt! *Error!*"

Matt's fingers flew across the console. Harry watched, paralyzed, as the boost burn went past 13.77 seconds and kept right on going.

"Negative cancel! That was a goddamned seventy-six-point-two-second boost, Harry! You sequenced seventy-six-point-two seconds!"

Matt stabbed at the console and plucked away a red circular plastic seal that covered a button larger than the others. His finger hesitated for just an instant before he let it strike. Suddenly, a gridlike array of flashing yellow lights came up on the big screen. In the distance, a single warning tone began to pulse. Matt spoke now for the benefit of others, God knew how many or how far away: "Miscue—repeat—miscue—"

"Oh shit!" Harry withered into his seat. "Matt—"

Matt's eyes jumped from screen to screen. "Give me the cancel, Harry! The cancel code!"

Harry was immobile, staring at the upper right-hand corner of his screen as the burn time passed 26.73 seconds and kept going.

Matt frantically scrolled to find the boost cancel command. Every extra second of boost consumed precious, vital hydrazine— wasted it by uselessly pushing the satellite into a progressively more eccentric orbit. It would take still more hydrazine to get the KH-12 back down into a productive trajectory again.

As Harry watched, his hand splayed over his open mouth, Matt finally located the command, loaded it, and transmitted the sequence into space. A moment later, high over the other side of the world, the satellite dutifully stopped the boost burn at a staggering 72.129 seconds.

It was a class-A fuck-up, the kind that would be talked about for years in hushed tones.

Harry immediately, feebly, attempted to deflect responsibility: "I can't see it. I mean, we had the seven-point-six loaded in plenty of time. You checked it, right?"

Matt let the question die where it belonged and Harry's mouth sagged open just a little wider. There was nothing really to say and so they were quiet; the only sound the distant bagpipe-droning of the alarm.

Satellite control was a game played out to the thousandth of a second. A several-second thruster mistake was considered big. What Matt and Harry had just been party to was titanic. There was a limited amount of hydrazine on each KH-12. A significant portion of this satellite's maneuvering fuel had just been carelessly destroyed, severely cutting back on its present operational lifespan and making it an early candidate for the costly, exacting, and dangerous task of shuttle refueling.

The yellow lights on the large projection stopped flashing. All three of Matt's screens went dead. The operator monitor at Harry's station blinked out a coded user sequence and then went blank as they were officially excised from the system. The Big Blue Cube in Sunnyvale had just taken over.

Matt stayed within himself, staring straight ahead. He didn't need to turn and look to know exactly the head-back, face-kneading, agonized posture that Harry had assumed.

One long minute passed.

Matt took off his glasses, cleaned them, and then found himself fooling absently with the latch on the plastic case.

Two minutes passed.

They waited, as the realization of what they'd done grew and grew until finally it seemed so large there was no longer any air in the small room.

Harry slammed his hand against the arm of his chair and stood, presenting a pathetic figure of defiance. "Where the hell are they?"

Matt decided he wasn't getting into it.

"How long are we supposed to wait?" Harry as the injured party. "This is insane!"

Matt wasn't going to touch it.

"Don't isolate me, Matt," Harry hissed. "*Don't.*"

A moment later, the steel door clicked open and the deputy section director on duty stepped in. He tersely dismissed them for the night. Hearings were scheduled for eight the next morning.

Matt fled the room, leaving Harry behind, and numbly walked as quickly as possible the length of the empty hundred-yard hallway.

It was just after two in the morning, seven and a half minutes since the accident, and Matt knew that all over Washington phones were softly buzzing and insistently beeping and loudly ringing as the momentous news of the satellite miscue was sucked into the cloaked, fragmented, vacuumlike world of U.S. intelligence.

Matt sharply turned the corner and continued down another long hallway. He passed dozens upon dozens of seamlessly shut, white steel doors. Each door was marked with a colored seal denoting the security clearance needed to pass inside. Most of them were fitted with combination-cipher locks that required the pressing of a sequenced group of five numbers before gaining entry.

Very few people, if anyone, knew what went on behind all the doors. The NSA was staggeringly compartmentalized. Every branch and service was fractioned, some duplicated, others simply fronts for even more clandestine work. The NSA was so veiled in code words, clearances, and secret organizations that it was virtually impossible for most employees to even grasp at its true functioning structure.

Matt had constructed a vast mental map of the NSA's interconnecting acronyms, and though he had a better idea than most how the various ultrasensitive departments functioned, he also understood that he was conscious of only the tip of the NSA iceberg and that anything could be happening behind the door he just passed with the "need to know" security seal on it—anything at all.

Anger was building with every echoing step Matt took. At thirty-two, he had built an exemplary seven-year record with the agency and now, because of Harry's laxness and idiocy, he might easily be fired tomorrow morning. At the very least his career prospects had just suffered a severe blow.

Matt balanced his chances like an equation: he was steady, reliable, professional. He couldn't remember a single incident in the past seven years that would've shaken that claim. He had Design, Application, and Systems references. He was a utility player, adaptable. He'd shown he could work alone and on team projects. He was young and dedicated and, most important for the NSA's desired personality profile—satisfied. Christ, there was even "The Thing." How many other people worked on voluntary outside projects?

On the downside he was a civilian.

Most of the NSA's fifty thousand employees were. But the military had their say in all hearing, evaluations, and clearance issuances—and this was an enormous screw-up. Here was human error of an inexcusable magnitude. The blue-suiters would want their pound of flesh. Probably several pounds. Someone was going to have to pay and Matt was right up at the front of the line, though he hoped he was behind Harry.

He came to the end of the corridor and took the elevator up eight floors to the headquarters tower lobby. Two young, well-armed Federal Protection Service guards silently watched Matt sign out and leave through the activated glass doors of Gatehouse 1.

It was August in Washington, D.C., and even at two in the

morning the air was hot and overloaded. He came out of the building quickly, lost in thought, and the temperature hit him like the exhaust fan from a bank of laundromat dryers. He kept pace for a few steps until the thickness of the heat made him realize just how fast he'd been walking. He caught a slower pace and a slight, false confidence returned. The habitual act—the reflex of unclipping and pocketing his green security card as he crossed the lot—fooled him for a moment into the thought that this was just the end of another shift. And then Matt remembered, and he cursed under his breath as he dug the car keys from his pants pocket.

Matt's car was a '73 BMW 2002, badly in need of a paint job and body work but as reliable as anything on the road. He eased the auto past the guarded entrance and left behind the razor-wire topped cyclone fence encircling the massive NSA complex. Matt drove the several dozen yards to Savage Road and hung the right. A quarter mile later, past the mall and expressway overpass, Matt was off Fort Meade property and heading south on the wood-lined Baltimore-Washington Parkway.

Matt drove, blending with the few others who were traveling at that strange hour, but the passing lights and the radio and even the air pushing past the open window seemed freakish. All these familiar, usually comforting things were piling onto what was becoming an overwhelming anxiety. The reality of what had just happened began crowding in. It was suddenly painfully clear to Matt that he didn't want to work anywhere but the NSA, and that he'd never really known that until just now—until it seemed a distinct possibility that everything could be pulled out from under him in the morning.

It wasn't that Matt felt patriotic about his job. He didn't think of himself—and there were those who did—as some frontline warrior in the noble battle for global dominance. Matt had no delusions that he was fanatically contributing his services to the winning of the Cold War. In fact, Matt had no strong political feelings whatsoever. He never voted. The few Russians he'd met he liked. The work itself, when you came down to it, was almost the antithesis of politics. It was unemotional, quiet, solitary, detached always. Every intricate task seemed to hang alone in midair as if it existed for only its own sake.

Matt liked the work because he was being paid to play games; games that had a unique and serious definition. And then, it wasn't just that either. There was also the mystique; the unspoken knowledge that you and those you worked with—from Engineering to Cryptanalysis to Computer Sciences to Linguistics to Telemetry to all the varied intelligence fields of the NSA—had taken oaths and vows to never mention the work outside these walls. It was the excitement of getting upped to a new GG security grade and the clearance to exotic words it gave. No Such Agency.

Never Say Anything.

Matt was part of a team, a team that he subconsciously considered benevolent and fair and worth playing on. Work was a game from which he desperately did not want to be ejected, especially for someone else's mistake.

II

The high-rise complex had been grandly named the Kingman Arms and was located in a cluster of new buildings along Fairfax Drive, just beside the Potomac, in Arlington. Matt's one-bedroom unit was on the tenth floor. The living-dining area was minimally furnished, almost empty save for a large particleboard workbench set in one corner of the room. Electronic parts, tools, and lengths of colored wire were chaotically spread across its scarred surface. The apartment's only decorative thoughts were a series of three framed underwater photographs bunched carelessly above the black leather couch and a large chunk of viceroy coral that was mounted and gathering dust on top of the television.

Matt couldn't sleep. Not even close enough to try. A sandwich, half-eaten, was going stale out on the balcony table. It was nearly four thirty in the morning and Matt sat facing three home-built chess computers that flashed red lights and spit back varied beep-tones as he played.

Matt grew tired of it. He rose, standing into a long, yawning, hands-above-the-head stretch. He walked to the open balcony door and looked out over the river to Washington, D.C. A siren was wailing somewhere, but otherwise the nation's capital was dark and silent on this hot August night. Leaning against the doorjamb, Matt gazed out over the sleeping city. He wondered what it might be like to live outside the safe, insulated existence of an NSA career. He suddenly began to think that maybe the future was totally out of his hands. A 727, tail-lit Federal Express logo clearly visible, came in low from the left, landing gear down, descending to nearby Washington National Airport. Leaving the balcony door open, Matt turned off the living-room lights and walked wearily back to the bedroom.

He felt like calling someone, but Matt's friends were few; a fact in part to blame on the highly classified, socially restricting nature of his job. There was Dave, his best friend, and Perri, Dave's wife of two years. There used to be several girlfriends of varying levels of intimacy, but Matt hadn't spoken to any of them in the last three months. For a moment, he entertained the thought of making a call, but Dave would most likely answer the phone and Matt could think of no credible excuse to ask for Perri at this time of night.

It would have been unfair to bother his parents. Matt simply could not explain the classified particulars of his dilemma. His mother, whose personality naturally tended toward worry, would have been left with a feeling of unease, while his father would have offered the advice he considered a panacea for all problems— work hard and save money. They were emigrants from Hungary, forced to flee in the aftermath of the 1956 uprising. Matt's father had been a pharmacist living in Debrecen when the students and factory workers flooded the streets in late October of that year. The Soviet Army crushed the uprising on November 4, and the next day Matt's father and mother, she seven months pregnant with Matt, left behind their families, friends, and possessions and fled the country. A month after arriving in the U.S., Matt was born prematurely in a hospital in Albany, New York.

The family last name was changed from Czelaw to Clarke, and after three years of working two menial jobs to support his family and attend night school, Matt's father opened a drugstore in Troy. Matt was put to use as soon as he could read well enough to take inventory.

His parents had only just retired last year—sold the store and bought a condo in Boca Raton. In America, Matt's father was fond of repeating, anything was possible. Matt decided to call them tomorrow, when he had a better idea of where he stood at work.

He turned off the lights, undressed in the dark, and lay down on his bed. He tried to fall asleep. Troubling images flickered by in the night: Perri's full, naked body falling into bed with him—surreal, dreamy sex—Dave watching silently from a chair—a satellite screaming through the sky—Matt trying to run from its path, blocked by a huge cipher-lock doorway—a loud alarm going off, over and over. Matt opened his eyes. He bolted up. His stomach tightened into a knot. Sleep, in this state, was an impossibility.

III

The conference room was dominated by a heavy oval table with seating for twenty. The floor was covered with a tight-weave, root-beer-colored carpet. An American flag hung limp from a spearlike staff in one corner of the room, beside which was a large, circular, wall-mounted rendering of the NSA's official seal—a keen-eyed eagle gripping an oversize key in its talons. Evenly spaced high-watt lights were recessed into brass bowls near the ceiling, making the room, whether planned or not, unusually bright.

At eight fifteen, Matt was nodded into the temporary court-room by a Federal Protection Service officer posted outside. Matt had been waiting for forty minutes in the robin's-egg blue hallway, seated beneath a poster that bluntly insisted: YOU ARE A SECURITY TARGET. He was scared. His heart was pounding and he knew his voice would quake when he spoke. Over the last seven years, the NSA had dominated his life. The intense secrecy that permeated its halls, the ongoing security checks, the rumored fate of those who'd stumbled, all these had distilled into a gut-wrenching dread of being called before its authority.

Matt took a chair near the center of the table and the guard, never once looking directly at him, shut tight the door from the outside. They made him wait another five agonizing minutes. The door finally opened and two men stepped in.

Air Force Colonel Norman Mills, in a crisp, cobalt-blue uniform and identified by a name tag, slid a metallic briefcase onto the table and took the central seat across from Matt. The second man, Charles Freid, his department head, nodded to the accused without expression and took the seat beside the colonel.

Matt had never seen Mills before but the species was familiar; a grave, flat-topped career officer—a blue-suiter with little tolerance for mistakes and the civilians who made them. Freid he knew and liked; a soft-spoken man nearing retirement who was generally regarded as competent and fair.

Freid folded his hands on the table before him. Matt thought he sighed.

Mills took his time removing a series of documents from the briefcase and Matt couldn't help but turn and check Freid's face for some indication of what was to come. The old man looked tired—no question he'd been up since the incident—but beyond that nothing.

Mills cleared his throat and abruptly began: "This is Miscue Hearing 4547, reviewing the events leading up to and following the mishandling of KH-12 Ikon number 5603 at two-hundred hours, three minutes, eighteen seconds, on this, August twenty-four, 1989. Air Force Colonel Norman Mills, Special Projects Directorate, presiding."

With a melodramatic gesture that hinted at humor, Freid raised his head and addressed the ceiling: "Charles Freid, cochair."

Matt didn't need to be told that, though there was no apparent apparatus in sight, the hearing was being recorded.

Mills focused directly on Matt for the first time since he'd entered the room. "Do you have any questions?"

"No, sir." Matt's voice quavered. He couldn't hide his fear.

Mills studied Matt briefly before his eyes fell back to a paper before him. "You are a civilian employee of the National Security Agency working in conjunction with Air Force Intelligence. As such, you do not fall under military jurisdiction. However, recommendations from these proceedings are considered final and binding, said proceedings and authority agreed to by you upon signing your NSA authorization documents when you began employment here approximately . . . seven years ago."

Mills dangled stapled copies of the forms in the air, as if they were an integral part of some fabulous trick he was about to perform.

Matt remembered signing them. He'd only just graduated from M.I.T. with a masters in electrical engineering when he was enlisted. NSA recruiters were always on the lookout for double-E's and they'd wanted him badly. A comment by a faculty adviser. A vague pamphlet in his mailbox and the strange little anonymous office in the Postal Building downtown. Questions. Hints. The first trip to Washington.

"I remember it," Matt said, his voice steadying.

"Regardless . . ." Mills let the paper fall to the table. "The subject, Matthew Selwyn Clarke, NSA ident number 977834, cleared SBI, May twelve, 1983. He received a GG-7 security classification and was assigned to R and D, spending six months in REMP before transferring to RADE where he specialized in microwave communications . . ."

Matt had enjoyed his days at Research and Development, but after two years he began to feel he was on a career plateau. When the opportunity arose to work in a new area, he took the job.

". . . Subject transferred to DDO as a SIGINT engineer.

". . . After eighteen months, subject transferred again," Mills said with a hint of disapproval, "to DEFSMAC, where the subject is now a KH-systems specialist. Current GG-17."

Matt felt a brief moment of satisfaction. His record was unusual but spotless. The NSA needed people like him. Freid knew it. Hell, Mills must know it, too.

The colonel squared and folded the papers he'd been reading.

"We reviewed the transmission tapes at Mr. Ingram's hearing

before coming here.'' He let his eyes wander across the table to Matt. ''I should tell you that this panel recommended his termination of employment on this project, which became effective immediately.''

Matt felt a buzzing in his ears. Harry was a civilian employee of TRW, which had been one of the chief systems contractors of the KH-12. Working with the NSA on an ultrasecret trial project had been a prestige assignment, as lofty an orbit as Harry could have hoped for. But now Harry was being sent back to TRW and a long fall from grace. Harry's career would be vaporized in the intense heat of an unscheduled reentry.

''I was not convinced that was the prudent decision,'' Freid said calmly.

Matt shifted his gaze between the two men. The bright room had suddenly taken on a sort of feverish, swollen dimension.

Mills, without emotion, gestured for Freid to continue.

''It's my opinion,'' Freid started, speaking clearly for the record, ''that Mr. Clarke came off well on the transmission tapes. His behavior and actions were professional and calm. I think he went by the book. It's obvious from the tape that Ingram's behavior was distracting. It's my feeling this is a case where the agency should distinguish individual responsibility.''

''On that point we disagree,'' Mills countered. ''The VICTOR sequence should've alerted Mr. Clarke to the anomaly—.''

''The codes change,'' Freid said. ''It was Ingram's job.''

Mills resisted the urge to volley back. He paused, then pulled another paper from the neat pile before him. ''Mr. Clarke, I've been apprised that in addition to your primary responsibilities, you've been involved with another engineering specialist in developing a COMINT microwave enhancement system . . .''

My God, Matt thought, ''The Thing'' was gonna save him.

''We have—yes, sir,'' Matt said eagerly. He paused, but neither of them spoke. ''It's worked out pretty well,'' he threw in.

''Maybe you've been spreading yourself a little thin. That a possibility?''

Matt shot a look at Freid, but there was nothing there to help him. His anxiety was evaporating slightly as his confidence grew, leaving an undercurrent of anger.

"Colonel Mills, if there'd been any problem, a scheduling problem, or a question of my being overworked, it should've been raised last year when we were in the development stage. We're just putting them in now. I've taken two one-week leaves for the installations. The late hours have been over for awhile."

His tone sounded more challenging than he'd intended.

"I see . . ." Mills's eyes thinned up a little. "And you're scheduled for this Pacific tie-in. What's the time frame for that?"

"We have a tech crew booked in October," Matt said hopefully. "About seven weeks."

Mills made a note, then turned to Freid. "Anything else?"

"I think my position's pretty clear," Freid said. "Clarke's a professional. I'll take him back if I can get him."

"Noted." Mills dug back through his papers; looking for something, not finding it.

Freid glanced at his watch and then leveled an impatient stare at Mills. "Look, I've got some major shuffling left this morning, Norman. Let's skip the pageantry."

Mills reddened. There was an awkward moment of quiet. Matt, confused, looked back and forth between the two men for some clue to his position in this sudden shift of moods.

"I'm sure there's a photostat of a committee decision somewhere in that briefcase," the old man continued. "Let's crack the cookie, read the fortune, and get back to work."

Mills was furious. His tongue clicked against the inside of his cheek. He was coloring deeply. He stared for a few long seconds at the Air Force Academy ring on his finger.

Was Freid with him or not, Matt wondered desperately. What the hell was he doing?

Freid turned in his chair to Matt. "I'm developing the kind of boldness that grows as one nears retirement," he said.

Matt nodded slightly, unsure of how to react.

"It is the abiding decision of this hearing," Mills announced stiffly, rushing the words, "that the subject, Matthew Selwyn Clarke, be placed on internal probation, to continue for an indeterminate period. This 'miscue' incident will be permanently tagged in his file, and he is reassigned, as of today, as of noon, to Imagery Analysis Section, until further notice. This transfer will not affect previously approved travel assignments. Miscue Hearing 4547 is hereby adjourned.''

Mills quickly began gathering his papers. Freid stood to leave. Matt slipped back in the chair, trying to reconcile his mixed emotions. Yes, he'd been spared termination, but what the hell had he been relegated to? Was he in or out? What was internal probation? He looked again to Freid for some indication. Freid shot him a faint smile and shrugged. Matt watched Mills lock up his briefcase and stand.

"Imagery Analysis, sir?" Matt said. "You mean, looking at pictures?"

Mills nodded, turned to leave.

"It's just that, I don't know, of all the options . . . it's not something I've been trained to do."

"Neither was the mishandling of an extremely valuable satellite," Mills shot back, already starting for the door, "but you managed to pick that up."

Freid waited until Matt took his eyes from the departing colonel. "One cautionary note," Freid said with the barest hint of a smile, "I met my wife on a blind date."

Chapter Two

Memoirs. They wanted memoirs.

For what? So that the bloodsuckers and simpering ineffectual academics could piss back over their shoulders on his grave? Explain himself to whom? To a willingly blind generation? To a country so groomed on passivity, so slippery with the lard of weakness, that sacrifice had become a memory in league with gaslights and dump rakes? Suffering fools was indignity enough. Wasting time, priceless time, explaining the world to them was madness.

And what were the memories anyway?

There was only activity!—Movement, Accumulation, Strength, Self-Preservation. What could possibly be said?

> . . . I was born poor. I beat myself harder than my father ever could. I left. And I returned with a vision and desire so strong that they lifted me beyond the smell of the scrap from which I was cut. So strong— and I say this without sadness—that they couldn't help but take me almost all the way. I served my

country. I had what passes for a family in this world.
And I will never be lonely as long as there are men
who fear the approaching sound of my voice . . .

Memoirs.

Were they looking for confessions? For some elderly eleventh-
hour appeal? A palsied voice croaking recantations to a tape
recorder? Or did they think he was finished, that this was some
sort of done sunset, some weakening final chapter of a vigorous
read? How mistaken. How typically, sickeningly mistaken they
were.

Was there any legitimate reason to expose his true beliefs?
Not the church-Sunday, parish-breakfast-invocation bullshit he'd
been scraped against since the first day he asked a man for his
vote, but the faith that clawed honestly at your guts when you
were alone in the dark.

Tell them what?

That of the whole cold, teeming bucket of advertised human
spirit only a few bubbles form at the surface, and the rest,
unknowing, unsightful, drown under the weight of their own
ignorance.

Memoirs, my patriotic ass!

Senator Claude Revis Screws, seventy-eight-years-old, the
senior senator of the proud state of South Carolina, chairman of
the Senate Armed Services Committee and longest-standing
incumbent in either house of Congress was in no way, shape, or
form relinquishing the mantle of his watch!

Galena brought breakfast in from the kitchen.

"I see your scratch here," he told her, tapping at the notepad,
"but I cannot read this."

She was deaf to his unpleasantness. Twenty-three years of
service, her and Ellis. Forty-six years between them. There was
a way to just let unpleasantness ride.

"It's Mr. Timmons in Columbia," she said, pouring tea.
"He called twice so far. That's just this morning."

Screws caught the twist in her tone. Let her rankle all she
liked. She and Ellis, pouting around, used to having this house—
his house—to themselves every August. Timmons calling every
twenty minutes, egging her on: "How's he doing?" "Gotta get

him down here.'' "People starting to talk.'' And she at the other end of the line pulling him along like some ancient lobbyist stroking a freshman punk.

She and Ellis wanted the house and Timmons wanted him to shore up a sinking ship back in South Carolina. He could read them like big print.

Too damn bad.

He was sick. Not dying! Not ready for the memoir closet yet! The doctor he trusted was here, in Washington. That was all. He needed to rest. Going back to state would burn him out faster than a straw wick. Picnics and dedications and all manner of the same vote-grabbing bunkum that he'd suffered for forty-six years. They were thundering for him, begging and rescheduling and practically threatening—as if they didn't know better!—and it was too damn bad but he was taking his own sweet time. He'd get down there by the end of the month, but he'd be damned if he was gonna run himself dry for the slate of thin-bloods the party committee had foisted on the state this year.

"You want me to cut the fruit?'' she asked.

"Not in that tone of voice,'' he said sharply. "Just clear what's left and get back out of my sight!''

"There's the medicine . . .''

"I'll minister to myself, thank you!''

He watched her suggest that familiar servile defiance, a slight stiffening as she moved back around the table.

"Tell him I'll want the car for eleven thirty.''

"That medicine's not to be fooled with.'' Her voice was sweet with warning, bustling in white starch to the door.

"This is not a discussion!'' he said, and the cough caught at the end of his wind.

She left him wheezing, fists clenched, alone at the head of the table.

Chapter Three

Matt wandered away from the headquarters tower, his mind running dozens of small consolations: He still had a job. Still had clearance. They hadn't touched his clearance. Surprising. But then it wasn't, really. What had he done? They could've though. Could've bumped him much worse. Hell, they could've iced him completely. But they didn't. He was here. He had time to kill. He had till noon. The Thing was still on line. Harry was gone. Too bad about Harry. Fuck Harry.

It was just after nine and the main buildings were beginning to hum with activity. The bank and dry cleaners and shops that ran the length of C Corridor were just opening for business.

Two young women, girls really, he could tell as he got closer, were struggling with the steel-roll night gate in front of the travel agency. Matt could see from fifty feet away that the chain was dangling off its track. The girls pushed weakly. The gate buckled but refused to move, and the girls stopped and fell toward each other laughing. Matt figured them for high-school kids from the base working a summer job. Such an uncharacteristic scene, he thought—spontaneous laughter, youth, the failure of a single machine amidst all this technology. No one else passing seemed to notice, if they did they left it alone. Matt loitered over, thinking he might help if it felt right, if there was an opening, but then an older woman ducked out beneath the gate and sent the girls giggling back inside.

Matt moved on.

He had nearly walked the length of the three-hundred-yard hallway when it occurred to him that he had no idea where he was going. He was drifting. He'd been slugging aimlessly around the hallways for half an hour. He kept moving because he was already moving, staring at hundreds of people on their way to work.

Matt felt suddenly lightheaded. He stopped, excused himself through the traffic, and eased off out of the way. All morning his stomach had been cramping slightly. He'd been thinking it was only nerves. He suddenly realized how hungry he was.

The coffee-and-doughnut crowd in the cafeteria was thinning out. Matt felt that he needed air and took his tray to the court-yard. It seemed hotter than it had been all summer. Even now, still only morning, it felt as if the heat and humidity of the last three days combined were sitting over Washington. There was a balmy yellow haze soaking into everything from the horizon on in, and the ground, the courtyard concrete underfoot, had been saturated to some thermodynamic point of ripeness where it was already sloughing back the gathered temperature of the day. This was the close, ugly heat that all of sensible, powerful, wealthy Washington fled in summer.

Other NSA employees sat at widely spaced tables around the open plaza, alone like Matt or talking in twos and threes. Some of them Matt recognized. You often saw familiar-looking people walking through guarded hallways or in the bank or the parking lot. You'd see someone around a certain department area or pass him on a regular schedule for a while. You'd nod hello, maybe say good morning. You might even get a feel for what he was up to, add another piece to your own personal NSA jigsaw puzzle. But unless you worked with that person or there was some legitimate interdepartmental reason, real conver-sation was out of the question. For all anyone knew the co-

worker you were bitching about work to was an M-5 security
plant testing you as a potential risk.

It just wasn't done.

Matt remembered that Dave would be at the lab by now.
They'd been recruited for Research and Engineering at the same
time. David Lakeman was three years older than Matt, a masters double-E from the University of Texas. At the beginning,
Matt hated him. He was too tan, too familiar, too physical. Matt
had slid without ceremony from the cocoonlike solitude of his
parents' house to the intellectual quarantine of M.I.T. Lakeman
was a west-Texas frathouse loony who was just too smart not to
succeed. Matt was used to working quietly, shyly revealing his
progress. Lakeman was into everybody's business; constantly
kibbitzing, constantly joking and announcing results.

Looking back now, Matt could only laugh at himself. What a
dry little shit-of-a-scientist he'd been. But at the time, he was
counting the days until one of them was transferred. They
worked nearly alongside each other for six months before there
was any thaw in this opinion. Finally, no one more surprised
than Matt, Lakeman won him over.

Dave took him on as a challenging project. A design assignment. "Personality Engineering" he called it. He shepherded
Matt around to bars and parties, loosened him up, introduced
him to some exciting women, drove him too fast, made him
sick, bought him cowboy boots for Christmas, taught him to
scuba dive and split car rentals with him when they went to the
Caribbean and got serious about it.

Matt corrupted nicely, perhaps too well in the light of recent
events, and began to give as good as he got and complimented
the friendship by reigniting Dave's fading interest in pure science.

It was easy at the NSA for people to lose themselves and their
ambitions in the projects to which they were assigned. Matt's
curiosity was passionate and contagious. It was impossible for
Dave—Dave the Enthusiast—to remain unaffected for very long.
After they'd known each other a year, the better part of the time
they were alone was spent talking, arguing, and double-teaming
theoretical engineering problems. It was during one of these
drunken late nights that The Thing was born.

Almost all long-distance telephone communications in the

U.S. are transmitted via broadband microwave transmissions. Overseas satellite calls are beamed by microwave. Even transatlantic cable messages have to be demultiplexed, decoded into microwave frequencies, and then broadcast to nearby AT&T relay stations. Telegrams, banking transactions, computer data, and electronic mail are all transmitted via microwave.

With a properly placed and sized listening dish it becomes a simple task to intercept those messages. All of them. They're in the air. The NSA just reaches out and grabs them on their merry way. The problem starts when one considers the number of calls. Tens of thousands of hours are logged every day in transmission. Picking out "useful" information was the stumbling block. Over the years, the agency had developed dozens of different strategies. There were tracer signals, random samplers, automatic scanners, even the archaic system of having thousands of Central Security Service employees listen in and log calls.

Matt and Dave, over the course of two years, developed "The Thing"—a system that integrated most of the useful technology into a single approach. It wasn't a major breakthrough in intelligence gathering. There was no new application of science or theory behind it. It was simply a dogged engineering effort that had been overlooked, was needed, and would eventually save the NSA a certain amount of time and money.

They made a small presentation for Dave's department head. Clearance, a GG hike, and a tech budget came fast. It was now a matter of field testing and installation. In the past six months, they had visited two Army Security Agency listening stations around the country.

California was next.

"Not to affect previously approved travel plans."

So far, The Thing was working out.

Matt's eyes followed the tight backside of a tall brunette as she passed his table and sat down with an older man reading a newspaper nearby. Yeah, Dave would be at work by now . . .

Matt left the table and went inside to a pay phone tucked beside a bank of vending machines. He didn't have a quarter and was forced to drop three dimes. Matt thought that if he lived to be a hundred he'd remember the seven digits that was

the phone number, so intricately intwined were the emotions
and physical memories it brought flooding to mind. Matt leaned
in close to the wall as the number rang once, twice—he had his
free hand poised over the receiver switch just in case Dave was
going in late—three times it rang. A woman's voice answered
and Matt's free hand dropped into his pocket.

"Hello—"

"Perri."

"Hi! I was gonna call you later, to see if maybe I could come
by for a few hours before you went to work—"

"I'm at work."

"I thought you were on a night schedule."

"I was."

". . . What's wrong?"

"Nothing."

"You sound upset."

"I'll tell you later." Matt stroked the side of the phone. "I
almost called you last night—"

"Dave and I had a huge fight. You could have called. He
was sleeping downstairs—when can I see you? Tomorrow?"

"Definitely."

"Can you get an hour off at lunch? Your apartment? Twelve
thirty?"

"I'll see you then."

"I miss you."

Matt leaned in close to the phone. ". . . I miss you, too."

II

Dave Lakeman was dark, with straight, jet-black hair combed
back slick and shoulders too broad for the lab coat he was
wearing. He sat on the Formica counter, thick legs dangling,
and shook his head sadly: "Good night, Harry."

"He's gone."

They were alone in the kitchenette that was shared by the labs in Dave's section. The door was closed. They had the sink running and spoke softly so as not to be heard over the sound of the water.

"You really gotta watch those decimal places," Dave said to him, leaning back against the wall.

Matt stopped pacing. "The idiot dragged me down the toilet with him." His irritation cut above the sound of the faucet.

Dave gestured with two palms for quiet.

Matt's voice dropped back to a hard whisper. "After a spotless seven-year record you'd think it was obvious to them that I was a guy who takes some kind of pride in his work. Am I right?"

Dave nodded, trying to contain his amusement at Matt's uncharacteristic indignation.

"You'd think," Matt said, "they'd realize that a thing like this, the fact it even happened, would be punishment enough. Really, the more I think about it . . . they call a hearing, put me on some vague probation, and exile me to stare at snapshots all day—it really pisses me off!"

"So you're on probation. They slap your wrist. What do you expect?"

"I expect to be treated like a professional, not some eight-year-old who let the dog loose."

"You screwed up," Dave told him. "So what it's Harry's fault? You were in the room. They want to keep you but they've got to do something."

Matt focused on the water spilling down the drain. He rapped a nervous beat with his fingers against the steel sink.

"Look, we're still going to California," Dave said. "That ought to tell you right there that everything's gonna work out all right. They've got way too much money invested to let you walk. It's a slap on the wrist."

"Do you know where Imagery Analysis is?" Matt's tone was challenging.

"Indeed I do."

"I didn't even know there was a Twelve B."

Dave smiled. "I hear they're down so far you just lean out the window to keep tabs on China."

"Funny stuff," Matt said, unamused.

"The good thing is, now you're back on nine-to-five, you can give me a ride home tonight."

"You've got three cars sitting in the driveway and you still need a ride home?" Matt said. "What were you gonna do if I wasn't here?"

"Whoa, if it's out of your way I guess you could just boost me up to a geosynchronous orbit."

Matt resisted the urge to smile.

Dave lifted himself up off the counter, stretched, and gently kicked at Matt's shoulder. Matt pulled away.

"Come on, man, it's not gonna be forever."

"No, it's only gonna seem like it."

Chapter Four

NSA Security Director Leonard Vanning scanned the "New Developments" list on the morning's M-5 Internal Investigatory Report.

—Two pressman from the Sensitive Materials printing office had been arrested by Maryland State Police on assault and disorderly-conduct charges.

—An ongoing investigation into the finances of a GG-13 SIGINT technician now revealed that he was more deeply in debt than previously reported.

—There were four updated medical reports on seriously ill employees.

—An S-Group investigator now had enough evidence to start hearings against three contract secretaries from the GENS administration office who liked to meet after hours at a nearby restaurant and gossip about Soviet Intelligence Estimates over too many margaritas.

—A former COMSEC employee was making noises about writing a book about his years at the NSA.

—Two ASOC station keepers had boosted a KH-12 into an

orbit that rendered it useless for the next four days. One employee, supplied by the contractor, had been terminated from the project with instructions for follow-up intelligence, the other transferred to Imagery Analysis pending further review.

—There had been fourteen cases of intraemployee suspicions. Of the nine investigated from the previous day, all but two had moved to a higher security status. These were listed along with the day before's forty-five approved changes in security clearance and the random financial spot-check codes and the Movement and Activity Reports and the priority projections for the day's events to come.

Vanning finished his coffee while it was still warm. After checking his messages, he rescheduled a squash game with an acquaintance from Naval Intelligence. Vanning had spent nine years in the Navy, the first three during World War II. He was now a vigorous sixty-five-year-old, seven and a half months away from retirement. His skin was taut and deeply freckled— not from time on the bridge, but bronzed on the patios and beaches that surrounded his vacation home on the Pacific coast of Mexico. The dramatic cast of his features, however, was the result of a lifetime spent in the darkest bureaucratic trenches of naval and national intelligence.

Vanning's assistant, Charles Grieve, a puffy, soft-shouldered young man, stood beside him ready with copies of the three other major daily security files.

"Is there something biographical that makes sense of this?" Vanning asked, indicating the entry that revealed the SIGINT technician's incredible debts.

"It's Drew's report," Grieve said, already making a note to himself. "Probably taking it for granted you remember his earlier entry."

"Call him," Vanning said, still reading, "ask him how this guy got down so far before we picked up on it."

Vanning flipped several pages.

"This thing last night, the satellite," Vanning said, "they managed to get a full committee?"

"They convened at five in the morning," Grieve answered.

"And then who did the . . . ?"

Grieve leaned in over Vanning's shoulder.

"It's, uh . . ."

"Oh, I see," Vanning said. "Mills. Lieutenant Colonel Norman Mills."

There was a pause. Grieve sensed some irritation. "Would you like a copy of the hearing notes, sir?"

"The Air Force is really something," Vanning said, dropping the report onto his desk. "They all get up at four in the morning and rush to this hearing as if it's the goddamn Dawn Patrol. Now wait and see how they run the follow-up on the guy they terminated."

"A review, sir?" Grieve asked.

"Assinine," Vanning continued, "an entire branch of military service based on a short attention span."

The U.S. Armed Services were a group of feuding fiefdoms. There was no love lost between the Navy and Air Force, or any of the constantly competing military services.

Grieve had his notebook ready. Vanning pulled the M-5 Morning Report on Great Britain and began reading it.

". . . See what they do in two weeks."

Grieve wrote it down and then hurried off to fetch Vanning's second cup of coffee.

Chapter Five

Matt took the Muzak-ambianced elevator to the Office of Administration. Any new assignment, change in GG level, or, in Matt's case, abrupt transfer, didn't officially happen until one reported to these businesslike offices.

He was ushered into a cubicle and was seated opposite a woman whose name tag identified her as one Mrs. D. Shaver.

Their transaction took place almost wordlessly. There was little to be said. Matt handed Mrs. D. Shaver his encoded security card. She ran it through a slot scanner attached to the terminal at her work station. Instructions appeared on the screen. Without expression, silently, as if she were bagging groceries, Mrs. D. Shaver tapped an amended Imagery Analysis code onto his security card and thrust an oath form across the desk at Matt.

In the course of his NSA career Matt had seen close to a dozen of these "Memoranda of Agreement." He'd stopped trying to read them the second time. Matt flipped to the third page and dutifully signed. Mrs. D. Shaver carefully affixed her signature as witness, handed him back his security card, and cleared the computer.

Matt stood to leave.

"*My pen,*" she said, her eyes on his shirt pocket. "Before you get too attached."

II

Time to clear out his desk.

Matt rarely came to or left the NSA with a briefcase or documents of any kind, including newspapers. First of all, almost everything he came into contact with was classified and wasn't permitted to leave the building. Second, bringing in or leaving with parcels necessitated a search at the gatehouse. Lines of NSA employees waiting to pass into the unsecured world invariably formed and Matt didn't like waiting on lines.

The result was that Matt had accumulated very little in the way of personal effects within the NSA's well-policed walls.

Up until yesterday, Matt had had a standard gray desk in a high-level DEFSMAC security wing. The few things Matt did keep in its drawers, including several technical journals, a commendation from his days as a member of SIGRADE (one of a number of Special Interest Groups within the NSA) and an address book, had to be picked up.

Matt dreaded the task. News of this morning's events had surely percolated through the wing and Matt steeled himself to endure the knowing glances and significant silence of anyone there while he went through the embarrassing motions of cleaning out his desk.

Luckily it was near lunch and a mail courier was the only one he encountered. He felt like a schoolboy as he quickly stuffed the items from his desk into a manila envelope. He paused when he came across an unsigned Valentine's Day card he'd dangerously saved. The card was scented with Perri's perfume, and Matt inhaled long and deeply at its edges before sliding it into the safety of the envelope. Matt surveyed the small room that had been his office for the last two years: the half-completed telemetry equations on the chalkboard walls that would never get finished, at least not by him; the black, high-backed swivel chair; the oversize desk.

Matt felt the anger and remorse of a ballplayer who's just been sent down to the minor leagues. To Matt, this had been the best job of his life. Nothing could replace the almost juvenile excitement that came from controlling the most expensive and ultimate of remote-controlled toys—the reconnaissance satellite.

In a moment of mild retribution, Matt angrily erased the equations on the chalkboard. He turned off the lights and sulked out of the office.

Matt walked through several guard stations to get to the tower lobby. He pressed the down button on the farthest of a bank of elevators.

The polished steel doors opened and Matt stepped in. "Twelve-B," Matt said.

The FPS guard was a tall kid with bad skin and a bowl haircut, twenty-five at most. The kid nodded gravely and pressed the appropriate button. Matt took him right away as one of those blunted NSA employees whose grand ideas about the secrecy and importance of their work led them to petty and officious behavior.

They dropped without saying a word. The kid, having staked out his hard ass, just-doing-the-job territory, refused to even return Matt's look. He fooled nervously with the buckle on his belt, sure in some dwarfed, solemn fantasy that even eye contact would risk a breach of security. Matt watched the lights of the floor numbers fall and then rise again as they descended into the ground.

The elevator stopped. The doors opened.

"Subbasement twelve, sir," the kid said. "Imagery Analysis'll be down this hall here, two rights, a left, and follow it to the end of the hall. Start with the right."

Matt stepped out into the hall. He paused, examining the vacant corridor. The kid waited. "You have any questions?"

Matt shot him a look. "What? About left and right?"

The kid, confused for a second, let the door slap against his hand.

"No, no questions," Matt said.

The kid was off balance. "Yeah."

The elevator doors shut.

Matt quickly got lost. Ten minutes later he had no idea where he was going or how to get back to where he'd started.

Here was an interesting place: brightly painted pipes of varying diameters were bolted to the ceiling, giving the disturbingly long and drab corridor a colorful hint of previous human presence. Other than that, it was a barren passage in which Matt's uncertain steps were the only sound.

The corridor leading to this one had been industrially carpeted and had doors distantly spaced and disconcertingly tall and wide, as if some race of overly large people were employed within.

The corridor before that one twisted and forked, and though its closed portals were of accepted human proportion, the identifying room numbers followed no logical sequence whatever, jumping from a teen to one in the tens of thousands in the space of five steps.

The corridor previous to the jumbled door numbers had been arrived at by walking down several flights of steep stairs and passing through another corridor, and another before that, and another before that, all leading to the fact that Matt was wandering somewhere in the massive basement of the NSA's Headquarters Operations Building, walking down a deeply buried hallway marked with brightly painted service pipes.

He suspected the young FPS guard had lied to him about the directions. He turned the corner down another long hall—flashing red lights and a piercing alarm suddenly erupted. His heart jumped. He froze like a deer caught in headlights.

"You have entered a restricted area. Identify yourself."

There was nobody but Matt in the long, empty corridor. The flat, metallic voice was coming from an overhead speaker that was mounted near a small video camera that was now aimed at Matt.

"Matthew Clarke—"

"Take two steps back."

Matt did so very carefully. The spinning lights and angry siren ceased abruptly.

"Where are you going, Mr. Clarke?"

"Imagery Analysis . . . I'm lost," Matt added, hoping it was obvious.

The speaker was momentarily silent, and then rattled off instructions on how to get where he was going.

Matt followed the route back to the elevators and tried again, this time succeeding. After running his card through the door slot, Matt entered the nether world of Imagery Analysis.

III

"Congratulations, Mr. Clarke. You found us." The man was tall and reedy, probably about fifty, balding from the top down and dressed in clothes that seemed cut for someone smaller. He took off his glasses, squinting in Matt's direction. "I'm Henry Sylbert." He offered a pale hand. "Director of Imagery Analysis."

They shook.

"Welcome. It's Matthew or Matt? Or is there . . . ?"

"Matt. Matt's fine."

"Matt it shall be." Henry Sylbert looked down at the bulky manila envelope in Matt's hand. He smiled thinly. "Bring your lunch, did you?"

Matt, unsure, turned and caught his line.

"Oh, no . . . tanning lotion."

Henry Sylbert laughed, a little too much, and then just as quickly stopped. The curious smile fell off a degree.

"Just kidding," Matt said, trying to cover any damage.

"Of course," Henry said. "Your personal things. No problem at all. We'll leave them here for the moment. Jean will keep an eye on it for you."

A heavy woman at a near desk looked up from her work, nodded. Matt followed Henry Sylbert from the reception area down a short hallway and through a set of double doors.

A dozen drafting tables were spread evenly across the large underground room. Every work station was lit by a single, high-intensity overhead fixture. The dim cast of the place and the sharp focus of the lamps formed bright islands of light around the men and women who sat hunched over their angled white boards. There was a nearly uniform posture, almost devotional; all heads were down, all vision directed through optical pieces attached to swivels on the desk frames.

If a single face turned, Matt missed it as his eyes adjusted to the contrast levels.

"Very quiet . . ." Matt observed, feeling he had to say something, aware that Henry was watching him.

"It's peaceful work . . ." Henry smiled again and then started away. Matt followed.

Matthew Clarke presented an odd case for Henry Sylbert. The sealed transfer memo had been on his desk when he arrived at work that morning. It gave the standard details: name, date, subject's security clearance, pay grade, previous department. A blue slip of paper stapled to the memo indicated that Matthew Clarke was on internal probation. Any unusual behavior was to be reported at once to M-5.

Henry had been running this section for almost ten years, been a deputy for six before that, and had never encountered a stranger transfer than this one. Here was a GG-17, pulling down more money with higher clearance than anybody in the department except himself. His prior section, Henry knew, accepted no one without superb engineering credentials.

What was he doing here?

Yes, people liked the work. Imagery Analysis had a history of high employee satisfaction, but the relatively quiet section was not one of the fast tracks at the NSA.

Henry weighed two alternatives as he led Matt through the dim room.

Matthew Clarke, this sharp young man with the easy smile and suntan jokes, was either here as a plant to observe the section—and that was a real possibility—or he had done something horrendously wrong and was being punished with this assignment in the basement. Neither choice was appealing. The section ran well and produced without problems. Were there complaints? Was there trouble that had gone unnoticed? Were reports floating around upstairs? If there was a leak he should've been informed.

On the other hand he didn't much like the idea of IA being used as a dumping ground for the mistake-makers of other sections.

Henry suspended opinion.

Matt followed him to an empty drafting table away from the others on the far side of the room. Several heads lifted slightly as they passed.

"This will be your work station," Henry told him, as he gently folded away the plastic dust cover. "A desk with a good bit of history."

"How's that?"

"This was Mrs. Childs's station," Henry paused, squared the stereoscopic viewer. ". . . Wonderful woman."

Matt detected a wistful tone.

"She was a cratologist, one of our best I'm afraid."

Matt's blank look brought an explanation from Henry. "A cratologist. From years of study, Mrs. Childs could estimate with a high degree of precision the contents of a crate, say on a Soviet frieghter or dock, by its size and shape. She developed cataracts which forced her departure. Analyzing photographs was her passion. She frequently worked ten, twelve hours a day. The result over a period of years was . . . inevitable."

"I'm sorry."

"Oh, please, no." Henry waved away Matt's concern. "She enjoyed her time here."

"I guess that's what counts," Matt said.

"We'll hope so," Henry said without expression. "You were a satellite systems specialist?"

"Yes," Matt said.

"And you've probably never seen the product."

"No," Matt admitted. "You mean the pictures, right?"

Henry nodded.

"No, I never have."

Henry smiled. He knew now. Just the way Matthew Clarke said "pictures" was enough. This young man had been exiled. No question about it, and no sense in making the worst of a bad situation.

"See, I've never liked the way they do it," Henry said. "All this compartmentalization. Someone, like yourself, works for years doing a job only knowing that piece of the work that comes before you. Should a man make tires his whole life and never once see a car?''

Henry turned on the lamp above the table and pulled close a tall, well-padded drafting chair. "Sit down. Please."

Matt took the seat. He wouldn't have wanted to sit there for twenty years, but it was comfortable enough.

"These are more than just pictures, Matt." Henry adjusted the easel as he spoke. "The photographs taken by your section, excuse me, former section, are an extraordinary thing. My God, from here, from this building, or from the Pentagon, or from the White House, a person decides he wants to see a thing halfway around the world. Really see it, in close to real-time. A Soviet soldier applying reactive armor to a tank in the field, or a weeping Afghani mother hunched over the body of a child killed by some forgotten mine—*we can see these things*. Hundreds of square miles captured on a single frame of film. Hundreds of thousands of details awaiting interpretation."

Henry paused, measured Matt. "I think you'll take to this kind of work."

"Well . . . I hope so."

"Look around you," Henry said, leading Matt's eyes around the room. "Professional curiosity and voyeurism often become difficult to distinguish, and the result is, well, as you can see—"

Indeed, there was an unusual, quiet intensity settled over the place. Each person seemed truly absorbed in the work.

"I'll be back in a moment."

Henry left Matt alone, shuffling off toward a series of offices that lined the far wall.

Mrs. Childs had been a good deal shorter than Matt. He adjusted the stool and sat and waited and wondered how in the world he could possibly stay rooted to this light table hours on end twelve floors beneath the ground. Maybe Harry was better off.

People kept working. Several stood and stretched. Two men joined a women at her desk across the room for a hushed conversation. Certainly, in a room full of people trained to spot details on photographs taken thousands of miles away, his presence was noted. Matt looked around but no one met his glance.

Henry returned with a poster-size folder and carefully removed a large photograph that nearly covered the entire surface of Matt's light table. Matt moved to one side as Henry deftly clamped and adjusted the print. This done, he lifted his glasses and peered down through the stereoscopic viewing piece, gently turning its position with two knobs on either side.

"There we go," Henry said, standing back. "This covers a small portion of Central Russia. I've got you cued in over an airbase outside Sverdlovsk. Go on."

He stepped away and motioned for Matt to look.

Matt leaned in.

Two mechanics working on a fighter plane bearing a dark black star leaped off the picture. It was incredibly clear. Both men wore dark coveralls. One stood on a ladder and was leaning into the open cockpit, adjusting something. The other man was caught ducking under the plane's swept wing. The detail was astounding. The stereoscopic viewing piece gave the scene depth of field and a tremendously lifelike aspect, and because of a two-to-three–fold vertical exaggeration, tiny details seemed to leap off the board. It was as if Matt were floating just above them. As if he spit they'd jump.

"Jesus . . ."

"You'll note it's in black and white."

"He's leaning into the plane," Matt murmured, almost to himself.

"That's a MIG-29—your first lesson," said Henry. "It was over Sverdlovsk, on a Sunday morning in May 1, 1956, that Gary Powers's U-2 was shot down. That was before satellites."

Henry leaned over and changed the setting: "Maximum detail."

Matt leaned back in. The landscape was now *astounding*. The mechanic leaning into the cockpit had short hair, his sleeves were rolled up, and he looked powerfully built. What must have been a tray of tools had been laid on the empty pilot's seat. The image was clear enough to see that the mechanic ducking under the wing was dragging wheel chocks behind him.

Matt had heard about the quality of high-resolution satellite photographs, but this—seeing what he was seeing now—was breathtaking. He didn't want to stop looking.

"It's something, isn't it?" Henry said, content with Matt's reaction. "Shall we see the rest of the facility?"

Imagery Analysis was smaller than he'd thought. Most of the nation's satellite photographs, referred to as "overhead assets" in the bureaucratic jargon of defense planners, were stored and analyzed by the National Photographic Interpretation Center, an innocuous, windowless building down by the Navy Yard.

IA was the NSA's own small, in-house version, much like the CIA's Imagery Analysis Section.

Matt was shown the computer facilities, introduced to the filing department and the clerks who kept track of the section's active material, glimpsed briefly the archival rooms, and met the office staff. Henry gave Matt a tour of the reference library, pointing out such page-turners as "Soviet Tank Profiles and Top Views," "Concrete Foundation Structures," and "Photogrammetry: Dimensions from Shadow Lengths." Matt was given the necessary cipher-codes, shown the men's room, the conference areas, the lounge.

Finally he was taken to the projection rooms. Henry led him to the second of five doors that ran the length of a narrow hallway. He knocked lightly, then entered, motioning for Matt to follow.

A small, energetic Asian man came forward from the darkness and greeted Henry. Behind him, on the wall, was the huge, detailed, black-and-white enlargement of some sprawling military installation.

"Reiko," Henry said, "I'd like to introduce our new addition. Matthew Clarke, Reiko Murata."

"Nice to meet you," Matt said, squinting into the room.

The little man edged closer. "How do you do?" he answered. His voice was high. His eyes were sharp and excited. He thrust forward a delicate hand and shook vigorously.

"Reiko's my deputy here," Henry said to Matt. "I'm going to put you slightly in his care."

"Sounds good," Matt said.

Reiko flashed a smile, glancing back and forth between the two men.

"Why don't you give Matt just a quick rundown on what you're doing?" Henry said.

"Certainly."

Matt watched as the man rushed back into the darkness. Suddenly he reappeared, bathed now in the light of the rear-projection. He held a pointer in his hand. He moved toward the screen and then, forgetting something, he hurried back to a console in the center of the room. He hit a switch and a grid was instantly superimposed on the photograph.

"This is a Soviet ICBM base near Yakutsk," he announced, gesturing broadly with the pointer. "We've been doing a concentrated series. There were reports that a recent earthquake damaged a couple of the silos."

He reached and tapped at a circular shape at the center of the blowup.

"There's been more seismic activity in the area. That's for certain. I guess they can test that pretty accurately. And now there's reports, conflicting reports, that the place is being scrapped. So what we're doing is looking for evidence to figure it out one way or another."

He danced back to a corner of the enlargement. He was pleased with the interruption, the chance to explain.

Remembering something, Reiko squinted through the light at Matt. "I normally wouldn't discuss my impressions of what's on a photo with you until after you'd had a chance to study it, so as not to bias your opinion of what's on the screen. But this *is* a demonstration."

Reiko returned to the screen. "These are the support troop sheds, here. And the officers' quarters. And here, we think probably the main kitchen, that's this, here . . ." He tapped at the locations as he spoke. "You see, a personnel count, a good one, is very important in this kind of problem."

Matt moved into the room, closer to the screen.

"We know, for example," Reiko went on, "it takes a crew of about fifteen to operate and maintain each—"

"That's fine, Reiko," Henry interrupted. "Don't want to scare him off first day out." He turned to Matt. "It's a lot to absorb all at once."

"Pretty interesting." There was a hint of surprise in Matt's voice. His eyes never left the screen.

"I think the best way to proceed, maybe Reiko has some

other ideas, is to get you started with some silhouette hand-
books. Get you studying. Shadow lengths. Supply indicators.
There's a lot to learn—''

"You can make this larger, right?" Matt asked. "I mean,
you can focus in on a certain piece of the grid."

"Of course," Reiko said.

Matt walked up to the screen and pointed at an area behind
the main kitchen. There was an indistinct cluster of shapes
beside an open halftrack. "I'm just curious," Matt said, "this
little crowd back here."

"I'll pull it up," Reiko told him. He darted back to the
console and a moment later the area behind the kitchen filled the
screen.

"Well," Henry laughed.

"I missed that," Reiko admitted, moving closer for a better
look. "It looks like a bottle of something."

"They're soldiers and it's cold," Henry offered.

"And probably bored," added Matt.

"Vodka," Henry said.

"You'd never guess they were working with nuclear weapons," said Reiko.

"Perhaps they're not," Henry threw out with significance.
"Anymore that is."

Reiko turned and tipped an imaginary hat in Henry's direction.

"Then again," Matt said, "maybe they are and they're just
smiling for the camera."

The way Matt said it made Henry's antennae jump.

This young man. These good eyes. The quick skill. The
complex deduction. The sudden transfer. Henry reopened the
mental file on Matthew Clarke he'd closed earlier that afternoon.

Chapter Six

On an estate several lazy kilometers outside Saint Maxime, a quiet town that hugged the crescentic southern coast of France, it was six hours ahead of the Washington, D.C., lunch hour. The sky was slowly fading from light blue to deep black, while on the ground shade was melting into shadow. Against this darkening light, a sparrow fell from a high eucalyptus tree and performed a graceful series of rapid stalls that brought it to the dewy grass several yards away from Jacques Seydoux's white wooden lawn chair.

It was the golden hour of a late-August day. The sun, having blazed furiously overhead from early morning on, had now cooled to a particularly tranquil shade of red in its last moments of life above the horizon.

Seydoux watched the sinking, peach-size disk from a chair pointed west on a promontory overlooking the Mediterranean. He had an orchestra seat in a gaudily lit amphitheater of orange and gold.

Unblinking, unmoving, he was suffused with an almost over-whelming calm by the sun's soft hues and the icy gin and tonic with lime resting in his right hand.

For two weeks each August, the ever-growing Seydoux family converged on their well-tended vacation estate by the sea. It was a rundown but spacious hillside villa when Jacques Seydoux purchased it in 1964, the year he was appointed an attaché to the French consulate in London.

Since then the house and grounds had grown with Seydoux's prosperity—each carefully planned addition and renovation over the passing years reflecting events in his healthy, thriving existence: the new wing constructed when the twin girls were born; the extra rooms added for the sons; a tennis court shoehorned into the increasingly landscaped property when Seydoux was named Minister Counselor to the French embassy in Washington, D.C.; and, at great expense, a guest cottage and sparkling pool installed two years ago, marking Jacques Seydoux's appointment as French ambassador to the United States.

Seydoux relaxed in the inclined chair, set at the end of the long sloping lawn, and stared out at the sunset-tinged sea. He didn't feel sixty-seven, and in the sun's rosy twilight glow he didn't look it. He had a long, handsome face, relatively unlined by the passage of time. The straight, once black hair, now streaked with a distinguished gray, was elegantly smoothed back from his high forehead. Sad, dark eyes and a mouth set into a permanent half smile gave Seydoux a detached, preeminent look.

It was a diplomat's face, and Seydoux, like a card player, had total control of the messages it could send. At this moment the face radiated genuine peacefulness. Seydoux was taking his family to dinner tonight; his stately wife, attractive sons and daughters, their assorted fiancés and spouses, and two grandchildren—eleven in all, with he their patriarchal head. Behind him, their various voices carried down the rolling expanse of manicured grass from the open windows and doors of the main house. Somebody, his son's fiancée most likely, was playing a haunting melody—Beethoven?—on the downstairs piano. A brief rise of laughter echoed from one of the upstairs bedrooms. The light splash of a running shower trickled through the evening air.

In this chair, in this place, at this instant, Seydoux was floating in a reverie of utter contentment. Even the distant thought of returning to Washington in two days—back to the tight budgeting of his time, back to the meetings dovetailed with conferences spliced to receptions—couldn't penetrate his dreamy state.

Seydoux was drifting. The past filled his mind's eye. Like a climber who's pulled himself to the top of a mountain and turned to embrace the view, Seydoux was thinking back on the long, twisting trail that had brought him to this spot.

His family had been farmers for generations in the Basses-Alpes, a tradition broken by his father, who, after being badly wounded in both legs during World War I, turned to a less physical calling and became a modestly successful provincial lawyer. He married. They named their first child Jacques.

Jacques Seydoux was sent off at a tender age to mature in a remote Swiss boarding school. He thrived there until September 3, 1939, when Hitler invaded Poland and France declared war on Germany.

It was then, at seventeen, that he joined tens of thousands of other grinning, jaunty young men who held a fatally inflated view of the state of the French war machine and enlisted in the Army in large, boisterous groups bellowing patriotic songs.

Assigned to the distinguished French 4th D.L.C., Seydoux was stationed with a detachment guarding the Yvoir bridge over the Meuse River.

Through a beautiful fall and very harsh winter, it wasn't much of a war. And then suddenly it was. No one was more stunned then Seydoux when, after eight long months of mind-numbing calm, the first elements of the German Army abruptly appeared late one May afternoon on the other side of the bridge, their armored cars belligerently racing to cross before it was blown.

The fractured seconds that followed earned Seydoux the Croix de Guerre, for when the span's set demolition charges failed to explode and destroy the vital link, he left his pillbox and, borrowing from the melodramatic account of the citation—"under a withering hail of bullets and shrapnel, did valiantly, and with no regard for his personal safety, charge forty meters of exposed railing to light the demolition charges by hand, and in so doing, greatly impede the enemy's progress."

By all rights he should have been killed. If not killed maimed. Nothing touched him.

He came through it all as well off as if he'd stepped out to get the morning paper. It was an absurdly heroic act, and only many years later, after giving much thought to his motives at the instant he stood up and stumbled into the slow-motion, sepia-tinged realm of valor, did Seydoux finally conclude with a shrug that he must have been temporarily insane.

Seydoux's unit fought and retreated until a reeling France fell an ignominious six weeks later, after which he remained in-country as a Resistance fighter until the Allied liberation in 1944.

Having relied on U.S. arms and agents with his life during the war, Seydoux was fascinated by America. He became obsessed with going there. He had a plan, and using the connections of his American liaison officer in the OSS, applied to and was accepted by Georgetown University.

Seydoux resolved to make the most of the situation, and once he set his mind to something, Jacques Seydoux was not to be detoured.

In 1951, after six years in Washington, D.C., Seydoux returned to France with a wife from Virginia, a perfect, though somewhat contrived, American accent, and a master's in political science. Back in Paris, Seydoux's war friends emerged from the grass. Cutting through their arcane probings, Seydoux realized he was being offered employment by the Service de Documentation Extérieure et du Contre-Espionnage, the French Intelligence Service.

He took the job.

To this day, there were many things Seydoux never discussed about his eleven years with the SDECE. There were incidents from that time, one incident—one decision in particular, he desperately tried to forget. After all, he was now a man of peace, a diplomat of the highest level. Deep down he believed he had earned the right of absolution.

It was ironic, Seydoux pondered, how drastically things change given time.

History.

He and his contemporaries had seen much violent history in

their relatively brief span; had lived to see yesterday's bitter enemies become today's undying friends. His son's fiancée, for example, was German.

Everything turns around.

A moment comes, the rules seem clear, and you act—committing something in the name of patriotism that at another time would be considered criminal.

Sitting in his white lawn chair, lost in that Elysian twilight, thinking back, Jacques Seydoux felt the sudden return of a familiar gnawing in his gut. He shifted uncomfortably in his seat.

There was no escaping the fact that at any time, maybe never, maybe long overdue, the reverberations from that one fateful act he'd been party to years earlier—committed in a different world, committed under different rules—the shock waves from that one act might suddenly make themselves felt. And in the light of the rules of the present, under the scrutiny of those who had no idea what the real circumstances had been when the act had been committed—a true act of patriotism, mind you—the act would be seen as heinous and unforgivable and would destroy Jacques Seydoux and all the good he had since created.

It was the events of one week, in mid-May 1954, that Seydoux dreaded would one day catch up with him.

Seydoux stared out at the sea . . . the sea . . . the sea. The memories of the atom bomb test he'd witnessed in the South Pacific and what followed immediately afterward blackened his thoughts like an ink drop. He involuntarily shuddered, awaking as if from a dream.

The moment was lost.

The sun, Seydoux realized with a start, had sunk from sight. It was dark. His hands were cold and his drink had gone warm. And from within the house, Seydoux noticed with a pang, the music of the downstairs piano had stopped.

Chapter Seven

The hallowed rite began with the sounding of a bell. A solemn incantation followed from the disembodied voice of the ceremony's high priest, the doorman: "Lady here to see you, Mr. Clarke."

After a zealous bound to the intercom, Matt would invariably respond with a quick: "A'right."

Next came a brief period of intense, almost spiritual introspection, as Matt paced his apartment awaiting the soft knock at the door. This was a time of raging emotions: overwhelming guilt warring with dizzying desire; giddy anticipation tossed by an undertow of dread.

Inner turmoil ceased in the face of Perri's arrival. The apartment door had barely closed before they were careening for the bedroom. It was a profound, explosive, almost violent gratification that afterward left them sheened and gasping.

She was small and thin with long black hair. Only twenty-four. She said it was the kind of love Dave was incapable of giving her. This was a remark Matt never explored. Out of some strange sense of loyalty he didn't want to hear her speak badly of his friend.

61

Their time was short. Following sex they lay silent in a doomed, empty calm—as if trapped in the eye of a storm—glancing at the clock like it was an approaching wall of clouds. Talk was relegated to the phone calls that preceded each meeting and rarely included analysis of their affair.

What could be said about it? She was guilty of adultery. He was guilty of much worse.

It had begun with fantasizing. Then stolen glances. Three months ago, Dave left Matt to squire Perri to a wedding. They danced. Drank. Suddenly kissed. Things happened rapidly after that.

It was continuing. Recently they'd fumbled to the conclusion that it soon had to end. It was just a matter now of one person pulling the switch. The other would understand, most likely be grateful. It had been going on, at least one such lunch-hour tryst a week, for three anxious months.

Perri was leaving and Matt walked her to the door. He had his hand at the small of her back.

"We should think about stopping," he said.

She kissed Matt quickly on the cheek and left.

II

Matt felt, as he looked down, as if he were all alone in a balloon.

For three weeks he'd meandered along at will as a silent, grainy, unmoving world went about its business below. It reminded him of the feeling he'd had while diving in the Caymans last year with Dave. The water had been so clear, so beautifully crystal clear, that Matt had had the sensation he was weightless and flying.

Staring down at the satellite photos, he felt he was flying again. A group of East German schoolchildren taking lunch at long tables set up beside a playing field . . . a busy Soviet military railway depot . . . a long line of shoppers waiting outside a store in the suburbs of Prague . . . a stalled nuclear reactor project in Pakistan . . . an automated copper strip mine in the Urals . . . four topless girls sunbathing on an apartment-house roof in Leningrad.

Every day was spent peering down into a miniature, perfectly detailed, unmoving world. A little over six weeks had drifted past and it hadn't been that bad. Matt was left alone to learn. The work *was* peaceful and there was, as Henry pointed out, a deep voyeuristic appeal. Matt's interest had never been confined to hard science and, once resigned to the assignment, he began to soak up everything they threw at him. He grew impatient quickly once a subject was exhausted, but Henry was sharp to this and there was a lot to learn.

Matt had never been so aware of his own vitality. The basement staff, the other analysts anyway, had a universally beaten-down quality. There was nearly obsessional attention paid to territory—lockers and desks and projection time—a trait that Matt thought suggested a slightly twisted communal nature. The place ran with the small-minded quiet of a parish reading room. Matt could only figure that it was the product of the recruitment process because there was nothing in the way the section was administered that seemed to encourage this. You were given a daily, weekly, or long-term assignment. You filled Henry or Reiko in on where you stood from time to time and the rest was up to you.

Matt wasn't shunned. Not exactly. But there was a further distance between him and the others than fell between themselves. He didn't sweat it. If it was going to be a temporary job then he didn't mind being an outsider.

The microwave installation, the California trip, was coming up over the weekend. Henry had seemed surprised, first at Matt's early release for two afternoons to finalize arrangements for the tech crew, and then at the approved travel waivers.

And now, after several weeks of reference books and file photographs, they'd thrown him his first assignment: doing comparative coverage of an ELINT station being constructed near Dushanke.

Matt looked up and realized that almost everyone had left for the day. He checked his watch. It was nearly six and he was due to meet Dave in the parking lot in fifteen minutes. He shut down his desk and ran the photographs back to the file room.

Coming back, past the projection area, Matt noticed Henry and Reiko sitting in the shadows of a darkened room. The door was open and Matt couldn't help but see the image flattened on the wall.

He quietly stepped in closer.

The screen was alive with the black-and-white details of an exhausted desert war scene. Some remote, ancient outpost was being overrun. Bodies and matériel were strewn about as if by some angry child in a sandbox. Abstractly, from the distance of the hallway, it held an unusual graphic appeal. Expressionist warfare. A pointillist battle. It was almost beautiful. Most of the section's photographs were dense with information and framed randomly. This was sparse and textured, with a quality and composition that looked staged.

"North Africa photographs well, doesn't it?" Henry asked over his shoulder.

"Sorry," Matt said, startled. "Couldn't help looking."

"Nonsense." Henry quickly half-turned in his seat. "It's the 'Photo of the Week.' Come in . . . come in."

Matt edged from the doorway into the shadows.

"A real candidate for 'Shot of the Month,' " Henry continued expansively. "You should see this."

Reiko, his head nodding affirmatively, turned back to Matt. "One of the year's ten best."

"Join us," Henry said. "Join us for 'Photo of the Week.' "

Matt noted some new melody in Henry's voice. His eyes jumped back from the screen and picked up on the bottle of Chivas between the two men.

"Do you drink good scotch?" Henry asked. "We've an extra glass and ice."

"A short one," Matt said. "Sure."

This resolved, Reiko turned back to the screen.

"Rituals of the basement," Henry said as he poured and handed the glass to Matt. "Salut."

Matt followed Henry's glass in a casual arc to his lips.

"Some photographs make it," Henry said, "because, well, not because they're such wonderful images—as this is, of course—but because they have a currency. Some immediate, pressing global importance. Breakthrough photos, if you like." Henry gestured to the screen. "Others have little use, but then . . . then there are . . ."

The picture simply pulled you in. It covered perhaps two hundred square yards of desert, and the edge, what seemed to be the perimeter, of a mud-brick low-walled enclosure. The charred shells of three large trucks were grouped at bottom left. They were pointed strangely, as if some chaotic retreat had been badly interrupted. Bodies and parts of bodies and burned sheets of canvas and bits of metal and twisted black scraps of debris spread out away from the blackened center—the dead trucks— like satellites fanning out in thinner and thinner orbits.

Above that, a long portion of the low wall had collapsed. This whole area, on either side of the rupture, was dotted with the deadly blossoms of grenade explosions. More men, the bodies of maybe fifteen, were weaved in among the stones and sand that had been kicked up by the battle.

But then, to the far right, just outside the earthwork, was where the drama climaxed.

It was tough to see at first. The shadows were harsh. But when you'd digested the rest of the scene it was obvious: three men were lined against the remnant of a wall facing a firing squad of five soldiers.

The shots had not yet been discharged but the guns were raised!

For an instant, Matt's senses were jolted—this was something private, something evil, something that was never really meant to be seen. It was an unchangable, merciless moment that had been captured and frozen by a silent machine circling two hundred miles up.

"Oh shit," Matt murmured as the shapes took hold.

"Afraid so." Henry answered from the dark.

As they stared in silence, it occurred to Matt that those men had, in all likelihood, died looking to the heavens—to a Greater Being—for salvation and miracle, and had instead been swallowed by a lens in the mouth of a system that represented man's greatest denial of spiritual modesty.

And here were the three of them, sipping scotch twelve floors

beneath the ground, thousands of miles and maybe half-a-cultural-
century removed, marveling in another language at the ability of
it, their distance from it, and teasing themselves with the false
sense of security that bound those ideas together.

"Where is this?" Matt found himself asking.

"This was taken Sunday last," Henry said, stopping to sip.
"The group outside the wall, the firing squad, are Ethiopian
government troops." He leaned in over Reiko's shoulder. "What
did Montone call them?"

"Brigands," Reiko answered plainly. "Mercenaries from the
Sudan."

"They represent the government," Henry continued. "The
losers are members of the Eritrean People's Liberation Front.
It's a battle for independence. A fight for sand. Been going on
for some time."

"Eleven years," Reiko said. "Tens of thousands of casualties."

Matt let his astonishment drift into a hard pull on the Chivas.
"Who wins?"

Henry crossed his legs. "Well, this is the loss of the outpost
in Teseny, which, if you're interested, is a hundred miles
southwest of Asmara."

"The Eritreans will take it back next week," Reiko said with
a knowing twinge of resignation. "I did coverage on this two
years ago. Classic seesaw conflict."

"Never heard of it," Matt admitted. "If I did, I . . ."

The specifics of it—Sunday last, the five raised rifles, the
three men on their knees—took the air out of his thought.

Reiko turned back and poured himself a finger of scotch.
"Twenty-two major conflicts in progress right now around the
globe. Over 400,000 deaths in '88 alone."

Matt could tell that Reiko had been one of those kids who
thrived on the squeamish reactions of others. Eagerly leading
friends to dead animals on the highway.

"That's not including lesser skirmishes and revolts and such,"
he added, offering the bottle before he capped it.

Matt declined. Henry freshened his own and they sat and
stared.

" 'Photo of the Month,' " Reiko said after a moment.
"Definitely."

Matt caught Henry watching him.

"A bit depressing, isn't it?" Henry's tone was soothing. "Much like watching ants killing each other."

Something from the recesses of Matt's mind surfaced and then he spoke, almost absently: "War, children, is just a shot away . . . it's just a shot away . . ."

Reiko nodded deeply.

"Burke?" Henry asked over his glass.

"Mick Jagger," it suddenly occurred to Matt.

III

Matt came up from the basement, out of the refrigerated air of the building and into the comfortable afterglow of a mid-October day. He threaded his way through the large parking lot to his car. Dave was already there, a gift-wrapped package in hand, leaning against the old BMW's door.

"Everybody else's mother was here to pick them up on time," he said, kicking a pebble for emphasis.

Matt glanced at the present. "What's that?"

"Perri's birthday's coming up."

They got into the car and Matt started the engine.

"She told me to tell you she wants some lace panties," Dave said and then turned to face Matt. He suddenly broke out laughing. "I love her sense of humor!"

Matt nodded, forcing a grin.

IV

The Cloverleaf Tavern in a suburban bar on M Street, a few blocks east of Georgetown University. People who go there are

attracted by its basic simplicity: a bar, tables in the back if you
want to sit and drink, and a TV mounted over the door. Years
ago, it had been just one of dozens of such unadorned drinking
establishments. But it had become an oddity—a dark saloon for
serious drinkers now surrounded by brightly lit fern bars serving
Perriers and lite beer.

The owner's movements were beyond economy of motion.
Duka Simms had developed an almost miserly attitude about the
expense of his energies behind the bar. He liked to roll into a
position and take care of as much business there as possible
before moving on. He spent little patience on customers who
changed minds or suddenly needed glasses for their beer or
wanted cigarette quarters where they sat. There was no arguing
about it. No court of higher appeal. He owned the Cloverleaf
and if you wanted some other kind of service then fuck yourself
and keep your money.

He was a huge man of fifty-eight and his body had given in
hard to gravity. The once-hulking foresquare shoulders and
ornamental chest had fallen down around his apron. His classic
pose, thirty years in the making, had those thick arms out to his
side, one at the taps, one at the register, and his head cocked up
at the TV set.

With the natural compensation that joins most handicaps,
Duka's reluctance to move was nearly balanced by his highly
developed bar-ear. This was not the kind of auditory skill that
doctors could measure. In fact, if anything, Duka had suffered
some hearing loss as a Marine Corps heavyweight contender.
This was a talent that only came with time behind the stick.
From his spot at the center of the rail, with the television blaring
a Bullets final quarter and the jukebox droning the same old
stale shit from across the tables in the back, Duka could hear,
distinguish, and provide caustic running commentary on almost
every bar conversation and order that carried above a whisper.

Matt and Dave were in their seats of choice at the far corner.
They'd been regulars for years, and Duka had a good enough
idea of what they did to steer clear when they were talking
business.

Matt shook his head. "I knew it was gonna get out," he said,
sounding wounded. "The jokes probably started last week."

"No, no, you could tell he had no idea what happened," Dave said. "He was fishing. I set him straight."

Matt stared at Dave, incredulous. "You told Feckler what happened?"

"He kept badgering me."

"*Feckler?*" Matt considered this for a second, then changed his mind and waved the whole idea out past the bar. "No way. I'm not falling for this."

"God's honest," Dave said. "When he asked me the third time I figured I had to tell him something just to get him off my back." Dave took a long smiling pull on his beer. He finished and wiped his mouth. "I told him you got kicked upstairs to a Deputy DIRNSA program and that he'd better be nice to you next time you meet."

"Very funny."

"Watch him bend over the next time he sees you in the hall."

"You're not the one whose career's been body-slammed into the basement."

"Relax already." Dave poured the last of his beer into his glass. He was just starting to get that look in his eye. A little more west-Texas was creeping back into his voice. "It's not that late. Why don't you call Lorraine, or Judy, or Ruth, or any of them, and maybe I can get the widow Lakeman to join us for dinner."

Matt inwardly winced. He'd purposely been avoiding being in the same room with Dave and Perri for some time, particularly now. He didn't think he could handle it. The girls Dave had just mentioned were all imaginary partners Matt had made up over the last few months in the misguided belief that Dave needed to be fooled into thinking he was too busy with other women to ever have an affair with his best friend's wife.

"It's seven thirty," Matt noted. "You're dinner's probably ready and waiting, besides, I got a date later on tonight," which was a lie.

"Duka," Dave called down the bar, "will you do me a favor and tell my friend here that if he doesn't start giving it a rest it's going to fall off and run away."

Duka's eyes never left the TV: "He should be so fortunate."

Matt sat back. "Duka, maybe you could do *me* a favor and tell Dave here that if he doesn't start minding his own business he's gonna end up taking a bus to work the rest of the week while he fixes his car."

"Hey, Jimmy!" Duka called to an older man at the end of the bar.

"Yeah?"

"Jimmy, do *me* a favor and tell these two senators to pay their tab, leave a big tip, and get the hell out of here before Dave's wife starts calling."

"Perhaps if I sing something . . ."

Dave stood. "Enough said."

Duka shifted his weight for the first time in five minutes. "Thank you, James."

Matt slapped a bill on the bar and followed Dave to the door.

"Whatever it is," Duka called after them, "it ain't enough."

V

"I'm gonna need a little help," Dave said, as Matt drove them the ten minutes from the bar to Dave's house. "She's not too keen on this weekend. She thinks we're rolling off to Vegas again for four days."

"Why don't you just tell her?"

Dave shook his head. "This is an area where national security and my need for marital independence clearly intersect."

"I think you could tell her," Matt said.

"What do you know about it?"

Matt went still, trying to sense the range of danger. ". . . Nothing." It came softly, timidly.

Dave smiled. "You're forgetting that I won this woman with the secret-agent routine."

"Right."

Dave had Matt pull slowly around the residential block from the blind side. They stopped just short of the clear view from the kitchen and Matt surveyed the house. Located in Chevy Chase—it was a forty-year-old white colonial suburban dream that Dave had mortgaged himself to his eyebrows to buy. He kept it up, mowed the lawn and all, but the driveway looked like a chop-shop. Three cars were in various states of repair. The centerpiece was a big-fin '59 Caddy on blocks.

"I'm hiding her stuff out in the Caddy," he told Matt. "The woman is a snoop. Every Christmas, birthday, same thing. Last year she just happened to have bought matching shoes and a coat for a dress I was giving her. This time I'm setting her up. I'm leaving junk hidden around the house for her to find."

Dave pushed the door open, stepped out.

"I was thinking," Matt said, watching him, "are your tanks filled?"

Dave had moved to the nearby Caddy. "Why?—you going diving?"

The idea had come to Matt out of the blue, from some residual feeling of nervousness and guilt. "I don't know, I started thinking what a shame—to go all the way out to California, get right up next to the Pacific, and not take a little dip. They're giving us a car, right?"

Dave lit up his maniac's grin. Matt was happy to see him smile.

"How close is Rock Ranch to the water?" Dave asked, as he opened the Caddy door and hid Perri's present under the car's front seat.

"I don't know," Matt said. "Can't be that far."

"Well, hell, don't lead me on. Look into it!" Dave, still smiling, checked the house again. "Christ, that's gonna go down great. Off on agency business carrying tanks and fins."

"Knocks out Vegas."

"Shit," Dave said, "there must be some kind of diving around there. *That* is a great idea."

"What amazes me, is that by the time you get up tomorrow morning you're gonna be sure that you thought of it."

"That's leadership ability for you, son," he drawled. "Watch and learn."

Dave quietly closed the Caddy door. He turned back to Matt. "Well, c'mon."

"What?"

"Dinner's waiting."

"I told you already—I got—"

"A date later on, I know. You're coming in for dinner now though. No excuses. Perri insisted."

"Perri did?"

Dave shrugged. "Doesn't think you eat enough. And when's the last time you saw her?—you haven't been over for months."

"I'm tired," Matt said, catching sight of a figure moving in the kitchen. "Really."

Dave followed Matt's stare. "Oh—look, she's waving. She sees us. No escape now. Stop being such an idiot about this— her cooking's not that bad."

Dave started up to the house.

Matt could see her in the window, motioning for them to come in. He turned off the engine, slowly got out of the car, and started up the drive. Dave had already trotted inside and could be seen in the foyer wrestling with their young, energetic black Labrador.

Matt walked the path and stepped through the screen door.

Perri suddenly appeared down the hall.

From Dave grappling with the dog on the floor: "You wanted him—you got him."

"Hi, Matt!"

"Hi."

She came quickly down the dark hall, sidestepped Dave and the dog, and kissed Matt on the cheek. The dog bounded into the living room. Dave chased after it, out of sight.

Perri gave Matt a quick kiss on the lips and Matt pushed her away, terrified.

From the living room: "Where's your ball? Where's your ball, boy? Perri—where's the dog's tennis ball?"

"In the back," she answered, watching Matt, smiling.

"Hell with it," Dave said. "I got time for a shower before dinner?"

"Uh-huh," Perri directed into the living room.

"Then I'm gonna take one." Dave went through the living room and appeared at the end of the hall. He trotted up the stairs, gone.

Matt and Perri stood motionless in the hall, staring at each other.

Perri took a step toward him. He had clear green eyes, she noted, as if for the first time. The left one was half-hidden by a length of longish, straight, sand-colored hair. He was wearing glasses. Thin rims. He looked good with glasses. And he had fine, soft skin, with an unfocused cluster of small freckles that spread out from the bridge of his nose to his cheeks. A boyish face. Fine profile. Young, sensuous mouth. She loved faces. The rest of him was long and lanky, which she liked as well, but she was particularly drawn to Matt's face.

Above them, from the second floor, the bathroom door could be heard closing. A moment later, the muffled running of a shower.

"No, not—"

But Perri had cut off the words with a kiss. Matt may have struggled for several moments, but not after that. His hands were suddenly under her shirt, then lifting her dress, grabbing her ass, fingers running between her thighs. Kissing her. Suddenly there was nothing in the world but his desire and her body. Matt pulled back to listen—the running upstairs shower muffled by the closed bathroom door. Perri's hand slid down his pants, stroked him, reached under. There was no thought of guilt then. No thought of not making love. This was a purely physical act. Perri pulled Matt into the living room. They performed swiftly, without speaking. He fumbled with the button of his pants, unzipped his fly. She pulled him hard down to the carpeted living-room floor. In seconds, her legs were clasped high around his waist and he was pushing inside her, there on the floor—a mere yard off the foyer. Her back was arched. He was kissing her hard to keep her from crying out—to keep him from crying out. Writhing on top of her. The shower was running above, capable of stopping at any moment. Purely physical. Deeper. Locked together. They couldn't have stopped if Dave had appeared in the doorway. Harder. Tighter. And together they climaxed there on the floor. Matt's eyes drifted open. The dog, head cocked, was watching nearby.

They lay there, panting, for several moments. Matt suddenly realized the shower had stopped. He leaped up, helped her stand. Zipped his fly. He was perspiring.

"I can't stay."

She was leaning against the wall, pulling down her dress, still lost in the intensity of the pleasure.

The bathroom door could be heard opening upstairs. He'd be getting dressed now.

"Tell him I had to go," Matt whispered, grabbing the knob of the screen door. "Tell him I had to meet this girl—"

She nodded, catching her breath.

He quietly closed the door behind him. Through the screen he whispered in parting: *"Jesus, Perri, we gotta end this thing."*

VI

Matt couldn't think of a better way to do it. He was in early anyway, so while he retrieved the coverage photographs he'd been using the day before, he had the clerk—the only other employee in at seven thirty—pull a northern-California series for him as well. He signed for it and took the folders and his coffee into one of the empty projection rooms.

It took a few minutes to set the easel and focus, and then longer when he had to change photos three times to locate the Rock Ranch listening post. He found it, finally, just where it was supposed to be, tucked in the heavily wooded coastline near Point Arena. From the compound's distinct silhouette of microwave dishes and transmitters, he traced access roads in several directions to a coastal two-lane fifteen miles away. He began framing and focusing a series of mile-and-a-half segments that ran the shoreline, looking for a place where he and Dave could get into the water.

"Good morning, Matt—"

Matt spun. Reiko was smiling politely in the doorway.

"Jesus, you scared me," Matt said. "Morning."

"I'm usually the first one in," Reiko stepped into the room. "Maya told me you've already been issued your series."

"I'm cutting out a little early," Matt said. "I didn't want to leave my first assignment go till Monday."

Reiko peered up at the screen. "You were doing the ELINT."

"Oh—this is California," Matt said. "This business trip, over the weekend, there might be some free time. I was just taking a quick look to see if there was a place in the area to go diving. Scuba diving. Something I like to do."

Reiko realized the business trip Matt was referring to must be some kind of NSA assignment. He wasn't sure at all how he felt about Matt Clarke, but he knew enough about the internal manners of the agency not to inquire further.

"I hope it's all right," Matt said. "I mean, I signed for them. For the photos . . ." Matt watched Reiko's eyes jump from the screen to him and then back again. "Have I done something really screwed-up here?"

"Oh, I don't think so." Reiko sounded pleasant enough. "May I see the folder?"

Matt quickly handed it to him. Reiko held the large manila square to the light from the projector and turned it around several times before finding the code markings.

"Oh, no," Reiko assured him, "these are just meteorological studies. You know, changing currents and all. Where is this?"

"Northern California."

"Yes, El Niño. All those storms. Lots of tidal shifting."

Matt relaxed and took the folder back. He pointed to the screen. "Well, that's where you'll find me Sunday afternoon. The water's supposed to be pretty cold but if you wear a wetsuit it's not so bad. You ever been diving?"

"No." Reiko shook his head. "I don't swim."

They both stared up at the screen for a moment.

". . . What is that?"

"What?" Reiko asked.

Matt moved away from the projector's glow and went deeper into the room.

"Three quarters down to seven thirty," he said. "That blur. Something underwater." He paused, then turned back to Reiko. "You see it?"

Reiko came around the other side of the console.

Matt pointed to the screen. "See that? It's angled about sixty degrees . . ."

"Oh, yes . . ." Reiko caught it and nodded. "I don't know, it's offshore. Could be an oil tank."

"No, no way,' Matt insisted. "It's underwater."

Matt moved back to the projector and pulled the frame out to the last degrees of magnification. The small blur became a slightly larger blur.

"No, there's no tubing. No pipes. It's not connected to anything." There was a rising energy in Matt's voice. "What *is* it?"

The scent of Matt's enthusiasm made Reiko back off and think. "A sunken garbage scow?" he offered without conviction.

"Or a Spanish galleon laden with gold." Matt smiled so broadly that Reiko was forced to summon a grin. "When was this taken?"

Reiko looked down and checked the folder. "It's fresh, eight weeks old."

Matt pulled a pen from his pocket and, by the light from the projector, began drawing a diagram on a piece of yellow legal paper. He stopped every few seconds to check the screen.

"What are you doing?" Reiko asked cautiously.

"A little triangulation," Matt said. "If I can get to it, that's where I'm going diving."

As Matt hunched over and concentrated on the work, Reiko had a series of chilling thoughts. Was this some kind of test? He knew Henry had suspicions about Clarke. Was he reading something into the situation because of that? But then . . . it was unusual enough that Clarke, if that really was his name, had discovered some unidentifiable underwater object—but diving for it?

Matt looked up and turned to him, smiling. "What do you say, Reiko? For a nominal fee I'll cut you in on a piece of the action."

Was he serious? Was this a bribe? Reiko's last handhold on paranoia slipped. The possibilities flew up around his ears. Matt had been drinking with them the night before. What had made him stop by then? And early, now, this morning, when it was known, everybody knew, that he came in then. This could well be some new-level security exam. He had to think, but there wasn't time. Clarke was staring right at him, expecting an answer.

". . . I'm kidding, Reiko," Matt said. "It was a joke."

"Ah, yes, of course." Reiko dropped the smile that was firmly, too firmly, set in place. Instinctively, he checked his watch. "It's on to almost eight. The priority pouch'll be ready." He glanced at the screen and then back to Matt. "I think this is Jonah's room today, Matt, so—"

"I was just leaving," said Matt, and he began gathering up his things.

Reiko walked slowly through the main room. A few people were just coming in. He traded good-mornings and kept on his stride, but he was moving on reflex alone. His imagination was running wild. What should be done? Matt seemed like a perfectly normal NSA employee, if there was such a thing. Hardly the cold-blooded M-5 type out to break the spine of careless careers.

But what if he was?

Reiko's breathing quickened. Clarke might just be the type security would send down to check on things, and if he didn't report what had just happened he'd be failing the test. What was he risking? If Clarke was innocent, then fine, he'd be proven so, and really, what did Reiko owe him anyway?

Henry appeared at the end of the hallway.

Reiko made up his mind. If they wanted to play games with him he'd deliver the desired response. Better that than the alternative.

"Morning, Reiko," Henry called, turning the corner to his office.

"Henry," Reiko said, hurrying up the corridor, "Henry, have you got a minute?" and without waiting for an answer, Reiko disappeared into Henry's office and closed the door.

Chapter Eight

A fat lazy fly the size of a nickel had somehow managed to get into the Senate Armed Services Committee chamber. Claude Screws angrily tried twice to crush it with a thick report detailing the latest performance figures for U.S. combat aircraft, but the fly had an early warning capability the envy of any aeronautical engineer and continued its irritating, purposeless flight around the committee chairman as if it sensed his decay.

The closed-door session was being conducted in room 212 of the Russell Senate Office Building. Outside, the smooth gray granite walls of the squat, solid structure were absorbing the dry heat of a mild October day in full Indian-summer bloom. A warm wind was rustling colored leaves over the heads of tourists and lunchtime passersby. Rolled-down car windows made narrow shelves for elbows and arms propped out in the light of a hot, white sun.

But not a degree of that life-giving warmth penetrated this high-ceilinged, windowless sanctum, and none of it certainly crept into the frigid environs of the classified topic under discussion before the United States Senate Armed Services Committee.

Four of the room's long, unwieldy wood tables had been placed together end to end, and Screws sat dead center, flanked on either side by a handful of half-attentive senators and their youngish respective aides.

Claude Screws was hunched and angled forward over the green leather-topped table like a dying palm tree about to topple into the surf. His once broad back was a mere smudge at the bottom of the dusty floor-to-ceiling mirror anchored to the wall behind him.

Heavy crystal chandeliers were securely chained high over-head and delivered a pale, undernourished light that gave up altogether as it approached the corners of the chamber. The air was neither warm nor cold, fresh nor stale. It was the trapped, uncirculating atmosphere found at the bottom of deep caves, and might have been the very same air around which the building was erected a half century earlier.

A round, gray man in a dark suit and a rust-red tie sat speaking into a desk-mounted microphone in the middle of the box-shaped room, facing nine senators and fourteen aides seated a shuffleboard-length of somber blue carpet across from him.

". . . what I'm trying to say, Senator Rosenbaum, if you'll stop interrupting me—"

"I wasn't interrupting you, sir, just for the record."

"Fine. —Is that you could make a very strong argument that yes, the United States both militarily and space-exploration-wise has suffered directly as a result of uninformed and overly cautious viewpoints with regards to nuclear reactors in space."

"Are you calling my viewpoint uninformed, Mr. Horne?"

"I don't know exactly what your viewpoint is, Senator Rosenbaum."

The pencil in Senator Lawrence Rosenbaum's nervous right hand stopped tapping against a stack of bound reports. He looked up from the disorganized pile of notes scattered before him.

Senator Rosenbaum, a liberal Democrat from New York, had a large, intelligent face set on a small, overweight body. A little circle of close-cropped black hair was balanced above his broad pink features not unlike a hat two sizes too small for its owner. Alert brown eyes peered out behind thick circles of glass set in fragile wire rims.

Somewhere down the line he'd been the class whiz; the mama's boy who got beat up for all his studying; the kid whose house always got the worst of it on Halloween.

Being thirty-three and the youngest senator on the Hill somehow took the edge off those painful memories now.

Rosenbaum's suit jacket was off and lay in a heap on the floor behind his chair. The sleeves of his wrinkled white shirt were haphazardly rolled up to his baby-soft forearms. Beneath the table, his black shoes were scuffed, his socks mismatched, and his belt barely held in the fourth and last new hole that could be punched into the finite piece of leather employed in the losing battle of ringing his waist.

Rosenbaum leaned forward toward his microphone and the witness sitting beyond it and spoke in a slow, nasal monotone that quivered with rising indignation. "My viewpoint, Mr. Horne, is that six months ago you sat in that very chair assuring this committee that space reactors, if deployed, would only be used in nuclear-safe orbits—"

"Design changes in the SP-100 have made that—"

"And now—"

"An unreasonably rigid yardstick."

"May I finish?—*May I?*"

"By all means."

"And now you want our approval to deploy and operate these space-based nuclear reactors in low-earth orbits. *My viewpoint,* Mr. Horne, is that that is an unacceptably dangerous proposition, a low-earth orbit, what you've cryptically referred to as," Rosenbaum scanned his notes, " 'maximum flexibility of deployment,' and one that could have catastrophic results in the case of an accidental reentry."

Nelson Horne, director of the Space Reactor Program at the Department of Defense, and Senator Rosenbaum sat staring at each other for several slow seconds. Papers rustled. Somebody coughed.

"Every conceivable problem you could come up with has been closely studied and taken into account, Senator," Horne said, crossing his arms defensively across his chest.

Rosenbaum conferred with an attractive young woman who kept whispering things in his ear. The woman's auburn-blond hair was parted at the side and fell across her downturned face. She sat so close to Rosenbaum their shoulders were touching. When not whispering she was quietly concentrating on a small notebook in her lap.

She was whispering now. Rosenbaum nodded, turned from the woman, and, looking down at his papers, addressed the microphone. "Could you please tell the committee what happened during the United States' first test of a nuclear reactor in space? That would be—"

"It was 1965, Senator, and not even remotely parallel to the technological—"

"It failed because of a ground control error, isn't that right, Mr. Horne?"

"The technological advances, Senator, since that time—"

"For the record," Rosenbaum raised his voice, continuing to look down at his notes, "*for the record,* the Air Force investigation into the incident listed ground control error as the primary reason we lost that satellite, which luckily was in an eight-thousand-mile orbit. I *have* that report in front of me."

Rosenbaum looked up sharply from his jumble of papers. "Do these wondrous technological advances of ours include a way to eliminate ground control error, Mr. Horne!"

"The effects of ground control error, Senator, can be minimized to the point that—"

"If that satellite in 1965 had been in a low-earth orbit when this happened we would have had one hell of a mess on our hands, would we not, Mr. Horne?"

"Can be minimized to the point that—"

"Yes or no, Mr. Horne? A hell of a mess."

"I don't know how you'd characterize that, Senator," Horne replied, absently smoothing his tie.

Rosenbaum turned and quietly spoke to his aide. "Where's that Soviet thing, Leslie? The thirty-three shots, that thing?"

Leslie Flood looked up. She was pretty. She was beautiful. She was bright green eyes, a perfect pinch of nose and full, inviting lips set in a pleasing oval of face. Her cheekbones were high and smooth, the kind fashion photographers with wind machines get excited about, and there was an alluring simplicity achieved by her not wearing makeup. What was she? Late-

twenties? Early-thirties? Thirty-five? It was impossible to tell.
She was a tough feminine professional isolationist. But there
was something more. More exotic. More complex. Something
at odds with the rest of her. Something that hinted at wildness.

Without a word she reached into Rosenbaum's pile of papers
and positioned the desired document before him. She looked
down again. The room got a little darker.

"Now then, Mr. Horne—"

"Yes, Senator?"

"The Soviets frequently use nuclear reactors to power their
satellites, do they not?"

"That's correct."

"They do?"

"Yes, particularly for ship-tracking platforms."

Rosenbaum scanned the document in his hands. "Out of the
thirty-three Soviet satellites that have been launched with nuclear reactors, three have malfunctioned and two, in reentering
the atmosphere that you and I breathe, have scattered radioactive debris over wide areas of the earth."

"It is my understanding, Senator, that there's only been *one*
confirmed Soviet uncontrolled reentry and that was with Cosmos 954, which did come down in an uninhabited section of the
Canadian arctic in, I believe, January of 1978."

"Fine. You're wrong, of course—"

"I don't believe I—"

"You're not counting Cosmos 1402, 1983—however—let
me finish, let's say it's only one. Just one. One. It's my
contention that *one* out of thirty-three is an unacceptable rate of
loss when the vehicle screaming back into the atmosphere becomes in effect a nuclear meteor—"

"There will be no rate of loss."

"That could land God knows where!"

"Nowhere. Because it won't happen. That was the Soviets."

"The Soviets figure prominently into this new request to drop
the nuclear-safe orbit criteria, don't they, Mr. Horne?" Rosenbaum
didn't wait for an answer. "Let's get down to brass tacks here.
The Pentagon wants to drop the nuclear-safe orbit criteria
because it wants to use space reactors in key components of
SDI, or Star Wars. Isn't that right, Mr. Horne?"

"The uses for space reactors go beyond—"

"Things like laser battle stations and other antimissile fantasy machines that will herald in a new and far more dangerous Cold War with the Soviet Union than any we've ever experienced. I'm against SDI, Mr. Horne. I'm against anything that leads this great country of ours in that direction. I'm against dropping the nuclear-safe orbit criteria because I think that's exactly where it does lead. A Cold War in space is the last thing this country needs—"

"I've had enough of you for one day, *Mister* Rosenbaum!"

Claude Screws's graveled voice came down on the room like a dusty landslide. Everything stopped. Heads turned. Someone claimed later the chandeliers tinkled.

Rosenbaum had to lean out around the other senators and aids who had suddenly swiveled on Screws's words to see the committee chairman's pale, side-turned head.

". . . Excuse me, Mr. Chairman?"

"Your views are not this committee's, *Mister* Rosenbaum, not as long as I sit here! And what you know about the Cold War couldn't fill this water glass." The words came loud, the tone as caustic as acid.

Rosenbaum sat very still as his attractive aide leaned over and whispered something in his ear.

Then, as if facing a man with a gun, he spoke with a quiet but shattered dignity. ". . . I'm told I still have three and a half minutes left under the ten-minute rule—"

Screws pounded the table hard. "That time is for questions—not far-left lectures from second-year senators!"

The half dozen people seated between them sat as motionless as if there were poisonous snakes on the floor. An aide at the far end of the tables secretly started writing down the dialogue for a friend at the *Washington Post*.

Rosenbaum's cheeks flushed and his forehead was suddenly beaded with sweat. ". . . The ten-minute rule is sacred, sir. I don't fully understand the chairman's—"

"You're yielding, and that's all you have to understand! Not another word from you today! Not about trying to hamstring our military efforts in space or what you think you know about the Cold War or how friendly the Soviets are or any other such

damn nonsense! You're through for the day here!'' The voice
was raspy enough to saw logs. Screws's bony hand pounded the
table once more for emphasis. His chest was heaving. He felt
slightly dizzy.

Rosenbaum slowly eased back in his chair, mind reeling.
Screws had just told him to shut up. Muzzled him. In committee. Rosenbaum was positive that wasn't allowed. Every senator
on the committee had the right to question a witness for ten
minutes.

They'd clashed before. Screws hated Rosenbaum in equal
measure for his politics and youth. He made Rosenbaum's life
on the committee almost unbearable.

But this was a new and more alarming tactic toward that end.

The old man was a tyrant. He was a son of a bitch. During
idle committee moments, Rosenbaum's thoughts drifted toward
various ways of killing Screws and getting away with it.

Still, there was nothing to be gained by a shouting match with
Screws. No matter how wrong he was. Seniority held sway, and
Screws had over forty years of it. Just keep your mouth shut and
let Screws look the fool.

Rosenbaum suddenly stood, saw his jacket on the floor, and
stooped to pick it up. As the others in the room watched in
silence, he gathered his papers into a loose mass and thrust them
under his free arm.

Senator Lawrence Rosenbaum walked out of the Senate Armed
Services Committee meeting with all the wounded pride he
could muster. As he stepped outside into the sun, he imagined
how satisfying it would be to pop up in the Senate parking lot
late some night with a gun and rid the world of Claude Revis
Screws.

Chapter Nine

Matt and Dave stood among a crowd of strangers as a steel carousel impulsively produced their flight's luggage in erratic five-bag groups. Three handlers in fluorescent red jumpsuits were tossing and arranging the luggage on the main belt as it came up the conveyor from below. Dave watched them strain to lift the two overpacked duffel bags, so heavy they could barely crest the rail. One guy cursed beneath his breath, and when the bag didn't sit well enough to get traction he leaned out and gave it a solid kick into place.

"I don't know about this," Dave said, grabbing the duffel bags as they came around, the tanks and gear settled heavily to the ground between them. "Awful lot of trouble for a few hours of diving."

Matt hefted the weight over his shoulder, balancing himself with his suitcase in the other hand.

"You might change your mind if we struck it rich."

Dave shuffled after him, toward the rental car counter. "Yeah? When's that?"

Matt waited until they were out of the crowd. "I wasn't

gonna tell you this," he said quietly, "but I saw something on one of the satellite pictures. Right off where we're going to dive—"

Dave burst out laughing so hard he lost his balance and had to stop and reshoulder the diving bag.

"What's so funny about that?" Matt stopped to ask.

"Why is it that you've got to turn every dive into a search for the lost city of Atlantis?"

"You asked me to check it out and I did." Matt stopped and struck a defensive pose. "There's something there that unless you've got a camera circling the earth you're probably not going to ever see."

"I'm thinking of two things," Dave said. "Know what they are?"

Matt started away. Dave followed; running commentary.

"I'm thinking buried treasure. I'm thinking about wasting half of a beautiful day, a beach day, waiting in some drunken maritime lawyer's office in Grand Cayman, for the guy to unfold a map and tell us we're not Mel Fisher and that the fortune we've found, the sunken British frigate that everybody's just been snorkeling by for years, is actually a junked fruit barge."

Matt shook his head and walked faster.

"I'm also thinking," Dave continued, "about the discovery of some *very* unique 'Spanish deck chains' off the coast of Cozumel . . ."

Matt spun around. "You got into that. That wasn't just me."

"Don't drink and dive."

"Now I remember why I wasn't gonna tell you about this in the first place."

II

They made the drive from Sacramento to Rock Ranch in two hours; the last fifteen minutes spent pacing an FPS escort patrol car up a perfectly paved mountain road that at its end revealed a large, concrete main building, several huge microwave dishes, and a number of smaller buildings tucked amidst the dense evergreens.

The installation went smoothly. The tech crew on this job had done two others with them since last February and knew what they were about. Matt and Dave spent the better part of Friday and Saturday going over the software with the office's supervisor and his staff. They tested Saturday night and it flew. There was a barbecue at the senior engineer's cottage. They drank some beer, talked shop, and found out there were a couple of salts who rented fishing boats down the Cape.

Matt wanted to know about the southern promontory.

". . . Yeah, there was a guy used to be open there, too."

III

Orin Marsh was hosing out the Boston Whaler when he heard the sound of a car struggling up the road off the point. He kicked over the draining bait trap and well water splashed down through the dock boards and cut patterns in the foam below. He rinsed his hands and then crowned himself with the spray, letting it flow down his back, through the straight gray-red ponytail that roped between his shoulder blades, and then, with a shivering movement, he leaned forward and let it wash across the broad angles of his face and bead into drops as it leaked through the kinked stretch of his bright red, grease-stained beard.

It was getting blustery. The tall, dense evergreens that covered the coast were bent to the wind. Scattered sunlight streaked between large, billowing clouds that came quickly off the ocean and sailed inland.

The car slowed coming up the driveway. Orin figured that right about now they'd be reconsidering, one of 'em at least, looking at the salt-beat house and the couple of rusted trucks up the shed and wondering out loud if this was what they had in mind, 'cause honey, or buddy, or whatever, we're out in the middle of nowhere and I just don't know . . .

More than one car had turned around in Orin's fifteen years.

Some made it through all that and then turned at the sight of his huge raw hands waving them into the driveway.

He twisted the hose in a rusted four-inch cleat and dried his face with the arm of an old plaid workshirt. The car stopped. A brand new LTD, looking plain like a rental, was all dusted and mucked from the ride up the point. Two clean guys, white, about thirty, casually dressed, got out and stretched and looked around through matching reflector sunglasses. How cute.

"Down here!"

Sound carried weak from the dock to the house, but Orin's voice moved two-hundred-fifty pounds' worth up the hill.

The two guys turned and figured it out. They talked and laughed easy to themselves as they came down the path from the house. They looked like they had money.

The skinny guy, doing the business, told him they wanted to go scuba diving.

"Off this boat here?"

"Unless you have another one."

Orin stroked at his beard and took a long look out at the ocean. "We don't do much diving. Used to go for abalone but the storms past couple years messed that all up."

"We're just around with our gear," the stockier, darker guy told him. "Thought we'd get wet."

"Yeah . . ." Orin looked at the boat and then back at them. "Sixty bucks." He said it firm, and smiled real casually, the way he knew people who were taken aback by his size liked to have him smile—the, sorry-there's-just-nothing-I-can-do, neighborly smile.

Stocky made a disappointed whistling sound.

"We don't want to go out for long," the other one said. "Take a ride off the point and get in the water's about it."

"The boy and I were gonna take some wood over to Lakeport this afternoon," Orin said, shaking his head sadly. "I've gotta make up at least part of what I'd lose on that. I'll change my plans for sixty."

Now they started whispering pros and cons back and forth for a minute. They pulled wallets and gave it another round.

"Look," Stocky told him, "we're a little cash-shy here. Like to keep something for the trip back. How do you feel about taking a check for half? I've got ID up the wazoo."

They finally settled on the sixty with Orin taking David H. Lakeman's Maryland check for twenty. They followed him back up the path to the house.

Matt and Dave assembled their gear and Orin called out into the woods for his nephew, Mark, who was going to take them out.

The boy was thirteen, in torn jeans with a length of waxed rope as a belt and a Portland Trailblazer's T-shirt that had been worn to the consistency of cheesecloth. The boy was stick-legged and sharp featured. His hair was short and sun-bleached blond, his skin freckled and deeply browned. He looked nothing like his uncle, but there was clearly a bond between them. He came out of the tall pines behind the house and glanced at Orin and before a word was spoken, he knew to smile and say nothing.

"Change in plans," Orin called over to him, and the boy just nodded.

Orin introduced him and they helped carry the tanks down to the dock. The boy was excited about the diving, asking questions while he prepped the Whaler. Matt and Dave stripped down to their bathing suits and handed on the gear.

"I don't know what you hope to see," Orin said, thinking about the sixty dollars. "Not much of a diving scene."

"I'll take 'em out to Bailey Cove," Mark said to Orin.

"Which way's that?" Matt asked, trying to keep his interest under control.

"South past the point," Orin said. "I'd take you myself, but my ear's acting up."

Matt nodded. That would be fine. He liked it better with the boy as it was.

Orin made sure it was all set, that the two men knew what they were about and that Mark felt comfortable; then he tossed the bowline into the shell and shielded his eyes, watching Mark gun the Whaler out over the two-foot swells.

"Storm coming in—don't stay out too long! Everybody back in one piece!"

And Mark waved to him and gave him a big thumbs-up and a mile-wide grin.

IV

The sun pulled back behind the clouds and as they cleared the point the breeze picked up. The Whaler scudded across the swells. Dave shivered, squeezing on the wetsuit. Matt was way ahead of him, arranging the gear on the floor of the boat.

"Hell, we don't need the camera, do we?"

"Sure," Matt said. "Why not?"

"It doesn't look like the clearest water in the world."

"For sixty bucks I want to try the new flash."

Dave shrugged and checked the pressure in the tanks. Twelve-hundred pounds. He took a loud, mechanical-sounding test breath from his regulator. Adjusted his weights. Donned his buoyancy compensator. Secured the Velcro straps of a shiny nine-inch diving knife to his right ankle.

Matt steadied himself and eased back to the helm. Mark was smiling broadly, getting into the rhythm, as the Whaler pounded against the swells.

"So Orin's your uncle," Matt said, loud enough to be heard above the engine.

"Yeah," Mark nodded. "I come out summers—from Sacramento."

". . . It's October now," Matt noted.

"I kinda got in trouble in school . . . end of last year."

"Ah."

"I was 'sposed to start school three weeks ago but I gotta wait till they let me. . ." Mark told him.

Matt surveyed the coast. "Looks like a pretty tough place to leave. Your uncle been here long?"

"Oh yeah, for . . ." he pondered the number for a couple

seconds, ". . . I think fifteen, sixteen, years." The boy was proud when it came to his uncle and didn't want Matt to have the wrong impression. "He doesn't look like it now but he was a corporal in the Marines in Vietnam, then he was in the Highway Patrol. He got the property first and then he paid it off and built the house himself with disability from being a cop, 'cause he was dragged behind a pickup truck after a robbery in Ukiah."

"Sounds like a pretty incredible guy."

The boy nodded seriously and then shifted the outboard, turning them in toward the cove.

"I'd like to head out a little farther," Matt said casually.

"But that's Bailey Cove, right up there." Mark pointed to an inlet on the south side of the point.

Matt had the hand-drawn chart tucked in the waist of the wetsuit. He unfolded it and tried to hold it steady against the wind. Mark cut the throttle back and leaned in with an interested look, as if Matt were selling fireworks.

"I'd like to go up here." Matt pointed to a place on the paper and then scanned the coastline. "I guess that'd be between these two coves, and then if we could, get even with the tip of the point."

Mark shook his head. "There's gonna be nothing to see. There's a shoal out there. Just a lot of seaweed. If you want, I don't think Orin'll mind, I could go out a little farther, there's a shelf that drops off real deep. Three, four thousand feet. Maybe you'd see some bigger fish off there . . . But there's sharks, too . . . Orin'd kill me if you got eaten."

"Come on," Matt said, flashing a conspirator's smile, "let's check this out. If it's no good, we'll go back to the cove."

Mark considered this, joined Matt's smile, and punched the throttle. Mark watched Matt steady himself as he moved up toward the bow. "Where'd you come up with this anyway?" he yelled.

"He makes 'em up as he goes along," Dave shouted from the back.

After another few minutes they eased into the spot. Mark double-checked Matt's map against the landmarks and signaled Dave to drop anchor. They shouldered the tanks and set their watches. The masks came down. The regulators were in their mouths.

They stepped over the side and dropped into the inviting black world of the sea. Mark watched them hover a few feet below the surface. Then they faded away like ghosts as they swam downward.

V

The water was biting cold. The suits were good, but the exposed hands and the back of the neck took a shocking slap of temperature.

The sun cast long, green, withering shanks of light that angled toward the unseen bottom. The regulators rasped with the rhythm of their breathing, which, as they slowly descended, grew louder and louder until that became the only sound.

Matt was in front, Dave trying to stay right on him. They floated down twenty feet and were suddenly surrounded by a school of thousands of small fish with a vein of silver along their sides that caught and then wildly remade the light as they swam by.

It grew progressively darker as they dropped—darker and colder, with each kick of the legs, until, at seventy-five feet, the visibility decreased to the point that Dave could see only Matt's fins swaying hypnotically directly below him—going steadily deeper. Up was now only a slightly lighter shade of dark than down.

They kept their arms at their sides, kicking rhythmically with their fins. Dave peered at the circular depth gauge strapped to his wrist—the red needle quivering at ninety-five feet and still heading down. The masks pressed tight to their faces, pushing into the skin by the crush of the sea. The regulators made breathing something harsh and mechanical.

Matt hit bottom before he saw it, a broad, flat rock almost knocking his mask off. Dave grabbed his leg. They floated there, an arm's length above the rocky ocean floor. Visibility was three feet at best, murky enough to make an active imagination worry about what might be circling just out of sight.

At this depth, they couldn't stay down long without decompressing. Matt had a direction in mind and quickly kicked forward. Dave followed, never more than a few strokes behind. They floated over the flat, rocky landscape—their field of view limited to that which passed directly below. The rocks gradually broke up and gave way to sand—sand rippled into long, small dunes by the action of the sea. Another field of rock. The sea floor angled slightly deeper.

Matt glanced up. A dark wall suddenly loomed before them. Seaweed—he reached for some—no, kelp. Matt paused at the edge of a junglelike kelp bed, Dave staying close beside him.

Long, slippery ropes of green-brown vines rose from the floor and tangled above them in the push-and-pull of the undulating current. The kelp thickened and choked off even the faint light coming from above. Dave grabbed Matt's arm and signaled they go back. Matt shook him off and motioned to continue. They stopped there for a moment, each of them pointing fingers in a different direction. A cloud must have passed, because the sun broke better through the seaweed and Matt gestured for just another fifty yards and then pulled away, without waiting for an answer, deep into the dense wall of swaying strands.

Dave was forced to follow.

Matt used his hands to gently push through the stuff. He frequently checked a compass attached to the diving watch on his wrist—as much to keep track of the way they'd come as to keep going in the desired direction.

Something big darted off right in front of him and Matt almost stopped, unsure what he had spooked.

Dave brushed beside him. Matt began swimming forward again, going faster now, conscious of the time. The kelp was thickening, making it difficult to push through. Matt could feel Dave tugging at his fin—gently at first, and then insistently. Dave wanted to go back. Matt decided to just swim another five strokes through the thickening tangle—just a little farther—almost ready to turn back—about to reverse direction—when the kelp suddenly thinned at a small clearing.

Dave saw Matt stop short. He pulled up beside him and angled perpendicular to the sea floor. They hovered upright, arms and legs treading water as if they were marionettes, staring.

A curved, heavily barnacled black-steel wall rose up out of the sand. The crippled light and sand and swaying seaweed put its true shape and dimensions beyond knowing, but it seemed organically bound to this spot, as if it had grown there, as if the sand had simply washed away to reveal some deeper, huge, more actual substance.

But the mind and eye revolted against that first opinion. This was unnatural and wrong. Some man-made object had sunk and laid here for a long time. Both divers stared for some half-dozen breaths, as if perhaps it weren't really there at all. Then they recovered enough to exchange excited, baffled glances through their masks. They were breathing harder now, ignoring the cold. Matt pointed back along the shell of the thing and Dave motioned with both hands for him to go slowly.

They felt their way along the rough exterior as it banked back into the kelp bed. As they moved along, the shape took on meaning.

. . . A submarine.

Dave stopped when it hit him. Matt kept swimming, rising higher, now above the hull. Dave pumped to catch up and drew even as Matt slipped his camera from its shoulder strap. Dave made a series of hand gestures to indicate a submarine tilted on its side and Matt nodded enthusiastically—Yes! He knew!

They rose together along the hull, higher and higher, passing over the main body of the craft and coming back down to a point where the steel shell began to fall away. The kelp's thick swaying strands silently parted and they were suddenly staring at the faded red star of the Soviet Navy.

Dave steadied himself against the turbulence and reached forward to touch the image. It was painted on steel. It was real enough. The flash of Matt's camera exploded. Dave was blinded for a second. When he turned around Matt was gesturing for his flashlight. Dave handed it to him and signed a question mark. Matt pointed down beyond the conning tower to a gaping hole on the underside of the hull. Dave signaled for calm, motioning to the stream of bubbles they were exhaling much too quickly.

Matt nodded in agreement, then gestured that he just wanted to look in the hole, and with that he swam off. Again Dave followed.

The hole was almost fifteen feet in diameter. The flashlight played over twisted pipes and metal that had been sheared outward in some kind of explosion. Everything inside was rusted, bent, unearthly. Sand had settled to the bottom and fish and small crabs darted silently about the hidden caves within the hull. Matt eased himself into the darkness and Dave angrily pulled at his fin. Matt jerked away and pointed deeper into the hole, beyond Dave's sight.

Dave leaned in and Matt focused the beam upon a hatch door that angled queerly into the chamber.

Matt handed him the light and, careful not to cut himself on the shards of metal petaled outward around them, moved to the door.

He shouldered the camera, gripped both hands on the latch hold, and wedged himself into position by levering his fin against a mangled length of six-inch pipe.

He put his back into it, and nothing.

Then, suddenly, as he relaxed, a *snap*—and the door separated from its thoroughly corroded housing, pulling free and forward, falling toward them.

Matt recoiled in terror, almost cutting his shoulder on a sharp piece of electrical tubing as he drew away.

An algae-coated skeleton, positioned against the inside wheel hatch, fell out past him as if from a dream and settled in loosely connected pieces on the sandy floor.

Dave wildly flashed the light around, between Matt and the skeleton and the dark hole that was now exposed before them. Matt was shaking visibly as he moved back to Dave and had him steady the beacon on the ground.

The skeleton had fallen into sections below them, the light sending dozens of small crabs scurrying for the safety of darkness.

Matt stretched gingerly down and removed a tarnished, rusty set of dog tags from beside the body's unattached, greenish-brown skull. He rapped the flat of the tags with the blade of the knife, rubbed with his thumb, and made out the letters USN. Matt passed the tags to Dave, then journeyed deeper.

Dave was frantic now—jerkily casting the flashlight's beam all around them.

Matt pointed into the black chasm of the open doorway.

Dave shook his head no. Emphatically no!

Matt tapped his watch and signaled that they had two minutes. He held up the camera and pointed for Dave to shine the light for him in the doorway.

Dave held up two fingers. Two minutes. Two minutes and that was it!

Matt nodded assent and moved back up to the open hole.

Dave braced himself beside the gaping entrance and sneaked the light around the corner as if he were pointing a gun into a dangerous alley. Matt tapped him excitedly and glided through on the flashlight's beam.

Dave looked in.

It was the control room. Matt was flapping his arms and legs to hover in the middle of the room. Dave directed the beam to the floor. Something was there but he couldn't make it out. Matt's flash suddenly exploded and Dave almost dropped the flashlight when he saw what it was. It took a moment for Dave's eyes to readjust, and then he focused the flashlight on the tilted floor—five, six—no seven!—algae-coated skeletons, here unmolested by the currents, were grouped around the ladder that led upward to the con.

. . . Huddled by the ladder—they'd been trying to escape!

Matt floated carefully down into the beam. He had his diving knife in his hand. Dave watched as Matt lifted up the dog tags beside the nearest skeleton and cut the thin rusted strand with his knife. In less than a minute, Matt had collected seven more dog tags from the tightly spaced skeletons.

Dave reached down and picked a small object off the tilted floor of the sub. A stainless-steel watch. Dave stuffed it into his diving bag.

Time was swiftly running out.

Dave pointed to a cracked gauge, over which, faded by the sea, were Russian markings. Matt took a picture.

Matt began firing off pictures as fast as the camera reset.

From Dave's point of view it was like being in some kind of

terrifying funhouse, a strobelight beating one horrifying image after another into your mind:

FLASH—A half-skeleton clutching at the ladder that ran up to the conning tower—

FLASH—The distorted, molten remnants of a navigation cockpit—

FLASH—A fire extinguisher lying beside one of the piles of bones—

FLASH—A thirty-year-old bottle of Coca-Cola.

Flash. Flash. Flash.

VI

The clouds were coming in dark now. The water was churning a deep blue and starting to chop heavily against the wind. The Whaler bobbed several hundred yards away.

Matt and Dave burst to the surface and ripped off the regulators.

"Jesus! Did you know that was down there!" Dave was overwrought, flushed, and gasping for breath.

"Of course not!" Matt yelled back, his teeth chattering from cold and fear. He took a sudden mouthful of salt water, gagged.

"What the fuck is this!"

"I don't know! I don't know what it is! How could I—"

"It's a Russian-fucking-submarine with an American crew!"

In the distance, the Whaler roared to life and began to move toward them.

"What the hell is going on, Matt!" Dave was nearly shrieking. *"What are we doing here?"*

"It was just a shadow on the picture!" Matt caught another mouthful of water and coughed. "I didn't know that's what it was!"

"I wanted to go diving! Nothing like this! Nothing!"

"It never happened!" Matt yelled, treading nearer. "It never happened! You understand?"

"I wish I understood! Why the fuck did you take the dog tags?"

"For proof!"

"You shouldn't have touched anything!"

"I was excited!"

"Well, it was a dumb-ass move!"

They went quiet, silent now, as Mark pulled the boat into hearing range.

"Where were you?" The boy was anxious "You all right? Your bubbles were gone for twenty minutes!"

Matt shook his head. "Nothing . . . Nothing at all. We're fine. Must've been the seaweed."

They clumsily pulled themselves onboard and caught their breath. Mark eyed them suspiciously as the Whaler tossed in the growing swells.

"C'mon, what was down there?"

"Dave thought he saw a shark," Matt said carefully.

"What?" Mark responded excitedly. "A big one? They're around here y'know."

Dave looked up at the threatening skies. "This weather's really coming up. Let's get the hell out of here!"

Mark shook his head and went back to the engine. Dave was inside himself, shivering and pulling off his belt. Matt hunched over and slipped eight sets of dog tags from inside his wet suit, burying them deep inside his diving bag.

The engines came to life and Mark turned the boat to head in. He kept his eye on the two men and, sure that they were not watching, reached beneath the seat and pulled a small yellow abalone buoy. He revved the engine full out and let the marker slip over the side.

The small boat raced for the shore. Behind it, along the entire horizon, thick, high clouds were heaving toward the coastline. Another of the season's monster storms was moving in to take over.

Chapter Ten

They came half scrambling, half walking the several hundred feet from the dock to their rental car parked up the path by the weather-beaten house.

They were late for their plane, Stocky told Orin, who watched silently from the sagging gray wood porch as the pair hurriedly tossed their tanks and wetsuits into the LTD's trunk.

A cold, damp wind that felt like somebody had left a distant freezer door open was coming in low from the northwest, pushing towering greenish-black clouds inland off the water. A fuzzy band of far away heavy rain obscured the line where the sea met the sky.

Still shivering, Stocky joked about thinking he saw a shark. His trembling fingers tried desperately to button the fly on his new jeans.

"Great dive, but you were right about not much to see. Waste a'time to bring the camera. Nothin' down there t'all."

For some reason, Stocky was sliding into a west-Texas drawl. Skinny said nothing, and moved with the methodical slowness of a guy who's just taken a nice sock to the jaw.

Five minutes later, Orin was still leaning against the same porch beam. He watched the LTD bounce down the rutted driveway considerably faster than it had come in. The big American car disappeared into the wind-twisted evergreens that carpeted this part of the coast and, just like that, Stocky and Skinny were gone.

II

A dazed quiet had replaced the angry flurry of talk that marked their tense, rainy drive down to Sacramento airport. They were on a red-eye that put you into Washington, D.C., at a little past six thirty in the morning and the plane, an L-1011, had just lifted off through a driving downpour.

It was uncomfortably crowded and the stewardesses had their hands full after takeoff. Dave got a double scotch from the cart that passed down the aisle, gulped it quickly, and leaned his head back heavily against the seat.

Matt was staring out the scratched Plexiglas window. He hated to fly. Persistent thoughts of freak mechanical failures made it an unpleasant experience even when the weather was clear and his mental outlook unclouded, neither of which was the case at the moment.

Matt watched as diffuse flashes of lightning erupted in the clouds around them. It reminded him of a camera strobe, and he suddenly felt trapped inside the plane, as trapped as one of the skeletons in that submarine.

"If you didn't know what it was there then why'd you bring the camera?" Dave asked it softly, beneath the low pitch of the engines and pockets of conversation around them.

"I had no idea what was down there. It was just a blur on a picture, an interesting place to dive." Matt spoke in a weary, nervous undertone. He continued looking out the window, fascinated by the dull silver wing flexing in flight.

"I don't understand. You just *happen* to see—"

Matt spun quickly around. "You keep suggesting that I did this on—"

"Wait a minute, Matt, and keep your voice down. We've known each other for a long time. You're just about the best friend I ever had. This would be one thing if we were just two guys, two stiffs, who stumbled across this thing. But this . . . *this* is different. Seven years at the NSA has made me one paranoid son of a bitch. These days I think conspiracy if someone follows me down a supermarket aisle. Now you said you saw this on a satellite photograph. A *classified* satellite photograph. I mean—"

"You're saying that I purposely tricked you down there for some reason. Is that what you're saying? Why? Why would I do that?" Matt's bright green eyes were wide behind his glasses.

Dave frowned. ". . . All I'm asking, Matt, is for you to tell me that you wouldn't lie to me."

A fleeting vision of Perri standing naked in his bathroom, looking in the mirror, played against Matt's mind. ". . . I wouldn't lie to you."

"Fine, I mean, what would you think if you were me? If I'd led *you* down there?"

Matt thought for a second. "I don't know . . . I probably wouldn't be sure."

"You'd be right."

They looked off in different directions. Matt loosened his seatbelt. "I should have gotten a drink."

Dave remained silent.

"Look—let's just walk through the facts," Matt said softly. "Can we do that?"

"Sure."

"You got a thirty-year-old Russian submarine."

"Maybe older."

"Maybe. With eight dead crewmen inside."

"Who knows how many? We saw eight wearing U.S. dog tags."

"Okay. Lying buried in sand under a kelp bed a mile off the coast of an isolated stretch of northern California."

"That's it."

The seat in front of Dave slowly reclined.

Matt removed his glasses and vigorously polished them with

a loose fold in his shirt. Without his glasses, Matt had the ageless look of somebody's younger brother.

". . . Okay," Matt continued, "so what probably happened is that during the mid-1950s, the Russians were trying to send in some saboteurs dressed in American uniforms and their sub sank, in a storm or something. The Russians couldn't go looking for it so close in American coastal waters . . . so they wrote it off and left it there."

Dave clinked the ice cubes around in his empty plastic cup. "But *all* those skeletons had U.S. dog tags."

"Part of the disguise," Matt said, returning the glasses to the bridge of his nose. "This guy I knew once, over in DIA, he said the Soviets are known for their detail—"

"But they *all* couldn't have been saboteurs, Matt. Using your scenario, if they were Russians—only some of them would have been dropped off on the California coast to do whatever it is these saboteurs were going to do. The others would have had to stay behind to run the sub. They wouldn't have just abandoned it. So it doesn't make sense that *all* of them would have been wearing them."

The plane took a sudden violent drop from turbulence and recovered. Matt tightened his seatbelt as if the plane's airworthiness depended on it. The NO SMOKING sign went on with a synthesized *bong*.

"How come the sign just flashed on?" Matt asked.

"Just relax. . . . Besides which," Dave picked up where he'd left off, "I don't see how they could have spared anybody. Didn't look like there were that many to begin with."

"There might have been more in the other compartments."

"Seems like if they all went down with the ship there should have been more in the control room."

"Maybe they'd already dropped off the people they wanted to drop off—*before* they sank. That's possible."

Dave shook his head, troubled. "It still doesn't explain why the others were wearing U.S. dog tags. They didn't *have* to. There wasn't any need. And that sub didn't sink in a storm. You saw the hole in its hull. Something inside exploded out and it sank fast."

"It looked like there'd been a fire," said Matt. "A bunch of stuff was charred. But my point is that none of this, the sub, the bodies, *none of it* makes sense if they weren't Russian seamen."

The liquor cart squeezed back down the aisle. Dave got two vodka rocks. He waited till the cart continued on its way, and Matt had taken a gulp of his drink, before going on. "I found this in the sand while you were taking pictures." Keeping it low, Dave held out the thin stainless-steel watch.

Matt took it and fingered it in his free hand. ". . . Russians can get Timexes—"

"Look what's inscribed on the back."

Matt rubbed the mottled steel casing on the back of the watch and made out a faint inscription. " 'To Carl, Love Julie. 2/16/53,' " Matt read aloud. He took another drink without taking his eyes off the inscription. "Well, what if they *were* Russians but they hadn't yet dropped off—"

"Matt—" Dave carefully looked around the crowded cabin and then lowered his voice to a sharp whisper: "those were dead *American* seamen—everything points to it. They weren't Russians."

"But the *sub* was Russian."

"The sub was Russian." Dave nodded as he spoke.

"So where would the United States just happen to get an intact Russian submarine at the height of the Cold War?"

Dave was nervously biting his lower lip, thinking. "I don't know . . ."

"The Russians wouldn't give us one without a fight, and if we stole it somehow they would have let the world know in a big way." Matt handed the watch back to Dave and then leaned in closer. "Look, we saw what we saw, right? We got eight dog tags. We got pictures if the camera worked. We got an old watch, and we know where the damn thing is. I don't think we should keep this to ourselves."

Dave stared at the back of the red seat in front of him until Matt thought he hadn't been listening. He finally looked at Matt. "I can think of a whole bunch of reasons why we should."

"Come on, Dave, you said yourself you're paranoid. We work for the government. For the NSA. We have to report this."

"Jesus, Matt, you don't think this is going to rock somebody's boat? You're too naïve sometimes. Your problem is that you live this cocoonlike existence—this ordered, set, sheltered life totally devoid of—"

There was a simultaneous explosion of lightning and thunder right outside Matt's porthole. The plane bucked violently, took a sickening drop, and then started tilting sharply left and down. Passengers not wearing seatbelts lifted at odd angles as their seats dropped beneath them. Those unlucky enough to be caught in the aisles hung weightless in midair for several surreal seconds. Matt white-knuckled both armrests, and for a brief instant watched his drink hang tantalizingly right before his face, close enough to possibly lean forward and take a sip from.

A loud bang!—and then the plane was suddenly going up like an express elevator and everything came crashing down. Oxygen masks dropped and danced like snakes from the ceiling. Overhead racks popped open and coughed out their cargo onto horrified passengers being pushed into their seats below. The terrifying up-and-down roar of straining engines filled the cabin for a relatively long moment, and then, after shuddering several times more, the plane slowly leveled off.

Silence. A child began crying hysterically. The stewardesses were soon staggering about from one group of deathly quiet passengers to the next. A laconic apology from the captain was drifting through the cabin.

Matt and Dave exchanged one eyebrow-raised frown, and then Dave reached out and lightly tapped the oxygen mask dangling in front of him.

Matt glanced back out the Plexiglas porthole to check the wing. It was a full, dreamlike minute before either of them spoke again.

". . . Anyway," Matt resumed, but then forgot where they'd left off. He was more shaken than he'd realized.

"You're right."

"About what?"

"We're not going to be able to keep this a secret." Dave said it with finality, as if that future course had somehow just played itself out on the seat cover he was staring at in front of him. "And if we're not positive we can keep this between ourselves,

and I ain't, we could get burned by not bringing this to somebody's attention right away . . . like tomorrow.''

"Tomorrow.'' Matt managed to repeat, absolutely convinced
another unexpected plunge into sheer and possible final terror
was about to occur at any second.

"Are you gentlemen all right?'' A stewardess was leaning
over them with obvious concern.

They nodded. She smiled bravely and moved onto the seats
behind them to repeat the question.

Dave looked squarely at Matt. "I think you should tell your
department head, what's his name?''

"My department head . . . Henry. Henry Sylbert.'' Matt
took a deep breath and tried to relax. Fear was loosening its grip
on his thinking. "Why Henry?''

"Because you saw it on a satellite photograph. Because he's
as good as anybody. Because, Matt, if we're not going to keep
it to ourselves, then the more people who know about this the
better. I'll hold on to the film and dog tags until Henry tells you
what to do. Let him pass the ball to the higher-ups.''

The plane was steady, things were back to normal, but when
Matt tried to think beyond the flight his stomach started tightening.

". . . I'm sorry, Dave.''

The flimsy oxygen mask was still hanging by its clear plastic
umbilical cord. Dave was staring at it again, as if it held some
meaning. "For what?''

Matt looked back out the window at the rain-streaked wing.
The red collision light flashed brightly at its tip.

". . . I don't know, I'm just sorry.''

He closed his eyes for only an instant. The broken images of
algae-coated skeletons in a dark silent world leaped to mind.
Matt quickly blinked them open.

"God, I wish we were there already.''

III

Matt had just, finally, drifted into an empty sleep when the jet
touched down at National under a clear blue sky that vaulted

over Washington, D.C., and most of the eastern seaboard. It was six thirty-seven on an October morning, the temperature was fifty-four degrees, and the disembodied captain's voice was telling, practically ordering, the weary line of passengers to have a nice day.

Waiting for their luggage, Dave buried himself in the sports pages of a *Washington Post*. Matt dozed off in an uncomfortable plastic seat that was bolted to the floor.

Once out of the terminal, they parted quickly, without saying good-bye. They took separate taxis: Matt to his apartment; Dave home to Perri. Both had to be at work in two and a half hours. The plan was for Matt to come up and see Dave after he'd spoken with Henry.

Things didn't seem so bad in the daylight, Matt decided in the cab. The vague but relentless phantoms of last night's tortured attempts to sleep were fading before the reassuringly routine elements of a sunny October Monday morning. The world seemed to be going about its business just as it should.

So calm down.

Just take a deep breath. In a few hours, after talking with Henry, everything would be fine. His cab was steadily weaving through early rush-hour traffic along the George Washington Memorial Parkway; one of tens of thousands of other vehicles taking respective passengers to myriad jobs and appointments that would intersect, fit together, and combine to become a subtle, fuctioning, productive whole, which Matt at the moment felt somehow outside of.

Everything was going to be okay, he kept telling himself.

Matt nodded pleasantly to the Kingman Arms doorman who helped him with his bags, and he smiled at a neighbor while in the elevator going up to his apartment.

Once inside he put the stove on under the kettle, and while it came to a boil he opened his mail.

His mom had sent a manila envelope containing a thick sheaf of newspaper clippings, each marked with cryptic comments in pencil beside circled pictures and articles he might be interested in. She'd collected an especially odd assortment this time, highlighted by a story about UFO sightings in Florida, under which was scrawled, "Is this what you do?"

After a long steamy shower and shave, Matt found a clean shirt and pants and put on a tie. The television was on in the background and a morning show was administering a pill of news. Matt watched briefly, picking up on some local disaster.

Matt turned off the television and took the elevator down to the garage.

He would go into Henry's office and tell him exactly what happened, just like Dave said to do. Henry would tell somebody else, who would then tell somebody else, who would then tell somebody else. And by the end of the day, Matt and Dave wouldn't be all alone in their knowledge of what lay beneath the waves at a certain remote point off the northern-California coast. By the end of the day, they'd be back to being little innocuous pieces of a greater whole.

Which was just the way Matt wanted it.

Chapter Eleven

"Just who in the hell are you, exactly?"

Taken aback, he didn't immediately respond.

Henry Sylbert spit the question again with frightening venom. This Matthew S. Clarke—if that even was his real name, which Henry severely doubted at the moment—this young, innocent-looking new man in his section had just cornered him outside the men's room, scarcely five minutes into an already hectic Monday morning, and calmly, almost pleasantly, told a story that began on Thursday, in IA, with a blur on a satellite photograph, and ended Sunday, yesterday, with a dive into a thirty-year-old Russian submarine with dead American crewmen inside—at least, everything pointed to them being American, when you thought about it—and he had—this Matthew Clarke concluded in a disquietingly unruffled tone.

"I don't understand—"

"I've had it with you, Mr. Clarke," Henry pressed on with unchecked hostility. "I don't know what sort of game, or test, or security check you're involved in and I don't *care* to know. You've been a disruption to this section since you arrived—and that's something you people don't factor into your elaborate stratagems to ferret out imagined leaks and potential cash-shy traitors—loss of productivity!''

"*What* people? Henry, I'm telling you the truth."

The young man's voice was no longer calm. In point of fact, the tone was rounded by a fuzzy edge of desperation. But that was also, Henry decided, most assuredly, all part of the role Matthew Clarke had been sent down by M-5 to play. And now that Henry recognized the man for what he really was, and what he was up to, there was really no point in continuing this disruptive charade.

"You've lied since you arrived here, Mr. Clarke. You're a plant, some kind of investigator, here to look for security violations, stir up trouble—make it up if you have to, I'm sure."

"Henry, that's crazy—"

"*Is it?*"

They stood facing each other in the quiet, dimly lit hallway while one of the section library clerks, practically a teenager, passed into the nearby women's room.

"Of course it is. It's absurd."

"Is it? *Is it?* Well, I don't think so," Henry stated with tight-lipped emotion, his voice ringing with contempt. "You arrive here on internal probation—"

"That had nothing to do with this, with what I just told you. I'm speaking to you because I saw the thing first on a satellite photograph. You never could have seen it any other way—"

"I'll not be made a fool of! I will not!"

Henry's wildest doubts about this man's presence in his section were coming to full boil. And rightfully so! The submarine story on top of everything else—the blur on the satellite photograph, the man's security grade, the way he'd arrived— damn him and the people who sent him here! This section ran smoothly! What more did they want?

"Henry, I didn't *have* to tell you about this. I didn't have to tell anyone. I could've just kept this to myself and nobody would have been the wiser."

"Ha!" Henry's left arm bent at the waist and his index

finger shot up triumphantly at an angle between them. "You *knew* I knew about this already, at least the blur on the satellite photograph!"

"But that's not true. How—"

"You purposely involved Reiko, one of the most loyal and hardworking people I have in this section, by showing that blur to him Thursday morning before you left, conveniently on some sort of business trip. You hinted at treasure and asked if he wanted to be cut in. The poor man's been worried sick all weekend, even though he reported it to me right away. *I've* been worried about it all weekend!"

"Worried about what? *I was joking*—I didn't know what was down there."

Henry shook his small head from side to side. He suddenly began rocking on the balls of his feet. "I was going to call you into my office—"

"But, Henry—"

"Let me finish! As I say, I *was* going to call you into my office and ask you about it, this incident with Reiko, as regulation demands—because I *do* follow regulations—but you've approached me first. And now you drop this, this ridiculous story into my lap, much the same way you dropped the sunken-treasure bit on Reiko, I believe, in order to see how I proceed—to see how, or even if, I'd follow it up—just to check up on how things are going down here in the basement. Well, everything here is running fine, I'm happy to report! Everything is running perfectly down here in IA, or was until you arrived! Have you people nothing better to do? Have you people no conscience?"

"Henry, Dave Lakeman and I were scuba diving and found an old Soviet submarine with bodies inside. I have pictures of it, dog tags from it—I could show you exactly where it is—you *must* believe me."

"You can drop the act, really, because I see through you like glass."

"You're being—"

Henry frantically waved a hand, cutting Matt off.

"I'm as security conscious as the next person here, probably more so, but if this is part of some new policy of trying to entrap hardworking, loyal employees—by God, I'll fight it to the top. I've been through this sort of thing before. In the late sixties, M-5 decided it was time for a witch hunt. I know how they operate. *I* was called before them on some nonexistent grounds!''

"Look," Matt said, his hands going up in a placating gesture as he slowly began backing away from Henry, "forget it. Just forget I ever mentioned it. Nothing happened. I didn't see a thing. All I want to do is go back to my table, just go back to work—''

"You'll do no such thing!" Henry closed the distance between them with one long, awkward step. "I'm reporting this to M-5, personally, right now, as soon as I'm through with you. It's quite plain to me that you work for them in some capacity, and I'm not leaving until I have somebody's word up there that you'll be transferred from my section immediately. You no longer work in IA, Mr. Clarke. You were on temporary assignment and I want you out of here right now. Leave. *Please!*''

Henry placed a shaking hand on Matt's shoulder and tried to turn him around toward the door.

"Henry—" Matt resisted. He brushed the hand away, but it quickly came back and resumed pushing, this time with tremendous resolve.

"Don't get violent with me, young man!" Henry had hold of Matt's arm and was walking him, practically dragging him, briskly toward the door.

"Henry, this is all some kind of mistake! I'm telling you the truth!''

Other people in the section were now looking up from their light tables as Henry pushed and pulled Matt through the main room.

"Yes, yes, yes! Just leave—*thank you!*" Henry could feel his heart pounding, too hard and too fast, but he had momentum and he couldn't stop now. The only thing that mattered was getting this man out of his section—immediately!

"Stop pushing me, goddamn it!''

They were at the door. Henry was shouldering Matt out now with demonic strength, employing his whole wiry body in the task.

"Please, Henry—you've got to listen to me! I don't work for anybody else—I'm not down here to spy on you—"

"I'll send your things on—check back after one—good-bye, Mr. Clarke—that's it—*good-bye!*" Henry gave one last frenzied push, and Matthew Clarke tripped backward, then fell to the floor in the hall.

The white steel door slowly swung closed, gradually blocking him off from view, and then locked with a satisfying click.

And that was how Henry always remembered Matthew Selwyn Clarke: in a heap on the floor, glasses off, trying to prop himself up on one elbow.

Sometimes you just had to put your foot down!

II

Henry marched back through the main room. All heads were downturned over respective light tables. They were pretending to work, no doubt, after having witnessed one of the most unusual spectacles to ever occur in the usually sedate and darkened quarters of Imagery Analysis.

Henry proceeded straight to the section's library annex. Taking deep breaths to try to slow his racing heart, he tracked down Thursday's assignment sheet and located the reference number of the satellite photograph that Matthew Clarke had seen the blur on. Henry removed the weather-satellite photograph from the files and signed for it with a hurried, uncharacteristically illegible scrawl.

He secured the poster-size print in a large manila envelope and walked swiftly back through the main room. Several people were huddled together over by the coffee machine, talking in excited, hushed tones. Henry paid them no mind.

He left Imagery Analysis section and strode down the hall to the elevators. After some impatient foot-tapping and absent toying with his bow tie, the elevator arrived. Henry stepped in and jabbed for the sixth floor. From the subbasement, the elevator rapidly ascended through the ground, then above it, and finally deposited Henry in front of two rows of small black plastic signs, one of which pointed the way to the Office of Security.

He clutched the large manila envelope as if it were a shield, tramping purposefully down one long hallway to the next. His indignant footsteps echoed through each successive passage, until he passed through a wide set of double doors at the conclusion of a dead-end corridor.

Henry stepped into a small, overly bright anteroom. The walls were painted white. Several security posters were hung about, including the ubiquitous bold-blocked order to SAFE-GUARD CLASSIFIED INFORMATION, and a new security witticism Henry had never seen before that read LOOSE LIPS SINK CRYPS. Against the far wall, beside a barren hatrack, sat a sturdy FPS guard behind a metal frame desk that was as clean as if he had, moments before Henry came in, swept everything off its surface into the adjacent wastepaper basket. The guard wore a crisp blue uniform. The tips of his shiny black shoes poked out from beneath the desk. His firm smile was almost as rigidly polite as his "Good morning."

"Yes . . ." Henry wavered, his resolve suddenly buckling under the numbing thought that he was on the threshold of making a terrible, terrible mistake. He'd acted rashly. There was still time to turn and leave. The room seemed to swim. Henry felt as if he, or the floor, were tilting.

"Can I help you?" The guard's smile was unwavering.

"Yes," Henry blurted, holding the large manila envelope out in front of him with a trembling hand as if it explained perfectly well the particulars of his unannounced visit. "Yes, I want to see the director, if he's available, of course."

"Leonard Vanning?"

"What?" Henry was distracted by a buzzing in his ears; the rush of blood to his brain. "Yes, of course."

"Your name, sir?"

"Henry Sylbert, director of Imagery Analysis."

It seemed like only a moment later, Henry was being led down a thickly carpeted hall by a rather pudgy, formal man. His name was Grieve, or something to that effect, and he was speaking.

"—without an appointment."

"Yes. I apologize. Perhaps I should come back—"

"No, no," this man Grieve was shaking his head gravely. "The director will see you now—as you insisted."

Henry looked down at the manila envelope in his hand, and for an instant couldn't remember what it contained.

Insisted?

He blindly followed Grieve through a confusing maze of hallways to an unmarked, closed wooden door.

"I think maybe I *should* come back another time," Henry stammered.

"Nonsense, here we are." Grieve knocked once, turned the polished brass knob, and politely ushered Henry inside.

The door swung closed behind him, and Henry was standing alone on a lawn-green carpet that flowed to a massive, ornately carved mahogany desk a short putt away.

There was a handsome man, in a suit—a beautifully tailored dark gray suit, sitting behind the desk, head down, writing something.

Against the right wall there was a white sofa, over which hung a large atmospheric sea scene reminiscent of Turner. The other three walls were lined impressively with books. A lone, straight-backed chair stood sentinel near the man's desk, facing it at a slightly off angle. The man looked up. His face was tan. He had exceptionally white teeth and piercing blue eyes. His black-and-gray hair was cut very closely, particularly at the sides. Henry realized the man was older than he seemed at first glance—probably near retirement age. The man wasn't physically strong, but he exuded a sense of power.

"Leonard Vanning, director of the Office of Security," the man said civilly without standing. "Please, sit down, Mr. Sylbert."

"Yes."

Henry took four steps and deposited himself, stiffly erect, in the chair opposite the director's desk. Up close it seemed the size of a pool table. Henry wondered how they got it into the room.

Vanning was staring at him.

Henry stared vacantly back, a detached smile attached to his face, not knowing how, or if, to proceed. His mouth was dry and he ached for a glass of water.

"I believe we met once at an IEC meeting several years ago," Vanning offered, studying Henry's face.

"Oh yes, yes, of course!" Henry nodded vigorously, having no memory of ever meeting Vanning. He crossed his legs, trying to get comfortable in the chair.

Vanning folded a pair of clean, manicured hands on the highly polished desktop. The white of his shirt peeked out a perfect half inch from under the sleeves of his suit jacket.

"So, Mr. Sylbert . . . you have some *urgent* matter to discuss?"

Henry glanced down at the stiff manila envelope in his lap. He gave a fidgety tug to his bow tie.

"Yes, I do have an issue—excuse me." His voice was quavering. "I'm a little nervous—an issue I'd like to bring up with you—if I may."

"An issue, by all means."

"Concerning the recent transfer to Imagery Analysis of one Matthew Selwyn Clarke . . ."

Henry watched Vanning's reaction closely. There was none. If Vanning knew who Clarke was, he certainly wasn't showing any sign of it.

". . . He was on internal probation."

The smooth, tan face was impassive. The teeth stayed white and the eyes stayed blue. His bare smile was as dangerously inviting as the lure of an angler fish.

"Perhaps it would help if I got the man's file," Vanning finally said. He picked up his phone and spoke briefly. A half minute later, during which Henry's eyes flitted about the room like those of a caged bird, Vanning's assistant, Grieve, entered with a folder and laid it open solemnly on the desk.

Grieve left the room.

"Here we are . . . um-hum . . . yes . . . right . . . Clarke." Vanning looked back up at Henry. "Conditional probation. Has there been a problem?"

"Well, I—I thought he worked for you." Henry said it

softly, and then strained to sit more erect in the oddly angled chair.

"For Security?"

Vanning impatiently returned to the file and scanned it once more. He let his gaze drift slowly back up to meet Henry's. ". . . I'm afraid I don't understand."

"I think I've made a mistake."

Henry's halfhearted chuckle came out sounding like a groan. He fingered the manila envelope nervously. Maybe it was the green carpeting, but he was feeling ill.

"I was under the impression that this Matthew Clarke might have been working for your section, in some capacity—ha!" Henry tossed a hand in the air and with a vague motion tried to fan the thought away.

"Did he *tell* you he worked for M-5?" Vanning leaned closer, as close as the huge desk would allow.

"Actually . . . no."

Henry tried shifting in the chair, but the back ended below the shoulder blades in a way that stopped you from leaning fully into it. All it lacked were straps for the wrists.

". . . No, in fact he denied emphatically that he worked for M-5. As I say, I believe I've made a mistake, and—"

"What made you think he was working for the Office of Security, Mr. Sylbert?" Vanning's tone left no room to maneuver.

"Yes, I should explain. He came to our section under unusual circumstances—high security clearance and pay grade, travel assignments, blue flagged, temporary assignment—and I became suspicious of him, why he was sent down to us and all that." Henry realized with a start that Vanning had closed Matthew Clarke's file and was staring at him balefully.

"I'm afraid I'll have to ask you to be more specific, Mr. Sylbert."

"Yes, of course. I apologize . . . I'm a little nervous."

Vanning wasn't returning his smile, so Henry quickly pushed on. "Thursday last, this Matthew Clarke came in early and my deputy director, Reiko Murata, came upon him examining a satellite photograph."

"And you found this to be unusual?"

There was sarcasm in the question, unmistakably. Henry was

too frightened to stop and respond. He galloped for the end of the story. "He pretended to spot, or rather, I realize now, *did* spot, a blur on the picture."

"A blur?"

"Yes. An underwater blur—something underwater."

Vanning's chin went up as if he were about to speak, but, oddly, he checked himself and remained silent.

After a moment's confusion, Henry continued. "The blur was on a recent satellite weather series, about a mile off a remote portion of northern California. The point is that Clarke told Reiko he thought he'd found an old galleon, or something along those lines, and that he planned to go scuba diving there over the weekend, during an NSA business trip of some sort. He asked Reiko if he'd like to split any possible treasure he found. I know it sounds ridiculous in this setting, but Reiko was extremely unnerved by the incident and reported it to me. Reiko became convinced it was part of some security test, a thought which I picked up, and I must confess, expanded on . . ."

Henry bowed his head. He stopped to let Vanning interject a rebuke.

Silence. Henry glanced up and was surprised to see Vanning had stood, and, back turned, was engaged in what must have been an examination of the bookshelves behind his desk. Henry found himself scanning the shelves as well.

From the spotless, gray-suited figure came a soft, "Go on."

"Of course. Well, this morning I walked into my office and was immediately confronted by Clarke. He told me an extremely bizarre story, which, in light of my previous suspicions about the man, heightened my belief that he worked for your office and was engaged in some sort of security exercise. I admit I got upset—"

"What did he say he found?" Vanning seemed to be looking up at a specific book several feet above his head, and had his ear cocked as if he were, at best, only casually interested in hearing the rest of the tale.

"What he found, yes. This Clarke said he went diving with a David Lakeman, a COMINT employee, with whom he was on this business trip, and that what they found, where this blur was, was a submerged thirty-year-old Soviet submarine with dead American crewmen aboard. Said he even had pictures and dog tags.'' Henry successfully managed a nervous laugh.

"And?'' asked Vanning, his back still turned as he idly reached up and pulled the book down to glance at its cover.

"And I became convinced he worked for the Office of Security, and that his story, in fact his very presence in IA, was part of some check on my section. I can see now from your reaction that that's not—''

"Congratulations, Mr. Sylbert,'' Vanning turned quickly and came around from his desk, "you passed!''

III

Stunned, Henry lifted his arm and let Vanning lead him in a vigorous handshake. The man was leaning over him so close that Henry could smell his cologne. He was smiling wildly, white teeth gleaming, and there was a look of reckless exuberance in his eyes. For a moment, Henry had the odd sensation that he was about to be kissed.

"Passed?"

"Certainly!'' Vanning dropped Henry's hand and was off pacing the room. "Of course, it *was* a rather elaborate and round-about way of getting the job done, I admit, but you've come through the process with flying colors.''

The phone rang. Henry watched Vanning fairly leap to pick it up.

"Hold all my calls!'' He quickly replaced the receiver.

"You're saying then, that Clarke *does* work for M-5, and this *was*, after all, a security test of my section?'' Henry asked it timidly, unconvinced this wasn't some sort of new progression in a nerve-racking game seemingly void of rules and reason.

Vanning hopped onto the edge of his desk. A tight black sock showed above his dangling shoe. Henry looked up at him hopefully.

"Let me ask *you* a question,'' Vanning said with a smile.

"Does anybody else know what you've just told me? Anyone at all? This Reiko Murata, perhaps?"

"No. Clarke said that other than David Lakeman, I was the only person he's spoken to—but I really don't understand what's going on here. I mean, I'm somewhat confused. I must have an explanation," Henry caught himself, "if that's at all possible, of course."

"Mr. Sylbert—Henry—of course you'll have an explanation. It's all really quite routine. You see, the idea is to temporarily place someone in a section as a silent observer. They stay for a few weeks, a few months on the outside, and we get a firsthand report for our files."

Vanning spun off the slippery desktop, stood, and clapped his hand together as if some large task awaited his personal direction. He went back and sat down in his chair.

"A report, of course. . . . What kind of report?"

Vanning put his elbow on the desk and rested his chin on his fist. "Just a routine report, a preventive measure, really. Try to catch any trouble before it occurs. A checkup, if you will."

"But what about this blur on the satellite photograph?" Henry asked, desperately wanting to believe. "What about this submarine business?"

"Ah, yes, well I'm afraid Mr. Clarke got a little *too* enthusiastic in his methods there. He had no instructions to fabricate such a story, I assure you, and I can guarantee he will be reprimanded."

Vanning was staring at the manila envelope balanced on Henry's lap.

"And is that the satellite photograph in question?" Vanning said carefully. "In that envelope there?"

Henry was about to ask something, forgot it, and answered, "Yes."

Vanning's hand was extended out over the desk and Henry automatically handed the poster-size manila envelope to him.

"Thank you." Vanning smiled as if he'd just been given a valuable gift. The manila envelope disappeared down into a cabinet that formed the whole right side of the desk.

"Now then, Mr. Sylbert. How did you leave the matter with Mr. Clarke?"

"Well." Henry's empty palms came up at his sides. "I told him to leave. I physically ejected him from the section. I was extremely upset at the time, as I said, and—"

"You had every right to be! Again, my apologies."

"Yes, well, I told him I was coming up here to report the matter and that he should come back at one to pick up his belongings. I was hoping he'd be reassigned to another section—"

"And so he will! So he will. As I say, we'll handle this from our end, since he was, *technically*, working for our section . . ."

Vanning's features shifted into a warm smile.

"Now, Henry, you understand the importance of keeping this incident under your hat, at least while we conduct a full investigation into the matter."

"Yes, of course." An ember of anger sparked to life. "I can't say I agree with this spying on fellow employees, however . . ."

Vanning remained silent.

Realizing he was still intact after this initial sally, Henry boldly charged ahead. "I mean, it's just so disruptive. I've been worrying about this all weekend—and Reiko, Reiko was practically sick about it. If this is some new policy to entrap hardworking—"

"It's a most unfortunate incident all the way around." Vanning was shaking his head in sympathy. He looked down at his heavy gold watch.

"Henry, it's going on ten thirty and I have a rather important staff meeting to attend. You'll forgive me if—"

"Certainly."

Henry stood, happy to be out of the chair's grasp. More than anything, he just wanted to get out of the room. Vanning came quickly around the desk. He firmly pumped Henry's hand as he led him across the green carpet to the door.

"This matter will get my full attention, I can assure you."

"There'll be no more of this kind of thing then—at least in my section?"

"No. I guarantee it."

Vanning flashed a winning smile and patted Henry on the back. He opened the door for him.

"Yes, thank you. Take care."

"You too, Henry. Good-bye."

"Will I be hearing from you?"

"I'll let you know how it all turns out."

"Yes, please," Henry said in parting.

Henry turned and walked briskly back down the hallway. *"Yes, please?"* He suddenly realized that he never wanted to see or hear from this Vanning again.

The hall intersected with another, and Henry stopped, trying to remember the way he'd come in. Right or left—here was something new to worry about.

Chapter Twelve

They were standing in the downstairs hallway: a stunned Leonard Vanning and Retired Admiral Ford Hulse's niece, Annie.

"You haven't called in six months," she stated simply. "If you'd stayed in touch you'd have known."

"But how bad?" Vanning asked. "How bad is he?"

". . . A month maybe. Two at the outside."

Vanning visibly sagged at the news.

"Today he's having a rough time of it. I've told him you're here. The nurse is almost done. You can go in then."

"Jesus, Annie," Vanning pleaded, "if I'd known I'd have come—in a second. No one ever called to tell—"

"He said not to. You know how stubborn he is. He didn't want to bother you with it."

"*Bother me?*" Vanning repeated, numbed. "He was like a father. *You* should have called, Annie." Vanning leaned against a wall and looked down at the floor, shaking his head. ". . . Not bother me with the fact he's dying?" he asked incredulously.

A short, round, starched nurse appeared from a room at the end of the hall. She was heading to the kitchen.

"He's asked for you to come in," she told Vanning as she passed. "But you'll have to keep it short."

Vanning drifted away from Hulse's niece.

"I'm sorry, Leonard . . ." he heard from behind.

Vanning trod slowly over creaking floorboards, down a long hall decorated in a naval motif: valiant sea scenes in oils and watercolors; intricately detailed and brightly painted models of ships and submarines; a cluster of framed citations; sunny photographs from the former warrior's days of command. These mementos stretched like a museum wing to the far end of the century-old farmhouse, to a half-open door at the end of the hall. Vanning paused just outside, collecting himself. He looked at the doorknob before taking it, and he moved slowly into the room.

Retired Admiral Ford Hulse was seated in a glass-enclosed sun-room. There was much sun today. The transparent walls and ceiling of the space let in all the bright cheerfulness of the cloudless morning. A spotlight-like beam fell over the man who was so deeply settled in the white wicker chair; a vastly different admiral from the rugged and vigorous figure found in the photographs in the hall. This Hulse was taut white skin over skeleton. The sharp lines of his skull grinned triumphantly behind sunken features. The neck choked down at the windpipe and seemed like a sculpture armature waiting for clay. Gnarled, useless hands lay upturned and painful on a distant lap. A very white, thick blanket covered his legs and he was wrapped in a new terrycloth robe of vivid blue that seemed horribly unnatural on his still, ravaged body. Here the forgotten warhorse collapsed in the pasture—punctured and deflating.

"Ford?"

". . . Live longer, Leonard . . . you'll die, too."

Vanning went gently across the room. He placed a light hand on Hulse's shoulder. "I didn't realize—" he choked. "Why didn't you call?"

"There was nothing you could do. Sit down, Leonard . . . it tires me to watch you stand."

Vanning pulled up a footstool and sat at Hulse's side.

"I should have stayed in touch," Vanning said.

Hulse was staring at him, studying him, looking for something. His moist eyes gradually widened.

"You found it . . ." he said suddenly to Vanning.

"How—"

"You must have found it!"

"Now don't get excited, Ford. I didn't come out here to get you upset. If I'd known how sick—"

"My God . . . have you seen it?"

". . . No," Vanning said after some hesitation. "I haven't. Two others have—two NSA employees. It's been found, Ford. It has definitely been found."

". . . Found. Finally."

Hulse closed his eyes. ". . . Avery . . . Sussman . . . Durso . . . Atkins . . ." he recited. "I still remember all those boys' names . . ."

His eyes opened, drifted to the sunny outside. "Tell me, Leonard. Tell me how it was found . . ."

"I don't think you should con—"

"Please, Leonard, don't make me beg."

". . . It was found by an NSA employee—from a satellite photograph. It showed up as a blur on a satellite photograph. It was found from the sky, Ford."

". . . From the sky it's been found," Hulse repeated in wonder. "All these years . . ."

"Are you okay? Jesus—you're crying, Ford."

". . . I'm fine," Hulse insisted, a tear running down his cheek. "Who, Leonard? Who found it?"

"That's not imp—"

"The names—I want the names."

"Why?"

"You'd deny me this?"

"Who cares what their names are? Matthew Clarke and Dave Lakeman—there. I didn't come out here to upset you, Ford. That's not why I came."

". . . Why then?"

"I didn't realize—"

"Why?"

Vanning stood. He began pacing before the retired admiral's chair.

Hulse summoned a fatherly tone: "Tell me, Leonard."

"You have—" Vanning paused, then tried another tack—"I thought we could work together on this . . . on wrapping this up. You and me."

Hulse remained silent, watching.

"You have access to some people, people I could use right now. I'm short on people like that. But, Ford, I didn't realize you were sick. I'd never have come out here like this if I'd known that you were so sick . . ."

When Vanning looked over at Hulse, the retired admiral was slowly shaking his head.

". . . Wash the wound, Leonard."

"What?"

"It was all a mistake . . . a horrible, murderous mistake."

"Calm down, Ford."

"I am."

"You look tired. I should go. I think I'll go—"

"What would you take back, Leonard? Anything? Line it all up—but then you always were a desk man . . ."

"I went inside it, Ford," said Vanning. "*I* pulled those bodies out."

"A gruesome task."

"I shouldn't have come. If I'd known—"

"You were so eager back then. So eager to please . . ."

"I should have stayed in touch. For that I apologize. Jesus, Ford—I didn't realize you'd slipped so far."

"I could have stopped it," Hulse said distantly. "I was on the bridge . . . next to Markwater. I could've stopped it."

"You did what you thought was right. We all did."

"Right? Seventy-six men—not counting Avery and his boys . . . for what? Do the right thing, Leonard. Come clean on this."

"That's easy for you to say," Vanning said, a note of rancor creeping into his voice, "you're dying—" Vanning regretted it as soon as the words left his mouth. "I'm sorry, Ford. I didn't mean that."

". . . These two who found it, they're dying, too, aren't they, Leonard?"

Vanning avoided Hulse's gaze.

"Screws?" Hulse asked.

"Let him come in and take charge? No. I'm crossing the T on this."

". . . At the hospital I told a doctor—"

Vanning looked at him now. "What?"

"A doctor, I told a doctor, everything . . . the whole story. Standing on the bridge . . . the call . . . it's out there . . . proceed with the test . . . the flash—"

"You told someone?"

"The doctor thought I was hallucinating, told me to go to sleep."

"You should. I'll be going now—"

"But I see it in my sleep, Leonard. The old footage just keeps on playing . . ."

Hulse was seized by a dry, hacking cough.

"Ford? I'll get the nurse, Ford!"

Vanning ran from the room. Several moments later, he returned trailing the nurse. She calmly put an oxygen mask over the patient's face. Hulse's eyes slowly closed.

"I didn't mean to upset him."

"The medication—he's very tired. Maybe you should go," she suggested politely.

"Yes . . . yes, I'll do that."

Vanning looked back one more time from the doorway. Hulse's eyes had reopened. The eyes said, *Wash the wound, Leonard.*

Chapter Thirteen

Matt's first instinct, like that of some wounded animal, was to bury himself in seclusion—a wooded bramble—or in his case, the nearest men's room (third stall).

"Oh, Jesus."

Matt's mind raced. He was hiding—from what, exactly, he wasn't quite sure—but there might as well have been a lunatic with a gun stalking the NSA halls.

Henry. Henry was stalking the halls.

"What am I gonna do what am I gonna do what am I gonna—"

Matt heard the door open. He stopped chanting. A pair of feet walked to the bank of urinals, relieved themselves, washed their hands, and walked out.

Safety in the bathroom. Black metal partitions, shiny lock on the door, soothingly ordered tile pattern. Always liked bathrooms.

"What the fuck am I supposed to do?"

Henry said he was going to M-5. Thought I worked for M-5. Don't be ridiculous. So they'll tell him he's wrong. They'll set

him straight. They'll tell him to get his act together and apologize to Clarke for the way you treated him. Son of a bitch.
Knocking me down! I should've punched him right there!

Matt listened. Another customer. Didn't wash his hands.

Some time passed, how much, Matt wasn't sure, but probably a lot. He finally, after much deliberation, decided it would
be safe to go see Dave.

Of course it would!

"I haven't done anything wrong," Matt reminded himself as
he unlocked the door and stepped out of the stall.

He stopped in front of the mirror. He looked tired, slightly
dark under the eyes.

Well, who wouldn't be after spending all night on a plane?

Matt ran a hand over his longish straight hair and adjusted his
glasses. Then he glared at the mirror.

"I haven't done anything wrong!"

II

"Way to go, buddy."

Dave was in his cluttered cubbyhole of an office in the
engineering lab of his section, drinking a cup of black coffee.

Matt had made a beeline to get there.

"What'd you mean?"

"I just got the call. We're meeting the director of Security at
one in his office. You held the big guy up, Matt."

Matt watched Dave as he took a sip of his coffee. He didn't
seem to be fooling.

"Security called you?"

"Yeah, forty minutes ago. Leonard Vanning himself. Said
your section head, Sylbert, had just left. Vanning wanted to see
you and me immediately. He tried tracking you down but he
couldn't find you, so he called back here, said he had to go out,
but that we should meet him at one in his office."

"In his office."

"Where were you?"

"Nowhere."

"Well, Vanning also said he was *'apprised'* of the situation and that we should keep *'it'* between ourselves until we meet with him this afternoon."

" 'It'?"

"Yeah."

"That's interesting."

"Why? You spoke to Henry, right?"

"Yeah, but . . ."

In something like the flat and halting tone of a poorly written letter, Matt gave Dave the details of what had happened.

Dave listened until Matt was done.

"You frightened him. He ran up to Security. This guy Vanning should be able to straighten everything out. So everything's going like it should."

"Vanning didn't say anything about me? —About where I was supposed to go?"

"Nope."

"Because I can't go back to IA. Henry kicked me out."

". . . Look, it's twelve now. Let's go get some lunch and we'll go up and meet Vanning at one. Okay? Good."

They went to the cafeteria. It was early for lunch and not at all crowded. Sitting at the table, Dave took a handful of shiny steel from his pocket and laid it in a small pile on Matt's tray.

"What's that?"

"The dog tags we found. I polished them up."

"These?"

Fascinated, Matt started separating them.

"Yeah, I wanted to see the names."

Matt picked them up and, one by one, examined them.

```
USN     BLOOD TYPE
LAMM, WALTER     AB
ST35525    667


USN     BLOOD TYPE
FURROWS, WILLIAM     AB
JU93002    772
```

```
USN     BLOOD TYPE
AVERY, CARL     A
RT40255     442


USN     BLOOD TYPE
ATKINS, LYLE     O
MN23156     717


USN     BLOOD TYPE
DILLING, JAMES     B
SD34312     445


USN     BLOOD TYPE
SUSSMAN, JAMES     O
RT36755     342


USN     BLOOD TYPE
LEONE, DAVID     A+
JU14522     667
```

"Holy shit . . ." Matt muttered.

"All polished up like that—they look practically new, don't they?"

"Strange to think of those skeletons having names."

"I got 'em all written down," Dave said.

"Why?" Matt stared at the glistening remains of the dead sailors, running them through his fingers like a metallic rosary.

"Now listen, Matt—"

"Dave, there's only seven."

Matt neatly laid the shiny tags back on his tray.

"We're walking into Vanning's office and we're giving him *seven* tags, Matt."

"But we found eight."

Dave took a bright red envelope from his jacket.

"I got the pictures developed this morning at the one-hour place downstairs."

Matt made no move for the packet in Dave's hand.

"You want to see them? They came out real clear."

"No."

"They came out real clear."

"I just don't want to."

"Okay." Dave put the photographs back in his pocket. "We'll give Vanning the seven dog tags, the negatives, which I made a copy of, but not the watch."

"Let's just give him everything and forget about it, Dave."

"Did you tell Sylbert about the watch?"

Matt thought back on the scene. "No."

"How many dog tags we found?"

"How many? No."

"I trusted you, now it's your turn to trust me. We have to cover ourselves. I'm not going in naked. We keep the one tag, the duplicate negatives, the watch—we keep them, Matt, for insurance."

"Insurance for what?"

"Until we find out how the land lies—"

"I want to forget this ever happened, Dave."

"Let's just see what Vanning has to say. Until then I'm protecting myself."

III

Vanning stood at the end of the hall, filling the doorway, as an assistant showed Matt and Dave into the office.

"Thank you, Grieve."

The assistant left, closing the door behind him.

Vanning broke into a wide smile and with strenuous sincerity shook hands with Matt and Dave.

"You must be Matthew Clarke—and David Lakeman, of course."

Somebody had checked somebody's files and pictures.

Vanning cheerfully led them to a large white sofa and bid them to sit, choosing, himself, to pull up a simple wooden chair that had been near his desk. He positioned it carefully opposite the sofa, so that a glass magazine table lay between them.

Watching the director's eager movements, Matt had the odd thought that Vanning was in actuality a game-show host, and that he and Dave had just won the grand prize.

"So, would you gentlemen care for anything to drink? A soda?"

Matt would have asked for a Coke, his stomach a mess of nerves, but Dave shook his head. Vanning quickly got down to business, leaning in very close to Matt. "I spoke with Henry Sylbert this morning, Matt."

Matt's eyes widened expectantly.

"Some unpleasantness there, eh?" Vanning queried with a paternal look of concern.

"He threw me out."

"I can straighten that. That won't be a problem at all. I think I can get you back into your previous position, the one you held before the, ah, satellite incident."

"That would be fantastic, Mr. Vanning, because all I want to do is get back to work and forget any of this ever happened, really."

Vanning was leaning in, elbows on his knees, lips pursed, nodding vigorously at Matt's words. "Good. That's just fine. We can do that."

That concluded, Vanning quickly sat back up to include Dave in his focused field of view.

"Now then . . . I understand you went diving . . ."

"We chartered a boat," Matt picked up quickly.

"And I gather you found something."

"It was very disturbing, to say the least," Dave said evenly.

"I can imagine. What, exactly, did you think you saw?"

Dave draped a leg over a knee. "We didn't *think* we saw anything. We saw it. It's out there, right now, where it's been for a long time, judging by what's inside."

"A submarine?"

Matt decided to be quiet and let Dave run with the ball.

"A Soviet submarine, about thirty years old—"

Vanning suddenly smiled.

Dave paused, and then continued. "With dead American seamen inside."

"Yes, well," Vanning said idly, "it *looked* like a Soviet submarine, I'm sure. Red star on the con and all that. No, it was an American submarine."

"American?" Dave repeated, just to be sure.

"Made in the U.S.A. Of course, it *was* built to look like a Soviet submarine, and from what I understand, not having seen it, the results were quite real."

"It definitely looks like a Soviet submarine," Matt happily agreed, glad to praise America's ship-building efforts.

At this point Vanning's face dropped into a grave frown. Here was the crux. "You see, and I must be absolutely sure you understand the classified nature of what I'm about to say before I continue . . ."

Matt shot out a quick, "Absolutely!"

"If it was a U.S. military operation," Dave qualified.

"It was."

"Fine."

Vanning regarded Dave for a brief moment and then picked up in an appropriately classified tone. "The submarine was built for a series of sea trials designed to simulate actual encounters with the Soviet Navy. I'm talking now about a period some time ago. Reality being the key to the exercise, the vessel was constructed to resemble as closely as possible a Soviet sub."

Even down to the Russian lettering inside? Matt tried to push the question from his mind, but he could sense the same thought going through Dave's.

"You have a questioning look on your face, Matt." Vanning was waiting on him with a polite, butlerlike expression.

"No. Not me. No questions here."

"Fine. As I said, these trials were extremely secret at the time, that being a particularly tense period in the Cold War—"

"What year was this?" Dave cut in.

At Dave's question, Vanning suppressed a distressed look by glancing down at the floor.

"Let him finish, Dave," Matt urged, a note of pleading in his voice.

"It was in the mid-1950s, I believe . . ." Vanning resumed,

openly pained. "The submarine in question, if I may continue, was lost at sea during one such trial, at the cost of all hands."

A moment's silence. Matt, appropriately, lowered his eyes.

". . . Despite being closely monitored, the sub went down during a particularly intense period of storm activity in the region. After a thorough and fruitless search, we, or I should say those involved, concluded the sub must have imploded in deep ocean off the continental shelf."

"We found it half-buried in sand," Matt said apologetically, as if high-pressure implosion might be preferable. "In a kelp bed."

"Yes. Very good. Now then, I understand you found dog tags, as well as took pictures . . ."

Vanning left the phrase hanging.

"I've got the film and dog tags here."

Dave reached into his jacket and took out the red envelope containing the underwater photographs. He leaned off the sofa and placed it on the glass table like he was playing a card.

Vanning scratched his nose. His eyebrows arched slightly. "You had them developed?"

". . . To be sure they came out." Dave seemed hesitant. "It was before I got your call." Dave shifted uncomfortably in his seat when Vanning didn't immediately respond. "Well, Matt was using a new flash and I wanted to be sure the pictures all came out—"

"It was a new flash," Matt concurred.

"And did they? Did they all come out?" Vanning asked evenly, staring at the envelope between them.

"Perfectly," Dave replied.

Vanning let the packet of pictures stay where Dave had placed them. "Good . . . That's fine. And the dog tags?"

Matt took the tangle of shiny tags from his pants pocket and, with a sweaty palm, dropped them into Vanning's waiting hand.

"I see you cleaned them, quite thoroughly . . . Was there some reason for that?"

Vanning, head down again, seemed to be concentrating on untangling the slithery steel beads. Matt gave Dave a pensive, questioning glance.

"We were curious, plain and simple," Dave said, looking around the room, waiting for Vanning to finish untangling the tags.

He did.

"You found seven?"

Matt nodded.

Vanning took the envelope holding the photographs and negatives and placed it snugly inside his jacket. The dog tags went into the right side pocket. He took his time, thinking.

". . . Very good then . . . I think we all understand each other. Am I right?" He was looking straight at Dave.

". . . We're not to ever say a word of this to anyone."

"In a nutshell, yes."

Vanning stood up. Clasping his hands officially behind his back, he regarded Matt and Dave on the sofa.

"I have it on the highest authority that those sea trials are still considered classified. You, as NSA employees, you both would be punishable to the full letter of the law if you ever spoke about it with anyone—a spouse, I know you're not married, Matt, or a girlfriend, in short—anyone."

Vanning kept his preacherlike stance, pausing to let the words sink in. "This is a national secret, and I strongly, strongly urge you both to forget you ever saw—"

"It's forgotten," Matt broke in.

"Do I make myself clear?"

"We won't say a word," Matt swore, looking at Dave for confirmation.

". . . Hell, I'm no traitor."

Vanning seemed unsatisfied with Dave's response. "You'll not speak about the matter, then, to anyone?"

"I won't say a word."

"Because I can guarantee you, in no uncertain terms, that if a word of this in any way leaks out—"

"We understand," Dave said, a slight note of irritation in his voice.

Vanning gave the barest nod of satisfaction. He turned and carried the chair back to its original position by the desk.

Matt followed Dave's lead and stood to go.

"One last thing," Vanning said, as he placed the red envelope and dog tags in a desk drawer. "You mentioned chartering a boat . . ."

"It was a Boston Whaler," Matt provided promptly. "We chartered it from a guy named Orin Marsh."

"And he knows what's down there?"

"No." Dave shook his head, watching Vanning lock the drawer. "We told you we haven't spoken to anyone about this. The boat guy doesn't know a thing."

Vanning didn't acknowledge Dave's answer, choosing instead to come smiling toward them from around his desk. "I'm very happy we had this talk. I think we all understand each other. Matt, take the rest of the day off and I'll call you in the morning at home. I'm fairly certain I can get you back to work by tomorrow."

"Thank you, Mr. Vanning, really. That would be great."

Matt grasped Vanning's extended hand.

". . . Dave, thank you."

Vanning gave Dave's hand a limp tug.

"Good-bye."

Vanning followed them to the door. Matt opened it and Dave followed him out.

"Take care," Vanning called in parting, as the two walked down the hall. "Good-bye . . ."

Vanning closed the door and locked it. His easy smile vanished, replaced by an expression of narrow-eyed, jaw-clenching intensity.

IV

Vanning spent the next four hours on the phone: talking, ordering, cajoling, pleading, threatening. After each call, he checked

off items on a list he'd made that ran the page-length of a
yellow legal pad. During the many calls, sharp, angular doodles
started to appear on the pad. Arrows with menacing oversize
tips shot out from the margins. Across the top, upon scalloped
waves, rode a crude drawing of a boat burdened with a large aft
winch. A downward zigzag became a deeply scored bolt of
lightning. An angry mushroom cloud with a thick, swirling stem
threatened to obliterate the upper right corner. A primitive
representation of a handgun materialized, then a small black
bug.

Beside Dave Lakeman's name was a check. After Matthew
Clarke's was a circled question mark.

At the end of it all, when the last call had been made and the
clock was inching toward five, Leonard Vanning leaned back in
his chair and desperately tried to remember if he was forgetting
anything.

. . . No.

There were some loose ends. There was tonight's rendezvous, another session of phone calls in the morning, but everything was on track. All aspects had been compartmentalized.

At this very moment, each element was being boxed in—
isolated from the others. The problem was being broken down
into its component parts. Each part would be carefully studied,
tagged, and attended to in an efficient, almost thoughtful way.

I was always good in a crisis, Vanning decided, as he tore off
the heavily marked piece of paper and neatly folded it into
squares. Other men, men like Hulse, or Markwater, or Seydoux,
or Screws, they had something, some far-seeing intelligence or
inner drive that took them higher than I'll ever reach—but put
me under pressure, challenge me, back me up against a wall and
force me to fight my way out, and I just believe you won't find
my equal. Vanning unlocked his desk and lay the folded piece
of paper beside the red envelope and anthill of dog tags.

A gruesome task.

Vanning slowly reached for the envelope, and, after some
hesitation, removed the dozen postcard-size photographs it
contained.

The pictures were amazingly sharp and quite well framed.

First, the conning tower (I remember it well) bearing a dull red star (still menacing after all these years). Then came a shot of a gaping hole in the hull, fringed with flower petals of jagged steel (some sort of explosion . . . fire perhaps . . . Avery was right to be worried about the sub's seaworthiness). Next were several other photos taken of the hull. What followed were the shots from within. The black, rusty, algae-coated control room.

Vanning swallowed back a gag.

. . . the control room . . .

It *had* been a gruesome task: hideous; nauseating; the unimaginable horror of what must have gone on in that stagnant metal box as it slowly became a coffin—and he was not thinking about the American seamen now, but of what had come before, of how the submarine had been obtained—thinking of the unheard, pleading screams; the grotesque and unsparing effects of decomposition; flesh sliding off in your hands; floor covered with a sticky flypaper coating of mingling, coagulating body fluids; and the smell—the thick, acidic, overpowering stench of rotti—

STOP IT! STOP IT!

Vanning took several deep breaths to keep from vomiting. Heart pounding, he tightly closed his eyes and tried to rein the stampeding thoughts. The memories of those sights and smells slowly sank into blackness.

Vanning opened his eyes. With remarkably steady hands he put the photographs back in their envelope and locked the desk drawer tight.

The intercom was buzzing. Vanning gently pushed a button on his phone. "Yes?"

"Your wife, sir. I told her you weren't taking any calls but—"

Vanning picked up the phone.

"Hello, Helen."

"I've been trying all afternoon to reach you."

He smiled wearily at the soothing sound of his wife's voice.

"It's about the party tomorrow night. There's a problem."

"I'm good with problems, dear."

"What's got into you?"

"Nothing . . . just a long day."

"Well, I do need your help on a few things . . ."

And Leonard Vanning luxuriously lost himself in the last-minute details of hosting a party for one hundred and twenty-five very important people.

For that was what this was all about, wasn't it?

Chapter Fourteen

"You know what I think?"

"I know what you think."

"I think it's a load of bullshit, that's what I think."

"So stop thinking and drink."

"I mean, who *is* this guy, really?"

Matt was carefully pulling away the wet napkin from around his glass. He thought briefly about Dave's question.

"Who is he? I dunno. He's the director of Security."

"So why did *he* take charge? Why would—"

"Because Henry went to him."

Matt admired the small circle of wet paper that now perfectly fit the bottom of his mug.

Unexpectedly, they were on their sixth beer, sitting in one of the dark corner booths—the one near the jukebox, way in the back—at Duka's.

Matt looked up. The whole low-ceilinged place was cavelike dim and practically empty. The hunched outlines of several inanimate alcoholics were lined at the bar, staring sullenly into their amber shots and flat chasers. One guy, the thin one down by the door, wearing a frayed plaid jacket and blaze-orange hunting cap, was painstakingly counting out change to Duka who watched unimpressed from behind the taps.

Diffuse sunlight slanted through the diamond-shaped Plexi-glas windows set in the front doors and fell, spent, in long faint rectangles across the yellowed linoleum floor. An inglorious end, thought Matt, to a ninety-three-million-mile sprint through deep space.

It was still afternoon, though not far from being evening, and Duka's had that unworldly, degenerate feel that comes with cheap drinking during the day.

And for some reason that Matt didn't fully understand, he *was* drinking, getting drunk, was drunk, with Dave.

"Well, I don't trust him," Dave said.

"Neither do I."

"Whoever he is."

"Nothing we can do," said Matt.

"And I think his story is a load of bull."

"Probably."

"If all this really did happen, why would he tell us? Why didn't he just say it's a matter of national security and there's no need for you to know? That would have been standard operating procedure. Instead he gives us this story about sea trials—"

"I thought it sounded kind of plausible," Matt cut in.

"Why would you put Russian markings on the controls?" Dave asked.

"I wouldn't," said Matt.

"Even if they were trying to be realistic about it all, you ain't gonna put a bunch of American sailors in a submarine and tell 'em they got to run the damn thing in Russian."

No. Another swallow of beer.

"And how come we only found eight crewmen?"

"Huh?"

"How come we only found eight? If they were going through these exercises like this Vanning claimed, they would've needed a full crew—probably something more like fifty, or sixty, or seventy guys—in which case we should have seen more!"

Dave was being loud.

"Not so loud, Dave—"

"I'll speak as loud as I want!"

Matt's eyes swung around the near empty bar, not sure who he was afraid would overhear, but positive it couldn't be a safe thing to do after what Vanning had said about keeping this quiet.

"Besides . . . I'm not talking that loud," Dave told him.

Matt was trying to think why they were even there, was about to ask, when he remembered. "Well, then talk more softly."

It had been Dave's idea to come to Duka's after the meeting with Vanning. He was hell-bent on getting off Fort Meade property and coming straight to Duka's to "thrash the whole thing out."

In Matt's case, leaving work early didn't really make any difference one way or another. He was between jobs, according to Vanning, and he'd just be wandering the halls. But Dave, Dave had to call his supervisor and, feigning illness, weakly report that he'd be out the rest of the day.

"Why? Why should I be quiet about this?"

Why? Matt was slouched in the darkness, staring at Dave. He heard the question—one word, the word *why*—but was too beaten down by beer and fatigue and a numbing sense of dread to give it more than a few futile seconds of thought. Reality seemed to be crumbling apart around him, exposing something frightening and unfamiliar.

"Just keep it down," Matt said.

"What's wrong with you?"

"What's wrong with *you*?"

"So, who's gonna hear us?"

"You never know."

"Bullshit," said Dave.

"Why?"

"You gonna have another beer?"

"I . . . I don't want another one." Matt took a swallow from his still heavy glass. For a moment, things seemed to come into focus.

"I *agree* with you, Dave—you keep thinking I don't but I do.

Vanning's not telling the truth. There's too many holes in the story. Not that I have any idea what the truth is. Not that I even want to know what th—''

"Well, I do," Dave cut in impatiently. "I do want to know. And I *plan* to know."

"But Dave, that's not wh—"

"You in or not?"

"In?"

"Or not?"

"In on what?"

Dave said: "You gonna help me or not? Because I'm gonna look around a little. You in?"

"Shit—"

Here's a Dave we haven't seen in awhile, thought Matt, not since last year, sparked by the deferral of an expected raise at work: here was righteous Dave, militant Dave, reckless Dave— the Dave that would hurl an ill-considered fist if called a liar, or slam his Caddy up to 120 on the Baltimore-Washington Parkway, or, well—here now, in what looked to be an extended appearance, was unpredictable Dave.

"In? What *'in'*? I'm involved in this, too, Dave. You go off and start making trou—"

"What trouble?" Dave said.

"Well, just don't do anything stupid."

"Don't tell me what to do," Dave shot back. "You, my friend, are the one who got me involved in this nightmare in the first place."

"Yeah, so, I'm also on conditional probation," Matt's voice rose uncontrollably in quick, drunken anger. "Any kind of problem and I'm out on my ass. The last thing I need is you going around shooting your mouth off about—"

"I'll do what I want—whatever I feel I have to do."

"You don't *have* to do anything. Christ, it was you who said we shouldn't even report it—on the plane, when we were talking."

Dave said: "Well, I'm not that kind of person."

"What kind?"

"I'm not going to blindly accept everything I'm told. That ain't me."

"But he said it was classified."

"Who's he?"

"Don't do th—"

"I'm gonna do a little checking around, with or without you."

Dave just finished his sixth beer.

"Dave, can't you get it through your thick skull—"

"Who the hell do you think you're talking to? Who in the *hell* do you think you're talking to?"

Dave's stare was frighteningly hard and cold. Matt suddenly felt trapped and anxious—but not anxious enough, or sober enough, to back down.

"We both swore to Vanning we wouldn't say a word about this."

"I'm not going to say a word! Not now anyway. That doesn't stop me from looking into it if I want to—if I think something weird's going on—and I do!"

"Shut up down there!"

Duka had stopped in midmotion wiping down the bar, and, with a mixed expression of mock anger and genuine concern, was looking back into the gloomy haze that enveloped Matt and Dave. "Quit arguing! If you're gonna fight do it someplace I can't hear you!" His gaze lingered on the pair, and then Duka went back to wiping down the bar.

"Dave—"

"I don't trust this guy Vanning. I don't trust *anybody* involved in this," Dave said bitterly, and then he turned his glass upside down.

"What about me?"

"It ain't so much I don't trust you . . . more like you've lost my respect. 'All I want is my job back.' " Dave whined in an unflattering, exaggerated imitation of Matt. "Fuck that."

"Fuck you."

"I don't need this."

Matt said: "Neither do I."

"I'm getting out of here."

Matt grabbed Dave's arm before he could slide out of the booth.

"I want some of that insurance."

"Oh, really?"

"Why should you get to keep it all?"

". . . I shouldn't, Matt. Like you said, we're both involved. Here—"

Dave pulled the single dog tag from his pocket and slapped it on the table. Matt didn't move to take it, realizing he'd only brought it up to try to keep Dave from leaving the bar.

"Listen, Dave—"

"No, no—you can have the duplicate negatives and pictures, too."

Dave dug a sealed red envelope out of his jacket and tossed that on the table as well: "Go on—check them—make sure the right pictures are in there! *Go on*."

"I trust you."

"*I'm* keeping the watch," Dave insisted.

"You can keep all of it. Here, I was just—"

Dave slipped from the booth.

"I was just—"

"You're pathetic," Dave said.

Dave just walked out of the bar.

Sometimes Matt imagined that everything in the world was black—not gone, not invisible—but velvety black—everything— and the things in that world—the insides of buildings, bars for example, and the people that moved through them—their forms and features were represented only by closely spaced green contour lines—all coming together to form a sort of moving computer graphic. And this was, for some reason, a silent world. It was a smooth, fluid, mechanical world. Here was a world reduced purely to its movements. It didn't allow anything more.

"Shit."

Matt was looking down at the dog tag and the red envelope on the table.

It sure as hell wasn't like this world.

For several blank moments Matt sat motionless in the booth. Then he got up and stood. His stance was unusually wide and he was staring down at the floor.

"Whew . . ."

This was interesting.

He started for the men's room, remembered the dog tag and envelope lying on the table, turned and got them, and then lurched down the dark hallway to the bathrooms in the back.

The men's room was cold and smelled of industrial cleaner. The sink tap was broken and an eternal trickle of water was coming down just hard enough to make the pipes hiss. A tangle of graffiti had been scratched into the blue-painted plaster walls over the urinals. The NSA has better bathrooms.

"Asshole."

Matt relieved himself for what seemed like a long time. He zipped his fly. He could feel the dog tag and envelope in his pocket.

Get rid of them.

Matt dropped them in the trashcan, buried them under a tossed section of a newspaper, decided to throw some paper towels on top of that, and then, after steadying himself, started out.

". . . Goddamn it."

Matt spun back. He reached down, dug through the trash, and pulled the dog tag and red envelope back out from under the garbage.

"What am I supposed to do with these?"

The tiles were ceiling . . . the ceiling was tiles. Flimsy tiles set in a metal frame.

Matt put one shoe-clad foot awkwardly on the slippery lip of the urinal and, gripping the handle for balance, pulled himself up near the ceiling.

Dirty acoustical tile. The bathroom looked like a cell from up here.

Matt pushed up a tile, peered into the still blackness, and placed the dog tag and red envelope carefully inside. He lowered the tile back into place.

He jumped to the floor, landing with his knees bent, and wiped his hands on his pants.

Matt made a significant effort to leave the bar looking as

sober as possible, cutting a fairly straight line for the door and offering a credibly casual nod to Duka on the way out.

It was kind of chilly outside. Matt felt his eyes watering. He saw his car in the small parking lot and walked rapidly to it. Got inside. Warmer here.

I can drive. Start the car. Turn on the radio—a little louder— put it in reverse—

Matt's head snapped back as his car rear-ended a light-pole stanchion. The crash seemed very loud from inside the car.

"Wha—"

Matt, stunned, turned slowly in the seat and saw a concrete pyramid standing surprisingly close to his trunk. A thick metal pole rose up from it, out of sight.

There must be a dent but he didn't get out to look. Matt put it in forward and drove off quickly.

A few seconds later, the engine of a nearby car came to life. The man in the car didn't hit anything backing up. He pulled out after Matt's car and began to follow, keeping a few vehicles between them as Matt weaved his way home.

Overhead, a solid, softly textured line of high cloud cover was steadily closing off the blue of the last few days. An unusually stubborn low-pressure system had stalled over the nation's capital, and the unbroken mass of clouds was being pulled across the sky like the closing of a window shade, as if some god somewhere high above did not care to witness the events that were about to unfold below.

II

Chilled, Leonard Vanning turned up the stiff collar of his shiny black overcoat and nervously, needlessly, smoothed down the perfectly obedient lapels.

A wounded day was rapidly sinking into the sea of night, and Vanning watched, exposed, sitting stoically like the captain of the ship from an old park bench around which grew a half-moon of tall, unruly bushes. It was a secluded place, picked for that reason, found at the bottom of a sharp drop in a little used path that snaked through Washington's National Arboretum.

The isolation of the pitlike, overgrown place created a double-edged element of danger and safety, the die cast depending on the purpose of your visit. Surely, at some time, some couple had used this arbored depression for an open-air bout of love-making. And just as surely, someone had paused at the bottom of the path, here, near the bench, for some reason darker, and less romantic in nature.

Vanning shivered in the unseasonable, winter-tinged cold that had spilled in with the coming storm. He tensed his left arm close to his body and felt the solid, reassuring bulge of the pistol he wore; a simple six-shot .38 that after thirty years of association had become like a wizened, silent friend.

All around him it was getting dark. The clouds had come in high and slow this afternoon, but they were dropping down now and moving fast; bringing on a hastened, gloomy dusk as they jockeyed across the sky.

An angry gust suddenly whipped overhead through the trees. Vanning looked up. The wildly swaying bare branches were like black, bony fingers scratching at the skin of an anthricite sky. The air was heavy with chilling moisture. It was going to rain soon, and probably hard.

Vanning had driven a long, circuitous route after leaving work, frequently checking the rearview mirror as he made sharp rights and lefts down Bladenburg Road and even a screeching U-turn on Mount Olivet for good measure. He could have been pulled over, but one look at his leather-bound, passport-size credentials—bearing a stern black-and-white photo of his un-smiling face, austere black lettering hinting at vast and ominous clandestine powers, and an impressive gold-embossed seal—was usually enough to get any policeman to put away his ticket book and walk away with a nervous—"Very good, sir, have a nice day."

Once positive he wasn't being followed, Vanning had driven to the dead end of T Street, where he'd left his car and sauntered gamely into the woods as if he were a birdwatcher and it was a beautifully sunny summer morning. A brisk half-mile walk over the rolling grounds, ducking through patchy stands of trees and scrub, had brought Vanning to the lonely bench where he was now.

At first Vanning had sat nervously erect, hands on his knees— the birdwatcher pausing to rest; but then he realized, almost regretfully, that there was no audience for the effort, probably no one at all in the whole park at this hour, and he settled heavily into the bench to wait.

Vanning checked his Rolex, forced to squint in the fast-fading dimness—six twenty-six—maybe twenty-seven.

Been waiting twenty-eight minutes.

He absently ran his index finger along the smooth, dark green slats of the bench, stopping at a faint X that, judging by the numerous coats of paint that considerably softened its definition, had been carved into the wood some time past.

I carved it, thought Vanning—eleven years ago, on a spring afternoon, while waiting just like this. I was waiting for the same man. He was late then too, remembered Vanning, and I took out my penknife and idly carved two crossed lines into the wood.

Vanning shivered again. The cold had seeped through his overcoat.

Where the hell is he? Just being late to show how important he is now. Assho—"Jack!"

A tall, dark figure had appeared like a specter from the deep shadows of the curving path and, seemingly pushed along by the blustery wind, came silently toward Vanning.

"Jack, my friend—" Vanning stood and instinctively opened his arms to embrace the figure, but a wooden Jacques Seydoux kept his distance and merely extended a limp, leather-gloved hand.

"Sorry to have to bring you out here in this—" Vanning glanced up at the bleak, threatening sky.

"Yes. I don't have much time," Seydoux responded flatly.

Night was crashing down around them. It was becoming so dark that neither man could clearly see the other's features—just black and gray, death-mask-like resemblances.

"It's been a long time—a lot of years," Vanning said.

"Yes, very."

"Eleven?"

"I haven't kept count."

"Michele?"

"Very good, thank you."

"I understand your youngest daughter—"

"Just got married, yes," said Seydoux.

"To a Navy man."

"Your sources are impeccable."

"We try."

The wind swept an eddy of pale fallen leaves around their feet. A few widely spaced drops of rain began to fall—the initial, random volleys of an advancing downpour.

Seydoux said: "You called—"

"I called you, Jack—"

"Yes?"

"I called you, see, because it's, ah, been found."

"Oh . . ."

"Yeah, found off a Cape in northern California, by two NSA employees."

". . . And I'll be reading about it in tomorrow's papers?"

"Ha!"

"No?"

"No, not at all, Jack," Vanning dismissed the suggestion with an awkward laugh. Then seriously: "No, of course not."

The rain was coming down harder and harder, a cold night rain. The falling drops seemed to be leaching the last vestiges of light from the sky. It was almost pitch black. Vanning and Seydoux were becoming just two voices in the dark.

Vanning said: "I called to tell you, Jack, because I thought it would be a weight off your shoulders."

"Well—"

"We're friends," Vanning said hopefully, "and you have the right to know, to not have to worry about this the rest of your life. It was my decision to call you, no one else's."

Seydoux let out a noncommittal "Ah."

"I've got almost everything under control . . ."

"You do," said Seydoux, his tone echoing from the uninspired hollow that lies between a statement and a question.

"Pretty much. For the most part, yes."

"I don't want to know any of this, Leonard."

"I think you should. The two who found it—a Matthew Clarke and one David Lakeman, they know, of course. They found it. They went scuba diving. One of them saw a shadow on a satellite photograph. Couldn't've seen it any other way. Now I've got those two covered. But there's another—"

"*No more*," Seydoux insisted from the dark.

"—Another guy," Vanning continued. "A guy named Orin Marsh. Once he's sorted out, you can just forget it ever happened."

"That's what you told me the first time," Seydoux said with a sudden, plaintive tone—sounding like a cheated lover.

The rain was stinging, angling in on the shoulders of the wind. Both men felt the cold rolling down their faces, but neither tried to brush it away.

"Yeah, well, we were all left holding the bag there, right?" Vanning said regretfully.

"I was told then to forget about it. And then, when it disappeared, I was called to be told it must have gone down in deep water—a fact I had no desire to know—and again I was told to forget about it. And now, yet again, I'm summoned—"

"Now, Jack—"

"And involved in this morass! *I ask you, Leonard—how can I forget when you keep reminding me?*"

Seydoux seemed to draw strength from the fury of the torrential downpour that had opened up on top of them.

Vanning forged on: "My point is we can get this—"

"*We?*" Seydoux shouted.

". . . We can get this under control once and for all, Jack. I say 'we' because you're involved in this. You are intimately involved."

"I never wanted to know what your plans for it were!" Seydoux said. "On that point you promised—"

"I think we've compensated you for it," said Vanning, peering into the dark where he thought Seydoux was standing.

"What you did you did on your own! I asked for nothing. I did it as a favor. If I had known then, that thirty-five years later I would be standing here now, still consumed by this god awful busin—"

"Now, you listen to me," Vanning said threateningly. "I don't have the manpower to take care of all this. The two NSA employees I can handle. But this other one—I can't."

"Neither can I!"

"Not directly you can't, I know. Over the years, I've kept track of the people who were involved in this. There's not many left. Very few. Who is still around, however, is LeClerc—Remy LeCler—"

"No!"

"What, no?"

"Impossible! I refuse to contact him!"

". . . Jack, there's no other way. This has to be done. LeClerc is perfectly suited for the—"

From the darkness, an hysterical: "I despise the man! Don't you understand that? You don't know what you're asking."

"LeClerc will listen to you. You've got to contact him."

"Absolutely not!"

Vanning ignored the refusal. "The man's name is Orin Marsh and he lives on Point Arena, that's in northern California. I've got the address right here with me—" Vanning held out a piece of paper, felt for Seydoux's hands.

"I'll not accept it!" Seydoux blustered. "I refuse!"

"This whole thing could unravel if he isn't taken care of. Unravel right back to the beginning. I wouldn't want that to happen, Jack. *You* wouldn't want that to happen either."

"I must—"

"It's the only way," Vanning interrupted.

"Must be going now . . ." Seydoux's voice trailed off, briefly, and then came back a brittle whisper. "There's someone there."

"We're alone—"

"Who's—"

Something *was* near, you could sense its pull. And then, frighteningly close, came a light, unmistakable footstep.

Vanning and Seydoux stood motionless, their hearts pounding, their ears cocked, trapped in that horrible, hushed, pregnant moment that separates the screech of brakes and a crash.

"This is a stickup! I'm not fooling around!"

The voice leaped from the darkness, a voice young and raw and dripping with fear. The voice had come very near, so near you could hear the rain striking its coat.

"I got a gun—gimme your wallets—now—I mean it!"

A murky object the size of a man was emerging from the rainy black.

"Hand it ov—"

A gun exploded with a sharp crack, spitting a dull orange spike of flame that for one nightmarish instant illuminated a closed, stark scene: a victim standing, then sharply doubling over like he'd been pulled by the waist from behind, then falling backward, swallowed by the night.

"*Leonard*—"

A shriek of agony. It was caught on the wind and spun crazily through the air around them.

"A mugger!"

Something was flopping on the ground. Another crack of the gun, this time pointed down, the muzzle flash disappearing in the victim's soggy dark clothes.

The shriek fell to a gurgling wail. The gun spat again, this time very low to the ground, and a hollow thump died in the rain—*similiar to the splat of a watermelon hitting the ground*, thought Seydoux—and the pathetic sound was silenced.

"Jesus!"

"A mugger—I got him, Jack! I had to—"

There was nothing but the sound of the falling rain and the wind clacking the branches of the trees. Then, intermittently, through the gusts, came the receding patter of shoes running on pavement.

"*Jack*—"

Seydoux had run off.

Vanning stood motionless in the rain, looking down at the ground but unable to see the bloody figure that must surely be sprawled there.

Shoot again? Call out? NO!

Vanning began to run, blindly, up the path. He took what he thought was the direction opposite to the one Seydoux had so quickly sprinted off in. It was impossible to see. The path went up steeply. Vanning was charging through the night, arms flailing crazily in front of him to brush away imaginary trees and branches. It felt like the path was leveling. He tripped, was going down, and then fell heavily to the wet pavement. It hurt. His gun was knocked hard from his hand and skidded some distance away. With a whimper, Vanning rolled onto his knees and began sweeping his hands in frantic circles along the rough, cold pavement immediately around him. *Have to find the gun! Have to get away! Have to*—his hand, his right hand, brushed against something warm—he lunged, grabbed, leaped up, and was again running blind, clutching the hot barrel of the gun.

Leonard Vanning careened through the blackness, away from the body he'd shot down and then shot twice again. He clumsily holstered his gun as he ran. After several moments, his adrenaline-charged sprint degraded into a huffing stagger as he lurched up what felt like a slippery, grassy hill.

Up—keep going—can't stop—can't get caught here—dear God—but the hill was steep and Vanning's smooth-soled shoes kept sliding back. Over and over. His legs were moving but he didn't move, like in a nightmare, only everything was real. He put out a hand and, crying for breath, dropped to the muddy hillside.

His sense of self slowly returned with his breathing. He struggled to his feet and started running again. In a few moments he scrambled over the top, all muddy and wet and terrified, and just kept on running through the night, as men have been doing since the race began.

Chapter Fifteen

They were good field glasses, with German lenses, and in steady hands you could see things pretty far away in okay detail. Orin had steady hands, and he stood as still as a sculpture at the end of his dock, peering out at the ocean.

It was night and there was no moon, which wasn't helping things, but Orin had the binoculars trained on a specific point of light, actually two lights that seemed close together because they were mounted on the bow and stern of a ship that was floating about a half mile offshore. Orin had been watching the ship continuously since the sun went down, probably going on four hours now, and it hadn't moved in all that time.

It had appeared in the afternoon—around three, according to Mark—while Orin was over in Willits getting a new prop for the Whaler. Mark said one diver went down for about a half hour and then came back out a little while before Orin returned. From then on, Orin kept Mark out back of the house with a variety of chores and he took up the watch himself. The diver went back over the side at about five, and a little while later, say about fifteen minutes, the ship started unspooling two heavy metal cables into the water. The one diver stayed down. Every hour or so they lowered him a few spare tanks of air, and once they sent down what looked to be an underwater welding rig. The guy was down there for five hours, alone, and there had to be an important reason for that because diving alone is nobody's idea of smart.

Orin tried but couldn't clearly make out the ship's name or her registry, there was too much rust and grease and grime covering the hull. It looked like some private outfit from God knows where. It was an unfriendly looking piece of scrap, and would be equally at home docked in some rough, small-town port, or pulling a shady salvage deal in open seas.

The diver was back up. That was him, barely visible, a little black figure climbing slowly up the stern ladder. There, he was back aboard, probably pretty damn cold, too, after being down that long.

I was, and I was only down there for twenty minutes.

Must have a good suit, Orin decided.

The two metal cables still ran into the water. Judging by the way they'd done things so far, chances were that something was going to happen soon. These boys looked to be in some kind of hurry to get this job over and done with. And when it was done, only one person on that ship would have actually seen what was down there. There was a highly professional air to the way things were being carried out—

"Orin!"

Orin pulled away the binoculars and turned sharply toward the house.

"I thought I told you to stay inside!"

Mark was barefoot, wearing just shorts, and he'd come pretty quiet down the dock because Orin hadn't heard him coming.

"They're getting set to move—I can see the winches tightening up through my telescope."

"*Get back up the house,*" Orin said harshly, more harshly than he intended.

Mark came no closer. Orin's voice was deadly serious and Mark almost lost his balance taking a step back.

". . . You scared me," Orin said gently.

"It's okay."

Orin grunted an apology and Mark nodded.

"Uncle Orin, they're moving."

On that, Orin quickly turned, fine-tuned the focus on the binoculars, and stared out over the black water. He watched for several moments, saw that it was so, and then slowly turned back to Mark.

"Get going," Orin said, nodding toward the house. "I'll be up there soon."

". . . You still gonna call the Coast Guard?"

Orin frowned. He looked down at the dock and ran a hand through his beard. "I don't think so."

"What're they doing out there, Orin?"

Orin's head came up fast. *"I thought I told you to go back inside—move it."*

Mark went. Orin watched to make sure he did as he was told, and then turned the binoculars back on the little points of light.

She was moving all right, moving slow, the cables taut behind her. She was churning up the water pretty nicely, too, using what must have been some mighty powerful engines. It may have been made to look like scrap, but that ship wasn't about to fall apart anytime soon.

Orin watched the ship crawl out to sea until he couldn't see the lights anymore and even then he stayed on the dock, peering through the binoculars, staring out into the darkness as if he might glimpse an answer to what was going on.

There was a drop-off out there, Orin knew, a sudden, sharp drop-off down to the real deep of the Pacific. The water changed color at that point—that deep, sunless blue that appealed to the soul. Orin couldn't see it, but the ship would have been out there by now. She'd be crawling along, diesels growling, those cables straining tight behind her, passing over that deep water that was the same color at night as it was at day.

Orin stopped watching at one in the morning, He wound the leather strap around the middle of the binoculars and walked down the dock toward the house. The lights were off and there was a blizzard of twinkling stars overhead. But Orin's thoughts were at the bottom of the sea. He walked up the path, climbed the porch stairs, went inside, and for the first time in fifteen years of living in the isolated house, Orin threw the lock on the door.

II

Within a tight circle approximately two miles in diameter, the Kingman Arms apartment building standing direct center, a light drumming sound was being broadcast through the air at 173 megaHertz, slightly above the business and police radio bands and slightly below those frequencies used for commercial television.

Tuned to 173 mHz and listening to the repetitive thumping beat was an audience of one: a man of about sixty (maybe older), not particularly strong (nor large), with the patience of a saint (an unlawful one), wearing an overcoat (tan), carrying false identification (name taken from the Arlington Cemetery), seated in a car (new, American, four-door) parked along the slope of Thomas Jefferson Street about a mile away from the Kingman Arms, calmly sipping a cup of black coffee (with sugar), a small earphone fitted into his ear (left).

The impatient drumming sound riding the signal was coming in loud and clear, despite the morning's heavy weather, from a four-watt, crystal-controlled radio-frequency repeater that was securely taped beneath a piece of decorative masonry an arm's length outside the Kingman Arms' tenth-floor closed hallway window.

The cigarette-pack-size repeater was boosting a much weaker signal that was being sent from a twelve-milliwatt, similarly crystal-tuned miniature radio-transmitting bug that had been placed inches from the source of the restless thump-thump-thump-thump—inside Matthew Clarke's apartment, carefully taped under an endtable on which sat the phone that Matt was drumming his fingers on.

There was a dull, tired ache in the back of Matt's head. This hangover looked like it wanted to stay.

After passing out for ten hours last night, Matt had bolted awake at seven this morning with a vise-press of a headache. He'd taken a fast shower, cut himself shaving, gulped two aspirin with a glass of orange juice, shoveled a bowl of cereal into his mouth, and raced through two cups of coffee—all so he could sit in the living room of his apartment and wait for the phone to ring.

He yawned long and deeply.

Rain was beating against the glass doors that led to the tiny balcony. It had been raining when he went to sleep after coming home from the Cloverleaf, and it was raining now, if anything harder. The clouds were thick and pressing right up against Matt's high apartment windows. The clouds looked like they were trying to squeeze inside.

Matt stared dully at the television, his fingers drumming away on the phone, as two rather dim hosts of a local morning show bantered on the screen.

Why the hell hadn't Vanning called? I clearly remember him saying he was going to call me this morning to tell me where I was working, if I even was working, and here it is approaching the time to go to work and I'm watching the goddamn TV.

". . . Maybe I should call him," Matt said out loud, as much to hear a voice in the quiet room as to express the thought. "He might be busy . . . maybe he forgot . . . I can't just sit here all day waiting for him to call . . . I'll call him . . . so call him . . . I will."

Matt stopped thumping his fingertips on the receiver and stared at the phone. He tried willing it to ring. He tried counting to ten, then twenty, then sixty, and it still didn't ring. Matt picked up the receiver and listened for a dial tone. It was working. He hung up the phone and waited some more, and then waited some more after that.

It didn't ring.

"I can't call him . . ."

Matt dejectedly turned his attention back to the television, where some clown, literally, had just manufactured a suggestive balloon animal to the clapping glee of those in the studio.

Matt got up and went to the bathroom. He rushed back out when he thought he heard the phone ring, but it must have come from the TV. Matt picked up the receiver and boldly dialed the main switchboard number of the NSA. He quickly hung up at the sound of the operator's voice. He got up and paced the apartment. After several minutes of leaning against a wall and staring out the rain-streaked windows, Matt slumped down into the sofa and stared at the phone.

He again grabbed the receiver and redialed the NSA switchboard, willing himself to stay on the line.

"Leonard Vanning, please . . . Vanning—V . . . thank
you . . ."

Matt cleared his throat several times while he was being
connected. He straightened up and took a deep breath. His head
hurt.

"Yes, good morning, Leonard Vanning please."

Pause.

"I see . . . Yes, Mr. Grieve? Yes, this is Matthew Clarke—we
met yesterday . . . right . . ."

Pause.

"Around ten . . . I see . . ."

Pause.

"No, he knows what this is about, I believe . . . Yes, if he
could call me at home when he gets in—that's 347-6982—right
. . . thank you very much . . . good-bye . . ."

Matt hung up. His heart was pounding. He began pacing the
apartment again, muttering to himself.

". . . Good . . . right. . . he can call me back . . . now he
knows I'm waiting . . ."

Much relieved, Matt sat back on the sofa. The local news was
being read. They were in the middle of a story about some man
who'd been found shot to death last night in the National
Arboretum—three times—unemployed construction worker—
criminal record—believe a robbery in progress—perhaps self-
defense—no witnesses—any information please call—

Matt grabbed the remote and changed the channel.

"I got my own problems."

Matt's words drew a thin smile from the man sitting patiently
in the parked car a mile away. "That you do," the man said
unemotionally to himself. He sipped the last of his coffee,
crushed the paper cup, and then began reading the paper he'd
bought early this morning, killing time until Matt left the safety
of his apartment.

Chapter Sixteen

Pain loves to travel, decided Remy LeClerc, stepping from the plane. Yes, he thought, pain's having a field day with this excursion.

Just the slightest bending motion made the pain in LeClerc's back explode into a kaleidoscope of excruciating patterns. He couldn't make it go away; locked, as he was, in a lopsided war. His chief weapons—Percodan, codeine, heroin, alcohol—bounced off pain's thick armor like rocks against a tank. He pictured pain laughing at him through the safety of the hatches. He could feel it rumbling through his body, leaving a ravaged nerve or muscle blazing in the background.

Pain was slowly expanding its perimeter, as LeClerc became more twisted and crazed.

LeClerc's only satisfaction was that he killed the fucking doctor who performed the first operation—a double fusion on his lower back that soon disintegrated into scores of tiny, sharp bone fragments—little knives, really, that quickly lacerated the surrounding nerves into a mangled mass of never-ending agony.

The doctor was drunk, LeClerc subsequently found out, when he'd worked on him. Retribution was called for.

The problem had begun when LeClerc herniated two disks

during a low-altitude parachute jump in the service of his country—a minor affair in Algeria. He was flown to a military hospital back in France, where the first operation was criminally performed.

Two years later, after three more painful operations failed to correct the original handiwork, LeClerc tracked the first doctor to a Navy hospital in Marseilles.

It was at night, and the man was going home by way of every bar that lay between the hospital and his apartment. LeClerc knew the man's routine. He had it all planned and was waiting in the shadows of a deserted street when the drunken doctor weaved out of an awninged bistro in search of a taxi. LeClerc walked right up to him, limped would be a more accurate description, and said, "Do you remember me, doctor?" The doctor's blank look slowly darkened into one of terror, for LeClerc felt he knew the purpose of the meeting, and in a frightened whisper he mumbled, "LeClerc . . . Remy LeClerc!"

The doctor trembled and pleaded as LeClerc pulled him, and then dragged him, into a foul-smelling alleyway. LeClerc quickly shut him up with a heavy blow to the throat—not that that was the extent of the punishment he had come to mete out—far from it. No, that was just LeClerc's own brand of anesthetic, for he had come to perform surgery, and felt it would have been inhuman not to somewhat stun the creature's senses before proceeding.

Proceed he did, and swiftly.

LeClerc severed the man's hamstrings with deep cuts to the back of his legs, this so he couldn't stand—and then poked around his back with a rusty old fishing knife, because this *was* emergency surgery—and dug down deep in the back of his upper right thigh to try to find the sciatic nerve. The operation looked like it might be a success, because he found the large nerve, he could tell from his patient's reaction. But LeClerc had no nurse, and it was getting hard to see the operating area because of all the blood and his hand must have slipped somehow—because the doctor died, there in the alleyway.

And a day didn't go by, usually at those times that LeClerc's back felt like someone was digging around with a pair of pliers, like now, that he didn't think about the doctor's demise and smile.

LeClerc was thinking about him in particular detail because he'd just gotten off a six-hour flight from Rabat, Morocco, to Washington, D.C, and poorly designed airline seats could be torture. Thanks to the prodigious quantity of heroin he'd snorted before take-off, the pain in his lower back was still like the low rumble of a distant storm. But it was wearing off.

LeClerc walked slowly through the busy terminal. He only had fifty minutes on the ground before he had to board another flight, still heading west—Sacramento to be exact, and he had to receive a call.

As he walked, the pain gradually began to awaken and return. The heroin had definitely run its course, and LeClerc paused at a water fountain to swallow several Percodans. Luckily he'd been trained to survive all manner of physical calamities, from bullet wounds to torture. His country had prepared him well, particularly the SDECE, though he'd left that institution some time ago.

LeClerc had since become a wealthy man. The mark-up in arms dealing was astounding. Aside from the money, and there was almost too much of that to ignore, he liked the work. His clientele was well educated and really quite interesting to socialize with.

LeClerc left the terminal and proceeded to a bank of pay phones on the lower level. He headed for the third phone from the left.

LeClerc stood there, waiting for the call.

"Are you using that pho—"

"Fuck off."

LeClerc normally didn't handle work like this himself anymore. As the head of a rather large and successful enterprise, there was no sense in the boss risking getting injured while taking out the garbage. But there was no way he could pass this up, both for personal and business reasons. That Seydoux would contact him after all these years, practically pleading in tone to come and save his exalted ass—moments like these are to be savored. And afterward, when LeClerc was through doing his dirty work, Seydoux would owe him huge, and LeClerc had several deals on which his influence would be invaluable.

The phone rang. LeClerc checked his watch—right on the minute, he noted. Seydoux always was anally punctual.

LeClerc let it ring for awhile, making the caller sweat. He took a healthy drink of brandy from his flask. It was running low, and LeClerc made a mental note to refill at the duty-free shop across the way.

He supposed he'd let the phone ring long enough. He picked up the receiver.

"Bonjour."

". . . Yes?"

"Shall it be English?" LeClerc asked.

"I've had to sneak away to make this call," said Seydoux anxiously. "I'm at a pay phone."

English it is.

"How exciting. No salutations after all these years?"

"I must be brief. You received my message?"

"Would I be here otherwise?" Sometimes LeClerc wondered how Seydoux had ever become an ambassador.

"Any questions," Seydoux asked quickly, "on the details? You know—"

"Name, that sort of thing? No, sir! I committed the details to memory and ate the cable. His name's Orin—"

LeClerc knew this last would provoke an intense response.

"Not over the phone."

"Oh, I apologize! Of course, sir!"

"What are you going to do?" Seydoux nervously queried.

"Me? Me, I'm going to go as ordered, *sir.*"

"It's not an order. Why do you keep calling me sir? I have no control over what you do. I merely asked if you could just look into it, that's all I—"

"Don't tell me how to do my job!" LeClerc shouted over the line.

A confused silence

". . . They asked me to contact you for this," Seydoux confided. "I'm being forced to do this. I have too much at stake not to comply. Any evidence could be severely—"

"Yes?"

"There's no one else to turn to. You were there—you found it."

"I found it, sir," LeClerc said, and as he said it, the sight came back to him—or more precisely—he went back to it.

LeClerc went back over thirty years, to a time before pain, a time when he was a young, fully functional specimen of man. A strange sight it was, too. Like a sleeping whale resting on the sandy ocean floor. LeClerc drifted down to it and tapped lightly on its side with his diving knife, but it didn't wake. Emboldened, he tapped harder and harder and then, excited by the strangeness of the scene, he pounded on its black steel hull until his arm grew weary of the effect. But still no return tapping from inside. LeClerc swam over the silent, unmoving submarine—the visibility very good—and felt like a Lilliputian floating over a sleeping Gulliver. They must all be dead inside, he decided—and at that point he realized what had happened. After seeing that giant fireball four days earlier—the light so bright it eclipsed the noonday sun—it was plain. LeClerc had kept quiet about it. Seydoux was just helpful enough the first few years to make it worth his while. And Seydoux, LeClerc suspected—he got something out of the deal from the Americans—though it wouldn't surprise him if Seydoux hadn't, because he would have done it for free. Seydoux always thought America was the greatest place since Eden.

"Now, you can contact me using the methods specified in my message—"

"Yes, sir!"

"Don't do anything drastic without first consulting—"

LeClerc hung up. He didn't need Seydoux telling him how to handle such things. LeClerc knew what the criteria were for executing each option to this problem.

His connecting flight would leave in thirty minutes. LeClerc went to buy some brandy across the way.

II

Dave was as excited as Matt had ever seen him, so excited that he didn't seem to remember their drunken, hostile parting last night—and Dave was the kind of guy who would remember an argument, usually for a long time. It was two in the afternoon and they were heading south toward Quantico. Dave was driving too fast down rain-slick U.S. 1, occasionally hydroplaning across small ponds that had formed over the leaf-clogged drains. He furiously worked a piece of gum as he drove.

Matt didn't know exactly where Dave was taking him. This was a secret, the nature of which Dave said would reveal itself very shortly. The windshield wipers were doing double time and Dave had the defrost on to keep the cold, wet-blanket humidity from fogging the windows.

"Did Vanning say when you'd be going back to work?" Dave asked, as if he already knew the answer.

"He thought next week," Matt said.

"Right," Dave said derisively.

"That's what he said."

"He's stalling, Matt."

"For what? He said I'd definitely be back at work next week. I—watch it—"

Matt instinctively pushed back in his seat as Dave cut back into the slow lane to pass a large truck on the inside. He barreled through the rooster tails of spray being kicked up by its dozen or so tires and swerved through a narrow gap, barely missing the back end of a car going the speed limit, to duck back into the fast lane. The semi blared its horn loud and long at the move.

"Why are you driving like this? Come on, slow down! I'm serious."

"I think I'm being followed."

Matt turned and looked out the back window, but all he could see was the receding truck through the spray and rain and gray.

"By who?"

"I dunno. I thought I was followed to work this morning, and then, when I left before, for lunch —to pick you up—I thought I spotted the same car tailing me over."

"You're being paranoid."

"I don't think so."

"Well, I don't see anything."

Dave had his eyes fixed on the rearview mirror. His gaze finally returned to the road. "I musta lost the son of a bitch."

He rapped his thumb against the steering wheel with nervous urgency as the car sped down the rain-clouded corridor of highway.

"Where are we going, Dave?"

"I spent all morning checking it out, Matt—I logged into the Pentagon system and spent all morning going on the computer—checking names, checking military records, checking dates, running cross-checks—" he cracked his gum, "—I should've been a detective or something, I'm great at this shit!"

Dave peered out the windshield to read an exit sign that flashed by. He let the car start drifting off to the right to catch the fast approaching ramp.

"What Vanning told us yesterday—total lie. I ran the names from those dog tags through the files—"

"Dave—"

"Let me finish! Just let me finish. Secret trials, my ass. First off I checked a reference book on submarines. That was a twin diesel, intelligence-gathering Soviet submarine circa 1950. It wasn't no simulated piece of American craftsmanship like Vanning said it was. Where we got it, I don't know."

Dave played the car around the long, curving exit ramp. The rain was coming down in sheets and the intersection seemed to appear from nowhere. Dave just managed to bring the car to a skidding halt in time. They waited at the light as the windshield wipers fought a losing battle against the deluge dropping from the dark sky above.

"So next I ran the names from those dog tags through the computer—remember how Vanning said these guys had been trained for this? Simulated sea trials and all that?"

Dave was looking at Matt for confirmation.

"I remem—"

"Lie! I know everything about these guys now—I read their files off the computer. Lamm, Furrows, Atkins, Sussman, and the others, each one of them was stationed on a different submarine—a couple in the Atlantic, a few in the Pacific, a few in drydock, a few on leave. These guys didn't know each other—they never served with each other before."

Dave swung a sharp left on green and sped up down a two-lane that headed into the heart of a residential suburb of Quantico.

"The one thing they had in common," Dave continued, "is that they all received immediate transfer notices on May 11, 1954. It's on record—one guy here, one guy there—but unless you had all their names like I had, unless you looked up each one individually—you'd never have seen it. It didn't arouse any suspicion. Just one man from eight different subs. See ya later, Sussman; bye bye, Dilling; nice crewing for you, Avery—and they're gone, transferred, and if you served with them you wouldn't think twice about it. But when you look at their files you can see what was really going on. One of them was an engineer, one of them was a first mate, one of them was a navigator, one of them was a captain—right down the line. Somebody pulled a crew together and they did it in a hurry. Total number is anybody's guess. For all I know it could have been just eight."

"Why?"

"I don't know why. The problem," Dave went on, "is that the transfer records don't have final destinations."

A pickup eased out of a Sunoco station and Dave went right up on his bumper.

"Asshole!"

"Dave—"

"I'm looking for a street, should be on the right—you see anything called Colonial Terrace Road? I can't see through this rain."

Matt watched the quiet residential streets roll by.

"Anything? Colonial Terrace—"

"I see it," Matt said. "Coming up on the right. Where the hell are we going?" he moaned.

"You'll see, you'll see." Dave turned onto Colonial Terrace and very slowly started up the steeply inclined street. "But, Matt, the thing I was leading up to is that not only didn't any of these guys know each other, not only didn't they have any special training like Vanning said they did, not only didn't their transfers have final destinations on them—but they were all reported as having died like three weeks later in totally separate ways—thousands of miles apart."

III

Colonial Terrace Road was like the trunk of a Christmas tree from which sprang small branches of pavement decorated with closely spaced, weekly mowed, middle-class, monotonously uniform tract homes. Though it was the middle of the day, there was nobody out in this storm. Matt looked hard for signs of life, but he could see no glowing lights in the passing windows, no cars backing out of driveways, no mailman making his rounds, no dogs, no repairmen, nothing. The place seemed ominously deserted and Matt was growing increasingly anxious about where he was being taken.

Dave's voice pulled his attention back into the car. "—One guy's listed as drowning on leave in Santa Cruz; another guy's supposedly caught in a storeroom paint fire at a base in Texas; this guy Durso's listed as AWOL later changed to missing person; Avery, the captain?—he's supposed to have died in a boating accident in Florida while being ferried to a new command! No bodies, and none of their families were told anything about them being killed in that sub . . ."

"If you don't tell me right now where we're go—"

"This guy Durso—his family probably still thinks the poor bastard's gonna walk through the door someday!"

"Right now, Dave—*where?*"

Dave seemed to spy something up ahead and accelerated toward it. "We're here, Matt. There it is—number 111, Colonial Terrace Road."

Dave eased the car up to the curb that separated the home's small yard from the street. It was a silent house, painted a depressing brown, with the obligatory picture window sitting over the standard scraggly row of twisted shrubs. The few spindly elms on the irregular half-acre lot had shed their muted foliage across the heavily overgrown lawn and no apparent effort had been made to rake them up—this in sharp contrast to the neighboring homesteads, where it appeared a bounty had been placed on stray leaves. The short blacktop driveway was badly cracked and led to a broad, rolling garage door that cried

for repainting. The mailbox was old and rusty and looked like it
fell down a lot. Matt barely managed to read the name off it
through the rain-streaked windshield . . . something that started
with an *A* . . . then a *v*—Avery—

"Oh shit, Dave!"

But Dave was already out of the car and slamming the door
closed on Matt's exclamation. Matt quickly got out on his side
and came around to Dave, who had started a brisk pace up the
rain-slick driveway.

"Dave—why? What's this gonna prove? Dave!"

"Let go of my arm, Matt . . . Thank you."

"You're scaring me, Dave—I don't, I have no idea what it is
you're doing—"

"I want to ask her a few questions and I want you to hear
what she has to say. She might know something. You'll be a
witness to this."

It was pouring and Matt was trying to walk in front of Dave,
trying to reason with him eye-to-eye. Dave left the driveway
and crossed the wet lawn for the front door. Matt kept looking
over his shoulder as he backed crablike toward the drab, gloomy
entrance to the house.

"Who, Dave? Who's *she?* Not Avery's wife, Dave—not
Avery's wife, Dave!"

"Of course it's Avery's wife—the one who gave him this."

He saw Dave lift the stainless-steel watch from his overcoat
pocket—the watch they'd found in the sub. Matt almost tripped
stepping backward onto the small, unadorned concrete slab that
served as a step to the door, and as he did so he remembered the
inscription on the watch—*To Carl, Love Julie.*

Dave stepped up from the lawn and stood next to Matt in
front of the door. He shook the water off his raincoat and
brushed his wet hair to one side with his hand.

"I took the home address listed in Avery's file, looked
through the phonebook, and found a J. Avery, must be his
widow, living in the same spot. This is where he lived, Matt—
right here."

For an instant, Matt saw how the place must have looked
thirty years ago—all new and raked and painted and paved and
sunny. And then the imagined scene was shattered when an

algae-coated skeleton appeared pushing a mower across the lawn.

"I'm going back to the car," Matt whispered harshly. "I have nothing to do with this."

At that, Dave grabbed Matt's windbreaker and simultaneously rang the doorbell. A mournful chime could be heard ringing deep within the house. Matt tried to pull away but Dave was strong and had a good grip on the thing and he rang the bell again.

"Let go!"

"Stop it! Someone's coming."

"Let go of me!"

Slow, faint footsteps could be heard from within the dark house. Matt froze. When he was young, there'd been one closet in his house that was always locked. It was the forbidden closet, a place where his parents stored things they deemed too dangerous to be left lying around out in the open. This lasted until Matt was fourteen, when one day, his parents out, Matt took a screwdriver and removed the hinges from the door. It turned out to be just a pile of junk inside—old books and uninteresting boxes, but Matt still remembered how the outside of that closet door looked—the molding on it—and it seemed to him, at this moment, that it had looked a lot like the door he was standing before now.

The footsteps were getting very near. And though he was scared, though everything seemed to be coming together like a bad dream careening to a climax, Matt realized that he *wanted* to see what was beyond the door—that there was no way he could pass up peeking inside this forbidden closet.

The door suddenly swung open and Matt felt Dave's hand let go of his windbreaker.

A wisp of woman was framed in the doorway; the black, murky interior serving as a dramatic backdrop. She was thin and small and had a round, heavily lined face. Her straight hair was short and disconcertingly two-toned—gray pushing out an unnatural orange-red that had been dyed in and forgotten about some time ago. She was probably over sixty, maybe over seventy, and her eyes were too far open—creating the distressing impression that she was blind or mad. She was wearing black pants and a red-and-white, vertically striped pullover, both of which hung very loosely from her matchstick body.

She stood there in the doorway and seemed to be looking right through Matt and Dave with those wide eyes, as she languidly brought the cigarette dangling at her side up to her mouth and inhaled deeply. *"What?"*

If the body was fragile, the voice was hard and raspy and came out on a steady stream of smoke.

"We're with the Navy," Dave said with deep, earnest officialness.

"Go fuck yourselves," was her immediate, hoarse response. Staring at them, she took a long, slow, quarter-inch inhale off the cigarette.

"Come on, Dave, let's go."

The woman's head barely turned and she looked at Matt with that wild, unblinking stare. He met her gaze for a moment and then had to look away.

Dave took the watch from his pocket and held it out to her. Her eyes shifted to it. She stared at it. She exhaled and smoke gradually enveloped it. And when the smoke finally cleared, Matt realized she was holding it, and she was crying—not sobbing or choking back gasps—just a fine solitary tear running down her left cheek. Her thin wrist turned and the back of the watch came into view. She blinked after reading the inscription and then she brought the watch up and pressed it to her chest.

". . . We found it," Matt said, because anything was better than this unnerving silence.

"You're not from the Navy." She held the watch close to her protectively, as if they might try to take it back.

"No."

". . . I gave Carl this watch right after we were married. Does it still work?" she asked with a soft laugh, as she pulled it away to look at the face. "No . . . no I guess not." She didn't seem to want to smoke in the presence of the watch, and dropped the half-smoked cigarette onto the wet lawn. Matt watched as the large raindrops beat it out.

"I know he didn't die in Florida," she suddenly offered. "I know that was a lie."

"How?" Dave asked.

". . . Because. Because he sent me a postcard from Hawaii."

"When?" Matt asked, before he realized he was getting involved.

"Between flights. He wasn't supposed to but he did. Just a line to say that he loved me. May 13, 1954—that's when it was dated. And they took the postcard, you know. After they told me Carl died in Florida while being ferried to his new command, I pulled out the postcard and told them it couldn't be Carl—because Carl had written me from Hawaii. And the man took the postcard and said he'd look into the matter. They never even had the decency to give it back—and I don't care if it was top-secret!" She looked out at the rain. "We'd only just been married."

"Did it say anything else?" Dave asked. "The postcard?"

"That he'd see me soon. But I knew where Carl was going. I knew because he'd told me before he left. He wasn't supposed to tell me but he did, as he was leaving. I didn't say it at the time, when the Navy was telling me he'd died in Florida. I didn't say it because I thought it might get Carl in trouble somehow. Because I really thought Carl was still alive. I convinced myself that this must be part of some secret exercise Carl was part of—this was at the height of the Cold War . . . a very bleak time. The Soviets had the bomb—Carl dug us a bomb shelter out back—still there . . . Carl truly believed we'd have to go to war with Russia—he was ready for it, told me to expect it. And I did. A lot of people did. So when they told me Carl was dead, I . . . I tried to deny it by coming up with this idea that Carl was involved in an operation so secret that wives had to be lied to and told their husbands had died. And I knew I was being lied to, because Carl wasn't anywhere near Florida. Carl told me where he was going. Carl was out at the atomic blasts."

She tilted her head and lightly touched her hair in back, and then her hand dropped to pull up the collar of her pullover as if she were suddenly cold. "You know—the Marshall Islands, Bikini and all those others. You might have been too young to remember—"

"I know what you're talking about," Dave told her.

"That's where they sent Carl. We were standing here, in the doorway right here, and we kissed good-bye. And then a car came up and took him away . . . like that car there—"

She said it in a dreamy way and Matt thought she was hallucinating, so Dave turned and saw it first. And there, through the rain, was the soft outline of a car. Matt almost jumped when he saw it—sitting across the street, its windows fogged, engine idling quietly. It was a new, four-door, American car. It was a car frightening for its standardness.

"Dave!"

Dave was off the concrete stoop and running across the lawn toward the car. The car started slowly forward as Dave ran headlong across the wet grass, changing his angle of attack to try to cut the moving vehicle off. But the car just slowly accelerated and casually headed farther up Colonial Terrace, Dave running for all he was worth behind it. He stopped after a good fifty-yard sprint and stood in the middle of the empty residential street, doubled over, hands on his knees, catching his breath as the rain beat down on his back.

Matt turned back to the woman but she was gone. He hadn't heard the door close. Matt thought about ringing the bell but didn't know what he would say to the woman when, and if, she answered. He thought she might have some questions about where they'd found the watch, but then realized it was probably unimportant now. At a certain point, Matt figured, after enough years have gone by, the loss created by a tragedy becomes so big that you probably just don't have room for the details.

Matt stepped off the stoop and walked across the lawn to the car. Dave was coming down the street, soaked. They got into the car and drove down the hill through the empty, silent neighborhood.

". . . The ball's in their court now," Dave said quietly, as he turned onto the highway and slowly headed back to Washington.

Chapter Seventeen

The momentous night of the Vannings's fastidiously planned, abundantly shopped, elegantly staged, and fashionably attended annual fall party was marked by near gale-force winds and torrential rain, the latter setting a record for this October day in the annals of Washington, D.C., weather history.

The raging elements became a lively topic of conversation within the crowded, brightly lit Georgetown mansion, surpassing less inclement subjects such as the trade deficit, the lack of parking on the Hill, and the prospects of this year's Washington Redskins. An expensive, suitably unobtrusive string quartet played from a distant corner of the high-ceilinged ballroom as tuxedos and evening gowns drifted through the perfectly appointed pink-and-gold décor, mingling with a variety of medal-bedecked military uniforms, vested waiters, and the occasional turban to create a rich scene of color and gaiety.

Leonard Vanning had married well. His wife, Helen, was out of one of the mainest of the Philadelphia Main Line oligarchies; their last name gracing a worthy chain of several thousand retail food stores. The family was loaded. To the gills. And to a young man from a poor Illinois town who'd clawed his way into the Naval Academy, wealth was a highly alluring quality in a woman. Vanning met her at a glitterball Annapolis dance only hours before he was to sail off into the heady final months of World War II. Romance and fate had little to do with their meeting, for Vanning had, weeks in advance, planned his assault in minute detail. Their first encounter, aided significantly by Vanning's dress uniform, the drama of his imminent departure, and the thorough intelligence he'd collected on his objective, went perfectly according to plan. Having gained a beachhead, Vanning left for the war. In fine martial tradition he softened the target, this with a fusillade of torrid correspondence from the steamy Pacific, and ultimately took the field by marrying his wealthy conquest shortly after the Japanese surrender. She was tall and tan and frosted and pearled and she was intelligent in matters that interested her, and though Leonard Vanning never loved her, his level of like had diminished little over their forty-two years. He was handsome, and conservative, and expertly clandestine in his extramarital activities, and she appreciated him for that.

Vanning edged toward the bar. The exhaustive effort Helen put into these affairs, specifically the conscription of a platoon of chefs, servants, valets, and bartenders, left him virtually unfettered from the harness of the host, and he moved supported by a cane through the cheerfully droning throng with the agreeable sensation of being a guest.

Yesterday evening's horrific episode had kept Vanning up for some time through the night in his study, a glass of scotch in his hand, anxiously meditating on the chances of his being identified as the man who shot the mugger. He quickly decided that though he'd acted hastily, his instinct to kill had been correct. The thief would have surely taken his wallet and credentials, as well as Seydoux's, leaving them both potentially open to explain the circumstances of their highly unusual appointment in the park. Vanning finally arrived at the conclusion that for lack of evidence, motive, and witnesses, he was in no danger of being connected to the body in the Arboretum. Since the purpose of their meeting had been executed, Vanning resolved not to contact Seydoux now or anytime in the foreseeable future.

The one truly regrettable result of the incident was that Vanning was forced with heavy heart to destroy his loyal, long-carried, .38, a ceremony performed in fine naval tradition with a heave into the Anacostia River.

Except for his knee, which had swelled magnificently from the pavement fall, tonight's Vanning was a healthy animal in a happy herd. He'd already drunk a significant quantity of expensive champagne to extinguish the brushfires of worry in the back of his mind, and with the support of an ornate but sturdy walking stick he moved through the crowd with a genuine smile on his face.

"Leonard—" a voice cried above the din of the party.

"Senator Rowe!" Vanning exclaimed grandly, and then he reached over someone's shoulder to grasp the heavy man's hand for a shake.

"Y'know my wife—" The man propelled a smiling, mature woman through the shifting assemblage.

"Raylene!" Vanning proclaimed. "You look wonderful." He leaned in rather unsteadily and kissed the air around her cheek. Though he'd only met the couple once before, and that several years ago at a diplomatic reception, Leonard Vanning had always, at least since his first week at the Academy, made it a point to remember people's names. It impressed. It created immediate intimacy. It could give you the upper hand in conversation while the other person, distracted and socially hamstrung, futilely racked his brain for your identity.

"Jus' got back from Ireland, Leonard," said the senator. "Beautiful country, simply beautiful. Best fishing I've ever seen."

"Junket?" Vanning asked, swirling the champagne in his glass.

"Now, Leonard, y'know we're not calling 'em junkets anymore. S'here was a 'fact-finding mission,' trying to determine the precise number a salmon a fella can catch in a day."

Vanning tilted his head back and opened his mouth and added to the laughter. He was about to push on to the bar when he felt a tap on his arm. A young man in a waiter's uniform spoke over the din.

"You're wanted at the door, Mr. Vanning."

"Eh? By who?"

"They didn't say, sir. The man refused to give his name, waiting for you outside. Ask him to leave, sir?"

Vanning tightened the grip on his cane. His heart was suddenly racing. The room seemed hot and he realized he might be drunk. *A man?* He fixed on the thought that the police would probably ask him to step outside rather than exercise their authority in this influential crowd.

". . . No, I'll see who it is. If you'll excuse me," to the senator and his wife.

Vanning stared straight ahead, stone-faced, as he hobbled through the bubbly throng. What if there had been a witness—an accomplice maybe, who was now cooperating with the police?

"You look like you're in pain, Leonard," someone called from his right. "How'd 'ya hurt your knee?"

"Squash," Vanning said hopelessly, not turning. He edged out of the ballroom and through the echoing, almost empty foyer. The house servant was waiting at the massive, studded oak front doors.

"Sorry to bother you, Mr. Vanning, but the driver in that car over there, next to the Mercedes, he said his passenger wanted to see you."

"Eh?"

Vanning followed the servant's outstretched arm and spied the long black limousine, one of a dozen such cars ringing the circular drive, parked in the inky darkness beyond the spillover light from the house. The rain was really coming down.

"He declined to give his name, sir."

The car's windows were smoked. It was too dark to see the plates. A black driver, uniformed and gray-haired, stood waiting at patient attention at the limo's back door. After a moment of near dizzying paralysis, Vanning stoically started down the half-moon shaped marble steps. He stopped when he felt the rain. "Borrow your umbrella?"

"Certainly, sir."

Fighting the wind for control of the large umbrella while trying to limp with the cane, Vanning gracelessly gyroscoped his way across the wet driveway to the car.

"Evening, sir."

The driver swung open the back door. Vanning veered toward it and dropped down to look inside.

"Just get in, Leonard—I don't need a cold!"

There was no question he'd have to get into the car. The croaking voice still had that sharp commanding ring to it. You did what this voice said and just hoped you could maintain a shred of dignity while doing it. Vanning collapsed the umbrella and slid into the deep-padded softness of the car. The door closed behind him with a solidly expensive *thunk*.

Screws was wedged into the far, rounded corner of the dimly lit limo, his frail body barely indenting the plush seat.

"Well, get to it!" Screws rumbled impatiently. "I don't have the time or inclination for pleasantries."

How the hell did he find out?

"I've got my sources," Screws cut in, reading Vanning's look. "*Just give me the facts.*"

". . . It was found," Vanning began resentfully. "They must have gotten choked in some kind of seaweed. Way off course . . . half-covered with sand—"

"How the hell did you find out about this?"

Vanning continued, coldly formal. ". . . An NSA employee was involved in a satellite mishandling several months ago. He had a hearing. He was put on probation and demoted to our satellite photograph analysis section. Everything he does while he's on probation is monitored because of his high clearance. The director of the section thought he was acting strangely and reported it to me. A thing like that gets high priority. It came across my desk right away—*thank God*."

"Go on."

"This NSA employee saw an underwater shadow off the coast of northern California, saw it on a satellite photo. He dove there with a friend. They took pictures and they collected the dog tags."

"Jesus Christ! And you never called me about this!"

Vanning studied the small, old, angry man sitting across from him. He was a pitiful little figure, and Vanning raised the corners of his mouth and smiled as if it was painful. "Claude, before you get yourself all started up, let me assure you that I've got this almost completely under control." He waited for the inevitable caustic comment, but none came. Screws was staring at him from the shadows with an intensity that was frightening. He went on: "I called the two in, got the pictures and dog tags, and told them it had been part of a simulated sea trial, top secret and all that . . . Now I have a couple people, three people from the original team who I've taken care of over the years—from my own pocket, Claude, at no small expense— people outside the Agency, loyal, trustworthy freelancers who know the rules—"

"*Who?*"

"What?"

"These 'freelancers'—who are they?"

Vanning regarded him. "Who are they? Well, there's really only three—actually quite fascinating. All late-fifties—early sixties, retired—two former Naval Intelligence boys, one who used to work for the Company. Great guys. They don't come cheap but they know their stuff. And trustworthy—real patriots. All three are family men, one's got a locksmith shop in Baltimore, does pretty well from what I understand. Other two . . . I'm not sure, I think just freelance stuff. I worked with all of them at one time or another. One asked me to be his second daughter's Godfather—I refused, of course—don't want the connection. You can meet them if you'd li—"

"No."

"There's a drop-off," Vanning resumed nervously, "a shelf right near there. They hooked it up and towed the thing. Only one man went down, only one from the ship, my man, actually saw it. Cabled it up and dragged it to the shelf. Gone for good—"

"What else have you done unsupervised, Leonard?" The question carried a strong undercurrent of rebuke. "*Don't omit a thing.*"

Vanning tried to get clear in his mind what more he could tell. Anything about Seydoux was definitely out. He unconsciously rubbed his swollen knee. Probably have to mention Hulse.

"The satellite photos were removed, there's no problem there . . . but these two who saw it, a significant problem, Claude. Unsettling. One seems to have dragged the other into investigating." He paused. "He's used the NSA computer to go back and check records. They were actually followed to Avery's widow's house today—"

"Son of a bitch!"

"They were there for five minutes tops. It's gotten to the boiling point. One's being taken out as a coronary in the morning . . ."

Screws didn't seem to disapprove.

"Other's earmarked for an accident soon as the opportunity arises. N'after that we're home free. I, ah, I've spoken to Admiral Hulse—"

"*You're not serious.*"

"He'd the right to know!"

"Have you lost your mind? Why on earth—"

"Because he's dying. Because he deserved to know, Claude. Admiral Hulse was one of the finest—"

Screws viciously cut in: "Ford Hulse is a babbling alcoholic—a weak sister! *He always was!* If this is your idea of how to handle this thing then we're in worse trouble than I thought!"

"Look, Claude, we don't much like each other and we never have. 'At's fine with me. But I've been over at the NSA for over twenty years. I think I know how to handle a crisis."

"The best way to handle a crisis is not to create one in the first place! You can skip the biography—I know all about you, Leonard. You've got this old Tudor monstrosity here and this wealthy little wife and you're out jogging every morning because you're afraid you might have to die and leave all this behind, and for the first time in your life you're starting to believe you might actually *be somebody!*"

". . . Y'know what's bothering you, Claude? *You need me!* You can't do it by yourself!"

"Contacting Hulse—"

"He's near death—"

"Was insane! While you've been squirreled away over at the NSA, going through people's garbage, listening to tapes, I've been up on the Hill. I may look old and small to you in the back of this car, *but don't try to run with me, Leonard.* I'll have your ass up the Capitol flagpole three times a day and no one the wiser—" It seemed like Screws tried to swallow and something somewhere got stuck. He heaved abruptly, rose forward, and was seized with a deep, frighteningly hollow cough. Vanning slowly gripped the door handle, about to alert the driver. His other hand automatically extended toward Screws.

"Get away from me, goddamn it!"

"Eh?" Eyes alert, mouth open, Vanning cautiously withdrew the errant hand. Screws forced himself back in the seat, managing now to draw breaths. He spoke quietly, but with a command that could not be ignored: "You, Hulse, Markwater—all you military boys; either you were bunglers who had balls or you were running from your shadows. . . . You, Leonard, you had the thinnest skin of all. That this has unraveled to the point that you've assumed control . . ." The thought seemed too depressing for him to finish.

A profound quiet followed, a moment's silence for that which had been.

To Vanning, the gloomy luxuriousness of the limo began to take on the claustrophobic outlines of a coffin. He was weary and in his heart of hearts knew Screws was speaking the truth. Contacting Hulse had been a huge mistake, one born of an unreasoned desire for acceptance from a former superior. To Hulse, the father figure, he'd gone sniffing for a pat on the back—good job, Leonard, keep up the good work. Instead, he'd found a man who fit perfectly Screws's babbling-wreck description. Screws was right. He wasn't up to the task at hand—single-handedly conducting the cover-up. He'd only briefly fooled himself into believing he was. That realization gently lowered Vanning back to the unspectacular plain that was his life. Rather than depress, it took a great weight from his narrow shoulders and brought an immediate sense of calm.

"You haven't left anything out have you, Leonard? Anything you've left out?"

For a moment, Vanning thought about telling Screws of his contacting Seydoux. Then decided there was no need.

"No."

"Are you sure?"

"Yes. What should we do, Claude? You tell me."

"You're sure about these two who saw the sub?"

"Gotta go."

"Then take care of them. That's unavoidable. I can only take your word that 'your boys' will do a professional job. So be it. I'll expect to hear from you tomorrow. From here on out I want information, Leonard, not faits accomplis. Do we understand each other?"

"Yes."

"What, Leonard?"

"I understand."

"Then run on back to your party—well, go on!"

Vanning swung open the heavy door.

"Leonard—"

"Eh?"

"It was Seydoux who called me. Don't even think about lying to me again . . ."

Cold air blew in from outside. He stepped awkwardly out of the car and took the borrowed umbrella from the waiting driver.

"Goddamn, it Ellis, close—"

Ellis swung the door shut on the words. Vanning hobbled on his cane back toward the house, not even bothering to open the umbrella. He'd been crazy to think he could keep Screws out of this. The man had more moles and informers and contacts than anybody in town.

Vanning handed the doorman the umbrella and started back into the party.

"Your cane, sir?"

"Eh?" Vanning turned back to the house servant standing at the door.

"You gave me your cane, sir—you're holding the umbrella."

Vanning looked down, saw that it was so, and exchanged the umbrella for the cane.

"I need a nice long vacation," Vanning muttered as he walked down the foyer. "Once this mess has blown over . . ."

II

Mark was where you could usually find him after helping

Orin clean up after dinner—down at the far end of the dock, an old stubby deep-sea-fishing pole in his hands, earphones on and vibrating with bass-heavy rock, a half-finished can of Coke at his side, sitting in one of those aluminum-and-plastic folding lawn chairs that always seem to be on sale at shopping centers.

He was bowing the fishing line with his hand in time with the music, making the jig jerk erratically twenty yards down. Heavy metal music seemed to have a particularly enticing beat when it came to angling in time, and Mark was considering writing a letter to a head-banger magazine to alert the world of his discovery.

It was getting kind of dark. He'd only caught a couple of undersize pollack that hadn't been worth keeping, and he was thinking about heading back up the house to maybe watch some TV. You could've strangled a cat behind his chair and he wouldn't have heard, so loud was the music from the headphones, and the man who walked with the stiff gait came down the dock much more quietly than that.

The man stood motionless behind him, so near he could have reached out and gently stroked Mark's close-cropped hair. The man quickly analyzed the layout of the place: the length of the dock, the distance to the house, the heavily wooded coastline that snaked off in either direction as far as the eye could see. Standing behind the boy, he breathed deeply the rich ocean air and looked out at the sea. The man calmly took a drink from a flask, put it away, and then lightly tapped Mark on the shoulder.

"Wha—" Mark spun around in the chair. He pulled off the headphones when he saw the man standing over him, smiling.

"Hallo."

"Where'd you come from?"

"Is Mr. Marsh here? Mr. Orin Marsh?"

The man wasn't so tall but he seemed pretty solidly built. He was bald on top but at the sides his hair was kind of long and straggly. His face had a lot of bone in it, and he had some mean dark circles under his eyes. It looked like he'd spent the last three days in the loose-fitting suit pants and jacket he was wearing. His shirt was open, no tie, and he had on a pair of new tennis shoes. He seemed foreign. For a guy his age, somewhere around fifty or sixty, Mark decided he looked pretty cool.

"I asked if Mr. Orin Marsh is in?"

The guy had a French accent, Mark noticed.

"Orin's out back the house chopping wood."

"Ah, and you are?"

"Mark—Orin's nephew. You lookin' to rent a boat or sum'em?"

The man again looked to the ocean, which was pretty calm, and shook his head. "I was interested in diving—scuba diving. Do you or your uncle do that sort of thing?"

"Orin dives, sure. I dive sometimes."

"Out there?" The man flicked a loose hand toward the water. Mark nodded. "Do others dive here?"

"Uh-huh."

"Recently."

"Yup. Just a few days ago two guys dove out there—I took 'em. Orin dove out there, too."

There it was then. The little ball had stopped rolling and the number was chosen. LeClerc's options had diminished to one.

"Where's your car? Say, don't you have a car?"

LeClerc had a car, a shiny, sporty foreign rental that was parked about a kilometer down the dirt road that led to the property. It had been painful to walk the distance, but LeClerc wanted to arrive unannounced, accompanied with the element of surprise.

Seydoux's cable had been cryptic and brief. The few pertinent facts concerned a location: Point Arena; a name: Orin Marsh; and a mission: reconnaissance. The parameters that Seydoux had placed on the assignment were admittedly vague, but LeClerc assumed Seydoux knew what his particular talents were and had called him for that reason.

After landing in Sacramento, LeClerc had spent about ten minutes with a phonebook. There were only four families named Marsh listed in that remote area of the Point, three hour's drive to the north, and several quick calls ruled out two of them. LeClerc then drove the rental out to the coast. It was a bit of a trip, but LeClerc immensely enjoyed driving at high speed on American roads, especially after spending three tortuous months negotiating the unpaved and rutted byways of Morocco.

He found the third Marsh existing with his battered wife in a rather squalid apartment complex near the sea. They were arguing when he knocked and the man yelled through the peepholed door that he didn't know anything about renting boats.

Which left this last Marsh to explore.

Turning off the coastal two-lane onto the dirt access road that led to the place, LeClerc was positive he'd found the man in question. He would've left peacefully if this boy's answers to his few questions had been different. But they hadn't, so there you were.

"How'd you get out here without a car?" the boy asked.

"My car broke down," LeClerc stated simply, having learned long ago that the short, unadorned lie works best; that one alibi was better than two. He looked down at Mark. "Your uncle, when was he diving out there?"

"Yesterday morning. There was a boat came last night, too, some kinda salvage rig. You want a hand with your car?"

The boy was in the process of standing, tall and lanky, getting up to help the stranded motorist, when his rod tugged violently.

"I got one!"

LeClerc watched, amused, as the boy began furiously reeling the line in. From the bend of the sturdy pole it looked as if he'd actually hooked something quite sizable.

"Oh yeah! I got a big one!"

"Keep the tension on," LeClerc offered with a smile. The line was slicing crazily through the water, tracing the life-and-death struggle being fought below. The boy was standing precariously near the dock's edge, desperately reeling in line as he peered down into the dark water for a glimpse of the reluctant leviathan.

"I think I see it!"

"Can you?"

"Maybe a bonita or something!" the boy shouted, flushed with the primeval ecstasy of the hunt.

"Very good—keep the tension on the line—"

LeClerc reached into his jacket and casually produced the .22 handgun he'd purchased at a sporting-goods store several hours earlier. A one-shot silencer improvised from a baby-bottle nipple was snuggly fitted over the tip of the finger-length, small-bore barrel.

"Reel," LeClerc repeated, suppressing a laugh, "keep reeling it in—"

"I am!"

"Good then."

The boy was reeling like a madman as he strained to pull the fish in. LeClerc could not help but grin at the excitement of the scene. The boy glanced back and gave LeClerc a pure, open-mouthed expression of joy. LeClerc flashed an encouraging smile and the boy turned back to the water. The gun barrel rose strangely into the scene. It came up to head level. LeClerc pushed it forward like a hypodermic needle. He lightly pressed the thick rubber nipple to the soft indentation behind Mark's left ear and immediately pulled the trigger. There was a very dull, wet *pop* as the boy's skull accepted the bullet. LeClerc took a slight step back as the boy's head snapped forward, sending a shockwave through his upright young body. The boy rose on the balls of his feet and was then pulled a half-turn around as the still struggling fish ripped the rod from his grasp. The boy's hands came up like he was trying to cover his ears, like he maybe had a headache, or was trying to protect his hearing from a loud noise. But there was no noise; it was a beautifully quiet evening out here by the water. The boy desperately tried to emit a groan. LeClerc looked into his contorted face as he continued the staggering turn. The eyes were bulged open, much like a fish that's been brought too quickly to the surface. There was no exit wound evident on the forehead (LeClerc took a keen interest in the details of his work), though he was fairly certain the bullet had come close to going all the way through. The boy's mouth was unnaturally far open, as if something large were trapped in his head and he was trying to give it an avenue of escape. LeClerc could no longer contain himself. This was as humorous as watching a mute try to scream for help—a memorable scene he had once played the protagonist in. LeClerc took pleasure in his work. How could you be good at anything if you didn't enjoy doing it—if you didn't get particular satisfaction from doing it well? Watching this boy go rigid with spasm and topple slowly off the dock was LeClerc's equivalent to an architect admiring a finished building or a golfer's hole-in-one.

The fishing rod went in first with a splash and disappeared just as the boy hit the water. His body twisted and rolled, as if trying to stay afloat, and then suddenly writhed downward and out of sight as if he thought some solution to his problem might be found at the bottom.

It had all taken maybe ten seconds at the most. The report of the gun had been very muffled, almost quiet. The baby-bottle nipple had worked quite well at baffling the sound.

LeClerc placed the handgun in his front jacket pocket. He walked stiffly down the dock to the house. He thought about the angry fish that was now cursed with dragging a heavy fishing pole around for the remainder of its shortened existence.

As he came off the dock and started up the rather steep dirt path, LeClerc could just make out the resonant, satisfying *kerchunk* of someone chopping wood. The light was fading off the ocean and LeClerc, rather than pause at the top of the path to catch his breath, continued around the side of the modest, weathered house.

By the frequency and volume of the chopping sound, LeClerc decided that Orin Marsh must be a powerful man. A powerful man wielding an ax. He took the handgun from his pocket and suddenly wished he'd purchased something with a larger cali-ber. This gun felt small and ineffectual in his hand. He assumed he'd made the purchase to increase the challenge; the hunter forcing himself to rely less on the weapon and more on the mind. Either that, or he'd been too cheap to buy something more substantial.

The wood chopping was very loud now—swift, sure, strong strokes. LeClerc could smell the fresh-cut wood as he pressed flat against the side of the house. The light was going and something had to be done fast. Adrenaline was coursing through him. He took several deep breaths, brought the gun out in front, and then sprang around the corner.

Maybe it was all the sitting on the plane, or the walk from the car, or the pent-up tension that comes with murder—but LeClerc's back went into spasm before his second leg even came around the house. His lower back exploded with a pain so intense he had to gasp.

Orin had just raised the ax for another stroke when he heard a grunting sound. He glanced up. For a brief instant he was confused—a man was teetering about ten feet away, half his body around the house, the other half hidden. His exposed arm was raised and in his hand was a small black object. The man was staring at him and grunted again, hesitated, and Orin realized what the black object was and hurled the ax in the man's direction.

LeClerc was unable to pull back around the house so he simply fell to the ground to avoid the spinning ax and handle. Orin ran for the safety of the other side of the house. LeClerc quickly fired off three shots from the prone position but this caliber gun wasn't built to hit anything more than ten feet away.

His back was on fire. Tears of pain welled in his eyes. He was lying with the leaves and twigs and started to crawl into the forest, clumsily at first, and then with increasing speed. He crawled because he didn't think he could walk.

All around were tall, sturdy trees and it soon grew dark. His hands and knees began to ache but still he crawled, pawing his way through the woods, back in the direction of his car. He wasn't worried about getting away. He'd cut the phone lines to the place and let the air out of the tires of the truck first thing. Right now Orin Marsh was probably conducting a desperate search for his beloved nephew—maybe even diving for the body in the hope of performing mouth-to-mouth resuscitation.

That image made LeClerc laugh so hard he had to pause in a dense stand of ferns. The laugh diminished to a chuckle. He took a long pull from his flask and resumed crawling across the forest floor.

III

Orin stayed with the dripping, sheet-covered body down on the dock. The night was slashed by the spinning red-and-white lights of a dozen hastily parked police cars. Radio chatter filtered from the cluster of vehicles. Flashlights moved jerkily through the surrounding forest. The coroner finally came to take the body away.

At first the police tried to be gentle, both to Mark's body and Orin, but both got bruised: Mark was dropped as they tried to slide him into the back of the wagon; Orin was accused of murder when he violently declined to confess.

It took a while for the two detectives at the scene to put their heads together and come up with the theory that Orin had committed the murder—all of about twenty minutes.

They arrayed the facts neatly before them and came up with what was, in the excited words of the younger of the two investigators, "A pretty darn good case! If he confesses . . ."

To start with, the boy had been a problem kid. The older detective gleaned this nugget—the cornerstone of their hypothesis —when he called Sacramento and notified the boy's parents of his death. The mother had to get off the phone because she was crying so hard, but the father stayed on the line and informed him that Mark was sent to Orin's to "straighten up," because Orin was a "no-nonsense" kind of guy and had helped keep Mark "in line."

The detective solemnly queried the father if he thought Orin could be violent. The man answered that Orin was his wife's brother. That he didn't know. Maybe.

Orin's hermitlike existence of the last ten years provided more grist for the detectives' rapidly developing idea. The guy lived out here in the woods—all alone. Word was some of the local kids claimed he was crazy. Made sense. Why else would you choose to live way out here in the middle of nowhere? Away from civilization. Something kind of suspect about it.

The young detective scribbled a note to himself about maybe getting a bulldozer out here to search for more bodies. Who knew what atrocities this bear of a man had been committing up here all these years?

Then there was the fact that Orin had extensive experience with firearms. He'd spent two tours in Vietnam as a Marine corporal and four years after that on the California Highway Patrol. Sure, he'd retired on disability after being dragged behind a pickup truck while breaking up a robbery in Ukiah—but that didn't mean he hadn't gone crazy-bad since. Lots of decorated vets and cops later turned their weapons on loved ones. You read about it in the papers every day.

They learned Orin had gone through extensive rehabilitation and had been on painkillers for some time after the accident—drugs.

"Probably still took 'em," the older detective sagely decided.

But most damning of all, in the detectives' keen view of things, was Orin's story about some foreign-looking guy spraying bullets with a handgun. Here was the alibi of a desperate man. Okay, so the phone line had been cut and the air let out of the tires in Orin's truck. But there was no evidence of a third person's recent presence—and it seemed more than likely, to the detectives anyway, that Orin had cut the phone line and flattened the tires himself after whacking the kid.

Come on, brother. How can you sit there and expect us to swallow this load?

Why would some foreign guy sneak up on this thirteen-year-old kid and plug him behind the ear? There was no motive. When they asked him about why he thought someone would have done such a thing, Orin refused to speculate. He was openly hiding something. He practically admitted that there was a matter he refused to discuss—even when they'd threatened to pin a murder rap on him.

So, after a huddled conference with the other policemen on the scene, after gathering all their damning (in their eyes) facts—the two detectives sat Orin down on the porch and announced they knew what had really gone on here. They dramatically walked Orin through a scenario that had him shooting Mark over a dispute—possibly drugs. They were absolutely positive that Orin had acted in the heat of anger, using a cheap .22 (one of a dozen guns, they pointed out, that had been found around the house), and then in desperation concocted this absurd story about a limping foreigner. They would be nice, they told Orin, and only charge him with second-degree murder—if he confessed right here and now. They tried to explain how much better he'd feel if he just admitted to the crime—Christ, they knew the nephew was a problem kid and probably had it coming—

It took five uniformed policemen to get Orin off the detective who'd let that line fly.

They put Orin in handcuffs and brought him up to the bar-
racks in Eureka. He was deathly quiet on the ride up, staring
straight, eyes of fire. He waived his right to call a lawyer and
they grilled him all night inside a small, high-ceilinged room,
ordering him again and again to repeat what happened. They
took turns at trying to catch Orin up. They contradicted him.
They told him to begin the story here, and then there, and then
had him skip around, and then tell it backward. And for eight
hours, in a flat monotone, Orin told the same story again and
again and again.

They gave him a paraffin test to see if he'd recently discharged a gun—negative—though one of the detectives pointed
out that an ex-cop might have thought about wearing a glove for
just that reason.

A patrolman was dispatched back to the house to search for a
glove.

They gave him two lie detector tests, both of which he
passed—a development for which no one present could offer an
explanation. They went back to rehashing the story and, one by
one, the half-dozen detectives grew tired. The only time Orin
wasn't forthcoming was when they asked him to speculate on
why the foreigner had killed Mark and tried to kill him. On that
point Orin refused to speculate. On that point he completely
clammed up.

At six the next morning, Orin quietly asked to be let go. He
had answered all their questions. He had passed all their tests.
There was no evidence he had committed the crime. If they
refused to let him go he was going to call a lawyer and get out
anyway.

They let him walk on the condition that he not leave the
county until their investigation was through. Orin nodded.

A squad car drove Orin back to the house. The sun was
coming up through the trees and blue sky stretched out like a
blanket over the sea. Everything seemed strangely quiet and
empty after last night's activity.

Orin went to the shoebox where he kept the records of his
few financial transactions and found the check he had yet to
deposit that the two guys, Stocky and Skinny, had given him to

charter the boat for their dive. He memorized the information on the check's upper left-hand corner:

David H. Lakeman
16 Garfield Drive
Chevy Chase, Md.

Orin took a cold shower. He got out and stood naked before the mirror. Orin spent the next half hour shaving off his unruly beard. With a pair of scissors he cut off his pony-tailed hair, tossing the foot-long rope of red and gray into a wastebasket. He got out his only suit and slowly, as if nursing a serious wound, dressed. Orin put on a tie. He methodically made breakfast and ate it. Orin took five hundred dollars he had hidden in a coffee jar, some of which was Mark's, and carefully put it in his old leather wallet.

Orin went outside, filled the tires on the truck with the compressor he used for the scuba tanks, and started driving to the airport in Sacramento.

In twenty minutes he had broken his word to the police about leaving the confines of the coastal county.

The day after Stocky and Skinny had come and gone, Orin had gone diving. He'd gone diving where Mark had dropped the buoy. He saw what was down there. That night he'd stood on the dock and watched a salvage boat tow it away.

There was one burning thought in Orin's mind: Stocky and Skinny would pay for what had been done to Mark. And if they weren't the one's responsible they better make him believe it, because unlike the police, Orin was prepared to use a number of rather inhumane methods to ensure they didn't hold anything back.

Orin was dry-eyed the whole drive down. He'd decided last night, while waiting for the police to come, that he was not going to let himself grieve until he'd killed the person responsible for killing Mark. After that he'd think about crying.

IV

Perri had gone off early to her sculpture class as she always did on Wednesday mornings, leaving some juice and cereal sitting on the kitchen table for when Dave got up. It was nine thirty already and Dave still hadn't come down. A depressing patter of rain pelted the kitchen windows. In the empty living room the stereo was blaring a disco beat, as a Jane Fonda Workout record spun on the turntable.

"Left arm—up—now the right—up—that's it—higher—and left two three four—"

The family dog, an exceedingly good-natured and loyal black Lab, was locked in the broom closet and had fallen asleep.

The narrow stairs leading to the second floor were dark, but if you'd bent down and looked closely you might have discerned the faint, moist impressions of two pairs of shoes that had recently ascended. The evaporating outlines of the wet shoes could also be found on the highly varnished wood flooring of the hallway leading to the bedroom, though here they reflected a faster gait—as if their wearers had been forced to run toward the bed that was visible down the hall. The bed itself was a jumble of sheets and blankets and pillows.

The bathroom door was open, however, and a light could be seen within.

Dave, still in the pajamas he'd slept in, was pinned to the cheerful yellow throw rug on the floor. A piece of duct tape firmly covered his mouth. One man had his arms securely spread-eagled across the cold tiled floor. A second man softly pinched Dave's nose so he couldn't breathe.

Dave tried frantically to break free—tried to kick up a leg or pull away an arm—but the others were stronger. His stifled cries were easily drowned out by the insistent din from the living-room stereo:

"—right leg—twirl—left leg—twirl—up two three—"

Dave was squirming with all the frantic energy of a person who is being suffocated. The men holding him down redoubled their efforts, as Dave's panic grew in proportion to the elapsed time without air. The man pinching his nose pulled a small pressurized canister from his overcoat pocket. Dave tried an old wrestling move to roll free but he was out of shape and things were going out of focus. The man on top suddenly ripped the duct tape from Dave's mouth. As Dave gulped desperately for oxygen the man whipped the lipstick-sized canister right up to his mouth. Dave was aware of a hissing sound. The air he drank in had a disturbing taste.

His heart suddenly skipped a beat and then thumped mightily twice. An excruciating pain erupted through his chest, so acute it arched his back off the floor and actually broke the grasp of the man pinning him down.

"Let go of him." The men stepped out of the bathroom and watched from the doorway.

Dave's heart was failing, squirming, misfiring horribly. A surge of hopeless terror swept through him. He was locked in the final, recognizable moment of violent death.

"—now the inner thighs—I want this to really burn—left leg—starting positions—"

A pulsing yellow haze crept into his vision. His heart machine-gunned four times more and then stopped. The blood paused, then froze in place. For an instant he was aware of being dead. His consciousness contracted in upon itself and merged, as a rain drop into the sea, with darkness.

Chapter Eighteen

Matt sobbed so on the drive to the hospital that he was given a warning. It was raining and the car was racing and his thoughts were a hopeless jangle of loss, fury, and fear. The young policeman who pulled him over seemed to sense he was dealing with a motorist who had just suffered a tremendous personal tragedy and let Matt off with a verbal rebuke for speeding.

Matt was prepared to lose it completely when he came screeching to an angled stop in an illegal parking space directly outside the hospital. So it was strange that upon storming through the emergency-room doors he was presented the task of consoling Perri. She was gone, lost, bouncing around inside some jagged, inaccessible place beyond hysteria.

Matt stopped crying for himself when he saw her: shunted off to a little curtained-off area, curled up in a chair, eyes tightly closed, jaw clenched, rocking rapidly back and forth like her life depended on it. He slowly approached and tried to put his arm around her but she practically screamed for him to stay away. Matt backed into one of the trolleyed curtains that formed

196

the walls and watched as a nurse entered with some pills and a tiny cup of water. Perri took the medication like a child.

Matt slipped out. He found a nurse who pointed to a doctor who, through the windows of a door, could be seen standing in a hallway writing on a clipboard. Matt went through the door and stood before the doctor—a black man, tall, about forty, with gray temples that gave him a distinguished air.

"Are you the doctor who worked on Dave?"

The man looked up from his writing. He'd dealt many times with people in Matt's state of mind, recognized it immediately, and spoke in a soft tone that conveyed understanding and sympathy: "We did everything we could . . . he was dead before he arrived here. I'm sorry."

"I think—" Matt fought back tears, "I think there's been a mistake."

The doctor remained silent, an expression of enormous compassion radiating from his face.

"The nurse said it was listed as a heart attack," Matt went on.

"Unfortunately . . . yes." The doctor shook his head ruefully; as if contemplating a tragedy of unique and unbounded proportion.

"Dave was only thirty-four. He was in good shape—didn't smoke—and had no history of any kind of heart trouble. Never ever. There must be a mistake. Maybe something was missed . . ." Matt was trying to be calm. You *wanted* to be calm in this man's presence.

"There's been no mistake. Mr. Lakeman died of a massive coronary and this is, however unfortunate, on the rise in men in his age group. Stress and high blood pressure can—"

Matt had to cut in: "You don't understand. Dave was murdered. You see we *found* something. We did. They told us not to say anything but I'll tell you—a submarine, with skeletons inside—"

The doctor gently placed a large hand on Matt's shoulder. "What's your name, son?"

"Matt."

"Matt," the doctor repeated in a deep, full, peaceful voice, "if there's any solace to be had here it's that your friend died a natural death."

"No. There's reasons, you have to believe me. There must be some kind of test you can run—"

"I don't know what kind of business you're in, Matt, but when you've seen something a couple hundred times you get so you can recognize what it is. He died of a heart attack."

"They must have done something to him—something to make it look like a heart attack, something—" Matt stopped in midsentence and studied the doctor's unchanging, benevolent expression. "You—you're one of them, aren't you?" he blurted. Matt pulled his shoulder from the doctor's hand.

"One of who? Matt, you're hysterical—realize it. It's a normal reaction to the situation."

"Dave Lakeman was my best friend and he was as healthy as I am and he was murdered because of what we found!"

Matt spun and crashed back through the double doors into the emergency room. He brushed through to the little area where Perri was. He'd tell her what she didn't know—everything that had been going on, and she'd believe him. Together they'd blow the top off this whole thing!

But Perri was sedated, fast asleep on a stretcher that had been wheeled into the room. She was lying on her side, pulled up tight into a fetal position, and Matt could hear a nurse just outside talking about possibly admitting her overnight for observation.

Matt had an overwhelming desire to punch something or somebody. An orderly came in. He started wheeling Perri out of the curtained room. They were admitting her for the night. As Matt watched them wheel her away down the hall he was hit with the overwhelming thought that he was responsible for it all. He tried to separate the numbing guilt he felt as a result of his affair with Perri from the intense grief of Dave's death, but they were somehow hopelessly interlocked.

He staggered back out through the emergency room and had to step out of the way when a team of doctors and nurses came running by to meet an ambulance that had just pulled up outside.

It wasn't until later that these seemingly permanent emotions fell away. It happened after he'd left the safety of the crowded hospital, just about the second he realized he would be killed as well.

II

It was official: Orin Marsh was wanted for the cold-blooded murder of Mark Conklin, his thirteen-year-old nephew. Orin heard the news just as he was pulling into the Sacramento airport parking lot that morning.

Evidently the police had returned to the house to ask a few more questions and instead found Orin and his truck gone. A long braid of hair in a wastebasket was proof he was on the run and trying to change his identity. A warrant for Orin Marsh's arrest was immediately issued and his description passed on to local TV and radio stations.

Orin was to be considered "armed and dangerous," and the radio news report wrapped the story on a lurid note by gravely announcing that bulldozers were being trucked to "the Vietnam vet's isolated home" to search for other "possible victims."

Being wanted by the police didn't create that much of a problem as far as Orin could see, which was pretty far. He had a good lead and wasn't really too concerned about getting picked up. If the intelligence of the two who'd grilled him last night was any indication he'd have all the time in the world. Orin continued into the airport parking lot and left the truck in one of the long-term spaces. The only thing he took from the vehicle was a large Phillips-head screwdriver. Orin casually turned to the car he'd parked beside, a spotless, white Lincoln Town Car, and easily broke the door lock. He climbed into the crimson velvet interior and closed the door. It had the crisp smell of a car with under five hundred miles. In two minutes the steering column and ignition wires were exposed and ten seconds later the engine was running.

It took Orin three uneventful hours to drive to Sparks, Nevada, where there would be less chance of being sought and he could pick up a bus to Salt Lake.

He stopped only once, and then to purchase a wide-brimmed Stetson. During the drive to Sparks, Orin listened to the radio to keep track of any new developments in the search for the crazed Vietnam vet. There were none.

Orin pulled into Sparks around noon and left the huge white Lincoln in the middle of a busy parking lot.

By this time the California police had probably stumbled upon his battered truck at the Sacramento airport. Orin knew the routine that would follow. The detectives assigned to the case would be putting all their energies into poring over departing passenger lists and delaying outgoing flights for searches. The airport was the only lead they had and they'd have to play it through to the end.

The most elusive fugitives are former cops, and Orin had worn a badge for four years.

From Sparks there was a twelve thirty-five Greyhound to Salt Lake City.

He was on it.

III

Ellis drove his grumbling charge with unwavering politeness. The harsher Screws's words, the more set became Ellis's broad smile and cheerful demeanor. He'd resolutely endured twenty years as Senator Claude Revis Screws's personal valet and driver. He'd endured them by learning to let the constant acidic commentary roll off him like water. Ellis guessed it was like any kind of work that involved harsh noise, say chicken farming or a factory job, both of which he'd tried—after awhile you just grew deaf to it.

Ellis eased the long limousine up a washed-out gray gravel driveway and came to a stop near the front door of an old Virginia farmhouse. It was large and solid and still white where the paint held. Probably a pretty productive place a few dozen years ago, Ellis decided, but the fields hadn't been farmed for a long time and the house was under seige by an encroaching sea of waist-high weeds that sloped down to a fuzzy outline forest where the trees, too, had decided to make a bid to reclaim the land.

"Quit gaping—I haven't got all day!"

Ellis got out of the car. He popped up a big black umbrella and then opened the back door for Screws.

"Well, give me your hand—"

Ellis held his arm steady while Screws used it to pull himself into a standing position. Holding the umbrella over Screws's bald, liver-spotted head, Ellis patiently walked him to the door and rang the bell.

It was answered almost immediately by a rather attractive, middle-aged woman wearing denim overalls. Her hair was pulled back in a ponytail, as if she'd been working. Ellis guessed she'd seen them approaching from a window.

"Good morning to you," said Screws with the slightest of bows. "I'm—"

"I know who you are," she said, blocking the doorway.

"I'd like to talk to the admiral."

"He's not available."

"You must be his niece . . ."

"I am."

"Then be a good little girl and go inside and tell your uncle I'm here."

"You go to hell!"

"I will *not* be turned away," Screws growled threateningly. "Now run along and tell him I'm here."

Ellis stood politely off to one side. Out of the corner of his eye, though, he watched—prepared to step in and quietly take the blow he was sure the woman was about to deliver. You could see she was debating whether to strike or slam the door closed, when a sound escaped out to the porch. Barely audible, almost lost in the heated air escaping from the half-open door, came a hoarse, feeble call: "Who is it, Annie . . . who's there?"

The woman stared icily at Screws, as if he'd just woken a

napping child who was difficult to put to sleep. "You son of a bitch." Several moments passed. Her gaze finally dropped in defeat to the floor. She opened the door and without looking up, let Screws pass.

Screws walked into the foyer. He spotted a nurse coming from an open door down the hall. Screws approached, looked into the room. Hulse was there, waiting for him.

Despite his obvious frailty, the eyes were wet and alive. The eyes followed Screws into a neighboring chair.

Hulse's breathing was labored to the point that it appeared he needed all his energy to continue with this one task. Then he started to speak.

"... Having a ... good day, Claude ... feel better than I've felt ... in weeks."

Screws didn't know what exactly was killing Hulse but it seemed to be doing its work in a slow, methodical manner.

"... After all this time ... still up there ... slugging away ... eh, Claude?"

"Someone's got to. I won't keep you long. I understand Leonard Vanning visited you the other day."

Hulse didn't seem to hear, just kept on trying to make his chest rise and fall, forcing air through his pale, parted lips. In this condition, Screws hoped, Hulse might not even remember Vanning's visit—in which case there was no need to stay any longer.

"... After all this time—"

Repeating himself. Good. Screws almost got up to go.

"... it's been found ..." Hulse suddenly wheezed, "... and now you're gonna have ... somebody kill these two ... aren't you, Claude?"

"... I don't know anything about that, Ford. I think you're imagining things."

"... Am I?"

"Yes, Ford—your mind's got things all twisted up. Your mind's gone, Ford. You're going crazy." Screws said it like an hypnotic suggestion, willing the words to be true.

"No ..." Hulse emitted with effort. "You're the one ... Claude ... who's twisted ..." That seemed to take something out of him, because he had to close those sparkling pale eyes for a moment. They reopened. ". . . You and your . . . fiery oratory . . ."

"You have gone crazy, Ford."

". . . When I close my eyes . . . I can see the blast . . . rising . . . like a wall . . . over the sea . . ." Hulse closed his eyes. ". . . A flash of light . . . brighter than the sun . . . and up rises this terrible . . . wall . . . A white wave . . . explodes across the water . . . and everything got dark . . . and somewhere down there . . . those poor Russian bastards . . . must have been . . . screaming . . . We knew . . . they were there . . . me . . . Markwater . . . and you . . ."

"Did it to themselves—sneaking around the site."

The eyes reopened and regarded Screws.

"You don't think they'd have done it to us?" Screws asked derisively. "You think they'd have called the blast off to shoo us away? Well, do you? Jesus, Ford, your mind *is* going. Think back on those times. It was war, goddamn it, still is! Sheer luck we got to put the thing to good use, or tried to, anyway."

". . . The whole thing was wrong—"

"We were trying to do what needed to be done—*what nobody else was willing to do*. Damn good plan turning the sub around, mighta worked, too, if you'd gotten some boys who knew what the hell they were doing."

". . . Everything else changes, Claude . . . but you . . . you stay the same . . ."

"I still believe in this country."

". . . You believe in fear . . . you still believe in fear . . . In all these movies . . . always some nut in uniform . . . going crazy and launching . . . the bomb . . ." Hulse paused for a tremendously agonizing swallow. ". . . But it took a politician . . . it took you, Claude . . . to orchestrate that scheme."

"It would have worked."

"Thank God it failed."

"*This* is preferable to the world we'd have created? This tortured, constipated, draining life-and-death stalemate that we've been backed into—*this* is better? The money we waste on defense—I see it, Ford—billions and billions. Money that we could have spent on schools and roads and—Christ, Ford—ours

would have been a productive world. You should die proud if
only because you had a hand in trying to bring it about."

". . . I won't die . . . until I've seen this . . . set right . . ."

Screws nodded. He stepped up to Hulse's chair and, rain
clouds looming over him through the glass ceiling and walls,
leaned in close to the wheezing man. "Vanning was a fool to
contact you. Do not—I repeat—do not get involved in this.
You're dying a slow death, Ford. I can see it. But sick or not,
you'll go to jail just like the rest of us. Good day, *Admiral.*"

Screws creaked back down the hall. The impertinent niece
was nowhere to be seen and he gladly got the door himself.
Ellis was waiting outside, standing on the porch, watching the
rain, humming to himself.

"Well, don't just stand there—open the damn umbrella and
get me to the car!"

Ellis smiled and opened the umbrella with an extravagant
flourish. You just gotta let that noise roll off you like water. You
most certainly do.

IV

It was mid-day and Matt was still at the hospital. It was
taking longer than expected to admit Perri. About an hour ago,
Perri's older brother arrived to be with her. His name was Bob.
The guy was a wide-tied high-school history teacher from New
Jersey. Matt had a cup of coffee with him in the hospital
cafeteria. Matt had thought about laying the whole story out to
him, but stopped short when he realized the guy was a pomp-
ous, overbearing jerk. They finally found Perri a room and Matt
moved down the halls, alone.

Hands fisted in his pockets, Matt moved through the fluorescent glare of the hospital. Half-closed doors opened on shadowy
rooms offering glimpses of the injured, sick, and dying. Young
and old seemed to be represented in almost equal measure here.
The bulky, elaborate machinery of late-twentieth-century medi-

cine took up wing after wing. Matt began agonizing over the possibility that Dave really might have died of a heart attack. A new grief crept over him. He couldn't decide which would be preferable: a heart attack at thirty-four or murder.

Matt suddenly found himself outside the hospital. He walked listlessly to his car and drove off through the rain, no clear direction in mind.

Man's works—roads and buses and buildings. Building's just a glorified pile of sand and steel and glass with squared edges. In the cosmic scheme of things the finished product's got all the permanence of a sandcastle. Road'll dissolve in the blink of a galactic eye. A bus may seem substantial but it's just a set of atoms that consist largely of empty space—

The bus horn blared Matt's car back into its proper lane.

He was driving north on the narrow expanse of asphalt that was the Baltimore-Washington Parkway. More powerful than grief or anger or any one emotion, force of habit was leading Matt back to the NSA. Undulating fields of fallow Maryland farmland rolled by between patches of wood. It was sometime in the afternoon, Matt wasn't at all sure when; cloudy-dark but not raining. Beads of water from the morning's deluge dotted the fringe of the windshield. The car radio chattered from the dashboard. It was supposed to rain again. It seemed to Matt that it had been raining forever.

He drove into the barbed-wire womb of Fort Meade and defiantly parked in an illegal space right outside the tower. The National Security Agency's tan, rectangular Headquarters Operations Building rose nine stories into a gray sky. The building's roof was crowded with antennae and radomes and microwave dishes. For the first time Matt was fearful of the place. The razor wire and electrical fence and closed-circuit cameras and armed guards that before gave comfort now loomed hostile and dangerous.

His steps were unsure as he approached the gatehouse and the two FPS guards waiting there. He was immediately stopped.

"Your security badge, sir?"

Matt remembered that he hadn't clipped on his laminated security badge. He dug into his pocket, found the badge, and clipped it on. He started through.

"Excuse me, Mr. Clarke—Mr. Clarke, sir!"

Matt turned back. The two guards were right on him.

"Yeah?"

"I'm sorry, Mr. Clarke, but you're to call M-5 before you go in. Mr. Vanning wanted to talk with you. Phone's right over there."

Matt looked from one guard to the other. They were young and clean-shaven and polite and seemed thoroughly dangerous. Matt let them escort him to their desk. Referring to a pink memo, one dialed the phone and handed Matt the receiver. Vanning answered directly.

"Mr. Vanning?"

"Matt—I got word this morning that Dave Lakeman died of a heart attack. I wasn't sure if you knew." The voice was deep with soothing, almost paternal concern.

". . . I just came from the hospital."

"Had he a history of heart trouble, Matt?" asked Vanning, shocked and deeply troubled.

". . . No."

"I tried calling you at home as soon as I heard. Believe me, I'm as shaken up about this as you. I was very . . . concerned about you, Matt. I was worried that under the grief and stress of the situation . . . your mind might possibly race to certain conclusions that have no basis in fact." There was a long pause, and then he added in a stronger tone, "Because the two are absolutely unconnected. It's very important that you understand that."

Phone to his ear, Matt watched a steady stream of men and women much like himself pass through the main entrance. For these people it was just another uneventful day at work—just one of thousands of uneventful days at work that stack up like blank file cards to form a career. Matt envied them terribly. He felt unclean with tragedy. He felt he didn't belong.

"You didn't have Dave killed?" Matt asked wearily.

"Course not! Exactly what I was worried about. Thoughts like that. Tragedy enough without thinking conspiracy. Pull yourself together, Matt."

"He was my best friend—" Matt choked on the thought and started to cry. He turned away from the passing flow of people, embarrassed. The tears came easily. The world seemed achingly empty.

"I know . . . I know . . . Matt? Matt, listen to me for just a moment if you can. Are you there, son?"

"Uh huh—" Matt took off his glasses and wiped his face with the back of his hand.

"Go home and get a good night's sleep. You'll see things more clearly in the morning. But come in sometime tomorrow so we can take care of some paperwork. I got you off probation. You're back at your previous job. Can start anytime. Matt?"

"Yeah?"

"Can't tell you how bad I feel about all this." Vanning waited for a response but all he heard was Matt fighting a losing battle with tears.

Vanning softly hung up and Matt swam through a watery world back out to his car.

Chapter Nineteen

Matt tumbled from sleep and awoke in a ball on his bed. Night beamed through the uncurtained windows. The apartment was dark and lonely. Matt lay still for several uncertain minutes, unsuccessfully trying to recall the plot of a not unpleasant dream, and then looked over at the faint glowing hands of the alarm clock.

It was eight in the evening. He'd lain down for a brief nap five hours ago.

Matt turned onto his back and folded his hands across his chest. He wondered if this was the position in which Dave would be buried, and then he quickly unfolded his hands. He grew very conscious of his heart beating. For a moment he tried to imagine what it might feel like if it stopped, but this had the opposite effect and his heart started to race. He immediately gave up.

There was no confusion about the earlier events of the day. Dave was dead. It was a great gray fuzzy weight of a fact that slowed his thoughts and desire to rise. Matt thought perhaps he should still be crying, but no tears came. As an oyster coats an irritant with nacre to produce a pearl, Matt's mind had already begun the process of smoothing the sharpness of the tragedy. Already the grief was dulling. Already he was thinking ahead.

He tried weighing his options like a chess game but grew fidgety when he couldn't think up a first move. Wildly disparate courses of action flickered against the bedroom darkness: Matt doggedly ordering endless autopsies to prove Dave had been murdered; Matt leading a scuba-clad team of investigators out to the site of the sub; Matt accepting Dave's death as a heart attack and returning to the NSA to pursue a loyal, gray-haired career; Matt ducking into the *Washington Post* to tell his tale to harried, coffee-charged reporters; Matt destroying the pictures and dog tag he'd hidden at Duka's; Matt eating a large meal.

Matt realized at least some of the emptiness he was feeling came from acute hunger. He had to do something, so he slowly got out of bed. Dressing, Matt resolved that he should get out of the apartment to think. These simple decisions, unique only for their immediacy, drained him. His head was slow with heaviness. He craved company, urgently felt the need to talk.

Matt sat on the edge of his bed. After a moment's thought, he picked up the phone and dialed his parents in Florida. He didn't know what he would say.

His father answered on the first ring: "Hello."

"Dad—it's Matt."

"Matt!" cried his father, his robust voice still heavy with a Hungarian accent. "You just missed your mother—out shopping. She would have loved to speak to you. So."

"How'y'doing?"

"We're both fine. It was a beautiful day. We're going out to eat tonight at a seafood place a few miles down the road—did I tell you about this place?"

". . . No."

Immediately: "What's wrong? You sound like something's wrong."

"Something's wrong, Dad."

Quieter: "What?"

"Remember Dave Lakeman? My friend. You met when we—"

"I remember—of course I remember!"

". . . He died this morning—"

Matt's voice was steady, in control.

". . . But how?"

Matt closed his eyes, thinking.

"Matt—how?"

". . . There's something going on."

"Going on?"

"At work—something's wrong. For all I know this phone line's tapped, but I don't care. Dave was killed. Last week I was at work, see, and—"

"But you work for the government! Don't speak on the phone if you get in trouble!"

"Somebody had Dave killed—they said it was a heart attack at the hospital but *I* know it wasn't—it wasn't. We found something, Dave and me. I saw something at work that—"

"Stop it, right now! I want to hear none of the secrets from where you work. You want to get in trouble? Matt, please, how can I listen to any of this? These heart attacks—you hear about this one having one, and that one—younger and younger it happens. About Dave, I am truly sorry. Is the widow provided for? That's what's important. Your work? I know what you do is secret secret, not for me to hear. I just don't want you to get in trouble. You understand. Trouble at work? Go to your boss. You do your job, I know you do. We raised you like that. Just work hard and save your money—"

"Dad."

"You okay? You understand what I'm saying."

"I'll call you in the next few days."

"Your friend—terrible. Younger and younger. Am I right?"

"Yup."

"Get a good night's sleep. Have a drink! I lost friends. Young men—during the revolt—very very close to me—your mother, too. Life goes on. Did I ever think at sixty-four I'd be in Florida? Me—from Debrecen? Never. I'm so sorry to hear about Dave. Should I have your mother call you when she gets back?"

". . . It's all right. I'll call again."

"You call her. She'll like that."

"I love you, Dad."

"I love you, Matty. I love you with all my heart."

Matt hung up and stared at the phone. He picked up the receiver and called the hospital to talk with Perri. Her brother answered the phone. She was sleeping. He was in touch with a funeral home. He was making arrangements for the burial. The funeral was scheduled for tomorrow. Please come.

Matt took the elevator to the garage and decided to go to a fast-food place down the street for a hamburger, maybe a side order of fries.

II

The car idled through the drive-in of the gaily lit fast-food franchise. Matt opted not to leave the refuge of his car, eating quickly and sloppily in the neon glow of the parking lot. A small import rolled to a stop nearby. Inside, a cute blond and a pudgy guy were sipping sodas.

Questionably fortified, home seemed the destination. But Matt drove past his building when he realized he didn't want to go back up to the hushed apartment. Thoughts of Dave led to a vision of Duka's. It was proposed, debated, and resolved in the space of a block that he'd go have a beer.

The streets were wet and windswept and slick with a dull orange sheet of dead leaves. Driving up 17th Street, Matt slowed before the prominence of the White House and the darkened masses of federal buildings nearby. In this proudly civic setting the idea of running around screaming of conspiracies seemed absurd. Undefined heroic action grew less and less realistic as Matt considered trying to assail these walls.

But when he thought of Dave he grew restless.

Dave was a void that seemed to scream for attention. It seemed like somehow something had to be done. Matt didn't know what. Matt didn't know how.

III

Duka reacted more as if he'd lost a son than a customer. The place was almost crowded, but for five minutes the big man wept openly into an old bar towel, lifting his head only once to moan: "Heart attack, y'say?"

He finally shook his head to stop, straightened with one massive inhale, and then walked down the bar without another word about it.

Matt slid off the stool with his beer. He wound up leaning against the plywood back wall. Smoke and jean jackets and splashes of hair were the view to the swinging front doors. The people here tonight seemed very young, or perhaps Matt felt very old. It crossed his mind that he probably wouldn't be coming here too much anymore.

Matt finished his beer and walked down the narrow dark hall to the bathrooms. He pushed open the door marked M. It was empty. Matt threw the lock. Using the lip of the urinal he pulled himself up to the ceiling tiles and raised the one directly overhead. He peered inside the space—the taped red envelope holding the photographs lay beside a shiny dog tag. Somebody pounded on the flimsy door. Matt almost slipped. He dropped the tile into place and jumped quickly to the ground.

An angry: "C'mon!"

Matt unlocked the door and left looking guiltily down at the floor. Pushing past loud conversations and whispering couples, Matt made his way for the door. He was suddenly tapped on the shoulder. A look back produced a very pretty face—model's features, set in a soft frame of blondish hair. Looked familiar. She was smiling pleasantly but Matt couldn't place her.

"You're Matt, right?"

" . . . Yeah."

Some dim memory made him feel vaguely uneasy, but she really was quite amazingly beautiful. She was probably almost thirty, but quick eyes and a mannish, too-big tweed jacket gave her a little-girl quality, like she'd raided daddy's closet before going out. Matt wanted to like her but something was telling him he shouldn't.

"My name's Leslie. There's someone I'd like you to meet."

A slight southern accent. Maybe an old girlfriend of Dave's? Should he tell her now of his passing? Matt didn't resist when she gently took his arm and led him toward the row of booths.

"Do I know you?" Matt asked over the noise of the bar.

She just looked back and flashed a disabling smile. She took him through the crowd and stopped before a seated, balding, red-faced, chubby man in glasses and a tie. The man was out of place here and knew it, but he smiled broadly when Matt appeared. "Matthew Clarke?"

" . . . Yeah."

"My name's Larry Rosenbaum, senator, New York—glad'a meetcha." The guy was trying too hard to be bar-friendly. He held out a baby-fat hand. "I won't bite."

Matt looked to the girl. She slid into the booth and patted the empty spot outside. Watching them very closely, Matt sat down beside her, facing the man. The guy took a sip of beer and Matt suddenly realized with a start that he recognized both of them, from the neon-lit, fast-food parking lot.

"You're the couple that pulled up beside me in the car!"

Matt fairly leaped out of the booth before the girl could take hold of his arm. Heart pounding, he looked down on the two as if they'd just played an injurious practical joke on him. Both the guy's hands were on the table, which was reassuring, and there were a lot of people in the bar, but Matt was terrified. He was ready to scream for help if they made any fast moves at all.

"Calm down, kid—hold on a sec. Sit down here."

"*I have to go.*"

"Calm down, for cryin' out loud! What're ya so spooked for? All we want to do is talk to you."

Matt continued standing. He glanced around and made sure Duka was in sight just in case.

"My name's Larry Rosenbaum and I really am a senator. This is Leslie Flood, my aide—"

"If you're campaigning or something I'm really not interested."

"We're not campaigning," the woman said impatiently, the smile instantly gone.

"I gotta go," Matt insisted.

"We're your friends, Matt," she said with a warmth that was hard to ignore.

"How'd you know my name?" Matt demanded. "Why are you following me?"

"Sit down and I'll tell you," Rosenbaum proposed.

"No. I'll stand."

"Okay. We wanted to talk to you about something you might have seen . . . something you might have seen recently . . ."

Rosenbaum paused between sentences like an artillery commander zeroing in on a target.

". . . Something you might have seen underwater."

"I don't have any idea what you're talking about," Matt said angrily, eyes darted between the seated pair. The thought of accomplices made him reel and scan the other patrons in the bar.

"Are you okay?" Leslie asked.

"Listen, you are Matthew Clarke, aren't you?" said Rosenbaum. "I mean, can't you just sit down and talk with us? This could be very important. We've been trying to reach Dave Lakeman all day but there's been no answer at his—"

"Dave's dead," Matt said bitterly, his tone flatly implying that he believed they might be responsible for it.

"Dead! But how—"

Matt didn't hear the question because he was practically running by the time he hit the swinging doors.

IV

By all rights Matt should have been killed. Horribly. It happened this way:

Matt left the Cloverleaf shaken by the encounter with the pudgy guy and the beautiful girl. All the way home he kept checking his rearview mirror to see if he was being followed. He probably should have been paying more attention to the road and most certainly can be faulted for not wearing a seatbelt, especially considering the wet road conditions, but he got back to the Kingman Arms without any problems whatsoever.

Matt brought the car down the short concrete ramp that led to the parking garage. He drove too fast all the way to the rear where his space was, passed over a slick patch of dripped oil, and parked without incident. Still anxious about being approached in the bar, Matt looked around the well-lit underground garage before getting out of the car—even rolling down the window and listening for strange noises. The car was still running and carbon monoxide began building up, but not nearly enough to cause any harm.

The garage seemed empty. Satisfied, Matt locked up the car and walked to the elevator, passing directly below a water pipe that had been improperly mounted to the ceiling, which didn't fall, though someday it might if not attended to.

It was quiet down here. A soothing patter of rain rolled through the large garage portal that opened onto the street. Matt tapped his foot while he waited. There was only one elevator that went to the garage and it was slow. A rattle of movement heralded its arrival and the doors finally parted open. Matt didn't step in until he was sure it was empty of men with guns. He pressed 10, the top floor, and the doors crawled closed.

The Kingman Arms was a modern high-rise apartment complex that tried desperately to convey in décor the boldness of spirit so lacking in its design. The floor of the elevator was covered with extremely durable carpet of a daringly loud leopardskin pattern. Every inch of wall, including the inner face of the doors, was audaciously graced with mirror, creating the nauseating effect of being in a tiny, vertically moving funhouse. The actual ceiling was hidden by what looked to be grated black steel but was actually rather brittle plastic.

The doors closed and the elevator had just begun ascending when everything abruptly stopped with a mechanical groan.

The lights suddenly went out.

". . . Shit—" Matt stood in the darkness and ran a hand through his hair, more indignant than concerned.

"C'mon!"

It wasn't moving. Matt gave the errant machine a few more seconds to correct itself and then, fumbling in the dark, found the protruding emergency button and pressed it. There was a sudden, ominous *whoosh* below and around the elevator, and the whole thing shivered delicately.

"Hey!" Matt yelled.

A dull-orange glow suddenly shot through the blackness. In a dozen identically reflected elevators, Matt could see smoke start wisping up through the corners of the floor where the carpet met the walls.

"Fire! *Fire!*" Matt yelled. His voice sounded weak, and he yelled it twice more at the top of his lungs. He started pressing every button on the panel—CLOSE DOOR, OPEN DOOR, floors 1 through 10—but he gave up when he saw they had no effect.

In that brief time the smoke had started to accumulate in a warm, hazy layer near the ceiling. Matt kicked the door, lightly at first so as not to damage the fragile-looking mirror, and then hard when the enormous gravity of the situation sank in. A dangerous cloud was filling the space. He, and the frantic reflected Matt facing him, tried to cram their fingers into the pencil-thin space where the doors met, but they were solidly closed and not about to open between floors.

Matt started to shout.

Bellowed *Help!* and *Fire!* quickly deteriorated into incoherent screaming and shrieking. He realized with no small surprise that he was banging his fists wildly against the door and slamming from one mirrored wall to the next like a terrified animal at the instant it realizes it's been trapped. Glimpses of other Matts reeling in the same orange glow made him feel as if he were watching the horror from outside himself.

What drew Matt back to reality was the heat—at first from below and then from all around him like an oven. Black sooty smoke began streaking the mirrors, closing him off from the other burning elevators around him.

The sudden acidic taste of angry fumes made him leap to the ceiling and grab at the decorative grating. The whole panel ripped off like it had been taped on, and Matt landed in a pile on the floor. Here it was so hot that Matt couldn't believe the carpeting hadn't ignited yet. Holding his breath against the dense chemical reek, he staggered to a standing position.

Matt stood there. The only thought he had was that he was suffocating. He had to breathe but he couldn't. The air was thick with poisons, and the result was a hacking that made him lean against one of the walls for support. The mirror burned the side of this face when it touched. The elevator, he realized, was suspended over some kind of fire, like a bucket over a well. He had to close his tearing eyes tight against the burning. Being blind was more frightening than not being able to breathe. His legs felt like they were on fire and he started jumping and ripping at his clothes. He tried to scream but was denied air for the task.

Doubled over and eyes closed, Matt's mind began spinning faster and faster and then something in his head exploded and he followed the stars into nothingness.

V

The next thing Matt was aware of was that he was coughing. Everything was black. He opened his mattered eyes and discerned a faceless crowd of people moving all around. Gradually his vision began to clear and he saw he was outside and it was night and he was lying on a stretcher.

A confused chorus of sirens was wailing all around. Matt blinked away the bluriness and a huge dark shape stretched before him like a giant pool. After a moment, he realized he was looking up at the Kingman Arms building from right outside the front entrance. Someone was taking his blood pressure and didn't seem overly interested in the fact Matt had just regained consciousness.

He suddenly turned to his side and vomited. Immediately someone was wiping his face. They lifted the stretcher and loaded it in the shiny bright back of an ambulance.

Matt felt almost fine by the time he got to the hospital. A cute Filipino nurse gently washed out his eyes and cleaned his face and hands and after a quick examination by a serious young doctor he was told he could go.

A policeman was there to take Matt's statement. Matt described what had happened but was more interested in how he'd been saved.

Two men, it seems, had been waiting for the elevator in the lobby. They smelled smoke and heard yelling. Unable to pry the sliding doors open by hand, they'd frantically searched the foyer for something to use as a wedge. The doorman had come up with a screwdriver, which proved woefully inadequate for the job. Finally, the leg of a wrought iron chair in the lobby had done the trick. The two had jumped down the few feet to the elevator roof, and, with smoke swirling up the shaft, they kicked in the elevator's ceiling-hatch cover. The hatch broke off and struck Matt in the head. One man jumped inside, handed Matt up to his friend, and together they got him into the lobby.

The cop said something about an electrical fire when Matt asked him how it started. He suggested Matt might want to consider taking the two men out to dinner sometime in repayment for saving his life. He gave Matt their names.

It was past midnight when the cop took Matt back to the apartment building. The police radio crackled with code numbers and street addresses as they drove. Matt felt safe in the front seat with the uniformed policeman and was disappointed when they arrived at the Kingman Arms.

The fire trucks and crowd were gone. Two white vans were now parked directly out front. The cop drove off and Matt walked inside the lobby where a half-dozen workmen were fussing with the charred elevator. The smell of smoke was heavy here. A sign apologized but residents would temporarily have to take the stairs. Matt walked up to a precise-looking man in spotless white coveralls and said he was the one who had been trapped inside.

"Lucky lucky lucky! Hey, Frank—this is the guy what was stuck in the lift!"

A soot-streaked face sporting safety goggles popped up from the open elevator doors. The rest of him must have been standing on the still stuck elevator roof. He looked Matt over and simply shook his head. The goggles popped back out of sight.

"How'd it happen?" Matt asked the man.

" 'Lectrical fire."

"But what started it? Exactly."

"Ain't no exactly about it. Was a couple things. Wiring in the panel shorted you to a stop. Best we figure, sparks dropped onto the garbage that collects at the bottom these shafts. Bingo—you got a fire."

"So the wiring was exposed?"

"Tough 'ta say. New elevator, ya know. Somebody maybe left sumthin' off on the assembly line. Maybe the installers don't do the job right. Wouldn't be the first time. Gonna take awhile to pin down."

"Can't you tell if somebody tampered with it?"

"I don't follow," the man said.

"Was somebody responsible for causing this?"

"The garbage in the shaft—at's the building's fault."

"No, what I mean is, it seemed to start the second I pressed the emergency button, like a *whoosh*. Could somebody have done this on purpose? You know, set it up to happen so it looked like an accident?"

The guy frowned. "I'm just a repairman, Bud."

"I'm asking if someone could have done this on purpose," Matt pressed.

"You talk to the fire marshals with questions like that, not me," he said uneasily. "They'll be here bright and early in the morning. You talk to them about that. Really. I'm just a repairman."

"It's vital I know what—"

"Like I say, you're a lucky son of a gun just to be alive. 'Scuse me, got work to do."

Matt left the lobby and began the long ten-story walk up to his apartment. He didn't mind relying on his legs. Even if the mirrored elevator had been working again, you'd have had to put a gun to his head to get him to take it.

Chapter Twenty

Heading east, the night fell fast. It was dark out now, and the green-and-silver Greyhound bus was speeding mightily down Interstate 80 toward the orange background glow of Salt Lake City.

Except for two widely spaced cones of light, one over an anxious young Morman man coming home after two years of missionary work in Japan, and the other illuminating the glossy pages of a teenage girl's glamour magazine, the bus was dark.

Orin sat in the second to last seat in back, where the dark was thickest, staring out the window. He wore a new Stetson and a suit and tie and heavy black shoes, and if you'd sat down beside him he would have happily drawled that his name was Charles Scott, rancher and damn proud of it, heading east to visit his younger brother Bob who sold insurance in Washington, D.C.

But the bus was half empty and nobody took the seat to hear the tale.

The door opened on a cool and cloudy night in Salt Lake City. Orin filed down the aisle with his fellow passengers and gave his hearty rancher thanks to the driver for a job well done.

Inside was a standard bus terminal equipped with the standard wooden benches and standard sprawled transients and standard out-of-order vending machines and even the standard lone, spiffy Army private proudly heading home for first leave.

Orin passed straight through with the shoulder-first gait of Charles Scott, the rancher. He climbed into a very clean taxi waiting outside the building, and he was driven the short distance to the Salt Lake City airport.

The airport's dozen terminals were aligned along an access ramp that stretched more than half a mile. Orin had the cab driver drop him off at the first of the buildings to find out which airline had the next flight to Washington, D.C.

In this terminal, a rival ticket agent whispered that United had a nonstop leaving in forty-five minutes. Orin slurred a "Thank'ee," tipped his hat, and walked out.

Half the terminal buildings were bunched together at the far end of the access ramp, but between the first of them, from which Orin had just departed, and the next, there was an unlit empty stretch of a few hundred feet.

He started walking down the road, breathing in the cool night air. Salt Lake City spread flatly out around him like a dinner setting on a tabletop. In the distance rose a ring of black mountains.

A car whizzed by, its taillights receding in the distance. An instant later it happened.

The lights of the next terminal were nearing. A sudden brush of gravel from behind. A sliver of glint. Orin instantly pivoted and the knife intended for his kidney instead punched a half-inch deep gouge into the thick of his waist.

Orin flexed to speed his spin and his whipping left fist caught in the soft part of the figure's throat, stopping the rotation. Orin brought in a shattering right on the counterturn and almost succeeded in removing the man's nose.

He glimpsed a bloody face as the body thudded off the graveled shoulder of the road. The man who killed Mark!

Immediately, Orin grabbed the man's belt with his right hand and the lapels of the man's shirt with his left and lifted with a sudden, wild energy. Before the man could react, Orin had him suspended at chest-level. He heaved the man down upon the three-foot-high metal ramp that lined the roadway and heard an audible *crack* as the body hit.

The figure went limp across the sharp-edged fulcrum it had been hurled upon.

Orin pulled the man's chest up so that his head wasn't against the ground.

"Who are you! Who sent you!"

A bloody face was smiling at him . . . actually smiling.

"Who are you!"

"You broke . . . my back," the man managed in a French accent. "I can't . . . feel . . . a thing—"

"Who are you working for!"

After twenty years of constant torture, Remy LeClerc was finally free of pain. He couldn't feel a thing below his neck. The tremendous agony that had so long racked his back was totally gone. His joy was colossal. Thanks to the man holding him off the metal road ramp he had, once and for all, triumphed over pain.

"Merci—"

And poor Orin, greatly confused, was suddenly supporting a smiling dead man.

A vehicle was approaching. Orin quickly dragged the body down the embankment and into a thick stand of scrub. He rifled the man's pockets and ripped out the jacket lining to be sure there was nothing hidden. After five minutes of searching, Orin's efforts had produced a scrap of paper bearing a phone number and a half-empty bottle of Percodan with what looked to be a French prescription.

He looked down at the body. Orin figured the guy had trailed him from the time he'd left the house that morning in the truck. The guy had probably been itching for the right moment to finish him off. He must have followed Orin to the Sacramento parking lot, watched Orin hot-wire the Town Car, decided because of others there that he'd have to wait, and then covered him to Sparks. Trailing the bus to Salt Lake would have been a breeze.

The guy had been waiting for just the right moment to make his move. He didn't wait long enough.

III

Pacing his apartment, the reluctant hero resolved it was finally time to act. Indecision and uncertainty were roughly cast aside. Forged in the heat of an elevator fire came a new and shining battle plan—attack!

Under the circumstances it seemed the only course left.

Matt had fought tooth and nail to avoid reaching a chilling, but obvious, conclusion. He'd entertained every possible explanation of recent events that might rule out foul play. But he was now firmly convinced that someone, or some group of people, or maybe even some sinister arm of the government, was trying to kill him.

Matt wasn't exactly sure what it was he was going to do. He hadn't quite figured out whose aid he would enlist or the means with which he'd tell the world his story. But come tomorrow he was going to do something—something big and bold and dramatic.

The only obstacle was surviving the night.

After changing his still smoky clothes, Matt began booby-trapping the apartment front door. Let them come, whoever they were. Just walk right in—a determined Matthew S. Clarke was ready and waiting to greet you.

Like a man possessed, Matt tore through a cluttered closet to locate an extension cord. He began running the long cord around the couch but the endtable was in the way. Kneeling down to get a grip on one of the legs, he spotted what seemed to be a thin wire peeking out from beneath the table's base.

Matt got on his knees for a closer look. Yes, it was definitely a very thin strand of wire. Matt peered under the table. The wire was connected to a small black disk the size of a dime. A piece of clear tape held the thing in place.

A radio bug.

Someone had come into this apartment when he'd been out—maybe even when he'd been sleeping!—and taped this thing under the table.

Matt froze.

His heroic mien collapsed in the presence of the tiny bug, and he was plunged once more into a storm of fear; coherent thought lost. *Why, only hours earlier he'd almost been killed. It was the dead of night. He was alone in his apartment, too scared to sleep or even think clearly, laying a booby trap to thwart what could be a legion of murderers, and he'd just found a radio bug right in the middle of his living room!*

It took everything in Matt's power to force himself to slowly back away from the small black bug and retreat into the bathroom and lock the door.

Fifteen minutes crawled by as only time can when it's night and you're terrified.

Finally, Matt reentered the living room. A braver act he'd never done. He left the tiny transmitter where it was, silently circling it as if it were a venomous insect capable of leaping twenty feet, and after several deep breaths he cautiously resumed his task.

Matt ran the extension cord across the living room to the apartment's locked front door. He cut off one end and separated and stripped the two sides of the cord to reveal the shiny copper wire within. With trembling hands, Matt carefully taped the exposed wires to the inside doorknob. He unlocked the front door.

Matt walked lightly to the back of the living room and positioned a heavy chair to face the front door some thirty feet away. Behind the Naugahyde barrier the extension cord's plug lay inches from an outlet.

Matt placed the phone on the floor nearby, in case he had to call for help. As an afterthought, he tiptoed to the bedroom and took a speargun from the duffel bag that held his scuba gear.

Matt came back in a crouch, surveyed his defenses, and turned off the lights. He crawled to the command post behind the chair and began waiting.

Sitting in the darkness, one hand near the electric cord's plug, the other clutching the speargun, Matt's senses had never been more finely tuned. He gradually became aware of every sound and shadow.

Too aware.

Matt started to see things after several exhausting hours of keeping his bloodshot eyes riveted to the outline of the door. Threatening shapes began to move stealthily through the darkened room. Shadowy figures started creeping silently around the apartment, coming to get him. The slightest noise became the footfall of a killer. Wide-eyed and panicky, hiding behind the chair, Matt became convinced he'd be shot if he moved. He was absolutely certain someone had somehow gotten into the dark apartment. It was only because the phantoms darted so quickly and noiselessly that he held back firing the long-shaft spear.

Day broke eternities later. The weak light of a cloudy morning gradually drove the apparitions from the room. But a tense and sleepless night had taken its toll. Matt felt like crying. He wanted to roll around on the floor, kicking and screaming, crying his eyes out and banging his fists on the floor. He wondered if he was losing his mind.

Still he waited, watching the front door. It was near seven in the morning. If the killers were going to make a move, now would be as good a time as any. They got Dave yesterday morning, Matt reminded himself. No time was safe. No place was safe. No one was safe. Who knows what they'd try next—whoever they were—or when they'd try it.

It appeared he had made it through the night.

As the minutes ticked by and the light grew stronger, Matt began to worry about what he would do next. He couldn't stay in his apartment forever, yet the thought of leaving terrified him.

He'd be killed as soon as he stepped outside. That is, if there really was anybody trying to kill him. But there had to be! Yet he couldn't be absolutely sure.

His nerves were shot and he was sure about nothing. Suddenly it seemed stupid to be sitting behind a chair waiting for an early morning visit by an imagined killer. Examined with a cold hard eye, there was, in fact, no actual physical proof that his life really was in danger.

But what about Dave's death? Well, the doctor was positive it had been a heart attack.

So what about the elevator fire? Repairman said it was a short.

How about the bug? He did work for the NSA—maybe it was just a security precaution.

Why not just call the police? But he couldn't. There was nothing concrete to support his theory. Besides, he'd been raised to believe in the system. His parents, his father, had drummed that into his head from the first—that he lived in a great, just, and glorious land—not like where they were born. It was one of the reasons he'd worked for the NSA in the first place.

But someone's trying to kill me!

He *was* going crazy.

A light knock at the front door sounded like an explosion to Matt's highly sensitive ears. They'd come! He lunged for the extension-cord plug and held it a fraction of an inch from the socket. The speargun was balanced atop the back of the chair, Matt's finger a millimeter away from the trigger.

Another knock at the door, this time more insistent. Go ahead! Open the door . . . it's unlocked . . . just step through the door . . .

A third knock, this time two solid raps. The door suddenly swung open. Matt jammed the plug into the socket. The speargun seemed to fire by itself. He ducked behind the chair and heard a soft *thud* as the yard-long spear buried itself in something across the room.

A pause, and then a downright cheerful voice called out: "Hello—anybody home?"

What trick was this?

A sunny: "Good morning . . ."

Ever so slowly, Matt peeked out from around the chair. There, in the half-open doorway, stood a smiling man in a dark blue suit wearing what looked to be a policeman's black-billed hat. He had a red face and a thick red mustache. He was heavy. He was holding a clipboard. Some sort of badge hung from his breast pocket. Matt leaned around the chair and watched the man use his clipboard to further push open the door. The man wasn't even touching the electrified doorknob.

"Hello," the man called out again in a friendly tone. "Anybody home? Your door's open!"

His view blocked by the half-open door, the jolly visitor was ignorant to the still quivering speargun bolt firmly embedded in the opposite wall.

Matt slowly stood up from behind the chair.

The man squinted in the dimness to see him. "Good morning!" he called with a smile.

". . . Yes?" Matt asked numbly, clutching the spent speargun in his right hand.

"I'm the fire marshal inspecting that elevator fire last night. Came up to talk with ya if I may. Your door was open. Repairman downstairs said you had some questions."

The man brought the clipboard down to his side and was about to lean on the still charged door handle. Matt dropped from sight and pulled the extension cord plug out just in time. He leaped back up.

The fire marshal noticed the speargun.

". . . Maybe I'll just come back another time," he muttered, backing away.

"No!" Matt cried. "Stay—please! I mean, I do have questions. I've got lots and lots of questions!"

III

Thursday. The rain was gone but the dawn broke bleak and gray over Washington, D.C. It was only just six thirty and most of the city was still asleep. At empty intersections, swaying traffic lights dutifully changed from green to yellow to red and then back again. The Potomac flowed black and choppy below the formal white rows of headstones of Arlington Cemetery.

In this gloomy morning's half-light, a long black limousine sped importantly down uncrowded Pennsylvania Avenue. Through Washington Circle it gently slowed, as if carrying eggs, then smoothly accelerated on its way.

Ellis silently drove the route to 24 Street. In the mirror he caught a glimpse of the Old Man. Hunched and lost in the enormity of the backseat, Claude Screws seemed like a child being driven to day school. Ellis felt sorry for him but didn't say it.

He'd expressed concern only once, after Screws's second visit, and gotten a "Keep your damn nose out of it!" for his trouble.

The limo rolled to a stop outside the doctor's office. Screws mumbled a curt, "Wait'ere."

Dr. Clay had evidently just arrived himself, because he was hanging up his overcoat when Screws, hat in hand, stepped into the empty waiting room.

"Mornin'," Screws grumbled as he slid off his coat and laid it on one of the room's idle chairs.

"Good morning, Claude," Dr. Clay responded pleasantly. "I know you're busy today. Why don't you just follow me on back."

Dr. Clay had achieved that aura of infinite patience and compassion that comes with a lifetime of treating the sick. A gilt-edged quality of peacefulness accompanied his every movement and word. He was a snow-haired sixty, with clear blue eyes and a face given to unblinking stillness. Tall and solid, he moved through this world slowly and deliberately, performing his work with unflagging thoroughness.

The nurse had yet to come in and the reception area and hallway and dreaded examination rooms were all silent and dark. Screws obediently trailed Dr. Clay back to his wood-paneled inner office. A desk light came to life.

"Have a seat, Claude."

Screws lowered himself into the high-backed, red leather chair positioned opposite the doctor's unadorned desk. While Dr. Clay carefully adjusted the room thermostat, Screws took in the familiar details of the spartan office: four framed diplomas, three shelves of heavy medical books, two wall-mounted opaque screens waiting to illuminate x-rays, one phone, and a single, rather small photo of his wife and children.

Dr. Clay went behind his desk. He sat. His hands gradually came together and folded upon the desk's green blotter top. Lifting his chin slightly, Dr. Clay regarded the seventy-eight-year-old man sitting across from him.

"How are you feeling today, Claude?"

"Shitty."

"I'm sorry to hear that."

"Why'd I come otherwise?"

"And over the last few weeks, since I saw you last?"

"Pretty bad, thank you."

Dr. Clay nodded thoughtfully at Screws's response. He carefully formulated another question and asked it slowly: ". . . Claude, would you say you're feeling worse today than you were the last time you came in?"

"Worse, better—I have a meeting in twenty minutes. Get to the point."

"Shall we say worse?"

"Say it."

These next queries came gingerly, as if just asking them might cause the patient pain:

". . . Bleeding from the gums?"

Screws nodded.

". . . Fatigue, perhaps?"

"Drop the 'perhaps.' "

". . . Persistent fever . . . loss of appetite—"

"Yes, yes, and yes—jump to the last page!"

Dr. Clay paused. ". . . It's not good, Claude. It's not at all good."

"There! Now we know what it's not."

"I want to schedule you for a test, Claude—a bone marrow test—as soon as possible."

"Just tell me what I have."

"I'm not absolutely certain."

"The results from the blood test?"

"I want to make absolutely certain."

"But you have some idea."

"I do have an idea."

"I pay your outrageous fees to share such information!"

"Claude . . ."

Dr. Clay blinked. Screws knew then he was in trouble.

"Well, go on!"

"There's a possibility," Dr. Clay went on, "a very strong possibility, that you have a rare form of cancer." Here his hands slowly unfolded and tactfully disappeared behind the desk, as if Dr. Clay wanted nothing, at this tragic moment, between him and his patient.

"A rare form of cancer?"

"That's correct."

"And what would that be?"

". . . Acute myelogenous leukemia."

"I'm dying? Well? Just say it!"

"We'll take this step by step, together, starting with a bone marrow—"

"No! No more tests! If you're going through the motions for my benefit, don't! And don't give me that *look*. There any treatment for this thing?"

"We'll certainly try chemotherapy—"

"The chances there—good or bad? The truth, damn you!"

". . . Not good."

"How long then?"

"That I can't say."

"Can't or won't?"

Dr. Clay relented: "Statistically not long, Claude. But I'd love you to prove them wr—"

"Can it." Screws pushed himself from the chair. "You're a good doctor and I'm a lousy patient. Let's just leave it at that."

"I won't lie to you, Claude. It's going to get very uncomfortable. Very grim. You're going to need care. You're going to need a lot of care and you're going to need it soon."

Screws was fumbling for something in his suit pockets, pretending not to hear the words.

Dr. Clay slowly stood. "This is one fight that you're going to have to let others help you with. Now I want you to call me this afternoon, Claude, so we can schedule this bone marrow test tomor—"

Screws violently shook his head.

"Then you tell me what to do."

"Just keep this to yourself."

The mere suggestion otherwise seemed to wound Dr. Clay: "I wouldn't tell a soul, Claude."

Screws turned and went out. Dr. Clay trailed him down the dark hallway. In the reception room he stood nearby, ready to help Screws don his overcoat, but Screws insisted he be left alone.

Screws was reaching for the doorknob, about to go, when a last question stopped him dead in his tracks.

"I meant to ask you, Claude—have you ever been in contact with or been exposed to high levels of radiation?"

"*Why?*" Screws demanded. "Why did you ask me that?"

". . . Exposure to high levels of radiation is a particular cause of this type of cancer. I wondered if perhaps you'd had such an incident in your lifetime?"

Had such an incident? Such as standing on the bridge of a Navy flagship to observe one of the largest aboveground atomic blasts ever? Such as doing so at a time when nobody knew a damn thing about fallout? Such as blithely boarding a still smoking test vessel anchored near ground-zero to see firsthand the military applications of atomic warfare? Such as remaining in the nuclear test area for a week afterward while a disabled Soviet submarine was secretly rid of its dead crew and eight Americans flown in as replacements?

Could the seeds of this fatal disease have been planted thirty years ago in the South Pacific—during that one week? The irony of it almost made Screws physically ill.

"You're pale, Claude—"

"Mind your own business!" Screws shouted. He practically ran from the office to flee Dr. Clay and his immensely compassionate gaze.

IV

Seydoux lay in bed, worrying.

His son's wedding was less than eight days, and a myriad of tasks, away. A breaking scandal involving the illegal sale of fissionable material to Iraq was creating a major headache for the administration back home. It was just seven in the morning, and in two hours Seydoux had to lead an important trade briefing for a business delegation of some twenty-five visiting French automakers.

But Seydoux was unable to concentrate on any of these things.

LeClerc was past overdue on calling. Far past due.

Last night Seydoux had waited three agonizing hours for LeClerc's call at a predetermined pay phone situated in a gargantuan mall in Alexandria. It was one of those deluxe versions of the species: with an anemic waterfall dribbling down fiberglass rocks in the central atrium; an upper level boasting a bastardized selection of ethnic foods from around the world; and a truly depressing array of garishly dressed and questionably raised young adults tramping the cavernous corridors in search of a sale or mate.

For three hours, Seydoux had anxiously awaited LeClerc's call, shooing away over-made-up teenage girls and under-shaved teenage boys insisting, quite rudely, that they had to use the phone. For three hours, he'd been forced to stand in the shadows of the phone booth, directly opposite the head-splitting sound effects coming from a monstrous video arcade.

But LeClerc had never called.

At the end of it—after three gut-wrenching hours of waiting for the call that never came—Seydoux had been roughly ordered to leave by a pimply security guard informing him the mall was closing, at which time he was unceremoniously swept out the main entrance with a tide bearing the dregs of the day's mall addicts.

Seydoux had spent an anguished night in bed with his wife; she sleeping peacefully, he worriedly staring at the ceiling.

If LeClerc had failed or been apprehended—

The thought was too chilling to contemplate, but too distinct a possibility to ignore.

Seydoux drifted into a strange state of unrest. The minutes ticked by and he found himself carried back to a dreamy, distant period in his life when he actually believed in things. It was long ago, when he'd been young. All that was left now was a pang.

Seydoux was suddenly consumed by a tremendous rush of self-pity. He almost, uncharacteristically, cried.

Wondering about LeClerc's whereabouts had consumed

Seydoux's night, and now, in the morning, it looked as if it would consume his day as well.

Seydoux lay in bed, a dim, gray light creeping through the blinds, worrying.

V

Vanning crossed his legs and chose to look out the tinted windows of the moving limo rather than face Screws during the ensuing briefing:

"There's been a number of developments. Good and bad. Dave Lakeman, one of the two who found the submarine, died of a heart attack yesterday."

A grunt of approval from Screws.

"The other one, Matthew Clarke, almost died in an 'elevator accident' last night. But for the timely aide of two good samaritans, he would no longer be alive."

Vanning turned from the window and began watching his right index finger run up and down the sharp crease of his crossed pants leg. He nervously resumed: "As you know, Ford Hulse killed himself yesterday. You didn't tell me you were going to see him, Claude. Going to see him was a big mis—"

"How'd he do it?" Screws suddenly asked.

"What?"

"Kill himself. How?"

Vanning was momentarily caught off guard by the question. ". . . Pistol shot to the forehead."

"Oh."

Vanning stopped himself from looking over at Screws. This next would be hard enough without his icy glare.

"Anyway, as I was saying, I could've told you that it was a mistake to see him, Claude—a big mistake. You pushed him over the edge—"

"I was hoping it would. That's why I went. He's out of the picture now."

". . . Not quite."

"What d'you mean?"

"Senator Rosenbaum and an aide were observed meeting with Matthew Clarke last night in a—"

"*Rosenbaum!*"

"Let me finish. Ford must have called him before he committed suicide. God knows what he told. Now I don't know what you said to him, Claude, but you really must have pushed him right over—"

"You're the one responsible for this! You, Leonard! Any idiot would've known better than to contact him in the first place! I was conducting damage control!"

"Apparently," Vanning continued quietly, "Rosenbaum and this aide met with Clarke last night in a bar. They followed him there. From what I understand, the conversation between them lasted a matter of seconds. Clarke left the bar looking scared."

"This aide a woman?"

"Yes, as a matter of fact she was."

"I'll handle Rosenbaum from my end. What else?"

Vanning was going to ask how, then decided against it. If Screws said he'd handle it, it would get handled, and quickly.

"Orin Marsh, the one who rent—"

"I know who he is."

"He's disappeared. There's a warrant out for his arrest for the murder of his nephew. We can only hope that LeClerc is still on his trail."

Screws shifted uncomfortably in the seat. "Can't you send one of your boys out there to—"

"If I had the manpower I would, Claude."

"This is a priority thing here!"

"As if Clarke isn't?"

"Well what about this Clarke? The one that survived the accident. He's the biggest threat."

"Today. Probably this afternoon. Gunshot, stabbing—my man'll try to make it look like a robbery if he can, but if not, it'll just be one more unsolved murder in Washington, D.C. As soon as he's out of the picture, I'll put my men on this Marsh guy . . ."

Vanning glanced at the old man for a reaction. Screws was

staring at the black partition, mind somewhere other than in the car.

"I guess that's it for now, eh, Claude?"

". . . What? Yes, that's it," Screws muttered.

He found the partition button and lowered the tinted shield of glass a fraction of an inch.

"Stop at the corner," he instructed Ellis.

The partition came back up. A moment later the car came to a stop. Vanning didn't want to wait for the driver to open the door and swung it open himself.

"Leonard—"

Vanning looked back over his shoulder.

"What was it that Hulse was dying of?" Screws suddenly asked.

Vanning regarded him curiously. "Ford? What Ford was dying of?"

"Yes."

"Well," said Vanning, "I thought you knew. Leukemia."

Chapter Twenty-one

The muted roar of take-offs and landings faded in the distance as the cab left the airport and took the highway to town. The man wanted for murder sat in the back, silently suffering the physical discomfort of a knife wound and the trying chatter of a talkative cabbie.

In a way the cabbie was worse.

"Nice hat. Whatcha here for, Cowboy—bizness or pleasure?" The cabbie's fast eyes studied Orin in the mirror.

"Business."

"I figured sumthin' like that 'cause a the no bags. Unusual to travel with no bags. Don't see it too often, least I don't anyways. Once in awhile maybe but not too much."

The taxi pounded into a pothole and bounced wildly for several seconds afterward, like a boat going over waves. Orin clenched his teeth. He looked down at his side to make sure blood hadn't started seeping through his shirt again.

The bandage of cocktail napkins, Saran Wrap, and duct tape seemed to be doing its job, but the puncture to his right side was throbbing angrily. Without the bottle of Percodan he'd rifled from the dead man's pockets last night, that hole in the road would have made him scream.

"Sorry 'bout that. Keep tellin' the guy who owns this rig to get new shocks—get new shocks I told him and I'm talkin' like a year ago—but still nothin'. Jerk owes me fifty bucks from tires, too."

Orin gave the universal half smile of forced interest. The cabbie seemed fascinated by the big man in the back seat with the Stetson and clenched jaw. His eyes spent more time watching Orin through the mirror than on the road.

"You was on 244 from Salt Lake, right?"

"What?"

"Flight 244. You was on it. Musta been. See, there's only three flights come in here from between six forty-five and seven o-five in the morning, which it is now. One's a Pan Am from London, one's the Eastern shuttle outa N.Y., and the third's United in from Salt Lake. You didn't have to claim no bags so you probably went through like a shot. I'm guessin' you came in from Salt Lake. I right, Cowboy?"

"If you say so."

"No bags from Salt Lake . . ." the cabbie repeated into the mirror, as if it could well be the most astounding thing in the world. "What kinda bizness you say you were in?"

"I didn't say."

"So what kind you in?"

"My own business," Orin said coldly.

The cabbie either didn't pick up on, or chose to ignore, Orin's unfriendly tone: "Most people, even if it's just one night, carry a briefcase or a little bag, but you got nothin'. I saw that right away. Not even a toothbrush. And you're tired, I saw that, too. I see all these things. I'm observant. Tired comes from no sleep and movin' around in a big—"

"What's the point?" Orin suddenly asked, cutting the cabbie off.

"No point, mister. No point at all."

"Then shut up and drive."

The cabbie regarded Orin for several moments through the mirror and then lifted his shoulders in a tremendous shrug.

He forced himself to watch the road for a hundred feet and

then, like nothing had happened, went back to looking at Orin.
". . . You said the Smithsonian, right?"

The cabbie continued to stare. Orin tried looking out the
window.

"Gotta know where I'm going, pal."

"Smithsonian," Orin was forced to concede.

"Not open yet, ya know. You know that?"

Orin crossed his arms and looked straight ahead.

"Guess ya knew. Which you want? You want I should drop
you off at the Air and Space or the Smithsonian?"

He didn't wait for an answer.

"Kinda funny a guy coming all the way from Salt Lake just
to go to the Smithsonian. Guess you got bizness in that area
though, huh? You're a big guy, ain't ya? I'm lookin' in the
mirror and I see one big guy. One big tired guy from outa town
without even a little tiny bag—without even a toothbrush or
nothin'—going to the Smithsonian before it opens. If I hada
suspicious brain I'd be curious about you."

"Unfortunately for both of us you've got no br—"

Orin stopped in midsentence. The cabbie had just flipped
open a small black leather case bearing a bright silver police
badge and was holding it over his shoulder for Orin to
see.

"Me? I got the two worst jobs in the world—I'm a cop and a
cabbie on my hours off. What was you sayin'?"

The rest of the ride was torture.

The cabbie had no intention of arresting Orin or anything of
the kind, though that course might have been preferable. Flashing the police badge merely ensured an attentive audience while
he asked inane questions and yapped infuriatingly about any
scrap of an idea that blew through his mind.

Pulling up to the Smithsonian twenty long and boring miles
later: "Here ya go, Charlie. Your rancher friends call you
Charles or Charlie? I asked you that already, didn't I? It's
Charlie. Sorry, Charlie—ha! Wanna receipt?"

Orin threw the fare money, which he'd been squeezing in his
fist for most of the ride, into the front seat and bolted from the
cab.

II

The only reason Orin had asked to be dropped off at the Smithsonian was because he knew it was in the middle of town.

A thick, misting rain hung low over the city, and except for a few early morning joggers, the Mall was empty at this hour. Orin ignored the sights—the Lincoln Monument and Reflecting Pool and the White House and Capitol Hill—and started walking. His game plan was simple: find a phone, buy a map, get a car, track down Stocky and Skinny.

Ten minutes passed before he found a phone in a long, narrow, greasy spoon of a coffee shop. Pale yellow light bulbs set in the ceiling struggled against a permanent haze of grill exhaust, cigarette smoke, and steam. An oily film seemed to coat every exposed surface, from the seats to the food. Crammed at the counter were people late for work, one more hostile and withdrawn than the next, carving a minute from their day to inhale eggs and coffee. The constant splatter of sizzling grease and rapid-fire orders barked from the waitresses to the cook lent a stomach-churning anxiety to the scene.

Standing in the back, observing it all in the relative quiet of a beat-up phone booth, Orin remembered why he'd decided fifteen years ago to live in the isolated beauty of northern California.

Orin took a scrap of paper from his wallet and laid it on the dented triangular metal shelf that jutted beneath the phone. It was the scrap of paper he'd found on the man he'd killed last night. On it was a phone number with a 703 area code.

What Orin couldn't get out of his mind was the man's dying smile and last words: *"Merci."*

Orin had spent all night on the plane trying to figure that one out, and got nothing but a headache for his trouble.

There was one obvious possible connection that Orin checked first. He called information and asked for the phone number of David Lakeman, 16 Garfield Drive. The operator gave him the number. Lakeman's phone number and the one on the scrap of paper didn't match. Not even the same area code. Orin dialed information a second time, and learned the 703 preceding the phone number on the scrap of paper was the area code for northern Virginia.

There went the obvious connection.

This didn't mean the guy hadn't been working for Stocky and Skinny—not at all. It just wasn't the same number as this guy Lakeman's.

In Orin's book, Stocky and Skinny were still the ones responsible for Mark's death and would be dealt with accordingly.

Orin dropped a quarter in the slot and dialed the number he'd taken off the dead man. He didn't know what he'd say if somebody answered.

The phone rang once . . . twice . . . three times . . . four times—someone picked up.

Strange, electronic noises could be heard in the background.

"Hello—" came a young man's voice.

Orin remained quiet, listening.

"I'm gonna hang up if you don't answer me . . ." followed by a laugh. Orin concentrated on the noises in the background. Video games?

"Where have I reached?" Orin suddenly asked.

"Where?" repeated the young voice on the other end of the line.

"Yes. Where have I called?"

"This is the Alexandria Mall, dude—where else would it be?"

III

In one recurring delusion, Larry Rosenbaum lived under a microscope through which his life would be minutely scrutinized by future generations and historians. Few had a stronger sense of destiny than he. He was bound for political greatness, positive of it and had been as far back as he could remember.

To Senator Lawrence Rosenbaum, the future stretched before him like a newly paved road on a summer morning.

The highlights went something like this: after a spectacular decade or two in the Senate, the result of which would forever link the Rosenbaum name with dozens of historic pieces of legislation, he'd mount a stunning presidential campaign marked for its tremendous cross-party support. An unprecedented landslide victory would sweep Rosenbaum smiling into the White House, where before taking office he'd pause to give the most inspiring inauguration speech since John F. Kennedy. Two terms as chief executive would follow, during which the country would prosper as never before. Like Augustus' reign, Rosenbaum imagined his presidency coming to be known as a "golden" time in American history, and he pictured himself displaying equal genius for both domestic issues and foreign affairs.

Despite increasing distance from the present, Rosenbaum's view of his later life was no less specific: forced to step down after eight years in the White House, by a law which in his case an adoring American public would fervently but unsuccessfully try to repeal, a white-haired Rosenbaum would retire to the role of Revered Elder Statesman, frequently called upon to apply his brilliant mind to settling international crises. A half-dozen bestselling books, most likely histories, would crown his stupendous career.

The very end needed some fleshing out, but he thought a peaceful death at a writing table, perhaps having just penned the last of his learned tomes, would be a fitting way to go.

Since in a way his glorious political future was practically assured, and this while only a thirty-three-year-old, second-year senator, Rosenbaum kept an eye on his biographers. He had copies of every speech he'd ever given, from the high-school debating club, over which he'd of course presided, to his most recent stirring oratory before the Senate.

He faithfully kept a detailed handwritten journal, entries to which a secretary on his staff spent part of each day typing up and filing.

In short, a more ambitious and driven man could not have been found in all of Washington, D.C., and though such people can be regarded as almost comic for their predictably self-aggrandizing ways, they do have a way of achieving lofty goals with a rather surprising frequency.

Already, in just his second year, still the youngest senator on the Hill, Lawrence Rosenbaum had gained a formidable reputation for his ungodly work habits. There were rumors he never slept; rumors Rosenbaum did little to dispel. It was said a light could be seen under his office door at the latest hour; and though he frequently worked till midnight, Rosenbaum now purposely left the light on even after he left so as to cultivate the workhorse myth.

Despite such artificial enhancing, Rosenbaum did toil as a man obsessed.

His daybook was choked for months in advance with appointments, meetings, speaking engagements, and some twenty-thousand miles of scheduled airline flights. Exhausting eighty-hour work weeks were not the exception but the rule. Weekends were passed reading pending legislation.

For pleasure, Rosenbaum studied the minutiae of Senate procedure.

He was not one to keep his light under a bushel. Keenly aware of the media, unlike many of his less farsighted colleagues, Rosenbaum actively courted the press. TV and radio talk shows were never turned down. Pithy, well-reasoned quotes were supplied whenever requested. A top public-relations firm was actively engaged in disseminating his every word and deed.

Rosenbaum's social life was governed by his career. Washington parties were only attended to further political aims; seen as a place to corner possible allies at the bar or pick up on potentially valuable rumors. If he attended a sporting event it was only with the hope of getting before a camera. Rosenbaum hadn't read a book for fun in more than three years, and he hadn't seen a movie in more than five. His only vice was coffee, which he drank black at an eight-cup-a-day clip.

You couldn't get far in politics without a wife, so Rosenbaum had one. She was smart, loving, understanding, patient, and much, much better than he ever deserved or appreciated. Despite employing perhaps the most alluring female aide on the Hill, Leslie Flood, he was unerringly faithful. To Rosenbaum, Leslie was simply the most intelligent and hardworking staffer he'd ever encountered. She'd joined his staff early in his first year, and she had gradually worked her way into overseeing every detail of Rosenbaum's life. She was that good.

The important result of all this was that Senator Lawrence Rosenbaum was gaining a reputation—that desired aura so vital in separating an achiever from the anonymity of the pack. In the rare moments he paused to take stock of his situation, Rosenbaum, like a punctual traveler speeding along in an on-time train, checked his master timetable and enjoyed the reassuring sense that everything was right with his world.

Lawrence Rosenbaum glanced at his watch as he strode purposefully down the empty second-floor hallway of the Russell Senate Building. It was almost eight thirty in the morning. Claude Screws's office door loomed a dozen steps away.

Twenty minutes earlier, Rosenbaum had been working alone in his closet of a space dictating responses to constituent mail. The phone had rung. Rather amazingly, the caller was Claude Screws. He wanted to meet. In his office. Immediately. Now.

It was the first time Screws had ever called, the first time they'd ever even spoken outside committee, and Rosenbaum's adrenaline was pumping as he headed to the Old Man's office.

Since the incident a month back, when Screws had cut off what he believed to be an impertinent line of questioning, Rosenbaum had been obsessed with getting revenge. Of course, imagining elaborate schemes to bring Screws down was more of a pastime than a serious pursuit. Screws wielded too much power too expertly to ever be hurt by a second-year senator like Rosenbaum. The prospect of actually somehow removing Screws from office seemed more than a bit absurd.

Until yesterday.

IV

Rosenbaum made a point of not knocking and chose a particularly jaunty walk with which to enter Claude Screws's private domain. As much as anything, he wanted to irritate the Old Man.

He closed the door behind him.

Inside, Rosenbaum cast a covetous eye on all he beheld. The reception room alone was twice the size of his own Murphy-bed of a work space. High ceilings created an impressive sense of proportion. Memorabilia spanning near fifty years in the Senate established an imposing quality of permanence. Dignified furniture and wallpaper gave a successful air to the place. It was, in fact, remarkably similar to the picture Rosenbaum held in his head of what his own office would look like in his later career.

Rosenbaum had to force himself to keep from smiling as he walked through the empty reception room and headed down the hall he assumed led to Screws's lair. Already he was thinking about how he could wrangle this space once he'd single-handedly ousted Screws from office.

A door at the end of the wide hall was ajar. Rosenbaum stopped outside it, savoring the moment, then gave a quick forceful knock.

"It's open," came a disappointingly uncombative voice.

Rosenbaum pushed in.

Screws's private office was surprisingly small and plain, smaller and plainer in fact than two aides' rooms Rosenbaum had just passed walking down the hall. There was a rather worn blue rug, a single-line phone on an antique desk that had probably been new when Screws purchased it fifty years ago, two green metal filing cabinets, two unremarkable wooden chairs for visitors, and an American flag graced with gold brocade standing guard in a corner behind the desk. There were no pictures on the walls of Screws shaking hands with dignitaries and ex-presidents, of which there could have been enough to fill a dozen offices, no framed awards and citations, none of the mementos found in the reception room.

This was a place of work.

Rosenbaum was more than a bit surprised by the starkness of the setting, and he was practically shocked when Screws asked, "Could you close the door?" in a semipolite tone.

He did so.

This morning the Old Man looked very old, skin pale as parchment. He was hunched behind his desk like a wrinkled baby in a highchair. His suit jacket hung loose as a shawl, as if tailored for a much larger man. His shirt collar and tie, meeting little resistance from the thin, sallow neck, settled on his shoulders like a harness collar on a swaybacked horse. The Old Man's hands were spread palms down on the desk before him, as if to check a possible tipping over to the floor.

"Have a seat, Lawrence," said the oldest standing senator to the youngest.

The youngest sat. Rosenbaum was not about to forget his biographers in the midst of perhaps the most dramatic moment of his career, and he began committing every word of Screws's to memory.

As for his own responses, those could be suitably punched up when transcribed in the diary.

"What can I do for you, Claude?" Rosenbaum asked with a broad smile.

"Don't get smug with me, son," Screws said instantly, though in an uncharacteristic, almost fatherly tone. "That's the sure sign of a fool. Permit me to think I was dealing with an intelligent man."

Rosenbaum cleared his throat. He crossed his legs. He was unnerved by this sudden, world-weary change in the usually fierce old man.

"I called you here so that we could talk."

"About what?" Rosenbaum asked warily.

"About things." A pause. "About you." Screws paused again. He looked at Rosenbaum for several moments, and then the corners of the Old Man's mouth rose ever so slightly to form a thin smile. "Second year's an exciting time in the Senate, isn't it, Lawrence?" he asked wistfully.

"Yes," Rosenbaum admitted, "yes it is."

". . . Very heady time . . . especially for a young, ambitious man such as yourself."

Rosenbaum didn't see how it could hurt so he bowed his head to the compliment.

"You begin to get the lay of the land by the second year," Screws continued. "Right about now's when a fella that keeps his eyes open and his mouth shut starts to make some sense of what goes on around here. First-year feeling of being out of your league just fades away. That constant fear of making an ass out of yourself becomes a thing of the past. A process that once seemed bewildering starts to make some sense. Pork-barreling for the folks back home don't seem like the mystery it once was. You begin to see there's ways of getting mileage out of a yea or nay. You even start thinking about drafting your own little piece of legislation . . ."

Rosenbaum found himself nodding in agreement at the Old Man's words and immediately stopped. He felt suddenly uncomfortable in the presence of a friendly Old Man.

"It's actually a dangerous time, Larry," Screws offered without a trace of menace. "It's a very dangerous time."

"And why is that?"

"Because, as they say, a little knowledge is a dangerous thing. You may think you know a lot in your second year, you may start thinking you got it all figured out, but in reality all you really know is enough to get yourself into trouble. You get antsy because it seems like the older senators have everything sewed up. You treat your more senior colleagues with outward respect, but inwardly you despise them for that which you do not have. You hate them, but the strange thing is that all you want in the world is to take their place. That dichotomy can lead to plotting and scheming based more on . . . personal, rather than professional, motives."

Screws paused to swallow. He seemed fatigued by the effort of speech. "It is, as I say, a very dangerous time."

Rosenbaum sat motionless. It was as if Screws had read his mind. He felt he was losing whatever edge he'd walked in with. He had to say something.

Rosenbaum slowly recrossed his legs, toyed with a loose thread on his sock, and then played his card.

"I got an interesting call from Retired Admiral Ford Hulse yesterday . . . before he killed himself."

The Old Man sighed deeply and frowned.

". . . You're not listening to me, son."

Rosenbaum pressed on: "Admiral Hulse had a very disturbing story to tell. Your name came up several—"

"Here we go," Screws growled. "I was wondering just how impatient a runt you were. I'm gonna warn you only once— *back off*. You're way out of your weight class, Senator."

"Are you threatening me?" Rosenbaum asked with a note of hysteria. "Is that what this is?"

". . . It's whatever you make of it. I only asked you up here because I truly believed you'd act smarter than what I'm seeing. You're too young to understand that certain people in this town don't play by the rules. I'm one of those people."

"You say it almost proudly."

"Don't fool yourself. We're more alike than you care to admit. I understand you, Rosenbaum—you'll do almost anything to get your point across. The difference is ammunition. *Don't* go trying to make a name for yourself at my expense."

"I have nothing in common with you," Rosenbaum declared angrily. "You're a dinosaur—a relic!"

"Son, what I am is you in forty years."

"Bullshit."

"Your ambition, your drive, your hostility—I'm written all over you."

". . . It must be terrible not to be able to step down at your age," Rosenbaum decided.

Screws leaned closer across the desk, as if to impart a secret. "This whole place—this whole city—politics? It's just like swimming; you can't make any headway with your fists clenched. It's all about how much water you can move. Your boat—*your submarine*—has a leak in it, and you're not a very good swimmer. You might want to be more careful."

"Spare me the anecdotes."

"Consider yourself warned. Class dismissed."

Rosenbaum rose to go. "I'll see you in committee, Senator," he said defiantly over his shoulder.

"So you shall, son, so you shall . . ."

V

Leslie at first tried to get him to talk, but he adamantly refused without Rosenbaum in the room. She told him she thought the senator would be back shortly.

After some confused pacing, he fretfully opted to wait.

He looked on the verge of a nervous breakdown and Leslie didn't want to push it, so she just sat at her desk typing up a report and watching him out of the corner of her eye.

He looked exhausted and energized and angry, but more than anything he looked frightened. He couldn't seem to sit still—nervously tapping his feet, then biting his lower lip, repeatedly running his hands through his hair, eyes darting all over the room.

"Can I close the door?"

Leslie looked up to see he was already moving for the open door.

"The door," he quickly repeated, "I'd like to close it."

"By all means," said Leslie, but by then it was closed.

He sat back down in the chair. Leslie resumed her work.

A moment later the front door suddenly swung open and he practically leaped out of his seat to better defend himself in a standing position.

"I was just over at Screws's," Rosenbaum said to Leslie as he burst into the office. "The Old Man threatened me!"

Rosenbaum waited for her response. Instead she pointed her finger to a spot behind him.

Rosenbaum impatiently turned to where she was indicating.

"Matt!"

Chapter Twenty-two

Matt was ushered like royalty into Senator Rosenbaum's closet-size private office.

"Can I get you anything?" Rosenbaum fawned. "Want some coffee or something? Or a soda? How 'bout a soda?"

Matt shook his head.

"Something to eat? Could order out for a bagel—or some eggs—you want some breakfast? No? Well, take that chair over there—the blue one—it's more comfor—"

Rosenbaum stopped talking. Matt had gone to his desk and was writing on a piece of paper. Matt thrust the finished note challengingly at the senator.

> Will discuss nothing until I've searched your office for bugs.

Rosenbaum's brows rose as he read. He passed the note to Leslie. Leslie read it and handed it back to Rosenbaum, who turned to Matt and shrugged as if to say, "If it'll make you feel better, go ahead, but I think you're wasting your time."

A thorough, fifteen-minute search for listening devices ensued.

Rosenbaum and Leslie sat as curious spectators, he behind his desk and she in one of two visitor's chairs, as Matt crept around the room peering under and around anything that wasn't nailed down, as well as a few things that were.

"What's this?" Matt whispered suddenly, picking up an inch-long black object that had been skulking on the floor behind a cabinet.

"That's . . . a pen cap," Rosenbaum answered in a suitably hushed tone. "Lost it a few weeks ago. Like to have it back if I may . . ."

Matt scrutinized the hollow piece of plastic.

"It's nothing, kid."

Matt reluctantly placed the errant pen cap on Rosenbaum's desk. He quietly resumed his quest for electronic eavesdropping equipment.

"And this?" moments later.

"My beeper."

Matt pried the battery cover off the back and examined the inside.

"Those are kind of expensive," Rosenbaum informed him.

It seemed to have the dimensions and qualities associated with a paging device, so Matt placed it back in the desk drawer from which it came.

A large, ornately framed watercolor of the Grand Canyon next came under scrutiny.

"Does the backing on this picture come off?" Matt whispered, holding the bottom of the painting away from the wall and examining the angled posterior.

"I don't think so," Leslie whispered back.

"You can take it off if you'd like." Rosenbaum leaned over and mouthed, "Never liked that picture much anyway."

Matt didn't rip the burlap backing off the picture, but he did proceed to pull up each corner of the room's carpeting. He also inspected the lampshades, the wastebasket, a coffee mug, and he asked, *told* might be more accurate, Rosenbaum and Leslie to stand so he could look under their chairs. Matt returned to pen and paper.

Beneath his previous composition he scrawled:

Have to check phone.

Rosenbaum slid his phone across the desk. Matt pulled out a pocket knife, popped up a flathead screwdriver, and rapidly dissected the instrument to its most basic components.

"Find anything?" Rosenbaum whispered, genuinely interested.

"Your hold button's broke," Matt quietly told him.

"I know."

"Do you want me to fix it?"

"Sure."

Matt performed the operation. After a final inspection of the wiring within, the phone was quickly reassembled.

"Do you have a radio with an FM band?" he asked, refolding the knife and putting it in his pocket.

Leslie went into the other room and came back with a portable radio. Matt switched it on and turned the volume all the way up. Over the static, he suddenly began whistling a rousing rendition of "The Bridge on the River Kwai." Rosenbaum and Leslie watched incredulously as Matt started slowly circling the room. He clutched the radio in front of him, moving the tuning dial up and down the band as he continuously whistled the song.

Matt circled the room in this manner for several unnerving minutes. Twice he paused, once by the bookshelves and another inside the office closet, and gingerly finessed the tuning dial while whistling as loudly as he could. By degrees, he arrived back at Rosenbaum's desk.

"FM's a popular band for bugs," he offered as explanation. "Eighty-eight to a hundred and twenty megaHertz. Sometimes you can pick 'em up just by playing a radio. If there was one in here I might have heard my whistle."

"Can we turn it off now?" Rosenbaum asked, worrying about what the sound of a blaring radio in the office might do to his hardworking reputation.

"No," Matt said over a country-western station. "I want some background noise."

He put the blaring radio square in the middle of Rosenbaum's desk and nervously sat down in the room's one spare chair. It appeared Matt was satisfied with the integrity of the office, yet he made no move to speak.

"How do you know so much about bugs?" Leslie inquired.

"I'm an electronics engineer."

". . . So—" Rosenbaum prompted.

"So how did you two track me down?" Matt asked suspiciously, eyes darting between the pair.

"You've heard of Ford Hulse?" Rosenbaum asked.

"No."

"Retired Admiral Ford Hulse?"

"No."

"He killed himself yesterday."

"I'm sorry to hear that."

"It's been on the news."

"I haven't been listening to the news. What's this guy got to do with me?" Matt asked impatiently.

Rosenbaum unlocked his bottom desk drawer and removed a yellow legal pad, the top page of which was dense with scribbled notes. ". . . Ford Hulse called me yesterday," Rosenbaum said. "We talked for close to an hour. I think I'm the last person he spoke to. He sounded very ill. At times he was clear as a bell, other times he was pretty hard to understand. A few times he cried. He told me a rather amazing story about a submarine. Among a lot of other things, he mentioned your name."

"How'd he know me?"

"He didn't know you, he knew of you."

"How?"

"I'll tell you that in a moment. He also gave me the name of your late friend, David Lakeman. Now, Matt, I'd like to start off with how Dave died—"

"Why'd this Hulse guy call you?" Matt cut in.

Rosenbaum managed a modest smile. "Said he'd read about me in the *Washington Post*, about a fight I had recently with the chairman of the Armed Services Committee—Claude Screws. That name mean anything to you? Claude Screws?"

"I know who he is—some old right-winger. Other than that, no."

A silence ensued that it seemed Matt had no intention of ending.

". . . Talk to us, Matt," Rosenbaum said gently. "Tell us what's going on."

"Why should I trust you? Either one of you?" indicating Leslie.

"Because you have to," said Rosenbaum.

"I don't *have* to trust anyone."

"I didn't mean it to sound challenging. I have a vested interest in seeing this thing through. I'll be perfectly honest with you, Matt—"

"You'd be the first in awhile."

"Well, I am being honest. I stand to gain if Claude Screws is dethroned. Bringing this thing to light will mean publicity for me. It'll mean prominence, up my chances of reelection—help me make a name for myself around here. It's that simple. It may sound mercenary, but there it is. I'm out to take down Screws, any way I can."

"There's no reason not to trust us unless you've done something wrong," Leslie added.

"I haven't done anything wrong, not yet, anyway."

"Meaning . . . you will?"

"Meaning I was explicitly told not to speak about this with anyone. I was told that it's a national secret and that I'd go to jail if I ever said a word about it."

"Who told you that?" Rosenbaum leaned closer.

"I'm not going to say."

"I'm a senator on the Armed Services Committee, Matt. If it's a national secret, I'm sure you could tell me without getting in trouble. How 'bout if I take responsibility? I'll order you to tell me. How's that?"

Rosenbaum assumed an official tone: "I order you to tell me what you know. There."

Matt rubbed his eyes and ran his hands through his hair. He took a deep breath. For several seconds he looked up at the ceiling, then the floor. When there was nothing left to stare at, it seemed, he reluctantly began: ". . . I work at the NSA. I've worked there for seven years."

"And what's your job there?" Rosenbaum asked, ready to write the facts on the pad.

"None of your business. If you don't believe me, here—"

Matt tossed his security badge onto Rosenbaum's desk. "This'll prove I work there."

Rosenbaum appeared pained. "I wasn't questioning your honesty, Matt."

"We might as well get this straight right here. I'm not going to tell you anything about me or the NSA that doesn't directly relate to this mess, so don't bother asking. You got that? Nothing classified."

"Of course. I wouldn't expect you to."

"Good. So anyway, I work at the NSA. One day last week I saw something, an underwater shadow, on a satellite photograph. Christ, it was only a week ago." Matt paused to ponder the rapidity of recent events.

He slowly resumed: "You see, I was going to California with Dave Lakeman, my friend, on business. I had this satellite photograph up and I was showing someone the area where we were planning to dive—sport diving—and I saw it, this underwater shadow thing. Well, I thought maybe it was a wreck or something, I mean, I don't know what I thought, but I marked the spot, checked off where it was and all, and when we went out there, to California, that's where we went diving."

"California?"

"Up north."

"Something underwater?"

"Yeah."

"What'd you find?" Rosenbaum asked.

"A sunken Soviet submarine with dead American servicemen inside, skeletons really, about a half mile off a remote section of northern California . . . kinda buried in a sandbar and lots of kelp . . . say a hundred feet down . . . except by satellite you'd never've seen it any other way . . . probably been there at least thirty years . . . red star still on the conning tower."

Rosenbaum swung around to Leslie and gleefully exclaimed: "So Hulse wasn't crazy!"

"There's this Hulse guy again," Matt protested. "You two seem to know more about this than I do!"

"Matt—"

"No! I'm not saying another thing until you tell me what this is all about! You ask me to talk when you got all the facts in front of you on that pad—I can see it from here! You talk! You tell me what's going on!''

"Matt . . ." Leslie laid a hand on his arm.

"I'm kinda high-strung right now."

"I sense that," said Leslie. "We're your friends. You're safe here.''

"I'm sorry."

"Nonsense!" Rosenbaum declared. "My own fault. I'll tell you everything I know, and then we can fill in the gaps together. How's that? That's fair, eh?''

". . . Okay."

A thick pair of thin-wire-rim glasses appeared and Rosenbaum put them on. His head moved energetically up and down as he scanned his scribbled notes.

". . . Right. Okay. This is what Hulse told me over the phone yesterday. I don't know how much of it's true, you understand—maybe all of it, maybe none of it—but this is what he said. Let's see here. Okay. Hulse said that in May of 1954, the United States scheduled an A-bomb test on the South Pacific island of Kili, part of the Marshall Islands—''

"You could check that easy," Matt broke in.

"Leslie already has. Happened. The largest Atomic bomb exploded up to that date. *Big one.* Now, before the test, the Navy tried to keep it a secret. Basically they just wanted to keep the press away because they were about to vaporize a beautiful little atoll with this huge bomb, but up until the blast it was supposed to be top secret—no advance word or anything.''

Rosenbaum looked up from his notes: "I'm paraphrasing now what Hulse told me yesterday, because his story was all over the place.''

The pink face dropped down to the yellow pad. "Let's see . . . okay. A guy named Admiral Charles Markwater was overseeing this thing. His second-in-command was Rear Admiral Ford Hulse. Also there, according to Hulse, was the newly named head of the Senate Armed Services Committee—Claude Screws.''

Matt thought he saw Rosenbaum smile here, but it came and passed so quickly he couldn't be sure.

"The Navy set up a small armada of scuttled warships around

this island, you know—so they could measure the effects of the blast, that kind of thing, and that's when the trouble started. Storms swept through, they had problems with the monitoring equipment—one delay after another. Every time they'd start a countdown, something new would crop up. A week of waiting— trying all the time to keep what's going on a secret. The pressure was really building to get this thing lit. Finally, it looks like they've got everything nailed down and they start another countdown . . .''

Rosenbaum paused to cough. "Something in my throat. That's better. So, they're all out there, everything looking good, when about fifteen minutes before the blast, Hulse said a sonar opera- tor on the flagship radioed up to the bridge where he was standing with Admiral Markwater and Senator Claude Screws. The sonar guy thinks he's picked up a submarine in the test area. He's not sure, you understand, but he thinks it might, judging by the sound patterns coming from the thing, be a Soviet sub. The problem is that the sonar operator isn't positive. Markwater and Hulse are in charge of this test, and now, on top of all this, they're faced with canceling again because some kid with earphones on 'thinks' he's heard something. Well, what with a week of delays and the threat of more bad weather coming through, Markwater and Hulse decide to take their chances and go ahead with the blast . . .''

Rosenbaum paused to jot a note to himself on the margin of the page. He resumed.

". . . Sonar operator is told to keep quiet, and the test went off as scheduled. Kaboommmmmm!''

Rosenbaum's hands gesticulated a sudden mushroom cloud rising off his desk.

"Hulse kept saying yesterday that he still sees the flash when he closes his eyes, that 'the old footage just keeps on running' —said it over and over—just thought I'd tell you that. But getting back to the story: for the next few days they stayed out there examining these blasted ships that were parked around this now nonexistent, radioactive island, which don't sound too safe to me but that's neither here nor there. Well, right about now a couple of Soviet intelligence-gathering trawlers start circling the fringe of the test area, quietly looking around for something.

Markwater and Hulse get scared. Is it possible that the blast actually destroyed a Soviet sub? Whatever the Soviets are looking for, they can't seem to find it. After a couple days, the trawlers just kinda sail away. At least that's the way Hulse made it sound—''

Rosenbaum lost his place on the page, coughed again, and refound it.

"Okay. About seven days after the blast, when things are starting to wind down and everybody's breaking stuff apart to go home, a French intelligence officer shows up at the flagship. Now this guy heads a French intelligence ship that was there to observe the blast, invited and all, and he insists on talking privately with Admiral Markwater. Markwater sits down with the guy. Turns out the French ship was leaving the area when they came upon an oil slick. The French intelligence officer sent down a diver to see what was what, and lo and behold this diver found a perfectly intact, but absolutely silent, Soviet submarine just lying on the sand. It's just lying there. The diver tries tapping on it, banging on it—but nothing—not a peep from inside.''

Rosenbaum looked up. "Anybody got any gum or anything? My throat's getting a little dry.''

Matt shook his head. Leslie searched her pockets.

"No? Forget it.''

Rosenbaum swallowed and stoically continued without the aid of gum. "Now, this French intelligence officer was a Resistance fighter during World War Two and he just loves America. The Cold War's in full swing and this guy's willing to cooperate on this—hand it over without telling his government. So Admiral Markwater immediately gets Admiral Hulse and Senator Screws up to his cabin because they were in on this thing with him, going ahead with the blast, and together they decide to send down a few guys to check it out—keeping it all a secret, you understand. So a U.S. naval intelligence guy dives down to the sub, Leonard Vanning—''

"Leonard Vanning?" Matt cried.

"I figured that'd get a rise out of you.''

"Leonard Vanning's the director of Security at the NSA!

He's the one who warned Dave and me we could be arrested if we ever told anyone about what we found!''

"'Exactly. It was Vanning who first contacted Hulse—but now I'm getting ahead of myself.''

Rosenbaum went back to reading from his notes. ''. . . So Vanning goes down there with a few U.S. Navy divers and they manage to get inside. What they find is absolute hell. Everyone dead. Hulse wasn't sure if it was radiation or suffocation or what, but the submarine was one big stinking coffin. The electromagnetic pulse from the bomb must have knocked out all the electrical equipment—radio, navigation, engines probably, and they sank to the bottom and all just . . . slowly died.''

Rosenbaum lifted his head for a moment at this grisly juncture, and then, after glancing at Matt and Leslie, continued the story in a more somber tone:

''. . . Well, when Markwater and Hulse find out these Russians are all dead, they start screaming at each other. They're terrified to all hell that people are going to find out about their decision to let the submarine get fried, I mean destroyed. The Old Man steps in—''

"Who?'' Matt interrupted.

"I'm sorry, Screws—Claude Screws stepped in. The Old Man. And Screws says what's the problem? Finding this submarine is a blessing in disguise. Well, Screws goes on to give a passionate speech about how the American public's growing complacent on the issues of defense spending, Soviet aggression, and preparedness for war. Screws thinks that a perfectly intact Soviet submarine could be used to change all that. Markwater and Hulse balk at the idea. They're in enough trouble already. But Screws keeps at them, and he finally wins them over to his way of thinking—''

"How?'' asked Matt.

"Just give me a minute, I'm getting there. So Markwater, Hulse, and Screws call in the French intelligence officer. They ask him to turn the sub over to them, to not tell his government that he found it, and basically to never speak about it again. The French intelligence officer and the diver he sent down, Hulse thought his name was LeClerc—''

Matt broke in: "Hulse had some memory.''

"On the past, yeah, but he kept calling me 'Rosenbloom.'
Anyway, the French intelligence officer and this LeClerc are the
only two people on his ship who know about it, and with the
promise of future help with their careers—at least that's what I
suspect was promised them—he agrees. According to Hulse,
that intelligence officer was Jacques Seydoux."

Rosenbaum looked up from his notes, awaiting a reaction
from Matt.

"Never heard of him."

"Jacques Seydoux?"

"He's now the French ambassador to the United States,"
Leslie supplied.

"An *ambassador*, Matt," said Rosenbaum.

"I don't really follow politics too closely."

"Oh. Well . . . anyway," Rosenbaum resumed, somewhat
disappointed by Matt's not recognizing the name, "the French
ship departs—off into the sunset. Now, Leonard Vanning and a
few of his men get the submarine going again and move it to an
isolated island. They drag the Soviet bodies out, like seventy of
them, and bury them in lime out there—this according to Hulse."

"Who helped him?" Matt asked.

"I doubt we'll ever find that out. Hulse just said a 'few of
Vanning's boys.' Vanning had little to worry about from them.
Back then it wasn't like now—people didn't talk about what
went on. They just didn't do it. This was fifteen years before
the Pentagon Papers. Different mind-set. Unthinkable. So Vanning
and a few of his boys, they clean the inside out, fix whatever's
broken on the thing, and, while they're doing that, a skeleton
crew is secretly flown in. They get these eight guys from—"

"Eight different subs," Matt completed the sentence.

"How'd you know that?"

"I'll tell you when you're done."

"Do you know all this already?"

"No—go on, please." Matt said. "I'll tell you when you're
done."

"Well, the Navy keeps a pretty close watch on its submarine
crews, particularly psychological profiles, what with these guys
being stuck inside a metal tube for weeks on end. And, after
looking through hundreds of service records, Admiral Markwater

and Rear Admiral Hulse pick eight crewmen—eight crewmen known for their gung-ho, all-American beliefs. So they fly these boys out, each one from a different sub. These boys are all excited about being picked for this special slot, and they happily take the assignment and disappear under the waves.''

"What was the plan?" asked Matt.

Rosenbaum stopped reading from the notes and pushed the yellow legal pad to one side. He took off his wire-rim glasses and pocketed them.

". . . The plan? The plan, according to Hulse, was to have this captain sail the sub to the California coast, go in real close, and surface a few times inside U.S. territorial waters. The idea was that people onshore would see the red flag on the submarine's conning tower. It would be conclusively identified as a Soviet sub. People would go nuts. Enough to get the public riled but not enough to start World War Three. After scaring the shit out of a few million Californians, they were supposed to then ditch the sub, get picked up by a ship supplied by Vanning, and each man in the skeleton crew would then be sent back to his respective assignment. Meanwhile, and this is how Screws sold the scheme to Markwater and Hulse, Screws would introduce a whopping defense spending bill which, with Soviet-American relations now at a new all-time low, would sail through Congress. Among the appropriations was a huge increase in Navy funding.''

"They thought a sighting would be enough to get this bill through?" Matt asked.

"Yup, and they were probably right. All it took during World War Two was one sighting of a Japanese sub off the California coast for us to decide to intern tens of thousands of Japanese Americans.''

Rosenbaum paused. "Anyway, they send the sub and its tiny crew off. But something happens. A few days go by—nothing. A week goes by, then two weeks—still nothing. No sightings, no contact where they were supposed to rendezvous afterward, nothing. Markwater and Screws and Hulse and Vanning—they know something went wrong by now, but they got big problems. They can't call a search for the damn thing, because if they do, and its found, they're up the creek. So the only thing they can do is wait.''

Rosenbaum rapidly clicked his ballpoint pen several times, deposited it in his breast pocket. ''After a week, they know something happened and these boys aren't coming back. What do you do? You've got to account for them somehow—they've got families, some of them did anyway—no small task. With Markwater and Hulse quietly pulling strings, Vanning visits eight separate sites—some bases, some small coastal towns— and lays in the proper paperwork—the transfers, accident reports, AWOL notices, or whatever was required for each particular man. He files the death certificates and sends off official letters of condolences to the next of kin. Most of them just accept it at face value. Hulse said one or two families asked for more, but that Vanning supplied whatever they wanted in the way of documentation—body unrecoverable, lost at sea, whatever. So a year goes by. Not a peep. Two years go by. Still nothing. Hulse and Markwater and Screws feel like they're walking around with an unexploded bomb in their pockets. Ten years go by. They decide it must have gone down in deep water and imploded, *but they can't be sure.* They continue with their careers because there's nothing else they can do, but they're living with the fact that some day they could wake up with this thing staring them in the face. Seydoux I don't know about, but Screws and Hulse and Markwater and Vanning, they start drifting apart. From what Hulse said, I guess they grew to really hate each other. Markwater died in 1966. Hulse became a full-blown alcoholic and retired from the Navy in 1971. Vanning climbed the ladder at the NSA. Seydoux went from French intelligence to diplomacy, got sent to London, then to Washington, and then got tapped ambassador to the U.S. And Claude Screws? Claude stays exactly where he was when the whole mess started and becomes one of the most powerful senators on the Hill. *Thirty years go by.* As far as they're all concerned it's a thing of the past . . . until one day a guy named Matthew Clarke sees something on a satellite photograph and decides to go diving there with his friend.''

A particularly melodramatic ballad on the country-western radio station was for several moments the only sound in the room.

"I think Vanning went to the NSA as much to keep his ear to the ground as anything," Rosenbaum told them. "The guy was in intelligence beforehand; there was always the chance he'd one day have to deal with this being found and the NSA's as good a place as any to conduct damage control. Vanning does pretty damn good there over the next thirty years—when bingo, he gets a report that an employee saw something on a satellite photograph! Vanning hits the ground running and goes to tell Hulse, because he's going to need help covering the tracks. What Vanning doesn't realize is that Hulse is dying. The retired admiral feels guilty as all hell about what they did to begin with, and when Vanning comes in and tells him that you and your friend have stumbled upon it, Hulse gets nervous that you're going to be the next casualties. Screws pays a visit and threatens Hulse to stay quiet. That decides it for him. Before he commits suicide, which he called an 'honorable death,' he calls me. Hulse calls me because he's read in the paper that Screws and I can't stand each other and he tells me all this, specifically mentioning your name and your friend Lakeman, because he insists you're both in danger. Leslie and I track you down last night, follow you to that bar, and here we are."

Rosenbaum's gaze rested squarely on Matt: "We're all on equal footing now, Matt. So how did you know they came from eight different subs?"

Matt told Rosenbaum and Leslie about Dave's foray into the Pentagon computer files. He told them about the visit to Captain Carl Avery's widow and about the car that mysteriously appeared while they were there. He told them about going to the hospital after Dave's death—

"They have drugs, you know," interjected Rosenbaum, "that accurately reproduce the effects of a heart attack. Drugs that don't leave a trace."

"What are you saying?" Leslie asked anxiously. "Are you saying he was murdered? I can't believe that."

"Dave was in perfect health," Matt told her.

"Maybe it was a congenital thing," Leslie suggested, "or high blood pres—"

"*Leslie.*" Rosenbaum was staring at her. "Let him finish."

Matt described how he almost died in the elevator fire after leaving the bar last night.

"Well it *could* have been an accident," Leslie offered. "If the repairmen said it was an electrical thing, I mean, they'd know—right?"

Rosenbaum was now regarding Leslie with concern. "I don't understand why you find this so hard to believe," he told her.

"I'm sorry," Leslie quickly backpedaled, "I was just looking for some plausible explanation . . ."

"When I got back to my apartment last night," Matt said, "I found a radio bug. It could have been put there by the NSA for all I know, because of my job, or by whoever killed Dave and set up that fire. I left it where it was."

"Good boy," Rosenbaum enthused. "Don't tip 'em off we know."

"Know?" Matt said sarcastically. "They probably followed me here, for chrissake."

"Did you see someone follow you here?" Rosenbaum asked, suddenly nervous.

"No, but that doesn't mean anything."

"Do you have any evidence from the submarine?" Leslie asked.

"I've got pictures from the sub inside and out," said Matt. "I've got one of the dog tags and the names of the others onboard. Avery's widow's got her husband's watch; we could get her to come forward with that."

"Well, let's not jump the gun here," Rosenbaum cautioned. "We can't do anything until we've got confirmation the sub's still there."

"Bullshit!" Matt spat. "That could take days—"

"Is there a problem with that?" Rosenbaum asked.

"I don't have days—someone's trying to kill me!"

"We can arrange some sort of protection for—"

"No! I've waited too long already! These guys are professionals—they know how to cover their tracks. The sub could be gone by now for all I know. I'm not going to wait any more. If you won't bring this out today, I'll go to someone else who will—networks, newspapers—I don't care where. I mean it!"

"Okay, okay," Rosenbaum said quickly. "Stay put. Let me think. Let me think. It's just I don't want to go off half-cocked on this thing. I don't want to get burned, you understand that, don't you?"

"I'll give you the pictures, the dog tag, my testimony, the names of the others that were onboard—I'll give them to you today—if you immediately announce what's been going on. If not, I'm going to ABC or NBC or the *Washington Post* with this. It's that simple."

Rosenbaum looked like a man in a high-stakes poker game stuck with either betting the kid's tuition money or folding with a full house.

". . . Ah . . . ah . . ." was all he could manage.

He rubbed his forehead and clenched his little hands into fists and for the next minute looked extremely uncomfortable as he desperately tried to decide what to do.

"You have pictures?" Leslie repeated. "Inside and out? Good, clear pictures?"

Matt nodded.

"And a dog tag?" she asked. "You do have one of the dog tags and the names of the others?"

Matt nodded again.

Rosenbaum's left cheek was twitching under the strain. Mouth open, he looked from Matt to Leslie several times.

". . . Ah."

Something was on the verge of coming out.

". . . Ah."

His forehead was shiny with a sudden sweat.

"Okay! Okay! I'll do it! I will do it!"

"Fine," Matt said calmly.

"This is what we'll do—now listen to me. Okay. This is what we'll do. Now then. Okay. Where're these pictures and dog tag now?"

"Hidden in a bar about twenty minutes from here. The Cloverleaf, where you were last night. In the ceiling tile of the men's room."

"Right! Okay. This is what we'll do. There's an Armed Services Committee meeting in an hour. Screws'll be in the room. You get me those pictures and the dog tag and the names of the others, and with the transcript of Hulse's phone call," Rosenbaum held up the notepad as if it were an Olympian torch, "I'll break this thing wide open! There! How's that?"

"What about press?" Matt asked.

"The press? The press'll pick up on it right away, believe you me! It'll be like dropping a bomb in the room! Somebody's aide'll sneak out and before you know it the place'll fill up! Every reporter on the Hill will be there! I'll show the pictures and the dog tag. I'll stand up there and read what Hulse told me. I'll call off those poor, dead U.S. submarine boys' names—"

Rosenbaum fairly shuddered, reveling in the drama of the imagined moment.

"And when I'm done, I'll look over at Screws and smile! Your move, Senator! Ha!"

"And then what?" Matt asked.

"Full-scale investigation! Seven o'clock news! Front page *New York Times*!"

Rosenbaum checked his watch. "Okay. Leslie, I want you to go with him—to this bar. I don't want him wandering around alone. And take your car—if he's being followed it might throw them off."

"I'll have to call and cancel your appointment with Eaton."

"Do it."

Leslie left to make the call. Matt was watching her as she walked out when Rosenbaum suddenly leaped out of the chair and pounded a fist on his desk to surprisingly little effect.

"My boy," he boomed to Matt, who was only three years his junior, "I'm gonna blow the lid off this town!"

Chapter Twenty-three

Matt took a good long look at her in the car. Any other kind of look would have been a waste. Leslie Flood had that understated self-contained thing that could drive a man nuts. She was a sharp woman. A committed woman. An absolutely beautiful woman. Very little makeup. What little there was was hard to discern, but seemed to accentuate her already striking green eyes. She was wearing a loose-fitting suede leather jacket over a red V-neck sweater over a plain white T-shirt. Pleated black pants seemed to stretch forever down to the gas and clutch pedals, where shiny black boots marked the end of a long pair of legs.

As an emotionally vulnerable patient can fall in love with his nurse or doctor, a distraught and exhausted Matthew Clarke had decided over the last twenty minutes that his escort was the most beautiful woman in the world.

In her, he'd found a temporary refuge from the horror of the last seventy-two hours. He openly stared.

"Do I stay on this?" she asked as she drove, indicating the street with a slight nod.

"Uh-huh—it forks up here but hang all the way to the right. Up there."

She had an old red Triumph Spitfire with cracked tan upholstery and a clock that didn't work. Matt took her for the type who drove fast and recklessly, but on this it appeared he'd read her wrong because she was driving much slower than the flow of traffic. Their shoulders pressed as the small car rounded the tight curve. Matt could smell the faintest trace of a balmy perfume.

"I'm going to have an accident if you don't stop looking at me like that," she told him without turning.

"I'm sorry," Matt said, and kept right on staring. ". . . So, how long have you been working for him?"

"Rosenbaum? I've been working for Senator Rosenbaum since last year."

"That's great."

"I like it."

"Must be exciting working for a senator at your age. You're so young—"

Her head suddenly bent down at the compliment and she cast a furtive sideways glance from around a loose tress of auburn blond hair. "I'm not," she said with a smile, "but thank you, anyway." The face returned to profile.

"Who'd you work for before? You must have had experience, right, to get hired by Rosenbaum?"

"I spent five years working on Senator Balfour's staff. Senator Thaddeus Balfour, Democrat from California."

"You quit?"

"He wasn't reelected."

"That's too bad."

"You might've read about it. Caught taking illegal campaign contributions? Big scandal. He claimed he'd been set up."

Leslie glanced at Matt to read his reaction. ". . . It was in all the papers."

"No, I didn't read about it. I guess you were pretty upset."

She didn't answer.

Matt thought that perhaps it had been too traumatic for her to discuss. He changed the topic: "You're from California?"

She shook her head.

"Where'd you go to school?"

"Georgetown."

"You grew up in Washington?"

"What do I do here?" she asked, ignoring the question.

The car was approaching an intersection. "Left," Matt instructed. "The Cloverleaf's about a mile down on the right. It's pretty much of a dive—"

"I was there last night, remember? I liked it. It's the kind of place you could lose yourself in," she said in a distant tone.

"Exactly. We should go there sometime."

"That's what we're doing now."

"I mean some night."

Her hand suddenly slid off the stick shift and gave Matt's thigh a quick gentle squeeze; at least that's what Matt thought happened, because when he looked down the hand was gone and she was shifting into the intersection.

Matt suddenly spun in his seat and peered out the sports car's small back window.

"What?" she asked.

"I should have been watching the rearview mirror instead of staring at you."

"I haven't seen anyone following us," she said immediately.

"You've been watching?"

"Since we left."

Matt kept his eye on the traffic behind them. He gradually settled back into the seat. "You were watching the whole time?"

She nodded.

"How come?"

"Because you said before that you thought you were being followed."

Her left hand came up and tugged at the neck of her T-shirt. Very softly she asked: "Do you really think somebody killed your friend?"

"Yes."

"But how can you be sure?"

"I can't. I realize that now. I can't be sure about the elevator fire either, but I *know* it was set."

"It *could* have been an accident, though . . ."

"No. It's weird. It's like one time in college, at M.I.T., I came back to my apartment one night and turned on the lights and there was a man standing in the middle of the living room. He was just standing there. And for like three or four seconds I tried to come up with some reasonable explanation why this person I didn't know was in my living room—like maybe he was a repairman, or someone who used to live there—I even thought I might have walked into the wrong apartment. You see, your mind doesn't want to believe something's wrong so it first tries to come up with an explanation why it's right. Well, in those few seconds the guy suddenly rushes me, knocks me over, and bolts out the door. He was a burglar. It was obvious. It's the same thing with Dave and this fire. My mind kept trying to come up with reasonable explanations why these things happened. It took me a while, but last night I finally realized there are none. Dave was murdered and that fire was set. I *know* it . . ."

Leslie was staring at a point somewhere far down the road. "After we get to the bar," she said uneasily, "promise me you'll go to a police station and stay there until Rosenbaum or I call."

"No, I'll come back with you."

"Please. I'll drop you off at a police station, and just stay there until Rosenbaum or I call."

"Why? What's wrong?" Matt regarded her as she drove. She refused to look his way. ". . . You're scared to be around me, aren't you?"

She continued staring straight ahead.

". . . That's what it is. You're scared something's going to happen to you while I'm around. You can say it, Leslie—I understand that. You're scared to be around me—just admit it."

"I'm scared," she said.

II

The parking lot was empty of cars but dotted with shallow black puddles that rippled in the blustery wind like miniature

lakes. The Spitfire's tires splashed violently through them, leaving twin tracks of muddy brown from the street to the Cloverleaf's front doors.

Matt trailed Leslie the short distance from the car to the bar,
practically walking backward to determine whether they'd been
followed. Autos of all shapes and sizes whizzed by on the
street, none any more suspect than the next.

"Is it open at this hour?" Leslie asked.

"Duka'll be here."

They reached the doors. Matt turned and followed her in.

Stepping from diffuse exterior light to a near black interior,
the pupil first hesitates and then adjusts; dilating to make sense
of the sudden shadows. Matt and Leslie stood at the threshold of
the dark rectangular space, for several seconds their sight blurred,
and then, like a photograph coming to life in a tray of devel-
oper, a strange scene emerged slowly from the dimness: the
place was in complete disarray—chairs up, tables pulled away
from the walls, boxes of liquor stacked up in the middle of the
room, and beer kegs strewn haphazardly along the floor. Bottles
covered the bar, and Duka was engaged in the laborious process
of placing them one by one back on the shelves.

He looked up at Matt and Leslie: "You believe this shit? Can
you believe this?"

Matt weaved through the tables and approached him. "What
happened?"

"Somebody put the Health Department on us—for no reason
at all! I had two fucking inspectors all over me—pardon my
language, lady. Look at this!" Duka demanded, his hand sweeping the premises: "Can you believe this? The Health Department, no less! It's goddamn harassment!"

"When?" Matt asked uneasily.

"They just left! Minutes ago. They sweep in here like
gangbusters, rip my place apart, and leave. I dunno who they
think they're messin' around with! I know people! I got some
pretty important customers come in here and if they think they
can just waltz in and rip my place—"

Matt was moving quickly to the back of the bar. He trotted to
the men's-room door and shouldered it open with a heave. It

was pitch-black inside. He found the switch after some frantic groping and flipped the lights on.

The bathroom was exactly as before: cold, empty, leaking tap, the bleachy smell of industrial cleaner. Matt vaulted onto the urinal and anxiously pushed up the ceiling tile directly overhead. His arm shot into the recess and he grabbed for that which should have been there . . . but wasn't.

Deeper and deeper he pawed the dusty shaft, his grabbing motions becoming increasingly frenzied. Matt finally stood tip-toe and popped his head into the gloom. There was nothing there. The package of photographs and dog tag were gone.

Matt ducked down to make sure he had the right tile. He was certain he did but he punched up the tile beside it, and the one beside that. He furiously knocked to the floor every tile within three feet of where he'd hidden the pictures and dog tag.

The floor became littered with broken bits of the stuff.

"What're ya doing, kid?" Duka asked behind him, watching from the doorway as the foot-square tiles fell noisily to the floor.

"They came in here!" Matt screamed. "They came in here!"

". . . The Health guys? Yeah, they were back here. Why you punching out the ceiling tiles, Matt?"

Duka used that tranquil tone of voice policemen employ with people who are balanced over bridge railings.

"You okay? You feel okay, Matt? Now, why don't you just hop down off that terlet and let me buy you a—"

Matt jumped to the floor and bounded past Duka. He dashed down the dark and cluttered bar to where Leslie was standing by the stacked boxes of liquor.

"What's wro—"

He grabbed her arm and directed her firmly out the door.

"*What is going on?* Let go of my arm, Matt—you're hurting me!"

They were suddenly back outside, moving across the parking lot. Matt made no move to release her as they approached the car. He seemed extremely disturbed and was talking to himself: "That's it . . . no more . . . end run . . . it's over . . . good-bye . . ."

"Will you just stop for one minute!" Leslie pulled up and wrenched her arm free.

"The stuff is gone!" he screamed at her. *"It's gone!* They came! They took it away! It's over! The whole thing's over! Dave's dead! I'm dead! The whole fucking thing is dead!"

"That doesn't mean they're going to kill you," she insisted, her face ashen. "I mean—that's crazy."

"Are you blind? Look how far they've gone already! They killed my best friend! They've got the pictures and dog tag—my insurance policy! I'm sure they've gotten rid of the satellite photographs this sub appeared on—they've probably even gotten rid of the sub by now! Lose me from the equation and this thing never happened!"

"What about the press? Maybe we could—"

"What?" Matt cut in mockingly. "A disgruntled NSA employee, on probation, distraught over the death of a friend? Talk about paranoid delusions!"

"But if Rosenbaum and I—"

"Rosenbaum isn't going anywhere without evidence! He's a senator, for chrissake! And you? You'd look like some ambitious peace-freak aide who wanted to believe in a conspiracy theory!"

It happened very quickly. Matt grabbed Leslie's pocketbook. She was astounded but instinctively clung to the strap. Matt yanked harder. A rip—and the contents of her purse tumbled to the wet pavement with a clatter.

"What are you doing?" she screamed.

Matt lunged for her car keys and got them. He jumped a step back, gripping them tightly in his hand.

"I'm taking your car!"

"Do you think *I* had something to do with this? Is that what this is all about?"

"No—I think there's a bug in Rosenbaum's office!"

"But you looked—"

"Big deal! They can be the size of a match, embedded in the wall! This guy Screws sounds like he'd keep track of an enemy like Rosenbaum—it makes sense he'd have one hidden well."

Matt started for Leslie's car.

"You can't just leave me here!"

"Go back inside. Tell Duka I said to make sure you get home safe."

Matt climbed quickly into the car. He started the engine. Leslie tried opening the door but he'd already locked it.

"You can't just take my car! At least let me come with you!"

Matt rolled the window down a crack. "Can't do it," he stated flatly.

"Where are you going? What are you going to do?"

Matt white-knuckled the steering wheel. He stared out the windshield and angrily revved the engine several times.

"You can't go home," Leslie said in a more sympathetic voice, sensing now how confused and far gone he really was. "Listen to me, Matt. I understand. I really do. If you get stuck you can go to my place. I'll give you the address."

Leslie went back to the objects scattered on the ground from her purse and retrieved a pen and scratch pad. She wrote rapidly on the paper and then fitted it through the window for Matt to have.

"Here's my home address and phone number."

Matt made no move to take it.

"You've already got the keys—they're on the same ring as the car's. You can take the car—it's okay. But please get in touch with me later. If I'm not there, just go in. Will you do that? Please."

Matt pocketed the piece of paper. He put the Spitfire in gear and squealed dramatically from the parking lot onto the road. The car grew smaller and smaller and was gone.

III

Like the flesh surrounding a surgical incision, the immediate area around the fresh excavation had been sanitized by covering. Instead of a bright red gash tightly framed by sterile white sheets, here was an earthy, ocher hole bounded by concentrically laid mats of soft-green carpet. The simulated lawnlike rugs ran right up to the edge of the grave, the inside walls of which were beautifully squared. Suspended over the six-foot hollow was a casket of dark wood and brass, superbly buffed and awaiting its electrically controlled descent into eternity. It was all extremely neat, allowing a downcast observer the more agreeable sensation that the deceased was being laid to rest in the floor of some strange, outdoor living room rather than the actual, more wormy, medium of dirt.

He was in an old, sprawling cemetery set on a golf-course-size piece of Maryland acreage. You needed intricate directions to get to the grave site of a specific burial, at least Matt did, and he still got lost several times.

By the time he arrived, a leaden sky was unleashing a terrific downpour, and the assembled mourners, some fifty in all, were clustered beneath a mushroom stand of dripping umbrellas—all black, save one violently bright red canopy that Matt had scrounged from the trunk of Leslie's car.

He was standing at the very back, where the keening from those closest to the coffin was barely audible over the patter of rain.

From here, Matt craned his neck over a small boulder-field of shoulders and heads and glimpsed the dark box bearing Dave's body. Off to one side, he could make out what he believed to be Perri's black-jacketed form and her brother standing sturdily beside her. The others there were mostly relatives of either Perri's or Dave's.

Matt didn't recognize any of them.

A young minister, younger than Dave it seemed, stood erect over the extravagant casket and conducted the service beneath a small umbrella held aloft by a very pale older man in a very severe black suit.

Matt had not wanted to come. He'd avoided coming. When he did finally decide to attend it was late and he had to rush to make it.

To say he was here, at his best friend's funeral, because he had nowhere else to go would have been more than partly true. In his own mind, Matt might have been able to justify skipping Dave's funeral with the pressing excuse of having to help Senator Rosenbaum and Leslie bring the murderous business to light—but with the tag and pictures gone, such was no longer the case.

Matt could also have rationalized bypassing the ceremony, perhaps, had he spied a closely following car and felt his life would be in danger if he allowed himself the luxury of stopping— but from the time Matt had peeled from the Cloverleaf parking lot till now, a period of roughly three hours, he'd observed no such tightly trailing auto. The killers had either been called off, which was highly unlikely, or were now so close to seizing their prey that obvious methods like tailing were no longer required.

Matt again caught sight of Perri, up near the front. The other reason he'd come was to speak with her.

Alone.

Beyond consoling words, Matt had to ask her about Dave: whether he might have told her anything, or hidden something, or given her a package to hold. It wasn't the best of moments to ask her such things, but then, from Matt's point of view, he didn't have that many moments left.

Showing up late, with the service almost finished, he was now hiding unobtrusively in the back under a bright red umbrella.

"It's this sudden nature of God's hand that makes it so difficult for us to understand," the minister was intoning over the grave. "For when one is called away as quickly, as suddenly as Dave was, it's the living, it's all of us who feel denied the moment of forgiveness . . . the punctuation of a simple good-bye."

The man in front of Matt shifted, the woman before the man lowered her head, and without seeking it, Matt momentarily had a clear view to the casket. Dave's casket.

The grief of loss, Matt was dealing with; the guilt of adultery and entangling Dave in something that took his life, he was not.

Matt stared at the coffin poised over the hole.

Dave's dead and I, Matt thought, am well on the way to joining him—if not there already. Matt *was* there already—merely playing out the final moments between a cause and its effect. Because as far as the end result is concerned, there really is no difference between when one begins a chain of events that lead to a specific occurrence and the final moment of the occurrence itself.

Dave was dead the moment Matt saw the shadow on the satellite photograph. Or, to be more chronologically precise, Dave was dead the moment Harry screwed up on the KH-12 boost-burn time, because it was that event that landed Matt in Imagery Analysis, which directly led to his seeing the shadow, which from that point until he was murdered, made Dave one of the living dead—just as he, Matt was positive, was now one.

He was unhinging. What made it frightening, however, was that he knew he was.

". . . For none of us liveth to himself," the minister was reading from a well-thumbed Bible, "and no man dieth to himself. For whether we live, we live unto the Lord; and whether we die, we die unto the Lord; whether we live therefore, or die, we are the Lord's . . ."

The service seemed to be nearing an end. Matt realized the coffin was slowly disappearing into the ground. He was crying. Everybody had their heads bowed. At any moment, these people, these mourners, would be turning to go, turning en masse in Matt's direction—all of them turning to face Matt. All those grieving people turning accusingly toward the person who slept with Dave's wife! The person there most responsible for Dave's death!

Matt started away from the wall of black before him.

As the minister delivered the final prayer, Matt walked briskly around the side of the group, trying to reach Perri.

From up front: "Amen."

The mourners were starting away from the newly dug hole. Perri, head bowed and sobbing, was being escorted on one side by her brother, and on the other, by an older woman dressed in black—her mother, thought Matt.

Matt was coming up behind the three, very close.

The brother glanced back, saw Matt, and glared. The brother whispered to the woman on Perri's left, and he dropped back to speak to Matt. "I wasn't sure you'd come," the brother said to him.

"I had to talk to Perri."

Matt could see Perri heading away across the grass, holding the woman's arm for support.

"If you'll excuse me." Matt tried to go around him.

"No, Mr. Clarke, I won't. She's very shaken up at the moment and I can't allow you to talk to her."

He was actually blocking Matt's way.

"What d'you mean? I came to talk with her. It's important. Why can't I talk with her?"

"Do I have to say it out loud?" he asked indignantly. "Here? Not ten feet from her husband's grave—"

The brother was trembling with rage. Matt took a step back.

"You adulterous son of a bitch!"

The brother lunged at Matt. It was all too much for him. Matt backed away, turned, and suddenly started to run—running as fast as he could across the thickly moist grass.

He reached a narrow path of asphalt. Matt ran down the rain-spattered path, past seemingly endless rows of varied tombstones to which he felt more connected than to the world of the living. He ran headlong through a gallery of carved angels, daggerlike obelisks, polished marble pillars, and eroded inscriptions. He ran for the quiet safety of the car, which he'd left on a busy street bordering the huge cemetery. He didn't look back once he reached the red sports car; just dove in, started the engine, and left.

Had he looked back, Matt most certainly would have spied a man running across the sloping lawn toward a car parked nearer the service.

The man was not Perri's brother.

In an odd way, Matt and the man had one thing in common— they were both thinking about the former's imminent and bloody death.

IV

It was a fashionable, tree-lined block on N Street in Georgetown; a street of solid doors and brass mail slots and faded brick and black shutters bordering dark windows and, behind it all, old money. Expensive cars, foreign for the most part, sat rain-beaded and idle on either side of the nicely paved thoroughfare. It was the kind of neighborhood that, if you didn't live there, made you feel like alarms might sound if you took a false step up one of the wide stoops. Matt cruised the street several times, referring to the address that Leslie had written on the piece of paper. Her address. On this street?

Matt tightly gripped the piece of paper that Leslie had slid through the window. Her address. It was a narrow, five-story brownstone, dull red in color. A driveway ran straight to the back. Matt turned the car into the driveway and parked out of sight from the street.

He came back around slowly, intently watching and listening. A nanny pushing a pram was passing across the way. The street seemed fairly deserted.

Matt took the steps three at a time up to the brownstone door.

He searched for a building directory, trying to determine which apartment was Leslie's. The only thing he found was a brass mail slot beside the door, a brass mail slot that read— LESLIE FLOOD.

She was the only tenant in the whole building?

Matt was confused.

An approaching car could be heard from a couple of blocks away. Matt fumbled with the keys, in a hurry to get inside. He found what looked to be a house key and jammed it into the lock. It turned. Matt stepped inside and the door closed behind him, just as the car came racing by.

V

It was five o'clock. Rosenbaum was clutching a glass of scotch. He nervously jiggled it so that the ice cubes made a continuous clinking sound.

Rosenbaum rarely drank liquor. He hated it. Leslie was watching with wry amusement as he tried to make the manly most of it: feet on his desk, tie loosened, the bottle set conspicuously before him.

He sipped minutely, experimentally. He had to stifle a gag after each taste.

This was not a celebratory drink. This was not a drink to get drunk. This was a drink to steel Rosenbaum's nerves, as much in a psychological as a chemical way.

Leslie had a theory. She believed she knew why Rosenbaum was drinking. She was probably much closer to the mark than Rosenbaum ever could have guessed himself.

If Leslie were to have explained it to you, and she wasn't big on explaining herself, it would have gone something like this: Lawrence Rosenbaum, like many intellectually strong but physically weak males, lived somewhere outside the sphere of virile, he-man-like habits that for all the noise to the contrary still pervades society's view of masculinity. The world of tough and territorial talk was not his. Never had been. Leslie's hypothesis held, however, that in stressful times, even cerebral men like Rosenbaum retreated to that world's props and language. It was instinctual. At this moment Rosenbaum felt threatened. His pulling out the booze and shot glass was the human male's equivalent to an elephant flapping its ears in the presence of some menacing beast, or a bird puffing out its plumage when confronted with danger, or a—well, there were countless such examples from the animal kingdom. The point was, that at the heart of such behavior lay a primordial fear. Fear for one's physical well-being. Fear of being mauled. Fear of being eaten. Leslie watched Rosenbaum. She could see that he was scared. He should be. He *was* in danger—of being eaten.

"Jesus! I ought to know better than to get involved in this conspiracy shit," he rattled on anxiously. "I mean, who is this guy Clarke anyway? Really. What do we know? We hear this story. A guy shows us some badge. I have to be more careful. Walking on eggs here . . ."

Leslie felt he wanted her to nod sympathetically. She did.

"I'm waiting there, in committee, for you and him to come back with the pictures and the dog tag. I try stalling for time, my heart's pounding, I'm about to drop a bomb on Screws—my political future's on the line. And I look over at him, at the Old Man, and he's watching me—smiling. Smiling! Like he knows exactly what I've got planned! Like he knows exactly what I'm going to do and he knows it's all going to fall apart."

Rosenbaum took something larger than a sip. Let it settle. "And he had this look on his face. The Old Man had this look on his face . . . this look like I was no more a danger to him than a bug. He threatened me this morning! I told you that. I gotta be more careful. I have a future to watch out for. I could get crushed."

He put down the glass. "I mean, did he make this whole thing up—this whole elaborate story, just to ruin me? Is that possible?"

"I think Matt's telling the truth," she told him.

"Well I don't have the luxury of being unsure! The last thing I need is to be branded a conspiracy wacko! If this thing isn't true, if it's made up and I jump up to tell the world, Screws will crucify me! Explode right in my face!"

Rosenbaum caught himself. ". . . I didn't mean to yell. I'm sorry. Have you heard from him—since he took your car?"

"No."

Rosenbaum leaned forward, cupping the glass in both hands. "Now *that* could be something. We could really distance ourselves from this guy fast if we called in and reported your car was stolen. We could say this guy came in, claimed he worked for the NSA, fed us this whole story, and that you drove him out to this bar and he stole your car. Then Screws wouldn't have anything on—"

"What are you so scared about?" she asked.

"You didn't see his face today, Leslie. I'm telling you, Screws has got something in the works here. *I could see it.* He's not worried at all. He was sitting there, looking at me with this expression like he held all the cards . . ."

Rosenbaum looked down into his drink, like a man with troubles and a glass of scotch in his hands is supposed to do.

"I don't think we should report my car as stolen," Leslie said. "Bringing the police in on this would be a mistake."

"I know—I'm just throwing out ideas. You got any? Ideas?"

Leslie shook her head.

A knock came at the door.

"Yeah?" Rosenbaum called out.

A young aide in his mid-twenties, wearing jeans, button-down shirt, and a tie, pushed open the inner-office door.

"Reporter here to see you, Larry."

"I can't talk to him now. Tell him to call tomorrow morning."

"It's Goodell from the *Washington Post*."

Rosenbaum immediately looked to Leslie. Her face was a blank. To the aide in the doorway, an apprehensive: "Tell him to wait a moment."

The kid closed the door.

"What the hell does he want?" Rosenbaum whispered harshly.

"I haven't a clue."

"Jesus!"

Rosenbaum jumped to his feet. He threw the bottle and glass in a drawer and quickly tightened his tie.

"What the hell does Goodell want? The guy's a shark! You don't think this could have anything to do with this other thing, do you?"

"I don't know, Larry," she told him, slowly standing as well.

"What should I do?" He was panicking. He wanted to bite his fingernails but caught himself at the last moment and thrust his hands in his pockets.

"Talk to him. See what he wants."

"Goodell no less!"

Leslie stepped out of the way. She watched impassively as Rosenbaum walked painfully toward the door. He opened it.

"Doug! Good to see you!" he feigned.

Through the open door, Leslie watched Rosenbaum step into the main office and shake the man's hand. The man was holding an open notepad and pen in the other.

"Am I the first?" she heard the reporter ask.

"First what?" Rosenbaum queried nervously.

"I am the first!" The notepad and pen came up like lightning. "Do you have a statement, Senator?"

"About what?"

"About your papers, sir."

The three aides who had been busily working in the room suddenly stopped. Rosenbaum searched their faces, like this might be some kind of joke played by a loving staff.

The reporter was speaking: "Your papers, Senator. I just got a call from my editor that some highly classified documents from the Senate Armed Services Committee—your copies, sir— were found in an intercepted envelope being delivered to the Bulgarian mission. Do you—"

"That's ridiculous!"

"Are you claiming the copies were stolen?"

It seemed like all at once the three office phones started to ring. Two more reporters, you could tell the occupation by their hectic entrance and hungry expressions, burst into the room.

Goodell, the first one there, saw his scoop slipping away. "Senator—a statement, please!"

"A statement?" Rosenbaum repeated dumbly.

In the Senate parking lot, a camera crew was ripping equipment out of a news van. The producer flew on ahead to check the directory for Senator Lawrence Rosenbaum's office.

"Whatever these accusations are," Rosenbaum said to the two reporters already there, "they are false! Totally unfounded!"

"Senator!"

"Did you keep your papers in a safe, sir?"

"When did you realize they were gone?"

The phones were ringing faster than the small staff could answer them. The reporters had backed Rosenbaum against a wall.

"Did you know they were classified, Senator?"

"Of course I did!"

"Then why did you let them leave your office?"

"I didn't!"

"Do you have a statement, Senator?"

"Just what I told Doug—that these accusations—"

"Have you been contacted by the police?"

"No!"

"How do you think your copies wound up in that envelope?"

"No idea. Leslie—"

"What did the papers deal with, Senator?"

"I don't know! I just found out about all this when you arrived! Now, please—I'll have to ask you all to leave! Leslie. Leslie! Where's Leslie?"

Rosenbaum ducked into his office.

"Leslie! Where the hell did she go?"

She was nowhere to be seen. Rosenbaum opened his arms wide and tried to steer the reporters toward the door.

"That's enough—enough now!"

"Senator!"

Rosenbaum looked to a nearby aide. He caught her eye just as she hung up the phone. She looked on the verge of tears and said very softly: "Senator Screws has just called for a full investigation . . ."

Chapter Twenty-four

Night had come. The Old Man was waiting for a call, sitting alone in his library, in his chair, surrounded by a long life's accumulation of books.

It would have been very difficult to define Claude Screws from an examination of his library.

The thousands of tightly packed titles that rose from the very floor to the twelve-foot ceiling had no common thread. Here was an eclectic mix that defied easy categorization. At first glance, one might take note of a preponderance of dry political tomes and think perhaps he'd been pinned down. But then came a disconcertingly thorough section of Victorian literature—pure fiction. Moving on, an impressive division of histories comes into view, only to be offset by five sweeping shelves of modern drama. Then a half wall of thick law volumes, sitting side by side with hundreds of slender works of poetry. Biographies stacked beside philosophy. A broadside of military tracts, stretching from Sun-Tzu's *The Art of War* to the most recent examination of the role of the supercarrier in modern combat, created an uneasy truce with a bordering land of crime fiction, spy novels, and popular thrillers. A language section, predominantly German and French, neighbored several shelves on gardening.

Who knows what one might find if the sliding ladder were employed for a look up near the ceiling.

The only conclusion to be reached was that the assembler of this library was a voracious reader.

And Screws was, or had been anyway. He'd pored through them all, many twice, and he remembered what he read. Screws had that kind of mind that retained specific information.

Of late, however, Screws had lost the desire or energy to read, and the only enjoyment he got from his library was sitting in his chair and scanning the titles, which was what he was doing now.

Ellis, ever smiling, came into the room.

"What will it take to get you to turn up the heat?"

"You should be feeling it any moment. Lots and lots of heat."

"I heard the door."

"She's waiting like you asked."

"Ellis."

"Yes, sir."

". . . Will you be smiling the day I die?"

Ellis regarded him.

"Sir?"

The phone on the stand beside Screws started to blink. He ignored it, continuing to stare at Ellis.

"You know what's going on—that I'm sick."

". . . I do know. Yes, I do."

"And what's your personal reaction to that, Ellis? You can tell me the truth. I'll tell you now that the will's made up and you're well taken care of. So, go on—tell me. Your personal reaction to my imminent passing."

". . . I believe I'll miss you, sir, when you're gone."

"The truth?"

Ellis nodded his head.

"Then you're a bigger fool than I thought you were." Screws turned abruptly toward the phone. "Send her in when I ring," he said curtly.

"Yes, sir," Ellis said, leaving with his smile.

Screws waited for him to close the door before picking up.

"This line clean?"

"Dedicated and approved," Vanning answered.

"So?"

". . . There's a problem. The pictures we got this afternoon from that bar. Turned out to be family snapshots of Lakeman and his wife. The dog tag we have, which makes eight all present and accounted for, but those pictures aren't what—"

"Nothing from the sub? Not one picture from inside or out?"

"No," Vanning told him.

"That leaves two possibilities . . ."

"That's how I see it."

"Either there are no duplicate pictures and there never were," Screws reasoned, "or there are and Lakeman didn't trust Clarke enough to give them to him."

"Yeah."

"If it's the first then there's no problem."

"No."

"If it's the second—"

"I can send my guy over to Lakeman's house to search."

"Using what excuse?"

"NSA business."

"Do it."

"Now, about Clarke . . ." Vanning paused. "He got away from my man. I don't know where he is. We lost him after the pictures. He practically stole that aide's car and took off like a bat out of hell. It's not that easy to trail a car, Claude," Vanning began to explain. "Especially if it's really flying like this one was and you hit a little traff—"

"Can it, Leonard."

Immediate, fuming silence.

"Stay on this line. I'll get right back to you."

Screws put the call on hold. He pressed for Ellis to send in the waiting visitor. Ellis showed her into the room several moments later. Not that she needed to be shown. She'd been here many times before.

Ellis left and closed the doors from outside. The woman crossed quickly over to Screws.

"Complicated, isn't it?" Screws asked her.

Leslie Flood paced before Screws's chair, avoiding his gaze.

"It's too complicated."

"Where is he?"

"You never said anything about killing people—that was never part of our relationship. *Never*."

"Nobody's been killed," Screws responded calmly.

"This Dave Lakeman—he was murdered!"

"He wasn't murdered. It was a *heart attack*. It was circumstance. A simple chain of events—poor eating habits, wrong set of genes. Sometimes things just get away from you."

Screws watched her drop heavily onto the sofa. She seemed to have reached some sort of decision about herself.

"I don't want any part of this. *Not this*. I just don't want— "

"*It's payday, Leslie*."

"That's what you said about setting up Balfour!" she challenged.

"You've profited since then. Your stock has risen very nicely. I foresee a blue-chip future. But for the moment, I, the broker, am taking some profits . . ."

Screws could see she'd been crying. She was trying to stay in control, barely managing.

"I've provided for you for thirty years," he said, sharply changing his tone. "This is called squaring up."

"Not—" she choked, "not if it involves people getting hurt!"

"It's a little late to start playing Snow White. As if Balfour and his family weren't hurt?"

"Not physically."

"You destroyed him, in every sense of the word."

"Because you ordered me to—he wasn't *physically hurt!*"

"You tell him that, see what he says."

"I don't want to do this anymore!" she pleaded.

"You know as well as anyone," Screws said evenly, "better than most perhaps, that everything you get, everything that you use—must be paid for. Do you remember where I found you?" Screws asked, eyes narrowing.

"At least my mother loved me . . ."

"*Do you remember?*"

"Yes! I remember!"

"Good! Then keep that place in mind at all times when I ask you to do something! *I* was the one who took you from there—

paid for your schooling, your clothes, your entire upbringing. I did those things.''

He watched her shoulders sag just a little more. She wasn't going to cry, he figured. She'd cry after she left, bawl most likely, but she wasn't going to give him the satisfaction of seeing her cry here.

"You've got a lot farther to fall these days, young lady. I put together your entire world. A very comfortable, very prosperous world. And you can go much farther still. But if I slip, if I miss a step, I'm going to take every brick of it with me! Do you understand? Do you understand what I'm saying? Stop nodding your head and answer me, damn you!''

She kept her head bowed: ". . . I understand.''

"Good! I'm moving fast on this and I don't have time to waste shoring you up. We're way past that stage, you and I. Now, where is he?''

"He's . . . he has my car and keys. I think he might show up at my place. He's very confused and very scared and—''

"It's seven thirty now,'' he cut her off. "I want you to go directly home. If I don't hear from you in one hour I'm going to assume he's there, with you. Do you understand?''

"Yes,'' she said to the carpet.

"The pictures we got from the bar were no good. It was family stuff—not what we wanted. If Clarke's at your place you keep him there. Do anything you have to do, and I know you can do a lot, to make sure he stays. You find out if there really are any duplicate pictures, and if so, where he's got them stashed. Make sure *you* answer the phone in the morning. The caller will identify himself as 'Warren from the office.' You have all that?''

"Yes.''

"I have to take a call.''

Leslie stood mechanically from the sofa. She started for the door.

"By the way,'' Screws said to her as she opened it to go, "you did an excellent job on the Rosenbaum thing. You should take pride in your work, Leslie. You do it exceptionally well.''

She walked out.

Screws closed his eyes for a moment, gathering his strength. He picked up the receiver and took Vanning off hold. "Leonard?''

"Still here."

"I think Clarke's going to show at the girl's place—the aide."

"The girl? But why?"

"Because he's got nowhere else to go."

". . . Where are you getting all this information?" asked Vanning.

"That's my business. Leonard, you're going to have to do them both."

"*Both?*"

"Yes."

"The girl as well?" Vanning asked, surprised. "Why the girl, Claude?"

"Because she knows what's going on."

"Now, wait a minute, Claude," Vanning said with rising indignation, "you're not the one who has to pay for all this! This isn't like thirty years ago. These aren't government guys I'm using. These guys don't work for free. I've only really got one guy who does this kind of thing—just one! He'll charge a fortune for this!"

"I'll pay."

"One is bad enough; I mean we have to knock this guy out of the picture—but the girl?"

"*I said I'll pay.*"

"You don't even know how much it is! It'll be somewhere in the neighborhood of twenty thou—"

"I don't care about the money! I've got more than I can spend! Christ, you can be an ass, Leonard!"

"You'll pay? If you say you'll pay, then I'll front it and you can pay me back."

"*Fine,*" Screws snapped.

"By the end of the week? Could you pay me back by the end of the week?"

"Yes!"

"I just wanted to get it straight, that's all. You don't have to yell at me . . ."

Vanning waited for an apology. Getting none, he asked: "What about Rosenbaum?"

"He's got enough troubles. Let him start babbling about

some Russian submarine. I don't want to hear from you unless
there's a problem. If I don't call you by nine, I'll contact you in
the morning. You know where the girl lives?"

"I can find out easy enough."

"This is the end game, Leonard. Get Clarke and we can put
this whole damn thing to rest."

"*I'll handle it.*"

"I'm trusting you on this."

"Only because you have to. Say, Claude, when you pay me
back . . . could you make it in cash? You know—small bills,
tens and twen—"

Screws slammed down the phone.

II

By the time Leslie got home it was dark. A cold wind was
sweeping out a high spiderweb of wispy clouds. Between the
wide, clear spaces shimmered tiny points of stars.

Lights glowed warmly through the curtained windows of the
other houses on the street. Families were home; in for the night.

The cab pulled away.

Leslie walked through the darkness around to the driveway.
There, in the shadows, was the Spitfire.

She came back around to the stoop. The brownstone was dark
and silent, melting in with the night.

Leslie retrieved a spare key hidden beneath the stoop and
climbed the steps. She listened at the door for some time before
unlocking it.

Slowly stepped inside.

The house was pitch black. Leslie let the door close behind
her. She took one creaking step into the foyer. A hesitant:
"Matt—Matt, are you here?"

The words died in the darkness.

She moved cautiously into the living room. Street light through the large uncurtained windows lent a dim silvery glow. She stood just inside, looking. It was empty.

She went down the hall, floorboards settling with each step.

To the right, the bathroom door was open. Peering through the gloom, she could see it was vacant. To the left, the staircase. She hovered at the landing, looking up, one ear cocked to the curving stairwell.

Unnerving silence.

She walked into the murky kitchen. Here the hum of the refrigerator. The stove clock glowed. She groped for the wall switch. Several rapid passes. Found it. Nothing. She pressed hard. Several times more. The light refused to come.

"*Boo.*"

From very near. She screamed a scream that had been years in the making. A light suddenly went on in the corner. Matt was sitting at the kitchen table, watching curiously.

"*What are you doing?*" she yelled. "You scared me half to death!" Leslie tried to catch her breath. "What the hell are you doing?"

"I'm hiding."

"Why are you sitting in the dark!" Her hands had flown to her head, holding either side like it was going to fall off.

"That was some scream."

"You could have turned on the lights, for God's sake!"

"I was thinking. I'm sorry. I like to think in the dark."

Leslie fiddled anxiously with the wall switch.

"I disconnected the fuse. It won't work."

"I said you could stay here," she responded, "not rewire the place."

"I didn't want anyone looking in through the windows and seeing me here."

"No one knows you're here."

"I don't see how they could, do you?"

Leslie took two candles from a cupboard. She found some matches in a drawer. Closed it hard.

"What the hell happened to Rosenbaum? I heard about it on the radio."

"I—" She struck a match. It went out. "The press just

showed up and . . . classified documents were found somewhere.'' She was having trouble striking another match.

''Let me do that.'' Matt crossed to her. He stood very close.
Lit the candles.

''Your hands are shaking.''

''You scared the hell out of me.''

Together they watched the candles sputter to life.

''What d'you think about this Rosenbaum thing?''

''I can't think about any of it right now.''

She turned away from Matt and opened the refrigerator,
stooping down into its light. ''I've got to sit down, eat something, and relax before I explode.''

''You okay?''

Leslie immediately straightened. She faced Matt with a sudden, odd smile. Brightly: ''I'm told I make the best omelets
in Georgetown.''

''I could eat something.''

The refrigerator was well stocked. She started pulling out
what she needed. Matt was leaning against a counter, watching
her in the flickering light.

''This is quite a place you've got here.''

''I'll have to turn on the stove light. I can't see with just these
candles.''

She turned on the light over the stove.

''I mean, it must be worth a fortune. Place like this—in this
neighborhood. I never realized senator's aides did so well.''

''Would you like a drink? I'm having white wine.''

''Yeah. I'll have a glass.''

She poured two glasses of white wine. Handed one to Matt.

''*Is* this your place?'' he asked.

''Yes. It's my place. I was left some money by my grandparents. Quite a bit.'' She tossed down almost the full glass and
poured herself another. Held out the bottle to Matt.

''I'm fine,'' he said. ''. . . So from Georgetown University
you stayed here and bought this with an inheritance? You did
say Georgetown before, right? In the car?''

''Yes.''

She began cracking the eggs into a light-blue bowl.

''There's no rush on dinner,'' said Matt.

"*I'm* hungry."

"Okay." Matt sipped his wine. "Judging by this house, I'd say you probably wouldn't even have to work if you didn't want to."

"I don't want to and I have to, if that answers your question."

"If you want me to go I will," he said suddenly.

"No—" She gave a sideways glance, smiled bravely. "Stay. Please. Rosenbaum today . . . it was horrible. I can't imagine where it's all going to end. I'm just upset. I'll settle down."

Matt sat at the table.

Leslie lost herself in making them dinner.

III

The plates had been pushed aside. A second bottle was almost gone. He was handsome, she'd decided. She was concentrating on staying in the moment. What came before, she'd forgotten. What might follow she refused to entertain. The only safe place to stay was the here and now. She was sitting in her kitchen with a handsome man. By candlelight. Her shoes off. That's all. And he was cute. Handsome, really. Youthful face— could pass for mid-twenties if he wanted. Nice hands. She liked that. She liked him. She did, she convinced herself. Perhaps she was feeling sorry for him. Maybe she felt guilt for what, despite repressing the violent specifics, she knew she was leading him to. Keeping him here. For others. For what they would do. Because something would be done, and she was going through with it. That was clear. But she felt a bond with him. A physical bond. Something was already being done and she was doing it. Keeping him here for others.

". . . and that was quite a shock because I'd practically grown up here."

"In Washington?" Matt asked.

"Right. But then suddenly Greg was issued orders for Germany and he was gone."

"Your ex-husband?"

"Did I say that?" she asked, pouring the last of the wine, spilling some. "And he was! I don't usually tell people I've been married is why I asked."

"That's what you said."

"And it's true. But he went to Germany—I told you that, too, didn't I? For all I know he's still there."

"You didn't go?"

"I was only eighteen."

"Your parents?"

"They didn't even know I'd married him. Why should they care? I left home years earlier."

". . . But they had money?"

"*Money?* They were dirt poor! My stepdad couldn't hold a job to save his life. Complete alcoholic. My mother had her hands full with us kids. I left there as soon as I could—boom—I was gone."

"But you said your grandparents left you an inheritance."

"I lied," she said immediately.

"So . . . so what about this house?"

"I rent it. Well, I don't *really* rent it. I take care of it. I'm like a house sitter. You know! These other people own it but they're away. In Europe somewhere. I get a break on the rent by watching it while they're away. Why do you keep asking all these *questions?*"

"I like you. I'm interested. So you went to college? To Georgetown then?"

She took a big gulp. Gave a terrific frown.

"It's *so* boring—really! I'm sick and tired of even thinking about it all the time."

Her movements were light and unfocused. She realized he'd had very little of the wine.

"How come you lied about the house?"

"Why? But who cares? Because I'm ashamed of my past. There. I don't want to talk about myself anymore."

". . . Okay."

He was sitting very near. Just the corner of the table lay between them. She reached out and ran her hand over his. He watched her fingers stretch softly over his.

"Would you like to see the rest of the house? The upstairs?"

". . . I'd like that."

She took one candle and stood.

"Take the other."

He did. Up the back staircase from the kitchen she led him. She giggled when she reached behind and took his hand. Two flights to the third floor. She stumbled only once. Around the landing and into the hall. The candle dripped warm wax on her hand. Matt held firmly on to the other. Their deformed shadows slid grotesquely along the walls.

A physical bond.

She led him gently into her bedroom. She liked the effect of the candles. Two little islands of light. She placed hers on the nightstand near the large bed. Matt's she extinguished with two moistened fingers. She turned and put her arms around him, drawing him near. He came willingly. She kissed him like her life depended on it. After just a moment he pulled away.

"Undress for me," he said.

She waited a beat. Locked in a dreamy stare, her arms dropped from his waist. Very slowly, she pulled off her sweater and T-shirt and let them fall to the floor—watching him. She unfastened her pants and stepped out of them, into his arms. He held her, inches away.

"Take off your bra and panties."

". . . You do it," she breathed.

He reached up and popped the snap of her sheer black bra. He slowly pulled the cups away to reveal her breasts. Her body was soft orange in the candlelight. Perfect. He held the parted bra, his face inches from hers, staring into her eyes. His hands rose from either side of her waist and encircled her breasts, caressing their firmness.

"You know what I can't figure out?" he whispered, his head dropping into the softness of her neck.

She pushed her pelvis tightly against his and pulled her chest back to let his hands roam freely.

"I can't figure out how those guys knew exactly where I hid the stuff . . ."

"*When?*" she moaned.

"In the bar," he whispered. He ran his tongue up behind her ear and pulled her tight. Kissing her there.

"I think it's strange," he said softly, darting his tongue onto her hot, arched neck, "that someone would think to look in a ceiling tile."

She moaned again. She was somewhere else. Her hand slid down to his pants. Rapidly undid the belt.

He kissed her full on the mouth as her hands frantically undid his pants. He drew her nearer, tighter against him. His head dropped back to her neck. His pants were about to fall. She could feel the hard bulge straining there.

"Leslie—"

"Uhhhh—"

"You didn't go to Georgetown."

He suddenly had both her arms pinned tightly behind her, encircling her from the front. She was panting, her eyes closed, writhing against him as if this were still foreplay.

"Matt—"

His lips brushing hers: "You *didn't* go to Georgetown. I checked. It was a lie."

She opened her eyes. Saw his face large in front of her, studying her, his eyes wide with a strange excitement. She tried suddenly to free her hands, slightly at first, and then really straining. But he had them tight together behind her.

"You made a call before we left Rosenbaum's office. You called someone before we left. That's how they knew where the stuff was."

She was trying to pull away from him with everything she had, but it was hopeless. They were locked as tightly as lovers.

"Who did you call before we went to the bar? *Who? Who the hell did you call?*"

He roughly pushed her away from him. She stumbled backward, and just as she did, just as she started to fall backward, a shot rang out from the darkness of the doorway.

Simultaneously, a small framed picture on the wall behind where she'd stood exploded in a splintering of glass.

Matt was dropping to the floor, exposed, no hope of hiding. He rolled desperately back and forth on the carpet. A second shot was overdue. Matt stole a glance at the door during his third frantic roll—looked at it from upside down—and saw a very strange sight: a man in an overcoat was staggering forward into the room—an older man, white, no hat—and his hands were at his throat, red hands, one still clutching a gun, as blood practically gushed through the fingers he had raised to his neck.

The man hit the floor face-down a dozen feet directly in front of Matt.

The man looked dead.

Looking low over the man's form, from floor-level, Matt could see someone else's legs still in the dimness of the doorway—as if the fallen man had left behind some supernatural double to finish the job.

Only this man was bigger and was holding a bloody knife in his hand, and he was coming straight for Matt.

Chapter Twenty-five

For four hours, Orin had been waiting outside the house—watching, biding his time until Skinny came back out. At around eight, a pretty young blonde had come down the sidewalk, checked the drive, and then gone in. All was quiet until twenty minutes ago, when an older, well-dressed man in a tan trenchcoat and brown felt hat had come ambling down the street and suddenly cut into the brownstone driveway. Orin quietly followed. He crept along the side of the house and watched from deep shadow as the man easily popped the back-door lock with a thin length of flexible steel. The man silently entered the house. After several moments, Orin went in after him. The room was pitch black, seemed to be a kitchen. Orin paused by the door, motionless, and heard faint footsteps—above—the man was going upstairs. Orin gave the figure two flights lead before following. Hunting knife in hand, Orin moved swiftly and quietly to the third-floor landing. Peeking into the hall, he saw the man, a mere ten feet away. The man was standing before a closed door, under the crack of which seeped a dim light. The man reached into his pocket and produced a pistol fitted with a long, black silencer.

Orin suddenly realized that the man was here to knock off

Skinny. The guy was obviously a pro; he was too casual and relaxed to be otherwise. The man, Orin decided, must have had something to do with Mark's death—either directly or indirectly—and was here to bump off Skinny—the one guy who probably had a line to what was really going on.

The man was putting his free hand on the knob. Orin tensed. The man's hand tightened and then turned—he quickly pushed the door open.

Orin flew around the corner into the hall, took two steps, and brought the knife deep across the man's throat. The man quickly fell forward onto the floor.

Orin stepped over the unmoving body. He was upon Matt. In one swift motion he kicked him square in the ribs. Another kick immediately followed, harder this time, in the stomach. Matt flew back against the bed frame.

He straddled Matt and lifted his head by his shirt collar. Orin cracked him hard in the jaw, letting go of the shirt at just the right moment to allow his head to bang to the floor.

"Wha . . . is this . . . ?" Matt managed.

"I'm the one who's gonna ask questions!"

Orin grabbed his arm and yanked him to a standing position. He punched him again, a quick powerful shot to the stomach. Matt collapsed onto the bed, sprawling beside Leslie.

"Look at me, you son of a bitch! I said, look at me!"

He grabbed Matt's hair and pulled his face up. Matt tried to focus. His eyes were squinting in pain.

". . . I don—"

"Look! You know who I am!"

". . . You?"

"Look!"

". . . You . . . you're . . . the guy—you were the guy from the dock . . ."

Mesmerized by the sudden association, Matt tried to prop himself on a wobbily elbow.

"That's right! The guy from the dock!"

In an instant, the knife's sharpened tip was pressing hard against Matt's neck, indenting the soft skin.

"Nuh!"

"I'm going to ask you a question, asshole—I'm only going to ask you it once. *Do you understand?*"

The blade pressed the indentation deeper into Matt's neck, the skin drew tighter—was a hair from slicing open.

"—Ah!"

"Now listen closely—here it comes—*Who sent you to me in the first place? Answer me!*"

"Stop!" Leslie screamed.

"Answer me!" Orin pushed the blade harder against Matt's neck. The skin cut, a trickle of blood ran quickly down his neck. Matt looked on the verge of passing out.

Leslie was screaming. She rolled off the back of the bed. Orin pulled his knife hand away to grab at her but she was quick.

He turned to cut her off, but she dodged around, going to the man on the floor. She grabbed for his bloody gun and quickly pointed it at Orin. Orin turned back to Matt and put the knife tight against his throat.

"Let him up," Leslie said. "Let him up now!"

Orin regarded the half-naked woman before him.

"I've come too fucking far, lady. You want to kill me? —fine, but he's going, too. You people killed my nephew. I don't know what for, but if I can't find out I'm gonna take as many of you out with me as I can—"

Matt's voice came out a whisper: "The people—the people who killed your nephew . . . are trying to kill me . . ."

Orin looked down at him, seething.

"That guy," indicating the man on the floor, "wasn't aiming at you, pal. He was aiming at *her!*"

It took a moment, but the gun in Leslie's hand dropped slightly as the realization of what Orin said hit home.

"Let him up," she said evenly. "I'll put down the gun, right on the floor, if you let him up and put away that knife."

"*No way.*" His grip tightened on Matt's collar. The knife stayed at his throat.

"I'm not the one you're after—" Matt croaked.

"Then who are you working for?"

"I can explain it to you."

"Go on," Orin said, eyes shifting between the two. "Explain it. Explain it as best as you can, because if I don't believe you I'm gonna slit your throat. I don't care what she does after that." Orin pulled the knife an inch away to let him speak.

And there, in the light of one candle, sprawled on the bed, a knife hovering at his throat, Matt quickly told what he knew: from the second he'd seen the shadow on the satellite photograph right up till the moment he was about to slap Leslie only minutes before.

He finished.

Orin looked over at Leslie. She had the gun trained on his head. She could easily have fired and then picked Matt off as well.

"You work for these guys, lady?" Orin asked, looking at her eyes and not the gun. "You're working for this old senator?"

Leslie stared back at him. ". . . Claude Screws," she began and then stopped. "Claude Screws is my father."

Matt struggled to see her face. *"Your father?"*

". . . I was an illegitimate child. My mother was a prostitute in South Carolina. Screws got her pregnant. She opted to keep the child, to sue for support. Screws paid her off after the birth, put me in a home, paid for everything—visited once every five years, got me a job, and put me in this house after college." She looked down at Matt. "I did what he told me to do . . ."

"I should've let that fuck on the floor blow your head off. That's what I should've done. You gonna shoot us now? Is that what you're going to do?"

Very precisely, Leslie laid the gun on the floor. "I don't work for him anymore," she said. She went into her closet and a moment later came out wearing a robe.

Orin took the knife from Matt's throat and put it in his pocket.

"You believe me?" Matt asked, rubbing nervously at the trickle of blood from where the knife had touched.

"I dove there, kid. After you left, Mark told me you'd seen something and he'd buoyed the spot where you went. I saw what was down there. It ain't there no more. The next night a salvage ship came around and towed the thing out to the shelf. If I *hadn't* seen it, I would think you were lying your ass off."

"But how did you find me?" Matt asked. "How'd you find me here?"

"Your friend's check had his address on it. I flew in this morning, got a car, and went to his house. I figured him and you were the ones behind Mark getting killed like that. So I followed some people from there to a funeral, then I figured out it was his. I saw you standing in the back. When you left I took off after you. I tailed you here. Once you were inside, I waited to see what was what. She came in two hours ago and I almost made a move. I decided to wait. Twenty minutes ago this guy breaks in through the back. I followed him inside. Bingo. I'd like to break your neck, lady," he said to Leslie, meaning it.

"I'm in the same boat as you two now," she said heavily, coming down from the wine. "You said yourself that man was aiming at me."

Leslie cowered as Orin seemingly started for her, but then he veered and was heading for the door.

"Where are you going?" Matt asked him.

"I'm gonna hurt this son of a bitch Screws is what I'm gonna do."

"How?" Matt asked.

"You don't want to know."

"If you really want to hurt him," Leslie said, "if you really want to hurt him where he lives—destroy him. Destroy him publicly."

Orin stopped at the doorway. He turned and regarded her.

Leslie looked to Matt: "You have the pictures from the sub, you've both seen the thing. Surely—"

"*What do you mean?*" Matt broke in. "I don't have the pictures. You were with me—the pictures were gone."

"The pictures from the bar were a fake," she said.

"What?"

"You didn't know that? It was family pictures of your friend."

"That can't be."

"Maybe your friend made a mistake when he gave them to you," she said.

"No way."

"Maybe he didn't trust you," Orin suggested from by the door.

A pause, then Matt tried to stand from the bed. He grimaced, holding his right arm tight to where he'd been kicked.

"You might have a broken rib," Orin told him.

Matt reached for the phone on the nightstand. He dialed a number. He looked over at the man on the floor while it rang. An unpleasant dark pool was forming on the carpet.

"Who are you calling?" Orin said.

Matt motioned for quiet. The line rang.

"Hello?" came a man's voice.

"Hello—is Perri there?"

"This is her brother. Can I help you with something?"

"Bob—This is Matt, Matthew Clar—"

"You've got one hell of a nerve!"

"I know this is a bad time, Bob, but it's really important that I talk to her. I'm sorry to bother you and all but I really have to talk with her."

"She's asleep and I have no intention of waking her—particularly for you!"

"Bob, I insist I talk with—"

"The answer is no. The doctor said—"

"*Bob!* Bob, I didn't mean to yell, but when I say something is *important*, I mean it."

"I'm sure it can wait till the morning. I will *not* wake her."

"I worked with Dave. Do you understand? Important work. Very, very classified and top-secret work! I have to ask Perri something very important about Dave's work. Now get her for me, Bob."

"I don't appreciate your tone. Not one bit."

"I don't really care."

"If it's about work, there's a man here from Dave's office right now looking for some papers or something. You can speak to him."

"A man from work?"

"Yes. What is it with you people over there? One's as rude as the next! Do you want to talk to him or not?"

"Uh, no. No, that's okay. Forget about it, Bob. I'll call Perri tomorrow. Good-bye."

Matt hung up the phone.

"There's someone already there searching the house. God-damn it!"

"Well, let's go," said Orin, immediately impatient.

"And do what?"

"Take the film and pictures away from them—what else?"

"You've got to be kidding."

"Why not?" Leslie asked. "This guy looks like he could handle an army."

"Just go in there? I don't even know where Dave hid them. They could be anywhere."

Orin had picked up the gun and was wiping the blood off on the dead man's tan overcoat.

"We're wasting time," he said.

"Let me get dressed," Leslie said. She stood and went into the closet. Orin spun and kicked the door closed on her. It was an old house with locks on every door. Orin turned the key and pocketed it.

"I don't want her around," he said to Matt. "She can stay in there until somebody comes back to let her out. She can die in there for all I care."

II

Orin was driving the Spitfire fast, Matt supplying directions. On the way, he mumbled an apology for batting Matt around. He offered Matt the gun, a token of his remorse, but Matt just shook his head and kept feeding the rights and lefts. Matt didn't turn down Orin's offer, however, of two Percodans.

Each breath caused Matt pain. Something felt wrong down there. A very sharp pain on one side.

"You should probably go to a hospital and get some x-rays or something," Orin said.

Matt nodded.

"Because broken ribs can be dangerous. I've had them. I know."

"I'll make it."

"Again, I'm sorry. I was sure you and Stocky were behind it all. Christ, I almost offed you on that bed. Really. You don't know. I was about to—"

"Slow down, slow down here—the house is on the next block."

Orin let off the accelerator and took the car out of gear. They coasted to the corner of the peaceful residential street, and Orin killed the headlights.

There was an empty car parked across the street from Dave and Perri's house. Lights shone from the downstairs living-room windows. Upstairs the house was dark.

Matt and Orin climbed out of the sports car. They stood in the shadows, under the low branches spreading from someone's huge old willow.

". . . That brown car parked in front—it's not theirs," Matt said. "Perri's brother said the guy was inside looking around. Must be his."

"C'mon."

Orin led Matt across the street. They followed a waist-high line of hedges that bordered a house two doors up from Dave's.

Orin stopped, crouching low. "What about those other cars in the drive?" he whispered to Matt. "Whose are those?"

"Dave was fixing up that Caddy and the Impala. The other one's Perri's. I guess the station wagon belongs to her brother."

"Yeah, that's the car I tailed to the funeral . . ."

"You think there's only one?" Matt asked.

"I don't know, kid. I don't see anyone else. That doesn't mean no one's there. We'll just stay low and try to get close to the house."

"And then what?"

"Catch this asshole coming out. Let him do the work. We'll take the pictures from him when he leaves."

They crawled around the hedge and stayed low going across the darkness of the lawn. Up to the side of the house. There were shrubs here. They stayed low behind them and crawled directly beneath the living-room window. Dead leaves had piled here, wet from the recent rains.

Matt started to get off his knees to take a look inside.

Orin firmly pulled him down. *"We'll get him going out.* No sense risking getting seen."

They waited. It was a cold October night, windy and very clear. Matt noticed that Halloween decorations had been put up on some of the neighboring houses. He was settled into the wet leaves, not caring that his pants were getting wet. Orin stayed in a crouch, ready to move in a moment.

Twenty minutes had gone by when the front door suddenly opened and a shaft of light angled across the lawn. The door closed again quickly and a thin, tall man wearing an overcoat and a hat came down the front steps. He started across the lawn toward the car.

Orin was moving before Matt knew it; darting low at an amazing speed. The man turned at the last moment and Orin came up and clasped a large hand over his mouth. With the other he gave four rapid-fire punches to the stomach and the man dropped to the wet grass like an empty sack.

Matt crawled up to where Orin had the man held to the ground. The man's eyes were wide.

Matt remembered the pain of Orin's punches.

"Let him breathe," Matt whispered to Orin.

"Check his pockets for the pictures."

Matt quickly checked the man's overcoat pockets. Other than a packet of tissues and a comb, they were empty. The man was lying still, accepting the fact that he had no hope of getting up if Orin didn't want him to.

"Inside—check inside."

Matt dug a hand under the overcoat and checked the man's jacket pockets. Nothing, not even a wallet. He checked the man's pants pockets with the same result.

"Where are the pictures?" Orin said to the man, and then lifted his hand slightly to allow a response.

"I couldn't find them."

"Then why were you leaving?"

"The lady's brother kicked me out—said she needed to rest."

Matt smiled in spite of the situation. He could easily picture the high-school history teacher from New Jersey getting indignant and tossing the guy out.

"*A car,*" Orin said to Matt, as he clamped his hand down hard over the man's mouth. Two headlights could be seen a block away. A third beam suddenly flashed on, pointing at the hedges they'd crawled beside—a patrol car!

Orin stuffed a glove into the man's mouth. "Move or make a sound and I'll kill you."

The man seemed to understand.

"Grab his arm," Orin told Matt, "we'll drag him to the Caddy."

They pulled the man across the last bit of lawn. The police car was barely a hundred feet away, moving slow and quiet, the search light scanning both sides of the street.

Orin eased open the back door of the Caddy. He climbed in and pulled the man in after him.

"Get in the front—stay low."

Matt climbed in the front and tried noiselessly, gently, to close the door. Just as he pressed himself flat against the floorboards, the driver door swung open several inches.

It hadn't closed.

The police car was too close to try to pull it shut now. Matt stayed where he was, head pushed under the passenger seat.

He could hear Orin breathing in the backseat. He could hear the patrol car stop very nearby. The searchlight suddenly swung through the Caddy, hitting the tops of the seats. Matt closed his eyes.

It seemed he could hear better that way so he kept them closed.

He could hear the radio chatter. A car door opened and closed. Shoes started a slow beat up the driveway, right past the Caddy. After a moment, he heard the cop knock on the front door. It opened. A muffled exchange:

"Yes, officer?"

"Sorry to bother you, sir. We've just had a report of prowlers in the neighborhood. In this vicinity."

"Really?"

A pause.

"Have you seen anything, sir?"

"Nothing unusual. No—nothing."

"It's probably not anything to get upset about, but we're checking it out."

"I'd certainly hope so."

"You might want to keep the doors locked and the windows, too."

"I'm very good about that."

"If you *do* see anything unusual just give us a call."

"Of course I will, immediately."

"Thank you, sir. Goodnight."

"Goodnight."

The steps came back down the driveway, blending with the sporadic radio chatter and the idling police-car engine. A car door opened and closed. The engine slowly faded into the night.

Matt opened his eyes. His pupils, now dilated, could see dimly in the dark. His head was pressed against the floor of the car and he was looking under the passenger seat. Right in front of him was a small, brightly wrapped box. He regarded it for a moment, trying to place it.

It came to him: Perri's birthday gift. He remembered watching Dave hide Perri's birthday present in the car. "She was a snoop," he'd said then.

Matt's heart suddenly started pounding. *Dave had hidden Perri's gift in the car.*

"I think they're gone," Orin whispered from the back.

Matt grabbed under the front passenger seat and pulled out the present. He ripped it open, looking for the duplicate pictures and negatives.

The box held a new leather belt.

Matt felt for anything else that might be there, but only found a candy-bar wrapper. He pawed under the driver's seat but that was clear as well.

Matt got up slightly, his head bumping the glove compartment.

From the back: "What are you doing up there?"

Matt turned to face the glove compartment. He pressed the latch. The lid dropped open. A small light went on. In the dim light he rifled through the junk: road maps, owner's manual, road flares, golfing magazine—and suddenly, beneath a clump of unpaid parking tickets, Matt found it—a red packet of photographs and a neat stack of computer printout.

Matt reached for them. He flipped through the pictures: thirty-six three-by-five-inch glossy underwater photographs. The computer printout was a copy of the research Dave had done on the dead sailors.

"Orin?"

"Yeah?"

". . . I found them."

Chapter Twenty-six

It was the first time in three decades that Claude Screws had been too ill to go in. Three uninterrupted decades of service. But this morning he felt bad, failing. It was as if the doctor's bleak diagnosis yesterday had hastened the physical onset of the disease.

He was lying restlessly in bed, feverish and weak. Ellis had brought up the papers but they lay unopened at his side.

Screws dozed.

Galena knocked, came into the room. He envied her health, would have snatched it had there been a way. She brought in a tray of cereal and juice and set it nearby on the nightstand.

"Do you need anything else?" she asked, her voice carrying a tint of genuine pity.

"I can manage myself, thank you very much."

He'd nip that nonsense in the bud.

She handed him a note from the tray and then started for the door. He looked at it.

"I can't read this. What is it? *Ten thirty, what—*"

Galena paused, turned. "They called from the office. Senator Rosenbaum, a press conference. I wrote it down."

Screws frowned, crumpled the note and tossed it feebly to the floor. She started to go.

"Tell Ellis to bring the car around," he told her, gathering his strength to try to rise.

Galena fixed him with a doleful look. "Is that wise?"

"Nothing from you! Not a word!"

He was pulling himself out of the bed, his emaciated frame emerging like a hermit crab from its shell.

She left shaking her head.

Screws steadied himself by the nightstand. He fingered through his address book and jabbed out a number on the phone. A wave of dizziness came, threatened to stay, and then passed.

"Hello."

". . . Give me Leonard Vanning."

"I'm sorry, sir, the Vannings are unavailable just now."

"He at work? That where he is?"

"No, sir."

"*This is Senator Claude Screws calling.* You find Leonard Vanning and you find him now!"

"I'm quite sorry, sir, but they've left."

"Wha—?"

"They've gone on what I was told would be an extended vacation."

"*Vacation?* What kind of vacation?"

"To be honest, Senator, I don't really know. The staff's been left no forwarding address."

Screws hung up the phone. He swayed, almost falling to the floor.

He forced himself, willed himself, to stand.

In fifteen minutes he was dressed.

Ellis came around with the car. Screws angrily shoved away Ellis's hand when it appeared under his elbow to help him into the back.

"The Senate! And I'm late."

Screws felt nauseated in the moving car. It was a cool

October morning, the kind he used to love. Washington looked all white as it passed quickly by his window. He was supremely fatigued.

". . . Open the windows."

From Ellis: "Sir?"

"Open the damn windows! I want some air."

The four windows dropped in concert as the car sped down Constitution Avenue and swung right onto Pennsylvania.

There was a jam on the circle around to the back.

"What's wrong?"

"Looks like they're repaving."

"I'll get out here."

Screws opened the door himself and tottered out.

The Capitol Building stood proudly before him in the clear morning light. He could see people going purposefully up and down its broad steps.

Screws moved across the soggy front lawn. He reached the bottom steps. Tourists taking pictures. It took all his energy but he started to climb. One hard stone step at a time.

He was soon flushed, a wild determination set on his face. He'd almost reached the top when his path was blocked by two people.

Damn tourists.

" 'Scuse me—" he labored.

They didn't move. He looked up at them.

"Get outa my way—"

"Look at my face," Matt said two steps above him.

"Move!"

"You don't know who I am, do you?"

Screws's eyes were very sensitive to the sun. He squinted up at the man and his big friend.

"I'm late! Get out of my way!"

"I've come to believe," said Matt, "that if you want to kill a man you ought to at least know what he looks like."

Screws tried to go around them.

"I'm Matthew Clarke."

Screws paused, looking down at the stone.

"This is Orin Marsh."

The dizziness was coming back. He had to bend over to keep from falling backward.

"What—" he managed, "what's the meaning of this?"

"You're wasting your time, Senator," Matt told him. "Leslie is inside with Rosenbaum. He's got the pictures, the names, the service records. Leslie's cooperating—the whole story. His office is packed with reporters."

Screws tilted his head, the only way he could see them.

". . . You! You think you're heroes? You think . . . think this is some kind of, kind of act of heroism?" He was draining the last energy he had. "Do you really think that your personal sacrifices are more important than the security of this country?"

His eyes were wet, shifting wildly between Matt and Orin. The enormity of his downfall was suddenly dawning.

"I don't need an air-raid siren going off to know there's a war on!"

His voice rang in his ears. The two men were only one step up on the Capitol steps, but they looked like giants.

"The strength . . . the willingness to look at your enemies—to look at them for what they are!"

Screws's world was slowly starting to spin.

Still he managed to stand.

"Russia had exploded the bomb—*we needed to build!* We knew, we all knew that the money we needed—the money the country vitally needed, wouldn't be appropriated without a kick in the ass—*I'm talking about an act of patriotism!*"

Everything was tilted now, the sun filling Screws's mind with a bright burning light.

"The sight of a red star off our coastline—that, people would understand!"

He sagged to one knee, tried to continue: ". . . People could see . . . they'd know . . . *they'd understand that we are locked in a life-and-death struggle . . .*"

Screws collapsed heavily onto the Capitol steps. His world

was rapidly growing dark. Something inside him had given way, something in his head.

To the stone he muttered finally, ". . . a life-and-death struggle . . ."

Epilogue

One Week Later

The earth seems small from twelve thousand five hundred miles up; a minor distance for mankind's ever growing reach to span.

From just such a height, one of eighteen Global Positioning System satellites was hovering far above the world, dutifully helping ships and planes navigate their way across the far-off blue ball's surface.

Below lay the outlines of North and South America, where a thin, white film—a major storm down there—coated the western edge of the United States.

A mile beneath the heavy clouds, off a remote cape of northern California, Orin Marsh was standing in the bow of a bobbing Coast Guard cutter, from which the FBI was conducting a search for pieces of a towed submarine.

A clear view held across the spit of land that formed Central America, along the Pacific side of which—on a palm-covered veranda in Costa Rica—Leonard Vanning was pleading with his wife not to leave him, terrified to play out his fugitive life alone.

315

From twelve thousand miles up, the enormity of Chesapeake Bay formed the barest of landmarks; and the nation's capital— none at all. In that tiny pinprick of land, however, Senator Lawrence Rosenbaum was realizing the destiny he'd always dreamed of: at the forefront of an investigation that would launch his career to the heights he'd always felt he belonged. Claude Screws lay unmoving in a private room of Walter Reed Memorial Hospital. Since suffering a stroke on the steps of the Capitol, he'd been kept alive by mechanical means. Ellis, true to his word, missed him when he was gone.

An opaque haze was settled over the thin line of Florida. Along the gulf side of the peninsula, Matthew Clarke was visiting his parents. Here he sought refuge from the myriad requests for interviews and the army of people trying to buy the book and movie rights to his story. He'd finally gotten a chance to talk with Perri. They'd both come to the conclusion that their affair and Dave's death was no foundation on which to build a permanent relationship. At the moment, Matt was on the phone with Leslie. She was free on bail. Her house had been sealed by court order and she was looking for a place to live. Neither of them were at all sure about how best to proceed with their lives, though Matt was seriously considering asking her to stay at his place.

From this satellite's vantage, France was blocked from view by the curvature of the earth. There, however, Jacques Seydoux— escorted by police—had just attended his son's wedding at the family estate in Saint Maxime.

Controlling this navigation satellite circling far above the world were two men in Sunnyvale, California. Due to an acute shortage of experienced satellite controllers and the relative stability of the satellites in the Global Positioning System, Harry Ingram was back on the job—actively trying to get his wife's visiting sister a date for next Thursday.